FULL DARK, NO STARS

'Stories of retribution and complicity . . . stories to linger in the imagination . . . fine stories to take with us into the night'
– Neil Gaiman, *Guardian*

'America's greatest living novelist' – Lee Child

'The genius of King is not the fecundity of his imagination, great though it is, but the empathy he can create between the reader and a character, and for all their horrors his books are accurate portraits of blue collar life. He is, I believe, our Dickens, and not a national, but global treasure . . . just buy the book. Trust me, you won't be disappointed' – *The Scotsman*

'Mr. King's gift of storytelling is unrivalled. His ferocious imagination is unlimited'
– George Pelecanos

'Never less than entertaining . . . Another of the prime pleasures of reading King is his ear for language . . . And from language, King builds character. This is the real reason that his readership stretches from adolescent boys to great-grandmothers' – *Daily Telegraph*

'Delivered with the skill we have come to expect from King in this form . . . King readers know that he is an absolute master of the long story and the proof of that shouts out from every page here' – *Daily Express*

'All of the stories . . . deal with people en-countering the darkest aspects of themselves and those they love. Through his mastery of detail and his deceptively effortless narrative voice, King transforms this disquieting material into a disturbing, fascinating book'
– *Washington Post*

'There is no doubt about it: Stephen King is the master of the short-form story . . . King relies on the monsters inside us, the ones which are faced with decisions to be good or evil every day, and the consequences of those deci-sions . . . FULL DARK, NO STARS is a brilliant scrutiny of humanity and inhumanity and only confirms that King is still king'
– *West Australian*

Author photograph © Dick Dickinson

STEPHEN KING is one of the bestselling writers in the world, *ever*. As the *New York Times* says in a review for *Full Dark, No Stars* he 'seems able to write compact tales or gargantuan ones with equal ease . . . whatever the length at which he writes, Mr. King leaves readers with a simple, one-word message: **Gotcha**!'

King is the author of more than forty books, all of them worldwide bestsellers, including *Different Seasons*, *Misery* and *Under the Dome*. Many of his books and novellas have been turned into celebrated films, including *The Green Mile*, *Stand By Me* and *The Shawshank Redemption*.

He was the recipient of the 2003 National Book Foundation Medal for Distinguished Contribution to American Letters. He lives with his wife, novelist Tabitha King, in Maine.

HAVE YOU READ . . . ?

DIFFERENT SEASONS

Four powerful long stories including those which were turned into the celebrated films *The Shawshank Redemption* and *Stand By Me*.

MISERY

Novelist Paul Sheldon is rescued from a car accident by his Number One Fan. She keeps him prisoner while forcing him to bring his romantic heroine Misery Chastain back to life.

DOLORES CLAIBORNE

Suspected of killing her wealthy employer, Dolores Claiborne has a confession to make to the police. But it's not the one they are expecting to hear.

THE GIRL WHO LOVED
TOM GORDON

Lost in the woods, nine-year-old Trisha Mc-Farland only has her portable radio for comfort. A huge fan of Tom Gordon, a Boston Red Sox relief pitcher, she fantasises her hero will save her. But there's something dangerous in the woods – waiting, watching . . .

HEARTS IN ATLANTIS

Composed of five interconnected, sequential narratives, set in the years from 1960 to 1999; each story is deeply rooted in the sixties, and each is haunted by the Vietnam War.

ROSE MADDER

After fourteen years, Rosie Daniels flees from her abusive husband. But Norman Daniels, a police officer, uses his law-enforcement connections to track his wayward wife.

GERALD'S GAME

Trapped in a lakeside cabin after a dangerous sex-game goes wrong, Jessie is mindful of the voice in her head: 'Women alone in the dark are like open doors . . . and if they cry out for help, who knows what dread things may answer?'

BAG OF BONES

When writer Mike Noonan returns to his lakeside retreat, which he will soon discover is haunted, he gets caught in a crossfire between a young widow and her rich father-in-law for custody of an innocent child.

LISEY'S STORY

Lisey's husband, a bestselling novelist, has died. And an unscrupulous character wants to get his hands on the author's papers, using whatever means necessary . . .

By Stephen King and published by
Hodder & Stoughton

STEPHEN KING

FULL DARK, NO STARS

HODDER

Copyright © 2010 by Stephen King.
'Under the Weather' copyright © 2011 by Stephen King

First published in Great Britain in 2010 by Hodder & Stoughton
An Hachette UK Company

This paperback edition published 2011

The right of Stephen King to be identified as the Author
of the Work has been asserted by him in accordance with the
Copyright, Designs and Patents Act 1988.

5

All rights reserved. No part of this publication may be
reproduced, stored in a retrieval system, or transmitted, in any form
or by any means without the prior written permission of the publisher,
nor be otherwise circulated in any form of binding or cover other
than that in which it is published and without a similar condition
being imposed on the subsequent purchaser.

All characters in this publication are fictitious and any resemblance
to real persons, living or dead, is purely coincidental.

A CIP catalogue record for this title is
available from the British Library

A format paperback ISBN 978 1 444 71257 5
B format paperback ISBN 978 1 444 71256 8

Typeset in Bembo by
Palimpsest Book Production Limited, Falkirk, Stirlingshire

Printed and bound by Clays Ltd, St Ives plc

Hodder Headline's policy is to use papers that are natural,
renewable and recyclable products and made from wood grown
in sustainable forests. The logging and manufacturing processes
are expected to conform to the environmental regulations
of the country of origin

Hodder & Stoughton
338 Euston Road
London NW1 3BH

www.hodder.co.uk

For Tabby
Still.

CONTENTS

*This new bonus story did not appear in
the original Hodder editions

1922

Magnolia Hotel
Omaha, Nebraska

TO WHOM IT MAY CONCERN:

My name is Wilfred Leland James, and this is my confession. In June of 1922 I murdered my wife, Arlette Christina Winters James, and hid her body by tupping it down an old well. My son, Henry Freeman James, aided me in this crime, although at 14 he was not responsible; I cozened him into it, playing upon his fears and beating down his quite normal objections over a period of 2 months. This is a thing I regret even more bitterly than the crime, for reasons this document will show.

The issue that led to my crime and damnation was 100 acres of good land in Hemingford Home, Nebraska. It was willed to my wife by John Henry Winters, her father. I wished to add this land to our freehold farm, which in 1922 totaled 80 acres. My wife, who never took to the farming life (or to being a farmer's wife), wished to sell it to the Farrington Company for cash money. When I asked her if she truly wanted to live downwind from a Farrington's hog-butchery, she told me we could sell up the farm as well as her father's acreage — my father's farm, and his before him! When I asked her what we might do with money and no land, she said we could move to Omaha, or even St Louis, and open a shop.

'I will never live in Omaha,' I said. 'Cities are for fools.'

This is ironic, considering where I now live, but I will not live here for long; I know that as well as I know what is making the sounds I hear in the walls. And I know where I shall find myself after this earthly life is done. I wonder if Hell can be worse than the City of Omaha. Perhaps it *is* the City of Omaha, but with no good country surrounding it; only a smoking, brimstone-stinking emptiness full of lost souls like myself.

We argued bitterly over that 100 acres during the winter and spring of 1922. Henry was caught in the middle, yet tended more to my side; he favored his mother in looks but me in his love for the land. He was a biddable lad with none of his mother's arrogance. Again and again he told her that he had no desire to live in Omaha or any city, and would go only if she and I came to an agreement, which we never could.

I thought of going to Law, feeling sure that, as the Husband in the matter, any court in the land would uphold my right to decide the use and purpose of that land. Yet something held me back. 'Twas not fear of the neighbors' chatter, I had no care for country gossip; 'twas something else. I had come to hate her, you see. I had come to wish her dead, and that was what held me back.

I believe that there is another man inside of every man, a stranger, a Conniving Man. And I believe that by March of 1922, when the Hemingford County skies were white and every field was a snow-scrimmed mudsuck, the Conniving Man inside Farmer Wilfred James had already passed judgment on my wife and decided her fate. 'Twas justice of the black-cap variety, too. The Bible says that an ungrateful child is like a serpent's tooth, but a nagging and ungrateful Wife is ever so much sharper than that.

I am not a monster; I tried to save her from the Conniving Man. I told her that if we could not agree, she should go to her mother's in Lincoln, which is sixty miles west – a good distance for a separation which is not quite a divorce yet signifies a dissolving of the marital corporation.

'And leave you my father's land, I suppose?' she asked,

and tossed her head. How I had come to hate that pert head-toss, so like that of an ill-trained pony, and the little sniff which always accompanied it. 'That will never happen, Wilf.'

I told her that I would buy the land from her, if she insisted. It would have to be over a period of time – eight years, perhaps ten – but I would pay her every cent.

'A little money coming in is worse than none,' she replied (with another sniff and head-toss). 'This is something every woman knows. The Farrington Company will pay all at once, and their idea of top dollar is apt to be far more generous than yours. And I will never live in Lincoln. 'Tis not a city but only a village with more churches than houses.'

Do you see my situation? Do you not understand the 'spot' she put me in? Can I not count on at least a little of your sympathy? No? Then hear this.

In early April of that year – eight years to this very day, for all I know – she came to me all bright and shining. She had spent most of the day at the 'beauty salon' in McCook, and her hair hung around her cheeks in fat curls that reminded me of the toilet-rolls one finds in hotels and inns. She said she'd had an idea. It was that we should sell the 100 acres *and* the farm to the Farrington combine. She believed they would buy it all just to get her father's piece, which was near the railway line (and she was probably right).

'Then,' said this saucy vixen, 'we can split the money, divorce, and start new lives apart from each other. We both know that's what you want.' As if she didn't.

'Ah,' I said (as if giving the idea serious consideration). 'And with which of us does the boy go?'

'Me, of course,' she said, wide-eyed. 'A boy of 14 needs to be with his mother.'

I began to 'work on' Henry that very day, telling

him his mother's latest plan. We were sitting in the hay-mow. I wore my saddest face and spoke in my saddest voice, painting a picture of what his life would be like if his mother was allowed to carry through with this plan: how he would have neither farm nor father, how he would find himself in a much bigger school, all his friends (most since babyhood) left behind, how, once in that new school, he would have to fight for a place among strangers who would laugh at him and call him a country bumpkin. On the other hand, I said, if we could hold onto all the acreage, I was convinced we could pay off our note at the bank by 1925 and live happily debt-free, breathing sweet air instead of watching pig-guts float down our previously clear stream from sun-up to sundown. 'Now what is it you want?' I asked after drawing this picture in as much detail as I could manage.

'To stay here with you, Poppa,' he said. Tears were streaming down his cheeks. 'Why does she have to be such a . . . such a . . .'

'Go on,' I said. 'The truth is never cussing, Son.'

'Such a *bitch*!'

'Because most women are,' I said. 'It's an ineradicable part of their natures. The question is what we're going to do about it.'

But the Conniving Man inside had already thought of the old well behind the cow barn, the one we only used for slop-water because it was so shallow and murky – only 20 feet deep and little more than a sluice. It was just a question of bringing him to it. And I *had* to, surely you see that; I could kill my wife but must save my lovely son. To what purpose the ownership of 180 acres – or a thousand – if you have no one to share them with and pass them on to?

I pretended to be considering Arlette's mad plan to see good cornland turned into a hog-butchery. I asked her to give me time to get used to the idea. She assented. And during the next 2 months I worked on Henry, getting *him* used to a very different idea. 'Twasn't as hard as it might have been; he had his mother's looks (a woman's looks are the honey, you know, that lure men on to the stinging hive) but not her God-awful stubbornness. It was only necessary to paint a picture of what his life would be like in Omaha or St Louis. I raised the possibility that even those two overcrowded antheaps might not satisfy her; she might decide only Chicago would do. 'Then,' I said, 'you might find yourself going to high school with black niggers.'

He grew cold toward his mother; after a few efforts − all clumsy, all rebuffed − to regain his affections, she returned the chill. I (or rather the Conniving Man) rejoiced at this. In early June I told her that, after great consideration, I had decided I would never allow her to sell those 100 acres without a fight; that I would send us all to beggary and ruin if that was what it took.

She was calm. She decided to take legal advice of her own (for the Law, as we know, will befriend whomever pays it). This I foresaw. And smiled at it! Because she couldn't pay for such advice. By then I was holding tight to what little cash money we had. Henry even turned his pig-bank over to me when I asked, so she couldn't steal from that source, paltry as it was. She went, of course, to the Farrington Company offices in Deland, feeling quite sure (as was I) that they who had so much to gain would stand good her legal fees.

'They will, and she'll win,' I told Henry from what had become our usual place of conversation in the hay-mow. I was not entirely sure of this, but I had already taken my decision, which I will not go so far as to call 'a plan.'

'But Poppa, that's not fair!' he cried. Sitting there in the hay, he looked very young, more like 10 than 14.

'Life never is,' I said. 'Sometimes the only thing to do is to take the thing that you must have. Even if someone gets hurt.' I paused, gauging his face. 'Even if someone dies.'

He went white. 'Poppa!'

'If she was gone,' I said, 'everything would be the way it was. All the arguments would cease. We could live here peacefully. I've offered her everything I can to make her go, and she won't. There's only one other thing I can do. That *we* can do.'

'But I love her!'

'I love her, too,' I said. Which, however little you might believe it, was true. The hate I felt toward her in that year of 1922 was greater than a man can feel for any woman unless love is a part of it. And, bitter and willful though she was, Arlette was a warm-natured woman. Our 'marital relations' had never ceased, although since the arguments about the 100 acres had begun, our grapplings in the dark had become more and more like animals rutting.

'It needn't be painful,' I said. 'And when it's over . . . well . . .'

I took him out back of the barn and showed him the well, where he burst into bitter tears. 'No, Poppa. Not that. No matter what.'

But when she came back from Deland (Harlan Cotterie, our nearest neighbor, carried her most of the way in his Ford, leaving her to walk the last two miles) and Henry begged her to 'leave off so we can just be a family again,' she lost her temper, struck him across the mouth, and told him to stop begging like a dog.

'Your father's infected you with his timidity. Worse, he's infected you with his greed.'

As though she were innocent of *that* sin!

'The lawyer assures me the land is mine to do with as I wish, and I'm going to sell it. As for the two of you, you can sit here and smell roasting hogs together and cook your own meals and make your own beds. You, my son, can plow all the day and read *his* everlasting books all night. They've done him little good, but you may get on better. Who knows?'

'Mama, that's not fair!'

She looked at her son as a woman might look at a strange man who had presumed to touch her arm. And how my heart rejoiced when I saw him looking back just as coldly. 'You can go to the devil, both of you. As for me, I'm going to Omaha and opening a dress shop. That's *my* idea of fair.'

This conversation took place in the dusty dooryard between the house and the barn, and her idea of fair was the last word. She marched across the yard, raising dust with her dainty town shoes, went into the house, and slammed the door. Henry turned to look at me. There was blood at the corner of his mouth and his lower lip was swelling. The rage in his eyes was of the raw, pure sort that only adolescents can feel. It is rage that doesn't count the cost. He nodded his head. I nodded back, just as gravely, but inside the Conniving Man was grinning.

That slap was her death-warrant.

Two days later, when Henry came to me in the new corn, I saw he had weakened again. I wasn't dismayed or surprised; the years between childhood and adulthood are gusty years, and those living through them spin like the weathercocks some farmers in the Midwest used to put atop their grain silos.

'We can't,' he said. 'Poppa, she's in Error. And Shannon says those who die in Error go to Hell.'

God damn the Methodist church and Methodist Youth Fellowship, I thought . . . but the Conniving Man only smiled. For the next ten minutes we talked theology in the green corn while early summer clouds – the best clouds, the ones that float like schooners – sailed slowly above us, trailing their shadows like wakes. I explained to him that, quite the opposite of sending Arlette to Hell, we would be sending her to Heaven. 'For,' I said, 'a murdered man or woman dies not in God's time but in Man's. He . . . or she . . . is cut short before he . . . or she . . . can atone for sin, and so all errors must be forgiven. When you think of it that way, every murderer is a Gate of Heaven.'

'But what about us, Poppa? Wouldn't we go to Hell?'

I gestured to the fields, brave with new growth. 'How can you say so, when you see Heaven all around us? Yet she means to drive us away from it as surely as the angel with the flaming sword drove Adam and Eve from the Garden.'

He gazed at me, troubled. Dark. I hated to darken my son in such a way, yet part of me believed then and believes still that it was not I who did it to him, but she.

'And think,' I said. 'If she goes to Omaha, she'll dig herself an even deeper pit in Sheol. If she takes you, you'll become a city boy—'

'I never will!' He cried this so loudly that crows took wing from the fenceline and swirled away into the blue sky like charred paper.

'You're young and you will,' I said. 'You'll forget all this . . . you'll learn city ways . . . and begin digging your own pit.'

If he had returned by saying that murderers had no hope of joining their victims in Heaven, I might have been stumped. But either his theology did not stretch so far or he didn't want to consider such things. And is there Hell, or do we make our own on earth? When I consider the last eight years of my life, I plump for the latter.

'How?' he asked. 'When?'

I told him.

'And we can go on living here after?'

I said we could.

'And it won't hurt her?'

'No,' I said. 'It will be quick.'

He seemed satisfied. And still it might not have happened, if not for Arlette herself.

We settled on a Saturday night about halfway through a June that was as fine as any I can remember. Arlette sometimes took a glass of wine on Summer evenings, although rarely more. There was good reason for this. She was one of those people who can never take two glasses without taking four, then six, then the whole bottle. And another bottle, if there is another. 'I have to be very careful, Wilf. I like it too much. Luckily for me, my willpower is strong.'

That night we sat on the porch, watching the late light linger over the fields, listening to the somnolent *reeeeee* of the crickets. Henry was in his room. He had hardly touched his supper, and as Arlette and I sat on the porch in our matching rockers with the MA and PA seat-cushions, I thought I heard a faint sound that could have been retching. I remember thinking that when the moment came, he would not be able to go through with it. His mother would wake up bad-tempered the following morning with a 'hangover' and no knowledge of how close she had come to never seeing another Nebraska dawn. Yet I moved forward with the plan. Because I was like one of those Russian nesting dolls? Perhaps. Perhaps every man is like that. Inside me was the Conniving Man, but inside the Conniving Man was a Hopeful Man. That fellow died sometime between 1922 and 1930. The Conniving Man, having done his damage, disappeared. Without his schemes and ambitions, life has been a hollow place.

I brought the bottle out to the porch with me, but when I tried to fill her empty glass, she covered it with her hand. 'You needn't get me drunk to get what you want. I want it, too. I've got an itch.' She spread her legs and put her hand on her crotch to show where the itch was. There was a Vulgar Woman inside her – perhaps even a Harlot – and the wine always let her loose.

'Have another glass anyway,' I said. 'We've something to celebrate.'

She looked at me warily. Even a single glass of wine made her eyes wet (as if part of her was weeping for all the wine it wanted and could not have), and in the sunset light they looked orange, like the eyes of a jack-o'-lantern with a candle inside it.

'There will be no suit,' I told her, 'and there will be no divorce. If the Farrington Company can afford to pay us for my 80 as well as your father's 100, our argument is over.'

For the first and only time in our troubled marriage, she actually *gaped*. 'What are you saying? Is it what I think you're saying? Don't fool with me, Wilf!'

'I'm not,' said the Conniving Man. He spoke with hearty sincerity. 'Henry and I have had many conversations about this—'

'You've been thick as thieves, that's true,' she said. She had taken her hand from the top of her glass and I took the opportunity to fill it. 'Always in the hay-mow or sitting on the woodpile or with your heads together in the back field. I thought it was about Shannon Cotterie.' A sniff and a head-toss. But I thought she looked a little wistful, as well. She sipped at her second glass of wine. Two sips of a second glass and she could still put the glass down and go to bed. Four and I might as well hand her the bottle. Not to mention the other two I had standing by.

'No,' I said. 'We haven't been talking about Shannon.' Although I *had* seen Henry holding her hand on occasion as they walked the 2 miles to the Hemingford Home schoolhouse. 'We've been talking about Omaha. He wants to go, I guess.' It wouldn't do to lay it on too thick, not after a single glass of wine and two sips of another. She was suspicious by nature, was my Arlette, always looking for a deeper motive. And of course in this case I had one. 'At least to try it on for size. And Omaha's not that far from Hemingford . . .'

'No. It isn't. As I've told you both a thousand times.' She sipped her wine, and instead of putting the glass down as she had before, she held it. The orange light above the western horizon was deepening to an otherworldly green-purple that seemed to burn in the glass.

'If it were St Louis, that would be a different thing.'

'I've given that idea up,' she said. Which meant, of course, that she had investigated the possibility and found it problematic. Behind my back, of course. All of it behind my back except for the company lawyer. And she would have done *that* behind my back as well, if she hadn't wanted to use it as a club to beat me with.

'Will they buy the whole piece, do you think?' I asked. 'All 180 acres?'

'How would I know?' Sipping. The second glass half-empty. If I told her now that she'd had enough and tried to take it away from her, she'd refuse to give it up.

'You do, I have no doubt,' I said. 'That 180 acres is like St Louis. You've *investigated*.'

She gave me a shrewd sidelong look . . . then burst into harsh laughter. 'P'raps I have.'

'I suppose we could hunt for a house on the outskirts of town,' I said. 'Where there's at least a field or two to look at.'

'Where you'd sit on your ass in a porch-rocker all day, letting your wife do the work for a change? Here, fill this up. If we're celebrating, let's celebrate.'

I filled both. It only took a splash in mine, as I'd taken but a single swallow.

'I thought I might look for work as a mechanic. Cars and trucks, but mostly farm machinery. If I can keep that old Farmall running' – I gestured with my glass toward the dark hulk of the tractor standing beside the barn – 'then I guess I can keep anything running.'

'And Henry talked you into this.'

'He convinced me it would be better to take a chance at being happy in town than to stay here on my own in what would be sure misery.'

'The boy shows sense and the man listens! At long last! Hallelujah!' She drained her glass and held it out for more. She grasped my arm and leaned close enough for me to smell sour grapes on her breath. 'You may get that thing you like tonight, Wilf.' She touched her purple-stained tongue to the middle of her upper lip. 'That *nasty* thing.'

'I'll look forward to that,' I said. If I had my way, an even nastier thing was going to happen that night in the bed we had shared for 15 years.

'Let's have Henry down,' she said. She had begun to slur her words. 'I want to congratulate him on finally seeing the light.' (Have I mentioned that the verb *to thank* was not in my wife's vocabulary? Perhaps not. Perhaps by now I don't need to.) Her eyes lit up as a thought occurred to her. 'We'll give 'im a glass of wine! He's old enough!' She elbowed me like one of the old men you see sitting on the benches that flank the courthouse steps, telling each other dirty jokes. 'If we loosen his tongue a little, we may even find out if he's made any time with Shannon Cotterie . . . li'l baggage, but she's got pretty hair, I'll give 'er that.'

'Have another glass of wine first,' said the Conniving Man.

She had another two, and that emptied the bottle. (The first one.) By then she was singing 'Avalon' in her best minstrel voice, and doing her best minstrel eye-rolls. It was painful to see and even more painful to hear.

I went into the kitchen to get another bottle of wine, and judged the time was right to call Henry. Although, as I've said, I was not in great hopes. I could only do it if he were my willing accomplice, and in my heart I believed that he would shy from the deed when the talk ran out and the time actually came. If so, we would simply put her to bed. In the morning I would tell her I'd changed my mind about selling my father's land.

Henry came, and nothing in his white, woeful face offered any encouragement for success. 'Poppa, I don't think I can,' he whispered. 'It's *Mama.*'

'If you can't, you can't,' I said, and there was nothing of the Conniving Man in that. I was resigned; what would be would be. 'In any case, she's happy for the first time in months. Drunk, but happy.'

'Not just squiffy? She's *drunk?*'

'Don't be surprised; getting her own way is the only thing that ever makes her happy. Surely 14 years with her is long enough to have taught you that.'

Frowning, he cocked an ear to the porch as the woman who'd given him birth launched into a jarring but word-for-word rendition of 'Dirty McGee.' Henry frowned at this barrelhouse ballad, perhaps because of the chorus ('She was willin' to help him stick it in / For it was Dirty McGee again'), more likely at the way she was slurring the words. Henry had taken the Pledge at a Methodist Youth Fellowship Camp-Out on Labor Day weekend of the year before. I rather enjoyed his shock. When teenagers aren't turning like weathervanes in a high wind, they're as stiff as Puritans.

'She wants you to join us and have a glass of wine.'

'Poppa, you know I promised the Lord I would never drink.'

'You'll have to take that up with her. She wants to have a celebration. We're selling up and moving to Omaha.'

'*No!*'

'Well . . . we'll see. It's really up to you, Son. Come out on the porch.'

His mother rose tipsily to her feet when she saw him, wrapped her arms around his waist, pressed her body rather too tightly against his, and covered his face with extravagant kisses. Unpleasantly smelly ones, from the way he grimaced. The Conniving Man, meanwhile, filled up her glass, which was empty again.

'Finally we're all together! My men see sense!' She raised her glass in a toast, and slopped a goodly portion of it onto her bosom. She laughed and gave me a wink. 'If you're good, Wilf, you can suck it out of the cloth later on.'

Henry looked at her with confused distaste as she plopped back down in her rocker, raised her skirts, and tucked them between her legs. She saw the look and laughed.

'No need to be so prissy. I've seen you with Shannon Cotterie. Li'l baggage, but she's got pretty hair and a nice little figger.' She drank off the rest of her wine and belched. 'If you're not getting a touch of that, you're a fool. Only you'd better be careful. Fourteen's not too young to marry. Out here in the middle, fourteen's not too young to marry your *cousin*.' She laughed some more and held out her glass. I filled it from the second bottle.

'Poppa, she's had enough,' Henry said, as disapproving as a parson. Above us, the first stars were winking into view above that vast flat emptiness I have loved all my life.

'Oh, I don't know,' I said. '*In vino veritas*, that's what Pliny the Elder said . . . in one of those *books* your mother's always sneering about.'

'Hand on the plow all day, nose in a book all night,' Arlette said. 'Except when he's got something else in *me*.'

'*Mama!*'

'*Mama!*' she mocked, then raised her glass in the direction of Harlan Cotterie's farm, although it was too far for us to see the lights. We couldn't have seen them even if it had been a mile closer, now that the corn was high. When summer comes to Nebraska, each farmhouse is a ship sailing a vast green ocean. 'Here's to Shannon Cotterie and her brand-new bubbies, and if my son don't know the color of her nipples, he's a slowpoke.'

My son made no reply to this, but what I could see of his shadowed face made the Conniving Man rejoice.

She turned to Henry, grasped his arm, and spilled wine on his wrist. Ignoring his little mew of distaste, looking into his face with sudden grimness, she said: 'Just make sure that when you're lying down with her in the corn or behind the barn, you're a *no*-poke.' She made her free hand into a fist, poked out the middle finger, then used it to tap a circle around her crotch: left thigh, right thigh, right belly, navel, left belly, back again to the left thigh. 'Explore all you like, and rub around it with your Johnny Mac until he feels good and spits up, but stay out of the home place lest you find yourself locked in for life, just like your mummer and daddy.'

He got up and left, still without a word, and I don't blame him. Even for Arlette, this was a performance of extreme vulgarity. He must have seen her change before his eyes from his mother — a difficult woman but some-times loving — to a smelly whorehouse madam instructing a green young customer. All bad enough, but he was sweet on the Cotterie girl, and that made it worse. Very young men cannot help but put their first loves on pedestals, and should someone come along and spit on the paragon . . . even if it happens to be one's mother . . .

Faintly, I heard his door slam. And faint but audible sobbing.

'You've hurt his feelings,' I said.

She expressed the opinion that *feelings*, like *fairness*, were also the last resort of weaklings. Then she held out her glass. I filled it, knowing she would remember none of what she'd said in the morning (always supposing she was still there to greet the morning), and would deny it – vehemently – if I told her. I had seen her in this state of drunkenness before, but not for years.

We finished the second bottle (*she* did) and half of the third before her chin dropped onto her wine-stained bosom and she began to snore. Coming through her thus constricted throat, those snores sounded like the growling of an ill-tempered dog.

I put my arm around her shoulders, hooked my hand into her armpit, and hauled her to her feet. She muttered protests and slapped weakly at me with one stinking hand. 'Lea' me 'lone. Want to go to slee'.'

'And you will,' I said. 'But in your bed, not out here on the porch.'

I led her – stumbling and snoring, one eye shut and the other open in a bleary glare – across the sitting room. Henry's door opened. He stood in it, his face expressionless and much older than his years. He nodded at me. Just one single dip of the head, but it told me all I needed to know.

I got her on the bed, took off her shoes, and left her there to snore with her legs spread and one hand dangling off the mattress. I went back into the sitting room and found Henry standing beside the radio Arlette had hounded me into buying the year before.

'She can't say those things about Shannon,' he whispered.

'But she will,' I said. 'It's how she is, how the Lord made her.'

'And she can't take me *away* from Shannon.'

'She'll do that, too,' I said. 'If we let her.'

'Couldn't you . . . Poppa, couldn't you get your own lawyer?'

'Do you think any lawyer whose services I could buy with the little bit of money I have in the bank could stand up to the lawyers Farrington would throw at us? They swing weight in Hemingford County; I swing nothing but a sickle when I want to cut hay. They want that 100 acres and she means for them to have it. This is the only way, but you have to help me. Will you?'

For a long time he said nothing. He lowered his head, and I could see tears dropping from his eyes to the hooked rug. Then he whispered, 'Yes. But if I have to watch it . . . I'm not sure I can . . .'

'There's a way you can help and still not have to watch. Go into the shed and fetch a burlap sack.'

He did as I asked. I went into the kitchen and got her sharpest butcher knife. When he came back with the sack and saw it, his face paled. 'Does it have to be *that*? Can't you . . . with a pillow . . .'

'It would be too slow and too painful,' I said. 'She'd struggle.' He accepted that as if I had killed a dozen women before my wife and thus knew. But I didn't. All I knew was that in all my half-plans — my daydreams of being rid of her, in other words — I had always seen the knife I now held in my hand. And so the knife it would be. The knife or nothing.

We stood there in the glow of the kerosene lamps — there'd be no electricity except for generators in Hemingford Home until 1928 — looking at each other, the great night-silence that exists out there in the middle of things broken only by the unlovely sound of her snores. Yet there was a third presence in that room: her ineluctable will, which existed separate of the woman herself (I thought I sensed it then; these 8 years later I am sure). This is a ghost story, but the ghost was there even before the woman it belonged to died.

'All right, Poppa. We'll . . . we'll send her to Heaven.' Henry's face brightened at the thought. How hideous that seems to me now, especially when I think of how he finished up.

'It will be quick,' I said. Man and boy I've slit nine-score hogs' throats, and I thought it would be. But I was wrong.

Let it be told quickly. On the nights when I can't sleep – and there are many – it plays over and over again, every thrash and cough and drop of blood in exquisite slowness, so let it be told quickly.

We went into the bedroom, me in the lead with the butcher knife in my hand, my son with the burlap sack. We went on tiptoe, but we could have come in clashing cymbals without waking her up. I motioned Henry to stand to my right, by her head. Now we could hear the Big Ben alarm clock ticking on her nightstand as well as her snores, and a curious thought came to me: we were like physicians attending the deathbed of an important patient. But I think physicians at deathbeds do not as a rule tremble with guilt and fear.

Please let there not be too much blood, I thought. *Let the bag catch it. Even better, let him cry off now, at the last minute.*

But he didn't. Perhaps he thought I'd hate him if he did; perhaps he had resigned her to Heaven; perhaps he was remembering that obscene middle finger, poking a circle around her crotch. I don't know. I only know he whispered, 'Goodbye, Mama,' and drew the bag down over her head.

She snorted and tried to twist away. I had meant to reach under the bag to do my business, but he had to push down tightly on it to hold her, and I couldn't. I saw her nose making a shape like a shark's fin in the burlap. I saw the look of panic dawning on his face, too, and knew he wouldn't hold on for long.

I put one knee on the bed and one hand on her shoulder. Then I slashed through the burlap and the throat beneath. She screamed and began to thrash in earnest. Blood welled through the slit in the burlap. Her hands came up and beat the air. Henry stumbled away from the bed with a screech. I tried to hold her. She pulled at the gushing bag with her hands and I slashed at them, cutting three of her fingers to the bone. She shrieked again – a sound as thin and sharp as a sliver of ice – and the hand fell away to twitch on the counterpane. I slashed another bleeding slit in the burlap, and another, and another. Five cuts in all I made before she pushed me away with her unwounded hand and then tore the burlap sack up from her face. She couldn't get it all the way off her head – it caught in her hair – and so she wore it like a snood.

I had cut her throat with the first two slashes, the first time deep enough to show the gristle of her wind-pipe. With the last two I had carved her cheek and her mouth, the latter so deeply that she wore a clown's grin. It stretched all the way to her ears and showed her teeth. She let loose a guttural, choked roar, the sound a lion might make at feeding-time. Blood flew from her throat all the way to the foot of the counterpane. I remember thinking it looked like the wine when she held her glass up to the last of the daylight.

She tried to get out of bed. I was first dumbfounded, then infuriated. She had been a trouble to me all the days of our marriage and was a trouble even now, at our bloody divorce. But what else should I have expected?

'*Oh Poppa, make her stop!*' Henry shrieked. '*Make her stop, oh Poppa, for the love of God make her stop!*'

I leaped on her like an ardent lover and drove her back down on her blood-drenched pillow. More harsh growls came from deep in her mangled throat. Her eyes rolled in their sockets, gushing tears. I wound my hand into her hair, yanked her head back, and cut her throat yet again. Then I tore the counterpane free from my side of the bed and wrapped it over her head, catching all but the first pulse from her jugular. My face had caught that spray, and hot blood now dripped from my chin, nose, and eyebrows.

Behind me, Henry's shrieks ceased. I turned around and saw that God had taken pity on him (assuming He had not turned His face away when He saw what we were about): he had fainted. Her thrashings began to weaken. At last she lay still . . . but I remained on top of her, pressing down with the counterpane, now soaked with her blood. I reminded myself that she had never done anything easily. And I was right. After thirty seconds (the tinny mail-order clock counted them off), she gave another heave, this time bowing her back so strenuously that she almost threw me off. *Ride 'em, Cowboy*, I thought. Or perhaps I said it aloud. That I can't remember, God help me. Everything else, but not that.

She subsided. I counted another thirty tinny ticks, then thirty after that, for good measure. On the floor, Henry stirred and groaned. He began to sit up, then thought better of it. He crawled into the farthest corner of the room and curled in a ball.

'Henry?' I said.

Nothing from the curled shape in the corner.

'Henry, she's dead. She's dead and I need help.'

Nothing still.

'Henry, it's too late to turn back now. The deed is done. If you don't want to go to prison — and your father to the electric chair — then get on your feet and help me.'

He staggered toward the bed. His hair had fallen into

his eyes; they glittered through the sweat-clumped locks like the eyes of an animal hiding in the bushes. He licked his lips repeatedly.

'Don't step in the blood. We've got more of a mess to clean up in here than I wanted, but we can take care of it. If we don't track it all through the house, that is.'

'Do I have to look at her? Poppa, do I have to *look*?'

'No. Neither of us do.'

We rolled her up, making the counterpane her shroud. Once it was done, I realized we couldn't carry her through the house that way; in my half-plans and daydreams, I had seen no more than a discreet thread of blood marring the counterpane where her cut throat (her *neatly* cut throat) lay beneath. I had not foreseen or even considered the reality: the white counterpane was a blackish-purple in the dim room, oozing blood as a bloated sponge will ooze water.

There was a quilt in the closet. I could not suppress a brief thought of what my mother would think if she could see what use I was making of that lovingly stitched wedding present. I laid it on the floor. We dropped Arlette onto it. Then we rolled her up.

'Quick,' I said. 'Before this starts to drip, too. No . . . wait . . . go for a lamp.'

He was gone so long that I began to fear he'd run away. Then I saw the light come bobbing down the short hall past his bedroom and to the one Arlette and I shared. *Had* shared. I could see the tears gushing down his waxy-pale face.

'Put it on the dresser.'

He set the lamp down by the book I had been reading: Sinclair Lewis's *Main Street*. I never finished it; I could never *bear* to finish it. By the light of the lamp, I pointed out the splashes of blood on the floor, and the pool of it right beside the bed.

'More is running out of the quilt,' he said. 'If I'd known how much blood she had in her . . .'

I shook the case free of my pillow and snugged it over the end of the quilt like a sock over a bleeding shin. 'Take her feet,' I said. 'We need to do this part right now. And don't faint again, Henry, because I can't do it by myself.'

'I wish it was a dream,' he said, but he bent and got his arms around the bottom of the quilt. 'Do you think it might be a dream, Poppa?'

'We'll think it is, a year from now when it's all behind us.' Part of me actually believed this. 'Quickly, now. Before the pillowcase starts to drip. Or the rest of the quilt.'

We carried her down the hall, across the sitting room, and out through the front door like men carrying a piece of furniture wrapped in a mover's rug. Once we were down the porch steps, I breathed a little easier; blood in the dooryard could easily be covered over.

Henry was all right until we got around the corner of the cow barn and the old well came in view. It was ringed by wooden stakes so no one would by accident step on the wooden cap that covered it. Those sticks looked grim and horrible in the starlight, and at the sight of them, Henry uttered a strangled cry.

'That's no grave for a mum . . . muh . . .' He managed that much, and then fainted into the weedy scrub that grew behind the barn. Suddenly I was holding the dead weight of my murdered wife all by myself. I considered putting the grotesque bundle down – its wrappings now all askew and the slashed hand peeking out – long enough to revive him. I decided it would be more merciful to let him lie. I dragged her to the side of the well, put her down, and lifted up the wooden cap. As I leaned it against two of the stakes, the well exhaled into my face: a stench of stagnant water and rotting weeds. I fought with my gorge and lost. Holding onto two of the stakes to keep my balance, I bowed at the waist to vomit my supper and the little wine I had drunk. There was an echoing splash when it struck the murky water at the bottom. That splash, like thinking *Ride 'em, Cowboy*, has been within a hand's reach of my memory for the last eight years. I will wake up in the middle of the night with the echo in my mind and feel the splinters of the stakes dig into my palms as I clutch them, holding on for dear life.

I backed away from the well and tripped over the bundle that held Arlette. I fell down. The slashed hand was inches from my eyes. I tucked it back into the quilt and then patted it, as if comforting her. Henry was still lying in the weeds with his head pillowed on one arm. He looked like a child sleeping after a strenuous day during harvest-time. Overhead, the stars shone down in their thousands and tens of thousands. I could see the constellations – Orion, Cassiopeia, the Dippers – that my father had taught me. In the distance, the Cotteries' dog Rex barked once and then was still. I remember thinking, *This night will never end*. And that was right. In all the important ways, it never has.

I picked the bundle up in my arms, and it twitched.

I froze, my breath held in spite of my thundering heart. *Surely I didn't feel that*, I thought. I waited for it to come again. Or perhaps for her hand to creep out of the quilt and try to grip my wrist with the slashed fingers.

There was nothing. I had imagined it. Surely I had. And so I tupped her down the well. I saw the quilt unravel from the end not held by the pillow case, and then came the splash. A much bigger one than my vomit had made, but there was also a squelchy *thud*. I'd known the water down there wasn't deep, but had hoped it would be deep enough to cover her. That thud told me it wasn't.

A high siren of laughter commenced behind me, a sound so close to insanity that it made gooseflesh prickle all the way from the crack of my backside to the nape of my neck. Henry had come to and gained his feet. No, much more than that. He was capering behind the cow barn, waving his arms at the star-shot sky, and laughing.

'Mama down the well and I don't care!' he sing-songed. 'Mama down the well and I don't care, for my master's gone *aw-aaay*!'

I reached him in three strides and slapped him as hard as I could, leaving bloody finger-marks on a downy cheek that hadn't yet felt the stroke of a razor. 'Shut up! Your voice will carry! Your——. There, fool boy, you've raised that God damned dog again.'

Rex barked once, twice, three times. Then silence. We stood, me grasping Henry's shoulders, listening with my head cocked. Sweat ran down the back of my neck. Rex barked once more, then quit. If any of the Cotteries roused, they'd think it was a raccoon he'd been barking at. Or so I hoped.

'Go in the house,' I said. 'The worst is over.'

'Is it, Poppa?' He looked at me solemnly. 'Is it?'

'Yes. Are you all right? Are you going to faint again?'

'Did I?'

'Yes.'

'I'm all right. I just . . . I don't know why I laughed like that. I was confused. Because I'm relieved, I guess. It's over!' A chuckle escaped him, and he clapped his hands over his mouth like a little boy who has inadvertently said a bad word in front of his grandma.

'Yes,' I said. 'It's over. We'll stay here. Your mother ran away to St Louis . . . or perhaps it was Chicago . . . but we'll stay here.'

'She . . . ?' His eyes strayed to the well, and the cap

leaning against three of those stakes that were somehow so grim in the starlight.

'Yes, Hank, she did.' His mother hated to hear me call him Hank, she said it was common, but there was nothing she could do about it now. 'Up and left us cold. And of course we're sorry, but in the meantime, chores won't wait. Nor schooling.'

'And I can still be . . . friends with Shannon.'

'Of course,' I said, and in my mind's eye I saw Arlette's middle finger tapping its lascivious circle around her crotch. 'Of course you can. But if you should ever feel the urge to *confess* to Shannon—'

An expression of horror dawned on his face. 'Not ever!'

'That's what you think now, and I'm glad. But if the urge should come on you someday, remember this: she'd run from you.'

'Acourse she would,' he muttered.

'Now go in the house and get both wash-buckets out of the pantry. Better get a couple of milk-buckets from the barn, as well. Fill them from the kitchen pump and suds 'em up with that stuff she keeps under the sink.'

'Should I heat the water?'

I heard my mother say, *Cold water for blood, Wilf. Remember that.*

'No need,' I said. 'I'll be in as soon as I've put the cap back on the well.'

He started to turn away, then seized my arm. His hands were dreadfully cold. 'No one can ever know!' He whispered this hoarsely into my face. 'No one can ever know what we did!'

'No one ever will,' I said, sounding far bolder than I felt. Things had already gone wrong, and I was starting to realize that a deed is never like the dream of a deed.

'She won't come back, will she?'

'*What?*'

'She won't haunt us, will she?' Only he said *haint*, the kind of country talk that had always made Arlette shake her head and roll her eyes. It is only now, eight years later, that I had come to realize how much *haint* sounds like *hate*.

'No,' I said.

But I was wrong.

I looked down the well, and although it was only 20 feet deep, there was no moon and all I could see was the pale blur of the quilt. Or perhaps it was the pillowcase. I lowered the cover into place, straightened it a little, then walked back to the house. I tried to follow the path we'd taken with our terrible bundle, purposely scuffing my feet, trying to obliterate any traces of blood. I'd do a better job in the morning.

I discovered something that night that most people never have to learn: murder is sin, murder is damnation (surely of one's own mind and spirit, even if the atheists are right and there is no afterlife), but murder is also work. We scrubbed the bedroom until our backs were sore, then moved on to the hall, the sitting room, and finally the porch. Each time we thought we were done, one of us would find another splotch. As dawn began to lighten the sky in the east, Henry was on his knees scrubbing the cracks between the boards of the bedroom floor, and I was down on mine in the sitting room, examining Arlette's hooked rug square inch by square inch, looking for that one drop of blood that might betray us. There was none there – we had been fortunate in that respect – but a dime-sized drop beside it. It looked like blood from a shaving cut. I cleaned it up, then went back into our bedroom to see how Henry was faring. He seemed better now, and I felt better myself. I think it was the coming of daylight, which always seems to dispel the worst of our horrors. But when George, our rooster, let out his first lusty crow of the day, Henry jumped. Then he laughed. It was a small laugh, and there was still something wrong with it, but it didn't terrify me the way his laughter had done when he regained consciousness between the barn and the old livestock well.

'I can't go to school today, Poppa. I'm too tired. And . . . I think people might see it on my face. Shannon especially.'

I hadn't even considered school, which was another sign of half-planning. Half-*assed* planning. I should have put the deed off until County School was out for the summer. It would only have meant waiting a week. 'You can stay home until Monday, then tell the teacher you had the grippe and didn't want to spread it to the rest of the class.'

'It's not the grippe, but I *am* sick.'

So was I.

We had spread a clean sheet from her linen closet (so many things in that house were *hers* . . . but no more) and piled the bloody bedclothes onto it. The mattress was also bloody, of course, and would have to go. There was another, not so good, in the back sheds. I bundled the bedclothes together, and Henry carried the mattress. We went back out to the well just before the sun cleared the horizon. The sky above was perfectly clear. It was going to be a good day for corn.

'I can't look in there, Poppa.'

'You don't have to,' I said, and once more lifted the wooden cover. I was thinking that I should have left it up to begin with – *think ahead, save chores*, my own poppa used to say – and knowing that I never could have. Not after feeling (or thinking I felt) that last blind twitch.

Now I could see to the bottom, and what I saw was horrible. She had landed sitting up with her legs crushed beneath her. The pillowcase was split open and lay in her lap. The quilt and counterpane had come loose and were spread around her shoulders like a complicated ladies' stole. The burlap bag, caught around her head and holding her hair back like a snood, completed the picture: she almost looked as if she were dressed for a night on the town.

Yes! A night on the town! That's why I'm so happy! That's why I'm grinning from ear to ear! And do you notice how red my lipstick is, Wilf? I'd never wear this shade to church, would I? No, this is the kind of lipstick a woman puts on when she wants to do that nasty thing to her man. Come on down, Wilf, why don't you? Don't bother with the ladder, just jump! Show me how bad you want me! You did a nasty thing to me, now let me do one to you!

'Poppa?' Henry was standing with his face toward the barn and his shoulders hunched, like a boy expecting to be beaten. 'Is everything all right?'

'Yes.' I flung down the bundle of linen, hoping it would land on top of her and cover that awful upturned grin, but a whim of draft floated it into her lap, instead. Now she appeared to be sitting in some strange and bloodstained cloud.

'Is she covered? Is she covered up, Poppa?'

I grabbed the mattress and tupped it in. It landed on end in the mucky water and then fell against the circular stone-cobbled wall, making a little lean-to shelter over her, at last hiding her cocked-back head and bloody grin.

'Now she is.' I lowered the old wooden cap back into place, knowing there was more work ahead: the well would have to be filled in. Ah, but that was long overdue, anyway. It was a danger, which was why I had planted the circle of stakes around it. 'Let's go in the house and have breakfast.'

'I couldn't eat a single bite!'

But he did. We both did. I fried eggs, bacon, and

potatoes, and we ate every bite. Hard work makes a person hungry. Everyone knows that.

Henry slept until late afternoon. I stayed awake. Some of those hours I spent at the kitchen table, drinking cup after cup of black coffee. Some of them I spent walking in the corn, up one row and down another, listening to the swordlike leaves rattle in a light breeze. When it's June and corn's on the come, it seems almost to talk. This disquiets some people (and there are the foolish ones who say it's the sound of the corn actually growing), but I had always found that quiet rustling a comfort. It cleared my mind. Now, sitting in this city hotel room, I miss it. City life is no life for a country man; for such a man that life is a kind of damnation in itself.

Confessing, I find, is also hard work.

I walked, I listened to the corn, I tried to plan, and at last I *did* plan. I had to, and not just for myself.

There had been a time not 20 years before, when a man in my position needn't have worried; in those days, a man's business was his own, especially if he happened to be a respected farmer: a fellow who paid his taxes, went to church on Sundays, supported the Hemingford Stars baseball team, and voted the straight Republican ticket. I think that in those days, all sorts of things happened on farms out in what we called 'the middle.' Things that went unremarked, let alone reported. In those days, a man's wife was considered a man's business, and if she disappeared, there was an end to it.

But those days were gone, and even if they hadn't been . . . there was the land. The 100 acres. The Farrington Company wanted those acres for their God damned hog butchery, and Arlette had led them to believe they were going to get them. That meant danger, and danger meant that daydreams and half-plans would no longer suffice.

When I went back to the house at mid-afternoon, I was tired but clear-headed and calm at last. Our few cows were bellowing, their morning milking hours overdue. I did that chore, then put them to pasture where I'd let them stay until sunset, instead of herding them back in for their second milking just after supper. They didn't care; cows accept what *is*. If Arlette had been more like one of our bossies, I reflected, she would still be alive and nagging me for a new washing machine out of the Monkey Ward catalogue. I probably would have bought it for her, too. She could always talk me around. Except when it came to the land. About that she should have known better. Land is a man's business.

Henry was still sleeping. In the weeks that followed, he slept a great deal, and I let him, although in an ordinary summer I would have filled his days with chores once school let out. And he would have filled his evenings either visiting over at Cotteries' or walking up and down our dirt road with Shannon, the two of them holding hands and watching the moon rise. When they weren't kissing, that was. I hoped what we'd done had not spoiled such sweet pastimes for him, but believed it had. That *I* had. And of course I was right.

I cleared my mind of such thoughts, telling myself it was enough for now that he was sleeping. I had to make another visit to the well, and it would be best to do it alone. Our stripped bed seemed to shout murder. I went to the closet and studied her clothes. Women have so many, don't they? Skirts and dresses and blouses and sweaters and underthings – some of the latter so complicated and strange a man can't even tell which side is the front. To take them all would be a mistake, because the truck was still parked in the barn and the Model T under the elm. She had left on foot and taken only what she could carry. Why hadn't she taken the T? Because I would have heard it start and stopped her going. That was believable enough. So . . . a single valise.

I packed it with what I thought a woman would need and what she could not bear to leave. I put in her few pieces of good jewelry and the gold-framed picture of her mama and poppa. I debated over the toiletries in the bathroom, and decided to leave everything except for her atomizer bottler of Florient perfume and her horn-backed brush. There was a Testament in her night table, given to her by Pastor Hawkins, but *I* had never seen her read it, and so left it where it was. But I took the bottle of iron pills, which she kept for her monthlies.

Henry was still sleeping, but now tossing from side to side as if in the grip of bad dreams. I hurried about my business as quickly as I could, wanting to be in the house when he woke up. I went around the barn to the well, put the valise down, and lifted the splintery old cap for the third time. Thank God Henry wasn't with me. Thank God he didn't see what I saw. I think it would have driven him insane. It almost drove me insane.

The mattress had been shunted aside. My first thought was that she had pushed it away before trying to climb out. Because she was still alive. She was breathing. Or so it seemed to me at first. Then, just as ratiocinative ability began to resurface through my initial shock – when I began to ask myself what sort of breathing might cause a woman's dress to rise and fall not just at the bosom but all the way from neckline to hem – her jaw began to move, as if she were struggling to talk. It was not words that emerged from her greatly enlarged mouth, however, but the rat which had been chewing on the delicacy of her tongue. Its tail appeared first. Then her lower jaw yawned wider as it backed out, the claws on its back feet digging into her chin for purchase.

The rat plopped into her lap, and when it did, a

great flood of its brothers and sisters poured out from under her dress. One had something white caught in its whiskers — a fragment of her slip, or perhaps her skimmies. I chucked the valise at them. I didn't think about it — my mind was roaring with revulsion and horror — but just did it. It landed on her legs. Most of the rodents — perhaps all — avoided it nimbly enough. Then they streamed into a round black hole that the mattress (which they must have pushed aside through sheer weight of numbers) had covered, and were gone in a trice. I knew well enough what that hole was; the mouth of the pipe that had supplied water to the troughs in the barn until the water level sank too low and rendered it useless.

Her dress collapsed around her. The counterfeit breathing stopped. But she was *staring* at me, and what had seemed a clown's grin now looked like a gorgon's glare. I could see rat-bites on her cheeks, and one of her earlobes was gone.

'Dear God,' I whispered. 'Arlette, I'm so sorry.'

Your apology is not accepted, her glare seemed to say. *And when they find me like this, with rat-bites on my dead face and the underwear beneath my dress chewed away, you'll ride the lightning over in Lincoln for sure. And mine will be the last face you see. You'll see me when the electricity fries your liver and sets fire to your heart, and I'll be grinning.*

I lowered the cap and staggered to the barn. There my legs betrayed me, and if I'd been in the sun, I surely would have passed out the way Henry had the night before. But I was in the shade, and after I sat for five minutes with my head lowered almost to my knees, I began to feel myself again. The rats had gotten to her — so what? Don't they get to all of us in the end? The rats and bugs? Sooner or later even the stoutest coffin must collapse and let in life to feed on death. It's the way of the world, and what did it matter? When the heart stops and the brain asphyxiates, our spirits either go somewhere else, or simply wink out. Either way, we aren't there to feel the gnawing as our flesh is eaten from our bones.

I started for the house and had reached the porch steps before a thought stopped me: what about the twitch? What if she had been alive when I threw her into the well? What if she had *still* been alive, paralyzed, unable to move so much as one of her slashed fingers, when the rats came out of the pipe and began their depredations? What if she had felt the one that had squirmed into her conveniently enlarged mouth and began to—!

'No,' I whispered. 'She didn't feel it because she didn't twitch. Never did. She was dead when I threw her in.'

'Poppa?' Henry called in a sleep-muzzy voice. 'Pop, is that you?'

'Yes.'

'Who are you talking to?'

'No one. Myself.'

I went in. He was sitting at the kitchen table in his singlet and undershorts, looking dazed and unhappy. His hair, standing up in cowlicks, reminded me of the tyke he had once been, laughing and chasing the chickens around the dooryard with his hound dog Boo (long dead by that summer) at his heels.

'I wish we hadn't done it,' he said as I sat down opposite him.

'Done is done and can't be undone,' I said. 'How many times have I told you that, boy?'

''Bout a million.' He lowered his head for a few moments, then looked up at me. His eyes were red-rimmed and bloodshot. 'Are we going to be caught? Are we going to jail? Or . . .'

'No. I've got a plan.'

'You had a plan that it wouldn't hurt her! Look how *that* turned out!'

My hand itched to slap him for that, so I held it down with the other. This was not the time for recriminations. Besides, he was right. Everything that had gone wrong was my fault. *Except for the rats*, I thought. *They are not my fault.* But they were. Of course they were. If not for me, she would have been at the stove, putting on supper. Probably going on and on about those 100 acres, yes, but alive and well instead of *in* the well.

The rats are probably back already, a voice deep in my mind whispered. *Eating her. They'll finish the good parts, the tasty parts, the* delicacies, *and then . . .*.

Henry reached across the table to touch my knotted hands. I started.

'I'm sorry,' he said. 'We're in it together.'

I loved him for that.

'We're going to be all right, Hank; if we keep our heads, we'll be fine. Now listen to me.'

He listened. At some point he began to nod. When I finished, he asked me one question: when were we going to fill in the well?

'Not yet,' I said.

'Isn't that risky?'

'Yes,' I said.

Two days later, while I was mending a piece of fence about a quarter-mile from the farm, I saw a large cloud of dust boiling down our road from the Omaha–Lincoln Highway. We were about to have a visit from the world that Arlette had so badly wanted to be a part of. I walked back to the house with my hammer tucked into a belt loop and my carpenter's apron around my waist, its long pouch full of jingling nails. Henry was not in view. Perhaps he'd gone down to the spring to bathe; perhaps he was in his room, sleeping.

By the time I got to the dooryard and sat on the

chopping block, I had recognized the vehicle pulling the rooster-tail: Lars Olsen's Red Baby delivery truck. Lars was the Hemingford Home blacksmith and village milkman. He would also, for a price, serve as a kind of chauffeur, and it was that function he was fulfilling on this June afternoon. The truck pulled into the dooryard, putting George, our bad-tempered rooster, and his little harem of chickens to flight. Before the motor had even finished coughing itself to death, a portly man wrapped in a flapping gray duster got out on the passenger side. He pulled off his goggles to reveal large (and comical) white circles around his eyes.

'Wilfred James?'

'At your service,' I said, getting up. I felt calm enough. I might have felt less so if he'd come out in the county Ford with the star on the side. 'You are——?'

'Andrew Lester,' he said. 'Attorney-at-law.'

He put his hand out. I considered it.

'Before I shake that, you'd better tell me whose lawyer you are, Mr Lester.'

'I'm currently being retained by the Farrington Livestock Company of Chicago, Omaha, and Des Moines.'

Yes, I thought, *I've no doubt. But I'll bet your name isn't even on the door. The big boys back in Omaha don't have to eat country dust to pay for their daily bread, do they? The big boys have got their feet up on their desks, drinking coffee and admiring the pretty ankles of their secretaries.*

I said, 'In that case, sir, why don't you just go on and put that hand away? No offense.'

He did just that, and with a lawyer's smile. Sweat was cutting clean lines down his chubby cheeks, and his hair was all matted and tangled from the ride. I walked past him to Lars, who had thrown up the wing over his engine and was fiddling with something inside. He was whistling and sounded just as happy as a bird on a wire.

I envied him that. I thought Henry and I might have another happy day – in a world as varied as this one, anything is possible – but it would not be in the summer of 1922. Or the fall.

I shook Lars's hand and asked how he was.

'Tolerable fair,' he said, 'but dry. I could use a drink.'

I nodded toward the east side of the house. 'You know where it is.'

'I do,' he said, slamming down the wing with a metallic clatter that sent the chickens, who'd been creeping back, into flight once more. 'Sweet and cold as ever, I guess?'

'I'd say so,' I agreed, thinking: *But if you could still pump from that other well, Lars, I don't think you'd care for the taste at all.* 'Try it and see.'

He started around to the shady side of the house where the outside pump stood in its little shelter. Mr Lester watched him go, then turned back to me. He had unbuttoned his duster. The suit beneath would need dry-cleaning when he got back to Lincoln, Omaha, Deland, or wherever he hung his hat when he wasn't doing Cole Farrington's business.

'I could use a drink myself, Mr James.'

'Me, too. Nailing fence is hot work.' I looked him up and down. 'Not as hot as riding twenty miles in Lars's truck, though, I'll bet.'

He rubbed his butt and smiled his lawyer's smile. This time it had a touch of rue in it. I could see his eyes already flicking here, there, and everywhere. It would not do to sell this man short just because he'd been ordered to rattle twenty miles out into the country on a hot summer's day. 'My sit-upon may never be the same.'

There was a dipper chained to the side of the little shelter. Lars pumped it full, drank it down with his Adam's apple rising and falling in his scrawny, sunburned neck, then filled it again and offered it to Lester, who looked at it as doubtfully as I'd looked at his outstretched hand. 'Perhaps we could drink it inside, Mr James. It would be a little cooler.'

'It would,' I agreed, 'but I'd no more invite you inside than I'd shake your hand.'

Lars Olsen saw how the wind was blowing and wasted no time going back to his truck. But he handed the dipper to Lester first. My visitor didn't drink in gulps, as Lars had, but in fastidious sips. Like a lawyer, in other words – but he didn't stop until the dipper was empty, and that was also like a lawyer. The screen door slammed and Henry came out of the house in his overalls and bare feet. He gave us a glance that seemed utterly disinterested – good boy! – and then went where any red-blooded country lad would have gone: to watch Lars work on his truck, and, if he were lucky, to learn something.

I sat down on the woodpile we kept under a swatch of canvas on this side of the house. 'I imagine you're out here on business. My wife's.'

'I am.'

'Well, you've had your drink, so we better get down to it. I've still got a full day's work ahead of me, and it's three in the afternoon.'

'Sunrise to sunset. Farming's a hard life.' He sighed as if he knew.

'It is, and a difficult wife can make it even harder. She sent you, I suppose, but I don't know why – if it was just some legal paperwork, I reckon a sheriff's deputy would have come out and served it on me.'

He looked at me in surprise. 'Your wife didn't send me, Mr James. In point of fact, I came out here to look for *her*.'

It was like a play, and this was my cue to look puzzled. Then to chuckle, because chuckling came next in the stage directions. 'That just proves it.'

'Proves what?'

'When I was a boy in Fordyce, we had a neighbor – a nasty old rip name of Bradlee. Everyone called him Pop Bradlee.'

'Mr James—'

'My father had to do business with him from time to time, and sometimes he took me with him. Back in the buckboard days, this was. Seed corn was what their trading was mostly about, at least in the spring, but sometimes they also swapped tools. There was no mail-order back then, and a good tool might circle the whole county before it got back home.'

'Mr James, I hardly see the rel—'

'And every time we went to see that old fellow, my mama told me to plug my ears, because every other word that came out of Pop Bradlee's mouth was a cuss or something filthy.' In a sour sort of way, I was starting to enjoy this. 'So naturally I listened all the harder. I remember that one of Pop's favorite sayings was "Never mount a mare without a bridle, because you can never tell which way a bitch will run."'

'Am I supposed to understand that?'

'Which way do you suppose *my* bitch ran, Mr Lester?'

'Are you telling me your wife has . . . ?'

'Absconded, Mr Lester. Decamped. Took French leave. Did a midnight flit. As an avid reader and student of American slang, such terms occur naturally to me. Lars, however – and most other town folks – will just say "She run off and left him" when the word gets around. Or him and the boy, in this case. I naturally thought she would have gone to her hog-fancying friends at the Farrington Company, and the next I heard from her would have been a notice that she was selling her father's acreage.'

'As she means to do.'

'Has she signed it over yet? Because I guess I'd have to go to law, if she has.'

'As a matter of fact, she hasn't. But when she does, I would advise you against the expense of a legal action you would surely lose.'

I stood up. One of my overall straps had fallen off my shoulder, and I hooked it back into place with a thumb. 'Well, since she's not here, it's what the legal profession calls "a moot question," wouldn't you say? I'd look in Omaha, if I were you.' I smiled. 'Or Saint Louis. She was *always* talking about Sain'-Loo. It sounds to me as if she got as tired of you fellows as she did of me and the son she gave birth to. Said good riddance to bad rubbish. A plague on both your houses. That's Shakespeare, by the way. *Romeo and Juliet*. A play about love.'

'You'll pardon me for saying, but all this seems very strange to me, Mr James.' He had produced a silk handkerchief from a pocket inside his suit — I bet traveling lawyers like him have lots of pockets — and began to mop his face with it. His cheeks were now not just flushed but bright red. It wasn't the heat of the day that had turned his face that color. 'Very strange indeed, considering the amount of money my client is willing to pay for that piece of property, which is contiguous with Hemingford Stream and close to the Great Western rail line.'

'It's going to take some getting used to on my part as well, but I have the advantage of you.'

'Yes?'

'I know her. I'm sure you and your *clients* thought you had a deal all made, but Arlette James . . . let's just say that nailing her down to something is like trying to nail jelly to the floor. We need to remember what Pop Bradlee said, Mr Lester. Why, the man was a countrified genius.'

'Could I look in the house?'

I laughed again, and this time it wasn't forced. The

man had gall, I'll give him that, and not wanting to go back empty-handed was understandable. He'd ridden twenty miles in a dusty truck with no doors, he had twenty more to bounce across before he got back to Hemingford City (and a train ride after that, no doubt), he had a sore ass, and the people who'd sent him out here weren't going to be happy with his report when he finally got to the end of all that hard traveling. Poor feller!

'I'll ask you one back: could you drop your pants so I could look at your goolie-bits?'

'I find that offensive.'

'I don't blame you. Think of it as a . . . not a simile, that's not right, but a kind of *parable*.'

'I don't understand you.'

'Well, you've got an hour back to the city to think it over — two, if Lars's Red Baby throws a tire. And I can assure you, Mr Lester, that if I *did* let you poke around through my house — my private place, my castle, my goolie-bits — you wouldn't find my wife's body in the closet or . . .' There was a terrible moment when I almost said *or down the well*. I felt sweat spring out on my forehead. 'Or under the bed.'

'I never said—'

'Henry!' I called. 'Come over here a minute!'

Henry came with his head down and his feet dragging in the dust. He looked worried, maybe even guilty, but that was all right. 'Yes, sir?'

'Tell this man where's your mama.'

'I don't know. When you called me to breakfast Friday morning, she was gone. Packed and gone.'

Lester was looking at him keenly. 'Son, is that the truth?'

'Yes, sir.'

'The whole truth and nothing *but* the truth, so help you God?'

'Poppa, can I go back in the house? I've got school-work to make up from being sick.'

'Go on, then,' I said, 'but don't be slow. Remember, it's your turn to milk.'

'Yes, sir.'

He trudged up the steps and inside. Lester watched him go, then turned back to me. 'There's more here than meets the eye.'

'I see you wear no wedding ring, Mr Lester. If there comes a time when you've worn one as long as I have, you'll know that in families, there always is. And you'll know something else as well: you can never tell which way a bitch will run.'

He got up. 'This isn't finished.'

'It is,' I said. Knowing it wasn't. But if things went all right, we were closer to the end than we had been. *If.*

He started across the dooryard, then turned back. He used his silk handkerchief to mop off his face again, then said, 'If you think those 100 acres are yours just because you've scared your wife away . . . sent her packing to her aunt in Des Moines or a sister in Minnesota—'

'Check Omaha,' I said, smiling. 'Or Sain'-Loo. She had no use for her relations, but she was crazy about the idea of living in Sain'-Loo. God knows why.'

'If you think you'll plant and harvest out there, you'd better think again. That land's not yours. If you so much as drop a seed there, you will be seeing me in court.'

I said, 'I'm sure you'll hear from her as soon as she gets a bad case of broke-itis.'

What I wanted to say was, *No, it's not mine . . . but it's not yours, either. It's just going to sit there. And that's all right, because it* will *be mine in seven years, when I go to court to have her declared legally dead. I can wait. Seven years without smelling pigshit when the wind's out of the west? Seven years without hearing the screams of dying hogs (so much like the screams of a dying woman) or seeing their intestines float down a creek that's red with blood? That sounds like an excellent seven years to me.*

'Have yourself a fine day, Mr Lester, and mind the sun going back. It gets pretty fierce in the late afternoon, and it'll be right in your face.'

He got into the truck without replying. Lars waved to me and Lester snapped at him. Lars gave him a look that might have meant *Snap and yap all you want, it's still twenty miles back to Hemingford City.*

When they were gone except for the rooster-tail of dust, Henry came back out on the porch. 'Did I do it right, Poppa?'

I took his wrist, gave it a squeeze, and pretended not to feel the flesh tighten momentarily under my hand, as if he had to override an impulse to pull away. 'Just right. Perfect.'

'Are we going to fill in the well tomorrow?'

I thought about this carefully, because our lives might depend on what I decided. Sheriff Jones was getting on in years and up in pounds. He wasn't lazy, but it was hard to get him moving without a good reason. Lester would eventually convince Jones to come out here, but probably not until Lester got one of Cole Farrington's two hell-for-leather sons to call and remind the Sheriff what company was the biggest taxpayer in Hemingford County (not to mention the neighboring counties of Clay, Fillmore, York, and Seward). Still, I thought we had at least two days.

'Not tomorrow,' I said. 'The day after.'

'Poppa, *why*?'

'Because the High Sheriff will be out here, and Sheriff Jones is old but not stupid. A filled-in well might make him suspicious about *why* it got filled in, so recent and all. But one that's still *being* filled in . . . and for a good reason . . .'

'What reason? Tell me!'

'Soon,' I said. 'Soon.'

All the next day we waited to see dust boiling toward us down our road, not being pulled by Lars Olsen's truck but by the County Sheriff's car. It didn't come. What came was Shannon Cotterie, looking pretty in a cotton blouse and gingham skirt, to ask if Henry was all right, and could he take supper with her and her mama and her poppa if he was?

Henry said he was fine, and I watched them go up the road, hand-in-hand, with deep misgivings. He was keeping a terrible secret, and terrible secrets are heavy. Wanting to share them is the most natural thing in the world. And he loved the girl (or thought he did, which comes to the same when you're just going on 15). To make things worse, he had a lie to tell, and she might know it was a lie. They say that loving eyes can never see, but that's a fool's axiom. Sometimes they see too much.

I hoed in the garden (pulling up more peas than weeds), then sat on the porch, smoking a pipe and waiting for him to come back. Just before moonrise, he did. His head was down, his shoulders were slumped, and he was trudging rather than walking. I hated to see him that way, but I was still relieved. If he had shared his secret – or even part of it – he wouldn't have been walking like that. If he'd shared his secret, he might not have come back at all.

'You told it the way we decided?' I asked him when he sat down.

'The way *you* decided. Yes.'

'And she promised not to tell her folks?'

'Yes.'

'But will she?'

He sighed. 'Probably, yes. She loves them and they love her. They'll see something in her face, I reckon, and get it out of her. And even if they don't, she'll probably tell the Sheriff. If he bothers to talk to the Cotteries at all, that is.'

'Lester will see that he does. He'll bark at Sheriff Jones because his bosses in Omaha are barking at him. Round and round it goes, and where it stops, nobody knows.'

'We never should have done it.' He considered, then said it again in a fierce whisper.

I said nothing. For awhile, neither did he. We watched the moon rise out of the corn, red and pregnant.

'Poppa? Can I have a glass of beer?'

I looked at him, surprised and not surprised. Then I went inside and poured us each a glass of beer. I gave one to him and said, 'None of this tomorrow or the day after, mind.'

'No.' He sipped, grimaced, then sipped again. 'I hated lying to Shan, Poppa. Everything about this is dirty.'

'Dirt washes off.'

'Not this kind,' he said, and took another sip. This time he didn't grimace.

A little while later, after the moon had gone to silver, I stepped around to use the privy, and to listen to the corn and the night breeze tell each other the old secrets of the earth. When I got back to the porch, Henry was gone. His glass of beer stood half-finished on the railing by the steps. Then I heard him in the barn, saying 'Soo, Boss. Soo.'

I went out to see. He had his arms around Elphis's neck and was stroking her. I believe he was crying. I watched for awhile, but in the end said nothing. I went back to the house, undressed, and lay down in the bed where I'd cut my wife's throat. It was a long time before I went to sleep. And if you don't understand why – *all* the reasons why – then reading this is of no use to you.

* * *

I had named all our cows after minor Greek goddesses, but Elphis turned out to be either a bad choice or an ironic joke. In case you don't remember the story of how evil came to our sad old world, let me refresh you: all the bad things flew out when Pandora gave in to her curiosity and opened the jar that had been left in her keeping. The only thing that remained when she regained enough wits to put the lid back on was Elphis, the goddess of hope. But in that summer of 1922, there was no hope left for our Elphis. She was old and cranky, no longer gave much milk, and we'd all but given up trying to get what little she had; as soon as you sat down on the stool, she'd try to kick you. We should have converted her into comestibles a year before, but I balked at the cost of having Harlan Cotterie butcher her, and I was no good at slaughtering much beyond hogs . . . a self-assessment with which you, Reader, must now surely agree.

'And she'd be tough,' Arlette (who had shown a sneaking affection for Elphis, perhaps because she was never the one to milk her) said. 'Better leave well enough alone.' But now we had a use for Elphis – *in* the well, as it so happened – and her death might serve an end far more useful than a few stringy cuts of meat.

Two days after Lester's visit, my son and I put a nose-halter on her and led her around the side of the barn. Halfway to the well, Henry stopped. His eyes shone with dismay. 'Poppa! I *smell* her!'

'Go into the house then, and get some cotton balls for your nose. They're on her dresser.'

Although his head was lowered, I saw the sidelong glance he shot me as he went. *This is all your fault*, that look said. *All your fault because you couldn't let go.*

Yet I had no doubt that he would help me do the work that lay ahead. Whatever he now thought of me, there was a girl in the picture as well, and he didn't want her to know what he had done. I had forced him to it, but she would never understand that.

We led Elphis to the well-cap, where she quite reasonably balked. We went around to the far side, holding the halter-strings like ribbons in a Maypole dance, and hauled her out onto the rotted wood by main force. The cap cracked beneath her weight . . . bowed down . . . but held. The old cow stood on it, head lowered, looking as stupid and as stubborn as ever, showing the greenish-yellow rudiments of her teeth.

'What now?' Henry asked.

I started to say I didn't know, and that was when the well-cap broke in two with a loud and brittle snap. We held onto the halter-strings, although I thought for a moment I was going to be dragged into that damned well with two dislocated arms. Then the nose-rig ripped free and flew back up. It was split down both the sides. Below, Elphis began to low in agony and drum her hoofs against the well's rock sides.

'*Poppa!*' Henry screamed. His hands were fists against his mouth, the knuckles digging into his upper lip. '*Make her stop!*'

Elphis uttered a long, echoing groan. Her hoofs continued to beat against the stone.

I took Henry's arm and hauled him, stumbling, back to the house. I pushed him down on Arlette's mail-order sofa and ordered him to stay there until I came back to get him. 'And remember, this is almost over.'

'It'll never be over,' he said, and turned facedown on the sofa. He put his hands over his ears, even though Elphis couldn't be heard from in here. Except Henry still *was* hearing her, and so was I.

I got my varmint gun from the high shelf in the pantry. It was only a .22, but it would do the job. And if Harlan heard shots rolling across the acres between his place and mine? That would fit our story, too. If Henry could keep his wits long enough to tell it, that was.

Here is something I learned in 1922: there are always worse things waiting. You think you have seen the most terrible thing, the one that coalesces all your nightmares into a freakish horror that actually exists, and the only consolation is that there can be nothing worse. Even if there is, your mind will snap at the sight of it, and you will know no more. But there *is* worse, your mind does *not* snap, and somehow you carry on. You might understand that all the joy has gone out of the world for you, that what you did has put all you hoped to gain out of your reach, you might wish you were the one who was dead – but you go on. You realize that you are in a hell of your own making, but you go on nevertheless. Because there is nothing else to do.

Elphis had landed on top of my wife's body, but Arlette's grinning face was still perfectly visible, still tilted up to the sunlit world above, still seeming to look at me. And the rats had come back. The cow falling into their world had doubtless caused them to retreat into the pipe I would eventually come to think of as Rat Boulevard, but then they had smelled fresh meat, and had come hurrying out to investigate. They were already nibbling at poor old Elphis as she lowed and kicked (more feebly now), and one sat on top of my dead wife's head like an eldritch crown. It had picked a hole in the burlap sack and pulled a tuft of her hair out with its clever claws. Arlette's cheeks, once so round and pretty, hung in shreds.

Nothing can be any worse than this, I thought. *Surely I've reached the end of horror.*

But yes, there are always worse things waiting. As I peered down, frozen with shock and revulsion, Elphis kicked out again, and one of her hoofs connected with what remained of Arlette's face. There was a snap as my wife's jaw broke, and everything below her nose shifted to the left, as if on a hinge. Still the ear-to-ear grin remained. That it was no longer aligned with her eyes made it even worse. It was as if she now had two faces to haunt me with instead of just one. Her body shifted against the mattress, making it slide. The rat on her head scurried down behind it. Elphis lowed again. I thought that if Henry came back now, and looked into the well, he would kill me for making him a part of this. I probably deserved killing. But that would leave him alone, and alone he would be defenseless.

Part of the cap had fallen into the well; part of it was still hanging down. I loaded my rifle, rested it on this slope, and aimed at Elphis, who lay with her neck broken and her head cocked against the rock wall. I waited for my hands to steady, then pulled the trigger.

One shot was enough.

Back in the house, I found that Henry had gone to sleep on the couch. I was too shocked myself to consider this strange. At that moment, he seemed to me like the only truly hopeful thing in the world: soiled, but not so filthy he could never be clean again. I bent and kissed his cheek. He moaned and turned his head away. I left him there and went to the barn for my tools. When he joined me three hours later, I had pulled the broken and hanging piece of the well-cap out of the hole and had begun to fill it in.

'I'll help,' he said in a flat and dreary voice.

'Good. Get the truck and drive it out to the dirtpile at West Fence—'

'By myself?' The disbelief in his voice was only faint, but I was encouraged to hear any emotion at all.

'You know all the forward gears, and you can find reverse, can't you?'

'Yes—'

'Then you'll be fine. I've got enough to be going on with in the meantime, and when you come back, the worst will be over.'

I waited for him to tell me again that the worst would never be over, but he didn't. I recommenced shoveling. I could still see the top of Arlette's head and the burlap with that terrible picked-over tuft sticking out of it. There might already be a litter of newborn ratlings down there in the cradle of my dead wife's thighs.

I heard the truck cough once, then twice. I hoped the crank wouldn't kick back and break Henry's arm.

The third time he turned the crank, our old truck bellowed into life. He retarded the spark, gunned the throttle a time or two, then drove away. He was gone for almost an hour, but when he came back, the truck's bed was full of rocks and soil. He drove it to the edge of the well and killed the engine. He had taken off his shirt, and his sweat-shiny torso looked too thin; I could count his ribs. I tried to think when I'd last seen him eat a big meal, and at first I couldn't. Then I realized it must have been breakfast on the morning after we'd done away with her.

I'll see that he gets a good dinner tonight, I thought. *I'll see that we both do. No beef, but there's pork in the icebox—*

'Look yonder,' he said in his new flat voice, and pointed.

I saw a rooster-tail of dust coming toward us. I looked down into the well. It wasn't good enough, not yet. Half of Elphis was still sticking up. That was all right, of course, but the corner of the bloodstained mattress was also still poking out of the dirt.

'Help me,' I said.

'Do we have enough time, Poppa?' He sounded only mildly interested.

'I don't know. Maybe. Don't just stand there, help me.'

The extra shovel was leaning against the side of the

barn beside the splintered remains of the well-cap. Henry grabbed it, and we began shoveling dirt and rocks out of the back of the truck as fast as ever we could.

When the County Sheriff's car with the gold star on the door and the spotlight on the roof pulled up by the chopping block (once more putting George and the chickens to flight), Henry and I were sitting on the porch steps with our shirts off and sharing the last thing Arlette James had ever made: a pitcher of lemonade. Sheriff Jones got out, hitched up his belt, took off his Stetson, brushed back his graying hair, and resettled his hat along the line where the white skin of his brow ended and coppery red took over. He was by his lonesome. I took that as a good sign.

'Good day, gents.' He took in our bare chests, dirty hands, and sweaty faces. 'Hard chorin' this afternoon, is it?'

I spat. 'My own damn fault.'

'Is that so?'

'One of our cows fell in the old livestock well,' Henry said.

Jones asked again, 'Is that so?'

'It is,' I said. 'Would you want a glass of lemonade, Sheriff? It's Arlette's.'

'Arlette's, is it? She decided to come back, did she?'

'No,' I said. 'She took her favorite clothes but left the lemonade. Have some.'

'I will. But first I need to use your privy. Since I turned fifty-five or so, seems like I have to wee on every bush. It's a God damned inconvenience.'

'It's around the back of the house. Just follow the path and look for the crescent moon on the door.'

He laughed as though this were the funniest joke he'd heard all year, and went around the house. Would he pause on his way to look in the windows? He would if he was any good at his job, and I'd heard he was. At least in his younger days.

'Poppa,' Henry said. He spoke in a low voice.

I looked at him.

'If he finds out, we can't do anything else. I can lie, but there can't be anymore killing.'

'All right,' I said. That was a short conversation, but one I have pondered often in the eight years since.

Sheriff Jones came back, buttoning his fly.

'Go in and get the Sheriff a glass,' I told Henry.

Henry went. Jones finished with his fly, took off his hat, brushed back his hair some more, and reset the hat. His badge glittered in the early-afternoon sun. The gun on his hip was a big one, and although Jones was too old to have been in the Great War, the holster looked like AEF property. Maybe it was his son's. His son had died over there.

'Sweet-smelling privy,' he said. 'Always nice on a hot day.'

'Arlette used to put the quicklime to it pretty constantly,' I said. 'I'll try to keep up the practice if she stays away. Come on up to the porch and we'll sit in the shade.'

'Shade sounds good, but I believe I'll stand. Need to stretch out my spine.'

I sat in my rocker with the PA cushion on it. He stood beside me, looking down. I didn't like being in that position but tried to bear up patiently. Henry came out with a glass. Sheriff Jones poured his own lemonade, tasted, then gulped most of it down at a go and smacked his lips.

'Good, isn't it? Not too sour, not too sweet, just right.' He laughed. 'I'm like Goldilocks, aren't I?' He drank the rest, but shook his head when Henry offered to refill his glass. 'You want me pissing on every fencepost on the way back to Hemingford Home? And then all the way to Hemingford City after that?'

'Have you moved your office?' I asked. 'I thought you were right there in the Home.'

'I am, aren't I? The day they make me move the Sheriff's Office to the county seat is the day I resign and let Hap Birdwell take over, like he wants to. No, no, it's just a court hearing up to the City. Amounts to no more than paperwork, but there it is. And you know how Judge Cripps is . . . or no, I guess you don't, being a law-abiding sort. He's bad-tempered, and if a fellow isn't on time, his temper gets worse. So even though it comes down to just saying so help me God and then signing my name to a bunch of legal folderol, I have to hurry right along with my business out here, don't I? And hope my God damned Maxie doesn't break down on the way back.'

I said nothing to this. He didn't *talk* like a man who was in a hurry, but perhaps that was just his way.

He took his hat off and brushed his hair back some more, but this time he didn't put the hat back on. He looked at me earnestly, then at Henry, then back at me again. 'Guess you know I'm not out here on my own hook. I believe that doings between a man and his wife are their own business. It has to be that way, doesn't it? Bible says the man is the head of a woman, and that if a woman should learn any thing, it should be taught by her husband at home. Book of Corinthians. If the Bible was my only boss, I'd do things the Bible's way and life would be simpler.'

'I'm surprised Mr Lester's not out here with you,' I said.

'Oh, he wanted to come, but I put the kye-bosh on that. He also wanted me to get a search warrant, but I told him I didn't need one. I said you'd either let me look around or you wouldn't.' He shrugged. His face was placid, but the eyes were keen and always in motion: peeking and prying, prying and peeking.

When Henry asked me about the well, I'd said, *We'll watch him and decide how sharp he is. If he's sharp, we'll show him ourselves. We can't look as if we have anything to hide. If you see me flick my thumb, that means I think we have to take the chance. But we have to agree, Hank. If I don't see you flick yours back, I'll keep my mouth shut.*

I raised my glass and drank the last of my lemonade. When I saw Henry looking at me, I flicked my thumb. Just a little. It could have been a muscle twitch.

'What does that Lester think?' Henry asked, sounding indignant. 'That we've got her tied up in the cellar?' His own hands stayed at his sides, not moving.

Sheriff Jones laughed heartily, his big belly shaking behind his belt. 'I don't know *what* he's thinking, do I? I don't care much, either. Lawyers are fleas on the hide of human nature. I can say that, because I've worked for 'em – and against 'em, that too – my whole adult life. But . . .' The keen eyes fastened on mine. 'I wouldn't mind a look, just because you wouldn't let *him* look. He's pretty hot under the collar about that.'

Henry scratched his arm. His thumb flicked twice as he did it.

'I didn't let him in the house because I took against him,' I said. 'Although to be fair, I guess I would have taken against John the Apostle if he came out here batting for Cole Farrington's team.'

Sheriff Jones laughed big at that: *Haw, haw, haw!* But his eyes didn't laugh.

I stood up. It was a relief to be on my feet. Standing, I had three or four inches on Jones. 'You can look to your heart's content.'

'I appreciate that. It'll make my life a lot easier, won't it? I've got Judge Cripps to deal with when I go back, and that's enough. Don't need to listen to one of Farrington's legal beagles yapping at me, not if I can help it.'

We went into the house with me leading and Henry bringing up the rear. After a few complimentary remarks about how neat the sitting room was and how tidy the kitchen was, we walked down the hall. Sheriff Jones had a perfunctory peek into Henry's room, and then we arrived at the main attraction. I pushed open the door to our bedroom with a queer sense of certainty: the blood would be back. It would be pooled on the floor, splashed on the walls, and soaking into the new mattress. Sheriff Jones would look. Then he would turn to me, remove the handcuffs that sat on his meaty hip across from his revolver, and say: *I'm arresting you for the murder of Arlette James, aren't I?*

There was no blood and no smell of blood, because the room had had days to air out. The bed was made, although not the way Arlette made it; my way was more Army-style, although my feet had kept me out of the war that had taken the Sheriff's son. Can't go kill Krauts if you have flat feet. Men with flat feet can only kill wives.

'Lovely room,' Sheriff Jones remarked. 'Gets the early light, doesn't it?'

'Yes,' I said. 'And stays cool most afternoons, even in summer, because the sun's over on the other side.' I went to the closet and opened it. That sense of certainty returned, stronger than ever. *Where's the quilt?* he'd say. *The one that belongs there in the middle of the top shelf?*

He didn't, of course, but he came forward with alacrity when I invited him to. His sharp eyes – bright green, almost feline – went here, there, and everywhere. 'Lot o' duds,' he said.

'Yes,' I admitted, 'Arlette liked clothes and she liked the mail-order catalogues. But since she only took the one valise – we have two, and the other one's still there, see it in the back corner? – I'd have to say she only took the ones she liked the best. And the ones that were prac-tical, I suppose. She had two pairs of slacks and a pair of blue denims, and those are gone, even though she didn't care for pants.'

'Pants're good for traveling in, though, aren't they? Man or woman, pants are good for traveling. And a woman might choose them. If she was in a hurry, that is.'

'I suppose.'

'She took her good jewelry and her picture of Nana and Pop-Pop,' Henry said from behind us. I jumped a little; I'd almost forgotten he was there.

'Did she, now? Well, I suppose she would.'

He took another flick through the clothes, then closed the closet door. 'Nice room,' he said, trudging back toward the hall with his Stetson in his hands. 'Nice *house*. Woman'd have to be crazy to leave a nice room and a nice house like this.'

'Mama talked about the city a lot,' Henry said, and sighed. 'She had the idea of opening some kind of shop.'

'Did she?' Sheriff Jones regarded him brightly with his green cat's eyes. 'Well! But a thing like that takes money, doesn't it?'

'She's got those acres from her father,' I said.

'Yes, yes.' Smiling bashfully, as if he'd forgotten those acres. 'And maybe it's for the best. "Better to be living in a wasteland than with a bitter-tongued, angry woman." Book of Proverbs. Are you glad she's gone, Son?'

'No,' Henry said, and tears overspilled his eyes. I blessed each one.

Sheriff Jones said, 'There-there.' And after offering that perfunctory comfort, he bent down with his hands braced on his pudgy knees, and looked under the bed. 'Appears to be a pair of woman's shoes under there. Broke in, too. The kind that would be good for walking. Don't suppose she ran away barefooty, do you?'

'She wore her canvas shoes,' I said. 'Those are the ones that are gone.'

They were, too. The faded green ones she used to call her gardening shoes. I'd remembered them just before starting to fill in the well.

'Ah!' he said. 'Another mystery solved.' He pulled a silver-plated watch from his vest pocket and consulted it. 'Well, I'd better get on the roll. Tempus is fugiting right along.'

We went back through the house, Henry bringing up the rear, perhaps so he could swipe his eyes dry in privacy. We walked with the Sheriff toward his Maxwell sedan with the star on the door. I was about to ask him if he wanted to see the well – I even knew what I was going to call it – when he stopped and gave my son a look of frightening kindness.

'I stopped at the Cotteries',' he said.

'Oh?' Henry said. 'Did you?'

'Told you these days I have to water just about every bush, but I'll use a privy anytime there's one handy, always assuming folks keep it clean and I don't have to worry about wasps while I'm waiting for my dingus to drip a little water. And the Cotteries are clean folks. Pretty daughter, too. Just about your age, isn't she?'

'Yes, sir,' Henry said, lifting his voice just a tiny bit on the *sir*.

'Kind of sweet on her, I guess? And her on you, from what her mama says.'

'Did she say that?' Henry asked. He sounded surprised, but pleased, too.

'Yes. Mrs Cotterie said you were troubled about your own mama, and that Shannon had told her something you said on that subject. I asked her what it was, and she said it wasn't her place to tell, but I could ask Shannon. So I did.'

Henry looked at his feet. 'I told her to keep it to herself.'

'You aren't going to hold it against her, are you?'

Sheriff Jones asked. 'I mean, when a big man like me with a star on his chest asks a little thing like her what she knows, it's kind of hard for the little thing to keep mum, isn't it? She just about has to tell, doesn't she?'

'I don't know,' Henry said, still looking down. 'Probably.' He wasn't just *acting* unhappiness; he *was* unhappy. Even though it was going just the way we had hoped it would.

'Shannon says your ma and your pop here had a big fight about selling those hundred acres, and when you came down on your poppa's side, Missus James slapped you up pretty good.'

'Yes,' Henry said colorlessly. 'She'd had too much to drink.'

Sheriff Jones turned to me. 'Was she drunk or just tiddly?'

'Somewhere in between,' I said. 'If she'd been all the way to drunk, she would have slept all night instead of getting up and packing a grip and creeping away like a thief.'

'Thought she'd come back once she sobered up, did you?'

'I did. It's over four miles out to the tarvy. I thought for sure she'd come back. Someone must have come along and given her a ride before her head cleared. A trucker on the Lincoln-Omaha run would be my guess.'

'Yep, yep, that'd be mine, too. You'll hear from her when she contacts Mr Lester, I'm sure. If she means to stay out on her own, if she's got that in her head, she'll need money to do it.'

So he knew that, too.

His eyes sharpened. 'Did she have any money at all, Mr James?'

'Well . . .'

'Don't be shy. Confession's good for the soul. The Catholics have got hold of something there, don't they?'

'I kept a box in my dresser. There was 200 dollars put by in it, to help pay the pickers when they start next month.'

'And Mr Cotterie,' Henry reminded. To Sheriff Jones, he said: 'Mr Cotterie has a corn harvester. A Harris Giant. Almost new. It's a pip.'

'Yep, yep, saw it in his dooryard. Big bastid, isn't it? Pardon my Polish. Money all gone out'n that box, was it?'

I smiled sourly — only it wasn't really me making that smile; the Conniving Man had been in charge ever since Sheriff Jones pulled up by the chopping block. 'She left twenty. Very generous of her. But twenty's all Harlan Cotterie will ever take for the use of his harvester, so *that's* all right. And when it comes to the pickers, I guess Stoppenhauser at the bank'll advance me a shortie loan. Unless he owes favors to the Farrington Company, that is. Either way, I've got my best farmhand right here.'

I tried to ruffle Henry's hair. He ducked away, embarrassed.

'Well, I've got a good budget of news to tell Mr Lester, don't I? He won't like any of it, but if he's as smart as he thinks he is, I guess he'll know enough to expect her in his office, and sooner rather than later. People have a way of turning up when they're short on folding green, don't they?'

'That's been my experience,' I said. 'If we're done here, Sheriff, my boy and I better get back to work. That useless well should have been filled in three years ago. An old cow of mine—'

'Elphis.' Henry spoke like a boy in a dream. 'Her name was Elphis.'

'Elphis,' I agreed. 'She got out of the barn and decided to take a stroll on the cap, and it gave way. Didn't have the good grace to die on her own, either. I had to shoot her. Come around the back of the barn I'll show you the wages of laziness with its damn feet sticking up. We're going to bury her right where she lies, and from now on I'm going to call that old well Wilfred's Folly.'

'Well, I would, wouldn't I? It'd be somethin' to see. But I've got that bad-tempered old judge to contend with. Another time.' He hoisted himself into the car, grunting as he did so. 'Thank you for the lemonade, and for bein' so gracious. You could have been a lot less so, considering who sent me out here.'

'It's all right,' I said. 'We all have our jobs.'

'And our crosses to bear.' His sharp eyes fastened on Henry again. 'Son, Mr Lester told me you were hidin' something. He was sure of it. And you were, weren't you?'

'Yes, sir,' Henry said in his colorless and somehow awful voice. As if all his emotions had flown away, like those things in Pandora's jar when she opened it. But there was no Elphis for Henry and me; our Elphis was dead in the well.

'If he asks me, I'll tell him he was wrong,' Sheriff Jones said. 'A company lawyer don't need to know that a boy's mother put her hand to him while she was in drink.' He groped under his seat, came up with a long S-shaped tool I knew well, and held it out to Henry. 'Would you save an old man's back and shoulder, Son?'

'Yes, sir, happy to.' Henry took the crank and went around to the front of the Maxwell.

'Mind your wrist!' Jones hollered. 'She kicks like a bull!' Then he turned to me. The inquisitive glitter had gone out of his eyes. So had the green. They looked dull and gray and hard, like lakewater on a cloudy day. It was the face of a man who could beat a railroad bum within an inch of his life and never lose a minute's sleep over it. 'Mr James,' he said. 'I need to ask you something. Man to man.'

'All right,' I said. I tried to brace myself for what I felt sure was coming next: *Is there another cow in yonder well? One named Arlette?* But I was wrong.

'I can put her name and description out on the telegraph wire, if you want. She won't have gone no farther than Omaha, will she? Not on just a hundred and eighty smackers. And a woman who's spent most of her life keepin' house has no idea of how to hide out. She'll like as not be in a rooming house over on the east side, where they run cheap. I could have her brought back. *Dragged* back by the hair of the head, if you want.'

'That's a generous offer, but—'

The dull gray eyes surveyed me. 'Think it over before you say yea or nay. Sometimes a fee-male needs talking to by hand, if you take my meaning, and after that they're all right. A good whacking has a way of sweetening some gals up. Think it over.'

'I will.'

The Maxwell's engine exploded into life. I stuck out my hand – the one that had cut her throat – but Sheriff Jones didn't notice. He was busy retarding the Maxwell's spark and adjusting her throttle.

Two minutes later he was no more than a diminishing boil of dust on the farm road.

'He never even wanted to look,' Henry marveled.

'No.'

And that turned out to be a very good thing.

We had shoveled hard and fast when we saw him coming, and nothing stuck up now but one of Elphis's lower legs. The hoof was about four feet below the lip of the well. Flies circled it in a cloud. The Sheriff would have marveled, all right, and he would have marveled even more when the dirt in front of that protruding hoof began to pulse up and down.

Henry dropped his shovel and grabbed my arm. The afternoon was hot, but his hand was ice-cold. 'It's her!'

he whispered. His face seemed to be nothing but eyes. '*She's trying to get out!*'

'Stop being such a God damned ninny,' I said, but I couldn't take my eyes off that circle of heaving dirt. It was as if the well were alive, and we were seeing the beating of its hidden heart.

Then dirt and pebbles sprayed to either side and a rat surfaced. The eyes, black as beads of oil, blinked in the sunshine. It was almost as big as a full-grown cat. Caught in its whiskers was a shred of bloodstained brown burlap.

'*Oh you fuck!*' Henry screamed.

Something whistled inches past my ear and then the edge of Henry's shovel split the rat's head in two as it looked up into the dazzle.

'She sent it,' Henry said. He was grinning. 'The rats are hers, now.'

'No such thing. You're just upset.'

He dropped his shovel and went to the pile of rocks with which we meant to finish the job once the well was mostly filled in. There he sat down and stared at me raptly. 'Are you sure? Are you positive she ain't haunting us? People say someone who's murdered will come back to haunt whoever—'

'People say lots of things. Lightning never strikes twice in the same place, a broken mirror brings seven years' bad luck, a whippoorwill calling at midnight means someone in the family's going to die.' I sounded reasonable, but I kept looking at the dead rat. And that shred of bloodstained burlap. From her *snood*. She was still wearing it down there in the dark, only now there was a hole in it with her hair sticking up. *That look is all the rage among dead women this summer*, I thought.

'When I was a kid, I really believed that if I stepped on a crack, I'd break my mother's back,' Henry said musingly.

'There – you see?'

He brushed rock-dust from the seat of his pants, and stood beside me. 'I got him, though – I got that fucker, didn't I?'

'You did!' And because I didn't like how he sounded – no, not at all – I clapped him on the back.

Henry was still grinning. 'If the Sheriff had come back here to look, like you invited him, and seen that rat come tunneling to the top, he might have had a few more questions, don't you think?'

Something about this idea set Henry to laughing hysterically. It took him four or five minutes to laugh himself out, and he scared a murder of crows up from the fence that kept the cows out of the corn, but eventually he got past it. By the time we finished our work it was past sundown, and we could hear owls comparing notes as they launched their pre-moonrise hunts from the barn loft. The rocks on top of the vanished well were tight together, and I didn't think anymore rats would be squirming to the surface. We didn't bother replacing the broken cap; there was no need. Henry seemed almost like his normal self again, and I thought we both might get a decent night's sleep.

'What do you say to sausage, beans, and cornbread?' I asked him.

'Can I start the generator and play *Hayride Party* on the radio?'

'Yessir, you can.'

He smiled at that, his old good smile. 'Thanks, Poppa.'

I cooked enough for four farmhands, and we ate it all.

Two hours later, while I was deep in my sitting-room chair and nodding over a copy of *Silas Marner*, Henry came in from his room, dressed in just his summer underdrawers. He regarded me soberly. 'Mama always insisted on me saying my prayers, did you know that?'

I blinked at him, surprised. 'Still? No. I didn't.'

'Yes. Even after she wouldn't look at me unless I had my pants on, because she said I was too old and it wouldn't be right. But I can't pray now, or ever again. If I got down on my knees, I think God would strike me dead.'

'If there is one,' I said.

'I hope there isn't. It's lonely, but I hope there isn't. I imagine all murderers hope there isn't. Because if there's no Heaven, there's no Hell.'

'Son, I was the one who killed her.'

'No — we did it together.'

It wasn't true — he was no more than a child, and I had cozened him — but it was true to him, and I thought it always would be.

'But you don't have to worry about me, Poppa. I know you think I'll slip — probably to Shannon. Or I might get feeling guilty enough to just go into Hemingford and confess to that Sheriff.'

Of course these thoughts had crossed my mind.

Henry shook his head, slowly and emphatically. 'That Sheriff — did you see the way he looked at everything? Did you see his *eyes*?'

'Yes.'

'He'd try to put us both in the 'lectric chair, that's what I think, and never mind me not fifteen until August. He'd be there, too, lookin' at us with those hard eyes of his when they strapped us in and—'

'Stop it, Hank. That's enough.'

It wasn't, though; not for him. '—and pulled the switch. I ain't never letting that happen, if I can help it. Those eyes aren't never going to be the last thing I see.' He thought over what he'd just said. '*Ever*, I mean. *Aren't ever.*'

'Go to bed, Henry.'

'Hank.'

'Hank. Go to bed. I love you.'

He smiled. 'I know, but I don't much deserve it.' He shuffled off before I could reply.

And so to bed, as Mr Pepys says. We slept while the owls hunted and Arlette sat in her deeper darkness with the lower part of her hoof-kicked face swung off to one side. The next day the sun came up, it was a good day for corn, and we did chores.

When I came in hot and tired to fix us a noon meal, there was a covered casserole dish sitting on the porch. There was a note fluttering beneath one edge. It said: *Wilf – We are so sorry for your trouble and will help any way we can. Harlan says dont worry about paying for the harvister this summer. Please if you hear from your wife let us know. Love, Sallie Cotterie. PS: If Henry comes calling on Shan, I will send back a blueberry cake.*

I stuck the note in the front pocket of my overalls with a smile. Our life after Arlette had begun.

If God rewards us on earth for good deeds – the Old Testament suggests it's so, and the Puritans certainly believed it – then maybe Satan rewards us for evil ones. I can't say for sure, but I can say that was a good summer, with plenty of heat and sun for the corn and just enough rain to keep our acre of vegetable garden refreshed. There was thunder and lightning some afternoons, but never one of those crop-crippling winds Midwestern farmers fear. Harlan Cotterie came with his Harris Giant and it never broke down a single time. I had worried that the Farrington Company might meddle in my business, but it didn't. I got my loan from the bank with no trouble, and paid back the note in full by October, because that year corn prices were sky-high and the Great Western's freight fees were at rock bottom. If you know your history, you know that those two things – the price of produce and the price of shippage – had changed places by '23, and have stayed changed ever since. For farmers out in the middle, the Great Depression started when the Chicago Agricultural Exchange crashed the following summer. But the summer of 1922 was as perfect as any farmer could hope for. Only one incident marred it, having to do with another of our bovine goddesses, and that I will tell you about soon.

Mr Lester came out twice. He tried to badger us, but he had nothing to badger with, and he must have known it, because he was looking pretty harried that July. I imagine his bosses were badgering *him*, and he was only passing it along. Or trying to. The first time, he asked a lot of questions that really weren't questions at all, but insinuations. Did I think my wife had had an accident? She must have, didn't I think, or she would either have contacted him in order to make a cash settlement on those 100 acres or just crept back to the farm with her (metaphorical) tail between her legs. Or did I think she had fallen afoul of some bad actor while on the road? Such things did happen, didn't they, from time to time? And it would certainly be convenient for me, wouldn't it?

The second time he showed up, he looked desperate as well as harried, and came right out with it: had my wife had an accident right there on the farm? Was that what had happened? Was it why she hadn't turned up either alive or dead?

'Mr Lester, if you're asking me if I murdered my wife, the answer is no.'

'Well of course you'd say so, wouldn't you?'

'That's your last question to me, sir. Get in yonder truck, drive away, and don't come back here. If you do, I'll take an axe-handle to you.'

'You'd go to jail for assault!' He was wearing a celluloid collar that day, and it had come all askew. It was almost possible to feel sorry for him as he stood there with that collar poking into the underside of his chin and sweat cutting lines through the dust on his chubby face, his lips twitching and his eyes bulging.

'No such thing. I have warned you off my property, as is my right, and I intend to send a registered letter to your firm stating that very thing. Come back again and that's trespassing and I *will* beat you. Take warning, sir.' Lars Olsen, who had brought Lester out again in his Red Baby, had all but cupped his hands around his ears to hear better.

When Lester reached the doorless passenger side of the truck, he whirled with an arm outstretched and a finger pointing, like a courtroom lawyer with a bent for the theatrical. 'I think you killed her! And sooner or later, murder will out!'

Henry – or Hank, as he now preferred to be called – came out of the barn. He had been pitching hay and he held the pitchfork across his chest like a rifle at port arms. 'What *I* think is you better get out of here before you start bleeding,' he said. The kind and rather timid boy I had known until the summer of '22 would never have said such a thing, but this one did, and Lester saw that he meant it. He got in. With no door to slam, he settled for crossing his arms over his chest.

'Come back anytime, Lars,' I said pleasantly, 'but don't bring him, no matter how much he offers you to cart his useless ass.'

'No, sir, Mr James,' Lars said, and off they went.

I turned to Henry. 'Would you have stuck him with that pitchfork?'

'Yessir. Made him squeal.' Then, unsmiling, he went back into the barn.

But he wasn't *always* unsmiling that summer, and Shannon Cotterie was the reason why. He saw a lot of her (more of her than was good for either of them; that I found out in the fall). She began coming to the house on Tuesday and Thursday afternoons, long-skirted and neatly bonneted, toting a side-sack loaded with good things to eat. She said she knew 'what men cook' – as though she were 30 instead of just 15 – and said she intended to see we had at least two decent suppers a week. And although I had only one of her mother's casseroles for comparison, I'd have to say that even at 15 she was the superior cook. Henry and I just threw steaks in a skillet on the stove; she had a way of seasoning that made plain old chew-meat delicious. She brought fresh vegetables in her side-sack – not just carrots and peas but exotic (to us) things like asparagus and fat green beans she cooked with pearl onions and bacon. There was even dessert. I can close my eyes in this shabby hotel room and smell her pastry. I can see her standing at the kitchen counter with her bottom swaying as she beat eggs or whipped cream.

Generous was the word for Shannon: of hip, of bust, of heart. She was gentle with Henry, and she cared for him. That made me care for her . . . only that's too thin, Reader. I loved her, and we both loved Henry. After those Tuesday and Thursday dinners, I'd insist on doing the washing-up and send them out on the porch. Sometimes I heard them murmuring to each other, and would peek out to see them sitting side by side in the wicker chairs, looking out at West Field and holding hands like an old married couple. Other times I spied them kissing, and there was nothing of the old married couple about that at all. There was a sweet urgency to those kisses that belongs only to the very young, and I stole away with my heart aching.

One hot Tuesday afternoon she came early. Her father was out in our North Field on his harvester, Henry riding with him, a little crew of Indians from the Shoshone reservation in Lyme Biska walking along behind . . . and behind them, Old Pie driving the gather-truck. Shannon asked for a dipper of cold water, which I was glad to provide. She stood there on the shady side of the house, looking impossibly cool in a voluminous dress that covered her from throat to shin and shoulder to wrist – a Quaker dress, almost. Her manner was grave, perhaps even scared, and for a moment I was scared myself. *He's told her*, I thought. That turned out not to be true. Except, in a way, it was.

'Mr James, is Henry sick?'

'Sick? Why, no. Healthy as a horse, I'd say. And eats like one, too. You've seen that for yourself. Although I think even a man who *was* sick would have trouble saying no to your cooking, Shannon.'

That earned me a smile, but it was of the distracted variety. 'He's different this summer. I always used to know what he was thinking, but now I don't. He *broods*.'

'Does he?' I asked (too heartily).

'You haven't seen it?'

'No, ma'am.' (I had.) 'He seems like his old self to me. But he cares for you an awful lot, Shan. Maybe what looks like brooding to you feels like the lovesicks to him.'

I thought that would get me a real smile, but no. She touched my wrist. Her hand was cool from the dipper handle. 'I've thought of that, but . . .' The rest she blurted out. 'Mr James, if he was sweet on someone else – one of the girls from school – you'd tell me, wouldn't you? You wouldn't try to . . . to spare my feelings?'

I laughed at that, and I could see her pretty face lighten with relief. 'Shan, listen to me. Because I *am* your friend. Summer's always a hardworking time, and with Arlette gone, Hank and I have been busier than one-armed paperhangers. When we come in at night, we eat a meal – a fine one, if you happen to show up – and then read for an hour. Sometimes he talks about how he misses his mama. After that we go to bed, and the next day we get up and do it all again. He barely has time to spark *you*, let alone another girl.'

'He's sparked me, all right,' she said, and looked off to where her father's harvester was chugging along the skyline.

'Well . . . that's good, isn't it?'

'I just thought . . . he's so quiet now . . . so moody . . . sometimes he looks off into the distance and I have to say his name twice or three times before he hears me and answers.' She blushed fiercely. 'Even his kisses seem different. I don't know how to explain it, but they do. And if you ever tell him I said that, I'll die. I will just *die*.'

'I never would,' I said. 'Friends don't peach on friends.'

'I guess I'm being a silly-billy. And of course he misses his mama, I know he does. But so many of the girls at school are prettier than me . . . prettier than me . . .'

I tilted her chin up so she was looking at me. 'Shannon Cotterie, when my boy looks at you, he sees the prettiest girl in the world. And he's right. Why, if I was his age, I'd spark you myself.'

'Thank you,' she said. Tears like tiny diamonds stood in the corners of her eyes.

'The only thing you need to worry about is putting him back in his place if he gets out of it. Boys can get pretty steamed up, you know. And if I'm out of line, you just go on and tell me so. That's another thing that's all right, if it's between friends.'

She hugged me then, and I hugged her back. A good strong hug, but perhaps better for Shannon than me. Because Arlette was between us. She was between me and everyone else in the summer of 1922, and it was the same for Henry. Shannon had just told me so.

* * *

One night in August, with the good picking done and Old Pie's crew paid up and back on the rez, I woke to the sound of a cow lowing. *I overslept milking time*, I thought, but when I fumbled my father's pocket watch off the table beside my bed and peered at it, I saw it was quarter past three in the morning. I put the watch to my ear to see if it was still ticking, but a look out the window into the moonless dark would have served the same purpose. Those weren't the mildly uncomfortable calls of a cow needing to be rid of her milk, either. It was the sound of an animal in pain. Cows sometimes sound that way when they're calving, but our goddesses were long past that stage of their lives.

I got up, started out the door, then went back to the closet for my .22. I heard Henry sawing wood behind the closed door of his room as I hurried past with the rifle in one hand and my boots in the other. I hoped he wouldn't wake up and want to join me on what could be a dangerous errand. There were only a few wolves left on the plains by then, but Old Pie had told me there was summer-sick in some of the foxes along the Platte and Medicine Creek. It was what the Shoshone called rabies, and a rabid critter in the barn was the most likely cause of those cries.

Once I was outside the house, the agonized lowing was very loud, and hollow, somehow. Echoing. *Like a cow in a well*, I thought. That thought chilled the flesh on my arms and made me grip the .22 tighter.

By the time I reached the barn doors and shouldered the right one open, I could hear the rest of the cows starting to moo in sympathy, but those cries were calm inquiries compared to the agonized bawling that had awakened me . . . and would awaken Henry, too, if I didn't put an end to what was causing it. There was a carbon arc–lamp hanging on a hook to the right of the door – we didn't use an open flame in the barn unless we absolutely had to, especially in the summertime, when the loft was loaded with hay and every corncrib crammed full to the top.

I felt for the spark-button and pushed it. A brilliant circle of blue-white radiance leaped out. At first my eyes were too dazzled to make out anything; I could only hear those painful cries and the hoof-thuds as one of our goddesses tried to escape from whatever was hurting her. It was Achelois. When my eyes adjusted a bit, I saw her tossing her head from side to side, backing up until her hindquarters hit the door of her stall – third on the right, as you walked up the aisle – and then lurching forward again. The other cows were working themselves into a full-bore panic.

I hauled on my muckies, then trotted to the stall with the .22 tucked under my left arm. I threw the door open, and stepped back. Achelois means 'she who drives away pain,' but this Achelois was in agony. When she blundered into the aisle, I saw her back legs were smeared with blood. She reared up like a horse (something I never saw a cow do before), and when she did, I saw a huge Norway rat clinging to one of her teats. The weight had stretched the pink stub to a taut length of cartilage. Frozen in surprise (and horror), I thought of how, as a child, Henry would sometimes pull a string of pink bubble-gum out of his mouth. *Don't do that*, Arlette would scold him. *No one wants to look at what you've been chewing.*

I raised the gun, then lowered it. How could I shoot, with the rat swinging back and forth like a living weight at the end of a pendulum?

In the aisle now, Achelois lowed and shook her head from side to side, as if that might somehow help. Once all four of her feet were back on the floor, the rat was able to stand on the hay-littered barnboards. It was like some strange freak puppy with beads of bloodstained milk in its whiskers. I looked around for something to hit it with, but before I could grab the broom Henry had left leaning against Phemonoe's stall, Achelois reared again and the rat thumped to the floor. At first I thought she had simply dislodged it, but then I saw the pink and wrinkled stub protruding from the rat's mouth, like a flesh cigar. The damned thing had torn one of poor Achelois's teats right off. She laid her head against one of the barn beams and mooed at me tiredly, as if to say: *I've given you milk all these years and offered no trouble, not like some I could mention, so why did you let this happen to me?* Blood was pooling beneath her udder. Even in my shock and revulsion, I didn't think she would die of her wound, but the sight of her – and of the rat, with her blameless teat in its mouth – filled me with rage.

I still didn't shoot at it, partly because I was afraid of fire, but mostly because, with the carbon lamp in one hand, I was afraid I'd miss. Instead, I brought the rifle-stock down, hoping to kill this intruder as Henry had killed the survivor from the well with his shovel. But Henry was a boy with quick reflexes, and I was a man of middle age who had been roused from a sound sleep. The rat avoided me with ease and went trotting up the center aisle. The severed teat bobbed up and down in its mouth, and I realized the rat was eating it – warm and no doubt still full of milk – even as it ran. I gave chase, smacked at it twice more, and missed both times. Then I saw where it was running: the pipe leading into the defunct livestock well. Of course! Rat Boulevard! With the well filled in, it was their only means of egress. Without it, they'd have been buried alive. Buried with *her.*

But surely, I thought, *that thing is too big for the pipe. It must have come from outside – a nest in the manure pile, perhaps.*

It leaped for the opening, and as it did so, it elongated

its body in the most amazing fashion. I swung the stock of the varmint gun one last time and shattered it on the lip of the pipe. The rat I missed entirely. When I lowered the carbon lamp to the pipe's mouth, I caught one blurred glimpse of its hairless tail slithering away into the darkness, and heard its little claws scraping on the galvanized metal. Then it was gone. My heart was pounding hard enough to put white dots in front of my eyes. I drew in a deep breath, but with it came a stench of putrefaction and decay so strong that I fell back with my hand over my nose. The need to scream was strangled by the need to retch. With that smell in my nostrils I could almost see Arlette at the other end of the pipe, her flesh now teeming with bugs and maggots, liquefying; her face beginning to drip off her skull, the grin of her lips giving way to the longer-lasting bone grin that lay beneath.

I crawled back from that awful pipe on all fours, spraying vomit first to my left and then to my right, and when my supper was all gone, I gagged up long strings of bile. Through watering eyes I saw that Achelois had gone back into her stall. That was good. At least I wasn't going to have to chase her through the corn and put a nose-halter on her to lead her back.

What I wanted to do first was plug the pipe – I wanted to do that before anything – but as my gorge quieted, clear thinking reasserted itself. Achelois was the priority. She was a good milker. More important, she was my responsibility. I kept a medicine chest in the little barn office where I did the books. In the chest I found a large can of Rawleigh Antiseptic Salve. There was a pile of clean rags in the corner. I took half of them and went back to Achelois's stall. I closed the door of her stall to minimize the risk of being kicked, and sat on the milking stool. I think part of me felt I *deserved* to be kicked. But dear old Achelois stilled when I stroked her flank and whispered, 'Soo, Boss, soo, Bossy-boss,' and although she shivered when I smeared the salve on her hurt part, she stood quiet.

When I'd taken what steps I could to prevent infection, I used the rags to wipe up my vomit. It was important to do a good job, for any farmer will tell you that human vomit attracts predators every bit as much as a garbage-hole that hasn't been adequately covered. Raccoons and woodchucks, of course, but mostly rats. Rats love human leavings.

I had a few rags left over, but they were Arlette's kitchen castoffs and too thin for my next job. I took the hand-scythe from its peg, lit my way to our woodpile, and chopped a ragged square from the heavy canvas that covered it. Back in the barn, I bent down and held the lamp close to the pipe's mouth, wanting to make sure the rat (or another; where there was one, there would surely be more) wasn't lurking, ready to defend its territory, but it was empty for as far as I could see, which was four feet or so. There were no droppings, and that didn't surprise me. It was an active thoroughfare – now their *only* thoroughfare – and they wouldn't foul it as long as they could do their business outside.

I stuffed the canvas into the pipe. It was stiff and bulky, and in the end I had to use a broomhandle to poke it all the way in, but I managed. 'There,' I said. 'See how you like that. Choke on it.'

I went back and looked at Achelois. She stood quietly, and gave me a mild look over her shoulder as I stroked her. I knew then and know now she was only a cow – farmers hold few romantic notions about the natural world, you'll find – but that look still brought tears to my eyes, and I had to stifle a sob. *I know you did your best*, it said. *I know it's not your fault.*

But it was.

I could hear Henry snoring. I thought I would lie awake long, and when I went to sleep I would dream of the rat scurrying up the hay-littered barnboards toward its escape-hatch with that teat in its mouth, but I fell asleep at once and my sleep was both dreamless and restorative. I woke with morning light flooding the room and the stench of my dead wife's decaying body thick on my hands, sheets, and pillow-case. I sat bolt upright, gasping but already aware that the smell was an illusion. That smell was my bad dream. I had it not at night but by the morning's first, sanest light, and with my eyes wide open.

I expected infection from the rat-bite in spite of the salve, but there was none. Achelois died later that year, but not of that. She never gave milk again, however; not a single drop. I should have butchered her, but I didn't have the heart to do it. She had suffered too much on my account.

The next day, I handed Henry a list of supplies and told him to take the truck over to The Home and get them. A great, dazzled smile broke across his face.

'The truck? *Me?* On my own?'

'You still know all the forward gears? And you can still find reverse?'

'Gosh, sure!'

'Then I think you're ready. Maybe not for Omaha just yet – or even Lincoln – but if you take her slow, you ought to be just fine in Hemingford Home.'

'Thanks!' He threw his arms around me and kissed my cheek. For a moment it seemed like we were friends again. I even let myself believe it a little, although in my heart I knew better. The evidence might be belowground, but the truth was between us, and always would be.

I gave him a leather wallet with money in it. 'That was your grandfather's. You might as well keep it; I was going to give it to you for your birthday this fall, anyway. There's money inside. You can keep what's left over, if there is any.' I almost added, *And don't bring back any stray dogs*, but stopped myself in time. That had been his mother's stock witticism.

He tried to thank me again, and couldn't. It was all too much.

'Stop by Lars Olsen's smithy on your way back and fuel up. Mind me, now, or you'll be on foot instead of behind the wheel when you get home.'

'I won't forget. And Poppa?'

'Yes.'

He shuffled his feet, then looked at me shyly. 'Could I stop at Cotteries' and ask Shan to come?'

'No,' I said, and his face fell before I added: 'You ask Sallie or Harlan if Shan can come. And you make sure you tell them that you've never driven in town before. I'm putting you on your honor, Son.'

As if either of us had any left.

I watched by the gate until our old truck disappeared into a ball of its own dust. There was a lump in my throat that I couldn't swallow. I had a stupid but very strong premonition that I would never see him again. I suppose it's something most parents feel the first time they see a child going away on his own and face the realization that if a child is old enough to be sent on errands without supervision, he's not totally a child any longer. But I couldn't spend too much time wallowing in my feelings; I had an important chore to do, and I'd sent Henry away so I could attend to it by myself. He would see what had happened to the cow, of course, and probably guess what had done it, but I thought I could still ease the knowledge for him a little.

I first checked on Achelois, who seemed listless but

otherwise fine. Then I checked the pipe. It was still plugged, but I was under no illusions; it might take time, but eventually the rats would gnaw through the canvas. I had to do better. I took a bag of Portland cement around to the house-well and mixed up a batch in an old pail. Back in the barn, while I waited for it to thicken, I poked the swatch of canvas even deeper into the pipe. I got it in at least two feet, and those last two feet I packed with cement. By the time Henry got back (and in fine spirits; he had indeed taken Shannon, and they had shared an icecream soda bought with change from the errands), it had hardened. I suppose a few of the rats must have been out foraging, but I had no doubt I'd immured most of them – including the one that had savaged poor Achelois – down there in the dark. And down there in the dark they would die. If not of suffocation, then of starvation once their unspeakable pantry was exhausted.

So I thought then.

In the years between 1916 and 1922, even stupid Nebraska farmers prospered. Harlan Cotterie, being far from stupid, prospered more than most. His farm showed it. He added a barn and a silo in 1919, and in 1920 he put in a deep well that pumped an unbelievable six gallons per minute. A year later, he added indoor plumbing (although he sensibly kept the backyard privy). Then, three times a week, he and his womenfolk could enjoy what was an unbelievable luxury that far out in the country: hot baths and showers supplied not by pots of water heated on the kitchen stove but from pipes that first brought the water from the well and then carried it away to the sump. It was the showerbath that revealed the secret Shannon Cotterie had been keeping, although I suppose I already knew, and had since the day she said, *He's sparked me, all right* – speaking in a flat, lusterless voice that was unlike her, and looking not at me but off at the silhouettes of her father's harvester and the gleaners trudging behind it.

This was near the end of September, with the corn all picked for another year but plenty of garden-harvesting left to do. One Saturday afternoon, while Shannon was enjoying the showerbath, her mother came along the back hall with a load of laundry she'd taken in from the line early, because it was looking like rain. Shannon probably thought she had closed the bathroom door all the way – most ladies are private about their bathroom duties, and Shannon Cotterie had a special reason to feel that way as the summer of 1922 gave way to fall – but perhaps it came off the latch and swung open partway. Her mother happened to glance in, and although the old sheet that served as a shower-curtain was pulled all the way around on its U-shaped rail, the spray had rendered it translucent. There was no need for Sallie to see the girl herself; she saw the *shape* of the girl, for once without one of her voluminous Quaker-style dresses to hide. That was all it took. The girl was five months along, or near to it; she probably could not have kept her secret much longer in any case.

Two days later, Henry came home from school (he now took the truck) looking frightened and guilty. 'Shan hasn't been there the last two days,' he said, 'so I stopped by Cotteries' to ask if she was all right. I thought she might have come down with the Spanish Flu. They wouldn't let me in. Mrs Cotterie just told me to get on, and said her husband would come to talk to you tonight, after his chores were done. I ast if I could do anything, and she said, "You've done enough, Henry."'

Then I remembered what Shan had said. Henry put his face in his hands and said, 'She's pregnant, Poppa, and they found out. I know that's it. We want to get married, but I'm afraid they won't let us.'

'Never mind them,' I said, '*I* won't let you.'

He looked at me from wounded, streaming eyes. 'Why not?'

I thought: *You saw what it came to between your mother and me and you even have to ask?* But what I said was, 'She's 15 years old, and you won't even be that for another two weeks.'

'But we love each other!'

O, that loonlike cry. That milksop hoot. My hands were clenched on the legs of my overalls, and I had to force them open and flat. Getting angry would serve no purpose. A boy needed a mother to discuss a thing like this with, but his was sitting at the bottom of a filled-in well, no doubt attended by a retinue of dead rats.

'I know you do, Henry—'

'*Hank!* And others get married that young!'

Once they had; not so much since the century turned and the frontiers closed. But this I didn't say. What I said was that I had no money to give them a start. Maybe by '25, if crops and prices stayed good, but now there was nothing. And with a baby on the way—

'There *would* be enough!' he said. 'If you hadn't been such a bugger about that hundred acres, there'd be *plenty*! S*he* would've given me some of it! And *she* wouldn't have talked to me this way!'

At first I was too shocked to say anything. It had been six weeks or more since Arlette's name – or even the vague pronounal alias *she* – had passed between us.

He was looking at me defiantly. And then, far down our stub of road, I saw Harlan Cotterie on his way. I had always considered him my friend, but a daughter who turns up pregnant has a way of changing such things.

'No, she wouldn't have talked to you this way,' I agreed, and made myself look him straight in the eye. 'She would have talked to you worse. And laughed, likely as not. If you search your heart, Son, you'll know it.'

'No!'

'Your mother called Shannon a little baggage, and then told you to keep your willy in your pants. It was her last advice, and although it was as crude and hurtful as most of what she had to say, you should have followed it.'

Henry's anger collapsed. 'It was only after that . . . after that night . . . that we . . . Shan didn't want to, but I talked her into it. And once we started, she liked it as much as I did. Once we started, she asked for it.' He said that with a strange, half-sick pride, then shook his head wearily. 'Now that hundred acres just sits there sprouting weeds, and I'm in Dutch. If Momma was here, she'd help me fix it. Money fixes everything, that's what *he* says.' Henry nodded at the approaching ball of dust.

'If you don't remember how tight your momma was with a dollar, then you forget too fast for your own good,' I said. 'And if you've forgotten how she slapped you across the mouth that time—'

'I ain't,' he said sullenly. Then, more sullenly still: 'I thought you'd help me.'

'I mean to try. Right now I want you to make yourself scarce. You being here when Shannon's father turns up would be like waving a red rag in front of a bull. Let me see where we are – and how he is – and I may call you out on the porch.' I took his wrist. 'I'm going to do my best for you, Son.'

He pulled his wrist out of my grasp. 'You better.'

He went into the house, and just before Harlan pulled up in his new car (a Nash as green and gleaming under its coating of dust as a bottlefly's back), I heard the screen door slam out back.

The Nash chugged, backfired, and died. Harlan got out, took off his duster, folded it, and laid it on the seat. He'd worn the duster because he was dressed for the occasion: white shirt, string tie, good Sunday pants held up by a belt with a silver buckle. He hitched at that, getting the pants set the way he wanted them just below his tidy little paunch. He'd always been good to me, and I'd always considered us not just friends but good friends, yet in that moment I hated him. Not because he'd come to tax me about my son; God knows I would have done the same, if our positions had been reversed. No, it was the brand-new shiny green Nash. It was the silver belt buckle made in the shape of a dolphin. It was the new silo, painted bright red, and the indoor plumbing. Most of all it was the plain-faced, biddable wife he'd left back at his farm, no doubt making supper in spite of her worry. The wife whose sweetly given reply in the face of any problem would be, *Whatever you think is best, dear.* Women, take note: a wife like that never needs to fear bubbling away the last of her life through a cut throat.

He strode to the porch steps. I stood and held out my hand, waiting to see if he'd take it or leave it. There was a hesitation while he considered the pros and cons, but in the end he gave it a brief squeeze before letting loose. 'We've got a considerable problem here, Wilf,' he said.

'I know it. Henry just told me. Better late than never.'

'Better never at all,' he said grimly.

'Will you sit down?'

He considered this, too, before taking what had always been Arlette's rocker. I knew he didn't want to sit – a man who's mad and upset doesn't feel good about sitting – but he did, just the same.

'Would you want some iced tea? There's no lemonade, Arlette was the lemonade expert, but—'

He waved me quiet with one pudgy hand. Pudgy but hard. Harlan was one of the richest farmers in Hemingford County, but he was no straw boss; when it came to haying or harvest, he was right out there with the hired help. 'I want to get back before sundown. I don't see worth a shit by those headlamps. My girl has got a bun in her oven, and I guess you know who did the damn cooking.'

'Would it help to say I'm sorry?'

'No.' His lips were pressed tight together, and I could see hot blood beating on both sides of his neck. 'I'm madder than a hornet, and what makes it worse is that I've got no one to be mad *at*. I can't be mad at the kids because they're just kids, although if she wasn't with child, I'd turn Shannon over my knee and paddle her for not doing better when she *knew* better. She was raised better and churched better, too.'

I wanted to ask him if he was saying Henry was raised wrong. I kept my mouth shut instead, and let him say all the things he'd been fuming about on his drive over here. He'd thought up a speech, and once he said it, he might be easier to deal with.

'I'd like to blame Sallie for not seeing the girl's condition sooner, but first-timers usually carry high, everyone knows that . . . and my God, you know the sort of dresses Shan wears. That's not a new thing, either. She's been wearing those granny-go-to-meetin' dresses since she was 12 and started getting her . . .'

He held his pudgy hands out in front of his chest. I nodded.

'And I'd like to blame *you*, because it seems like you skipped that talk fathers usually have with sons.' *As if you'd know anything about raising sons*, I thought. 'The one about how he's got a pistol in his pants and he should keep the safety on.' A sob caught in his throat and he cried, 'My . . . little . . . *girl* . . . is too young to be a mother!'

Of course there was blame for me Harlan didn't know about. If I hadn't put Henry in a situation where he was desperate for a woman's love, Shannon might not be in the fix she was in. I also could have asked if Harlan had maybe saved a little blame for himself while he was busy sharing it out. But I held quiet. Quiet never came naturally to me, but living with Arlette had given me plenty of practice.

'Only I can't blame you, either, because your wife went and run off this spring, and it's natural your attention would lapse at a time like that. So I went out back and chopped damn near half a cord of wood before I came over here, trying to get some of that mad out, and it must have worked. I shook your hand, didn't I?'

The self-congratulation I heard in his voice made me itch to say, *Unless it was rape, I think it still takes two to tango.* But I just said, 'Yes, you did,' and left it at that.

'Well, that brings us to what you're going to do about it. You and that boy who sat at my table and ate the food my wife cooked for him.'

Some devil – the creature that comes into a fellow, I suppose, when the Conniving Man leaves – made me say, 'Henry wants to marry her and give the baby a name.'

'That's so God damned ridiculous I don't want to hear it. I won't say Henry doesn't have a pot to piss in nor a window to throw it out of – I know you've done right, Wilf, or as right as you can, but that's the best I can say. These have been fat years, and you're still only one step ahead of the bank. Where are you going to be when the years get lean again? And they always do. If you had the cash from that back hundred, then it might be different – cash cushions hard times, everyone knows that – but with Arlette gone, there they sit, like a constipated old maid on a chamberpot.'

For just a moment part of me tried to consider how things would have been if I had given in to Arlette about that fucking land, as I had about so many other things. *I'd be living in stink, that's how it would have been. I would have had to dig out the old spring for the cows, because cows won't drink from a brook that's got blood and pigs' guts floating in it.*

True. But I'd be living instead of just existing, Arlette would be living with me, and Henry wouldn't be the sullen, anguished, difficult boy he had turned into. The boy who had gotten his friend since childhood into a peck of trouble.

'Well, what do you want to do?' I asked. 'I doubt you made this trip with nothing in mind.'

He appeared not to have heard me. He was looking out across the fields to where his new silo stood on the horizon. His face was heavy and sad, but I've come too far and written too much to lie; that expression did not move me much. 1922 had been the worst year of my life, one where I'd turned into a man I no longer knew, and Harlan Cotterie was just another washout on a rocky and miserable stretch of road.

'She's bright,' Harlan said. 'Mrs McReady at school says Shan's the brightest pupil she's taught in her whole career, and that stretches back almost 40 years. She's good in English, and she's even better in the maths, which Mrs McReady says is rare in girls. She can do triggeronomy, Wilf. Did you know that? Mrs McReady herself can't do triggeronomy.'

No, I hadn't known, but I knew how to say the word. I felt, however, that this might not be the time to correct my neighbor's pronunciation.

'Sallie wanted to send her to the normal school in Omaha. They've taken girls as well as boys since 1918, although no females have graduated so far.' He gave me a look that was hard to take: mingled disgust and hostility. 'The females always want to get *married*, you see. And *have babies*. Join Eastern *Star* and sweep the God damned *floor*.'

He sighed.

'Shan could be the first. She has the skills and she has the brains. You didn't know that, did you?'

No, in truth I had not. I had simply made an assumption — one of many that I now know to have been wrong — that she was farm wife material, and no more.

'She might even teach college. We planned to send her to that school as soon as she turned 17.'

Sallie planned, is what you mean, I thought. *Left to your own devices, such a crazy idea never would have crossed your farmer's mind.*

'Shan was willing, and the money was put aside. It was all arranged.' He turned to look at me, and I heard the tendons in his neck creak. 'It's *still* all arranged. But first — almost right away — she's going to the St Eusebia Catholic Home for Girls in Omaha. She doesn't know it yet, but it's going to happen. Sallie talked about sending her to Deland — Sal's sister lives there — or to my aunt and uncle in Lyme Biska, but I don't trust any of those people to carry through on what we've decided. Nor does a girl who causes this kind of problem deserve to go to people she knows and loves.'

'What is it you've decided, Harl? Besides sending your daughter to some kind of an . . . I don't know . . . orphanage?'

He bristled. 'It's not an orphanage. It's a clean, whole-some, and busy place. So I've been told. I've been on the exchange, and all the reports I get are good ones. She'll have chores, she'll have her schooling, and in another four months she'll have her baby. When that's done, the kid will be given up for adoption. The sisters at St Eusebia will see to that. Then she can come home, and in another year and a half she can go to teachers' college, just like Sallie wants. And me, of course. Sallie and me.'

'What's my part in this? I assume I must have one.'

'Are you smarting on me, Wilf? I know you've had a tough year, but I still won't bear you smarting on me.'

'I'm not smarting on you, but you need to know

you're not the only one who's mad and ashamed. Just tell me what you want, and maybe we can stay friends.'

The singularly cold little smile with which he greeted this – just a twitch of the lips and a momentary appearance of dimples at the corners of his mouth – said a great deal about how little hope he held out for *that*.

'I know you're not rich, but you still need to step up and take your share of the responsibility. Her time at the home – the sisters call it pre-natal care – is going to cost me 300 dollars. Sister Camilla called it a donation when I talked to her on the phone, but I know a fee when I hear one.'

'If you're going to ask me to split it with you—'

'I know you can't lay your hands on 150 dollars, but you better be able to lay them on 75, because that's what the tutor's going to cost. The one who's going to help her keep up with her lessons.'

'I can't do that. Arlette cleaned me out when she left.' But for the first time I found myself wondering if she might've socked a little something away. That business about the 200 she was supposed to have taken when she ran off had been a pure lie, but even pin-and-ribbon money would help in this situation. I made a mental note to check the cupboards and the canisters in the kitchen.

'Take another shortie loan from the bank,' he said. 'You paid the last one back, I hear.'

Of course he heard. Such things are supposed to be private, but men like Harlan Cotterie have long ears. I felt a fresh wave of dislike for him. He had loaned me the use of his corn harvester and only taken 20 dollars for the use of it? So what? He was asking for that and more, as though his precious daughter had never spread her legs and said *come on in and paint the walls*.

'I had crop money to pay it back with,' I said. 'Now

I don't. I've got my land and my house and that's pretty much it.'

'You find a way,' he said. 'Mortgage the house, if that's what it takes. 75 dollars is your share, and compared to having your boy changing didies at the age of 15, I think you're getting off cheap.'

He stood up. I did, too. 'And if I can't find a way? What then, Harl? You send the Sheriff?'

His lips curled in an expression of contempt that turned my dislike of him to hate. It happened in an instant, and I still feel that hate today, when so many other feelings have been burned out of my heart. 'I'd never go to law on a thing like this. But if you don't take your share of the responsibility, you and me's done.' He squinted into the declining daylight. 'I'm going. Got to, if I want to get back before dark. I won't need the 75 for a couple of weeks, so you got that long. And I won't come dunning you for it. If you don't, you don't. Just don't say you can't, because I know better. You should have let her sell that acreage to Farrington, Wilf. If you'd done that, she'd still be here and you'd have some money in hand. And my daughter might not be in the fam'ly way.'

In my mind, I pushed him off the porch and jumped on his hard round belly with both feet when he tried to get up. Then I got my hand-scythe out of the barn and put it through one of his eyes. In reality, I stood with one hand on the railing and watched him trudge down the steps.

'Do you want to talk to Henry?' I asked. 'I can call him. He feels as bad about this as I do.'

Harlan didn't break stride. 'She was clean and your boy filthied her up. If you hauled him out here, I might knock him down. I might not be able to help myself.'

I wondered about that. Henry was getting his growth,

he was strong, and perhaps most important of all, he knew about murder. Harl Cotterie didn't.

He didn't need to crank the Nash but only push a button. Being prosperous was nice in all sorts of ways. '75 is what I need to close this business,' he called over the punch and blat of the engine. Then he whirled around the chopping block, sending George and his retinue flying, and headed back to his farm with its big generator and indoor plumbing.

When I turned around, Henry was standing beside me, looking sallow and furious. 'They can't send her away like that.'

So he had been listening. I can't say I was surprised.

'Can and will,' I said. 'And if you try something stupid and headstrong, you'll only make a bad situation worse.'

'We could run away. We wouldn't get caught. If we could get away with . . . with what we did . . . then I guess I could get away with eloping off to Colorado with my gal.'

'You couldn't,' I said, 'because you'd have no money. Money fixes everything, he says. Well, this is what I say: *no* money *spoils* everything. I know it, and Shannon will, too. She's got her baby to watch out for now—'

'Not if they make her give it away!'

'That doesn't change how a woman feels when she's got the chap in her belly. A chap makes them wise in ways men don't understand. I haven't lost any respect for you or her just because she's going to have a baby – you two aren't the first, and you won't be the last, even if Mr High and Mighty had the idea she was only going to use what's between her legs in the water-closet. But if you asked a five-months-pregnant girl to run off with you . . . and she agreed . . . I'd lose respect for both of you.'

'What do you know?' he asked with infinite contempt. 'You couldn't even cut a throat without making a mess of it.'

I was speechless. He saw it, and left me that way.

He went off to school the next day without any argument even though his sweetie was no longer there. Probably because I let him take the truck. A boy will take any excuse to drive a truck when driving's new. But of course the new wears off. The new wears off everything, and it usually doesn't take long. What's beneath is gray and shabby, more often than not. Like a rat's hide.

Once he was gone, I went into the kitchen. I poured the sugar, flour, and salt out of their tin canisters and stirred through them. There was nothing. I went into the bedroom and searched her clothes. There was nothing. I looked in her shoes and there was nothing. But each time I found nothing, I became more sure there was *something*.

I had chores in the garden, but instead of doing them, I went out back of the barn to where the old well had been. Weeds were growing on it now: witchgrass and scraggly fall goldenrod. Elphis was down there, and Arlette was, too. Arlette with her face cocked to the side. Arlette with her clown's grin. Arlette in her *snood*.

'Where is it, you contrary bitch?' I asked her. 'Where did you hide it?'

I tried to empty my mind, which was what my father advised me to do when I'd misplaced a tool or one of my few precious books. After a little while I went back into the house, back into the bedroom, back into the closet. There were two hatboxes on the top shelf. In the first one I found nothing but a hat – the white one she wore to church (when she could trouble herself to go, which was about once a month). The hat in the other box was red, and I'd never seen her wear it. It looked like a whore's hat to me. Tucked into the satin inner band, folded into tiny squares no bigger than pills, were two 20-dollar bills. I tell you now, sitting here in this cheap hotel room and listening to the rats scuttering and scampering in the walls (yes, my old friends are here), that those two 20-dollar bills were the seal on my damnation.

Because they weren't enough. You see that, don't you? Of course you do. One doesn't need to be an expert in trig-geronomy to know that one needs to add 35 to 40 to make 75. Doesn't sound like much, does it? But in those days you could buy two months' worth of groceries for 35 dollars, or a good used harness at Lars Olsen's smithy. You could buy a train ticket all the way to Sacramento . . . which I sometimes wish I had done.

35.

And sometimes when I lie in bed at night, I can actually *see* that number. It flashes red, like a warning not to cross a road because a train is coming. I tried to cross anyway, and the train ran me down. If each of us has a Conniving Man inside, each of us also has a Lunatic. And on those nights when I can't sleep because the flashing number won't *let* me sleep, my Lunatic says it was a conspiracy: that Cotterie, Stoppenhauser, and the Farrington shyster were all in it together. I know better, of course (at least in daylight). Cotterie and Mr Attorney Lester might have had a talk with Stoppenhauser later on – after I did what I did – but it was surely innocent to begin with; Stoppenhauser was actually trying to help me out . . . and do a little business for Home Bank & Trust, of course. But when Harlan or Lester – or both of them together – saw an opportunity, they took it. The Conniving Man outconnived: how do you like that? By then I hardly cared, because by then I had lost my son, but do you know who I really blame?

Arlette.

Yes.

Because it was she who left those two bills inside her red whore's hat for me to find. And do you see how fiendishly clever she was? Because it wasn't the *40* that did me in; it was the money between that and what Cotterie demanded for his pregnant daughter's tutor; what he wanted so she could study Latin and keep up with her *triggeronomy*.

35, 35, 35.

I thought about the money he wanted for the tutor all the rest of that week, and over the weekend, too. Sometimes I took out those two bills − I had unfolded them but the creases still remained − and studied at them. On Sunday night I made my decision. I told Henry that he'd have to take the Model T to school on Monday; I had to go to Hemingford Home and see Mr Stoppenhauser at the bank about a shortie loan. A small one. Just 35 dollars.

'What for?' Henry was sitting at the window and looking moodily out at the darkening West Field.

I told him. I thought it would start another argument about Shannon, and in a way, I wanted that. He'd said nothing about her all week, although I knew Shan was gone. Mert Donovan had told me when he came by for a load of seed corn. 'Went off to some fancy school back in Omaha,' he said. 'Well, more power to her, that's what I think. If they're gonna vote, they better learn. Although,' he added after a moment's cogitation, 'mine does what I tell her. She better, if she knows what's good for her.'

If I knew she was gone, Henry also knew, and probably before I did − schoolchildren are enthusiastic gossips. But he had said nothing. I suppose I was trying to give him a reason to let out all the hurt and recriminations.

It wouldn't be pleasant, but in the long run it might be beneficial. Neither a sore on the forehead or in the brain behind the forehead should be allowed to fester. If they do, the infection is likely to spread.

But he only grunted at the news, so I decided to poke a little harder.

'You and I are going to split the payback,' I said. 'It's apt to come to no more than 38 dollars if we retire the loan by Christmas. That's 19 apiece. I'll take yours out of your choring money.'

Surely, I thought, this would result in a flood of anger . . . but it brought only another surly little grunt. He didn't even argue about having to take the Model T to school, although he said the other kids made fun of it, calling it 'Hank's ass-breaker.'

'Son?'

'What.'

'Are you all right?'

He turned to me and smiled — his lips moved around, at least. 'I'm fine. Good luck at the bank tomorrow, Poppa. I'm going to bed.'

As he stood up, I said: 'Will you give me a little kiss?' He kissed my cheek. It was the last one.

He took the T to school and I drove the truck to Hemingford Home, where Mr Stoppenhauser brought me into his office after a mere five-minute wait. I explained what I needed, but declined to say what I needed it for, only citing personal reasons. I thought for such a piddling amount I would not need to be more specific, and I was right. But when I'd finished, he folded his hands on his desk blotter and gave me a look of almost fatherly sternness. In the corner, the Regulator clock ticked away quiet slices of time. On the street — considerably louder — came the blat of an engine. It stopped, there was silence, and then another engine started up. Was that my son, first arriving in the Model T and then stealing my truck? There's no way I can know for sure, but I think it was.

'Wilf,' Mr Stoppenhauser said, 'you've had a little time to get over your wife leaving the way she did – pardon me for bringing up a painful subject, but it seems pertinent, and besides, a banker's office is a little like a priest's confessional – so I'm going to talk to you like a Dutch uncle. Which is only fitting, since that's where my mother and father came from.'

I had heard this one before – as had, I imagine, most visitors to that office – and I gave it the dutiful smile it was meant to elicit.

'Will Home Bank & Trust loan you 35 dollars? You bet. I'm tempted to put it on a man-to-man basis and do the deal out of my own wallet, except I never carry more than what it takes to pay for my lunch at the Splendid Diner and a shoe-shine at the barber shop. Too much money's a constant temptation, even for a wily old cuss like me, and besides, business is business. *But!*' He raised his finger. 'You don't *need* 35 dollars.'

'Sad to say, I do.' I wondered if he knew why. He might have; he was indeed a wily old cuss. But so was Harl Cotterie, and Harl was also a shamed old cuss that fall.

'No; you don't. You need 750, that's what you need, and you could have it today. Either bank it or walk out with it in your pocket, all the same to me either way. You paid off the mortgage on your place 3 years ago. It's free and clear. So there's absolutely no reason why you shouldn't turn around and take out another mortgage. It's done all the time, my boy, and by the best people. You'd be surprised at some of the paper we're carrying. All the best people. Yessir.'

'I thank you very kindly, Mr Stoppenhauser, but

I don't think so. That mortgage was like a gray cloud over my head the whole time it was in force, and—'

'Wilf, that's the *point*!' The finger went up again. This time it wagged back and forth, like the pendulum of the Regulator. 'That is exactly the rootin'-tootin', cowboy-shootin' *point*! It's the fellows who take out a mortgage and then feel like they're always walking around in sunshine who end up defaulting and losing their valuable property! Fellows like you, who carry that bank-paper like a barrowload of rocks on a gloomy day, are the fellows who always pay back! And do you want to tell me that there aren't improvements you could make? A roof to fix? A little more livestock?' He gave me a sly and roguish look. 'Maybe even indoor plumbing, like your neighbor down the road? Such things pay for themselves, you know. You could end up with improvements that far outweigh the cost of a mortgage. Value for money, Wilf! Value for money!'

I thought it over. At last I said, 'I'm very tempted, sir. I won't lie about that—'

'No need to. A banker's office, the priest's confessional – very little difference. The best men in this county have sat in that chair, Wilf. The very best.'

'But I only came in for a shortie loan – which you have kindly granted – and this new proposal needs a little thinking about.' A new idea occurred to me, one that was surprisingly pleasant. 'And I ought to talk it over with my boy, Henry – Hank, as he likes to be called now. He's getting to an age where he needs to be consulted, because what I've got will be his someday.'

'Understood, completely understood. But it's the right thing to do, believe me.' He got to his feet and stuck out his hand. I got to mine and shook it. 'You came in here to buy a fish, Wilf. I'm offering to sell you a pole. Much better deal.'

'Thank you.' And, leaving the bank, I thought: *I'll talk it over with my son.* It was a good thought. A warm thought in a heart that had been chilly for months.

The mind is a funny thing, isn't it? Preoccupied as I was by Mr Stoppenhauser's unsolicited offer of a mortgage, I never noticed that the vehicle I'd come in had been replaced by the one Henry had taken to school. I'm not sure I would have noticed right away even if I'd had less weighty matters on my mind. They were both familiar to me, after all; they were both mine. I only realized when I was leaning in to get the crank and saw a folded piece of paper, held down by a rock, on the driving seat.

I just stood there for a moment, half in and half out of the T, one hand on the side of the cab, the other reaching under the seat, which was where we kept the crank. I suppose I knew why Henry had left school and made this swap even before I pulled his note from beneath the makeshift paperweight and unfolded it. The truck was more reliable on a long trip. A trip to Omaha, for instance.

> *Poppa,*
> *I have taken the truck. I guess you know where I am going. Leave me alone. I know you can send Sheriff Jones after me to bring me back, but if you do I will tell everything. You might think I'd change my mind because I am 'just a kid,' BUT I WONT. Without Shan I dont care about nothing. I love you Poppa even if I don't know why, since everything we did has brought me mizzery.*
> *Your Loving Son,*
> *Henry 'Hank' James*

I drove back to the farm in a daze. I think some people waved to me – I think even Sallie Cotterie, who was minding the Cotteries' roadside vegetable stand, waved to me – and I probably waved back, but I've no memory of doing so. For the first time since Sheriff Jones had come out to the farm, asking his cheerful, no-answers-needed questions and looking at everything with his cold inquisitive eyes, the electric chair seemed like a real possibility to me, so real I could almost feel the buckles on my skin as the leather straps were tightened on my wrists and above my elbows.

He would be caught whether I kept my mouth shut or not. That seemed inevitable to me. He had no money, not even six bits to fill the truck's gas tank, so he'd be walking long before he even got to Elkhorn. If he managed to steal some gas, he'd be caught when he approached the place where she was now living (Henry assumed as a prisoner; it had never crossed his unfinished mind that she might be a willing guest). Surely Harlan had given the person in charge – Sister Camilla – Henry's description. Even if he hadn't considered the possibility of the outraged swain making an appearance at the site of his lady-love's durance vile, Sister Camilla would have. In her business, she had surely dealt with outraged swains before.

My only hope was that, once accosted by the authorities, Henry would keep silent long enough to realize that he'd been snared by his own foolishly romantic notions rather than by my interference. Hoping for a teenage boy to come to his senses is like betting on a long shot at the horse track, but what else did I have?

As I drove into the dooryard, a wild thought crossed my mind: leave the T running, pack a bag, and take off for Colorado. The idea lived for no more than two seconds. I had money – 75 dollars, in fact – but the T would die long before I crossed the state line at Julesburg. And that wasn't the important thing; if it had been, I could always have driven as far as Lincoln and then traded the T and

60 of my dollars for a reliable car. No, it was the place. The home place. *My* home place. I had murdered my wife to keep it, and I wasn't going to leave it now because my foolish and immature accomplice had gotten it into his head to take off on a romantic quest. If I left the farm, it wouldn't be for Colorado; it would be for state prison. And I would be taken there in chains.

That was Monday. There was no word on Tuesday or Wednesday. Sheriff Jones didn't come to tell me Henry had been picked up hitchhiking on the Lincoln-Omaha Highway, and Harl Cotterie didn't come to tell me (with Puritanical satisfaction, no doubt), that the Omaha police had arrested Henry at Sister Camilla's request, and he was currently sitting in the pokey, telling wild tales about knives and wells and burlap bags. All was quiet on the farm. I worked in the garden harvesting pantry-vegetables, I mended fences, I milked the cows, I fed the chickens – and I did it all in a daze. Part of me, and not a small part, either, believed that all of this was a long and terribly complex dream from which I would awake with Arlette snoring beside me and the sound of Henry chopping wood for the morning fire.

Then, on Thursday, Mrs McReady – the dear and portly widow who taught academic subjects at Hemingford School – came by in her own Model T to ask me if Henry was all right. 'There's an . . . an intestinal *distress* going around,' she said. 'I wondered if he caught it. He left very suddenly.'

'He's distressed all right,' I said, 'but it's a love-bug instead of a stomach-bug. He's run off, Mrs McReady.' Unexpected tears, stinging and hot, rose in my eyes. I took the handkerchief from the pocket on the front of my biballs, but some of them ran down my cheeks before I could wipe them away.

When my vision was clear again, I saw that Mrs McReady, who meant well by every child, even the difficult ones, was near tears herself. She must have known all along what kind of bug Henry was suffering from.

'He'll be back, Mr James. Don't you fear. I've seen this before, and I expect to see it a time or two again before I retire, although that time's not so far away as it once was.' She lowered her voice, as if she feared George the rooster or one of his feathered harem might be a spy. 'The one you want to watch out for is her father. He's a hard and unbending man. Not a bad man, but hard.'

'I know,' I said. 'And I suppose you know where his daughter is now.'

She lowered her eyes. It was answer enough.

'Thank you for coming out, Mrs McReady. Can I ask you to keep this to yourself?'

'Of course . . . but the children are already whispering.'

Yes. They would be.

'Are you on the exchange, Mr James?' She looked for telephone wires. 'I see you are not. Never mind. If I hear anything, I'll come out and tell you.'

'You mean if you hear anything before Harlan Cotterie or Sheriff Jones.'

'God will take care of your son. Shannon, too. You know, they really were a lovely couple; everyone said so. Sometimes the fruit ripens too early, and a frost kills it. Such a shame. Such a sad, sad shame.'

She shook my hand — a man's strong grip — and then drove away in her flivver. I don't think she realized that, at the end, she had spoken of Shannon and my son in the past tense.

On Friday Sheriff Jones came out, driving the car with the gold star on the door. And he wasn't alone. Following

along behind was my truck. My heart leaped at the sight
of it, then sank again when I saw who was behind the
wheel: Lars Olsen.

I tried to wait quietly while Jones went through his
Ritual of Arrival: belt-hitching, forehead-wiping (even
though the day was chilly and overcast), hair-brushing. I
couldn't do it. 'Is he all right? Did you find him?'

'No, nope, can't say we did.' He mounted the porch
steps. 'Line-rider over east of Lyme Biska found the truck,
but no sign of the kid. We might know better about the
state of his health if you'd reported this when it happened.
Wouldn't we?'

'I was hoping he'd come back on his own,' I said dully.
'He's gone to Omaha. I don't know how much I need to
tell you, Sheriff—'

Lars Olsen had meandered into auditory range, ears
all but flapping. 'Go on back to my car, Olsen,' Jones said.
'This is a private conversation.'

Lars, a meek soul, scurried off without demur. Jones
turned back to me. He was far less cheerful than on his
previous visit, and had dispensed with the bumbling
persona, as well.

'I already know enough, don't I? That your kid got
Harl Cotterie's daughter in the fam'ly way and has probably gone haring off to Omaha. He run the truck off the
road into a field of high grass when he knew the tank
was 'bout dry. That was smart. He get that kind of smart
from you? Or from Arlette?'

I said nothing, but he'd given me an idea. Just a little
one, but it might come in handy.

'I'll tell you one thing he did that we'll thank him
for,' Jones said. 'Might keep him out of jail, too. He yanked
all the grass from under the truck before he went on his
merry way. So the exhaust wouldn't catch it afire, you know.
Start a big prairie fire that burned a couple thousand acres,

a jury might get a bit touchy, don't you think? Even if the offender was only 15 or so?'

'Well, it didn't happen, Sheriff – he did the right thing – so why are you going on about it?' I knew the answer, of course. Sheriff Jones might not give a hoot in a high wind for the likes of Andrew Lester, attorney-at-law, but he was good friends with Harl. They were both members of the newly formed Elks Lodge, and Harl had it in for my son.

'A little touchy, aren't you?' He wiped his forehead again, then resettled his Stetson. 'Well, I might be touchy, too, if it was my son. And you know what? If it was my son and Harl Cotterie was my neighbor – my *good* neighbor – I might've just taken a run down there and said, "Harl? You know what? I think my son might be going to try and see your daughter. You want to tell someone to be on the peep for him?" But you didn't do that, either, did you?'

The idea he'd given me was looking better and better, and it was almost time to spring it.

'He hasn't shown up wherever she is, has he?'

'Not yet, no, he may still be looking for it.'

'I don't think he ran away to see Shannon,' I said.

'Why, then? Do they have a better brand of icecream there in Omaha? Because that's the way he was headed, sure as your life.'

'I think he went looking for his mother. I think she may have gotten in touch with him.'

That stopped him for a good ten seconds, long enough for a wipe of the forehead and a brush of the hair. Then he said, 'How would she do that?'

'A letter would be my best guess.' The Hemingford Home Grocery was also the post office, where all the general delivery went. 'They would have given it to him when he went in for candy or a bag of peanuts, as he often does on his way back from school. I don't know for sure, Sheriff, anymore than I know why you came out here acting like I committed some kind of crime. I wasn't the one who knocked her up.'

'You ought to hush that kind of talk about a nice girl!'

'Maybe yes and maybe no, but this was as much a surprise to me as it was to the Cotteries, and now my boy is gone. They at least know where their daughter is.'

Once again he was stumped. Then he took out a little notebook from his back pocket and jotted something in it. He put it back and asked, 'You don't know for sure that your wife got in touch with your kid, though – that's what you're telling me? It's just a guess?'

'I know he talked a lot about his mother after she left, but then he stopped. And I know he hasn't shown up at that home where Harlan and his wife stuck Shannon.' And on that score I was as surprised as Sheriff Jones . . . but awfully grateful. 'Put the two things together, and what do you get?'

'I don't know,' Jones said, frowning. 'I truly don't. I thought I had this figured out, but I've been wrong before, haven't I? Yes, and will be again. "We are all bound in error," that's what the Book says. But good God, kids make my life hard. If you hear from your son, Wilfred, I'd tell him to get his skinny ass home and stay away from Shannon Cotterie, if he knows where she is. She won't want to see him, guarantee you that. Good news is no prairie fire, and we can't arrest him for stealing his father's truck.'

'No,' I said grimly, 'you'd never get me to press charges on that one.'

'*But.*' He raised his finger, which reminded me of Mr Stoppenhauser at the bank. 'Three days ago, in Lyme Biska – not so far from where the rider found your truck – someone held up that grocery and ethyl station on the edge of town. The one with the Blue Bonnet Girl on the roof? Took 23 dollars. I got the report sitting on my desk. It was a young fella dressed in old cowboy clothes, with a bandanna pulled up over his mouth and a plainsman hat slouched down over his eyes. The owner's mother was tending the counter, and the fella menaced her with some sort of tool. She thought it might have been a crowbar or a pry-rod, but who knows? She's pushing 80 and half-blind.'

It was my time to be silent. I was flabbergasted. At last I said, 'Henry left from school, Sheriff, and so far as I can remember he was wearing a flannel shirt and corduroy trousers that day. He didn't take any of his clothes, and in any case he doesn't *have* any cowboy clothes, if you mean boots and all. Nor does he have a plainsman's hat.'

'He could have stolen those things, too, couldn't he?'

'If you don't know anything more than what you just said, you ought to stop. I know you're friends with Harlan—'

'Now, now, this has nothing to do with that.'

It did and we both knew it, but there was no reason to go any farther down that road. Maybe my 80 acres didn't stack up very high against Harlan Cotterie's 400, but I was still a landowner and a taxpayer, and I wasn't going to be browbeaten. That was the point I was making, and Sheriff Jones had taken it.

'My son's not a robber, and he doesn't threaten women. That's not how he acts and not the way he was raised.'

Not until just lately, anyway, a voice inside whispered.

'Probably just a drifter looking for a quick payday,' Jones said. 'But I felt like I had to bring it up, and so I did. And we don't know what people might say, do we? Talk gets around. Everybody talks, don't they? Talk's cheap. The subject's closed as far as I'm concerned – let the Lyme County Sheriff worry about what goes on in Lyme Biska, that's my motto — but you should know that the Omaha police are keeping an eye on the place where Shannon Cotterie's at. Just in case your son gets in touch, you know.'

He brushed back his hair, then resettled his hat a final time.

'Maybe he'll come back on his own, no harm done, and we can write this whole thing off as, I don't know, a bad debt.'

'Fine. Just don't call him a bad son, unless you're willing to call Shannon Cotterie a bad daughter.'

The way his nostrils flared suggested he didn't like that much, but he didn't reply to it. What he said was, 'If he comes back and says he's seen his mother, let me know, would you? We've got her on the books as a missing person. Silly, I know, but the law is the law.'

'I'll do that, of course.'

He nodded and went to his car. Lars had settled behind the wheel. Jones shooed him over — the Sheriff was the kind of man who did his own driving. I thought about the young man who'd held up the store, and tried to tell myself that my Henry would never do such a thing, and even if he were driven to it, he wouldn't be sly enough to put on clothes he'd stolen out of somebody's barn or bunkhouse. But Henry was different now, and murderers *learn* slyness, don't they? It's a survival skill. I thought that maybe—

But no. I won't say it that way. It's too weak. This is my confession, my last word on everything, and if I can't tell the truth, the whole truth, and nothing but the truth, what good is it? What good is anything?

It was him. It was Henry. I had seen by Sheriff Jones's eyes that he only brought up that side-o'-the-road robbery because I wouldn't kowtow to him the way he thought

I should've, but *I* believed it. Because I knew more than Sheriff Jones. After helping your father to murder your mother, what was stealing some new clothes and waving a crowbar in an old granny's face? No such much. And if he tried it once, he would try it again, once those 23 dollars were gone. Probably in Omaha. Where they would catch him. And then the whole thing might come out. Almost certainly *would* come out.

I climbed to the porch, sat down, and put my face in my hands.

Days went by. I don't know how many, only that they were rainy. When the rain comes in the fall, outside chores have to wait, and I didn't have enough livestock or outbuildings to fill the hours with inside chores. I tried to read, but the words wouldn't seem to string together, although every now and then a single one would seem to leap off the page and scream. Murder. Guilt. Betrayal. Words like those.

Days I sat on the porch with a book in my lap, bundled into my sheepskin coat against the damp and the cold, watching the rainwater drip off the overhang. Nights I lay awake until the small hours of the morning, listening to the rain on the roof overhead. It sounded like timid fingers tapping for entry. I spent too much time thinking about Arlette in the well with Elphis. I began to fancy that she was still . . . not alive (I was under stress but not crazy), but somehow *aware*. Somehow watching developments from her makeshift grave, and with pleasure.

Do you like how things have turned out, Wilf? she'd ask if she could (and, in my imagination, did). *Was it worth it? What do you say?*

One night about a week after Sheriff Jones's visit, as I sat trying to read *The House of the Seven Gables*, Arlette crept up behind me, reached around the side of my head, and tapped the bridge of my nose with one cold, wet finger.

I dropped the book on the braided sitting-room rug, screamed, and leaped to my feet. When I did, the cold fingertip ran down to the corner of my mouth. Then it touched me again, on top of my head, where the hair was getting thin. This time I laughed – a shaky, angry laugh – and bent to pick up my book. As I did, the finger tapped a third time, this one on the nape of the neck, as if my dead wife were saying, *Have I got your attention yet, Wilf?* I stepped away – so the fourth tap wouldn't be in the eye – and looked up. The ceiling overhead was discolored and dripping. The plaster hadn't started to bulge yet, but if the rain continued, it would. It might even dissolve and come down in chunks. The leak was above my special reading-place. Of course it was. The rest of the ceiling looked fine, at least so far.

I thought of Stoppenhauser saying, *Do you want to tell me there aren't improvements you could make? A roof to fix?* And that sly look. As if he had *known*. As if he and Arlette were in on it together.

Don't be getting such things in your head, I told myself. *Bad enough that you keep thinking of her, down there. Have the worms gotten her eyes yet, I wonder? Have the bugs eaten away her sharp tongue, or at least blunted it?*

I went to the table in the far corner of the room, got the bottle that stood there, and poured myself a good-sized hooker of brown whiskey. My hand trembled, but only a little. I downed it in two swallows. I knew it would be a bad business to turn such drinking into a habit, but it's not every night that a man feels his dead wife tap him on the nose. And the hooch made me feel better. More in control of myself. I didn't need to take on a 750-dollar mortgage to fix my roof, I could patch it with scrap lumber when the rain stopped. But it would be an ugly fix; would make the place look like what my mother would have called trash-poor. Nor was that the point. Fixing a leak would take only a day or two. I needed work that would keep me through the winter. Hard labour would drive out thoughts of Arlette on her dirt throne, Arlette in her burlap *snood*. I needed home improvement projects that would send me to bed so tired that I'd sleep right through, and not lie there listening to the rain and wondering if Henry was out in it, maybe coughing from the grippe. Sometimes work is the only thing, the only answer.

The next day I drove to town in my truck and did what I never would have thought of doing if I hadn't needed to borrow 35 dollars: I took out a mortgage for 750. In the end we are all caught in devices of our own making. I believe that. In the end we are all caught.

In Omaha that same week, a young man wearing a plainsman's hat walked into a pawnshop on Dodge Street and bought a nickel-plated .32 caliber pistol. He paid with 5 dollars that had no doubt been handed to him, under duress, by a half-blind old woman who did business beneath the sign of the Blue Bonnet Girl. The next day, a young man wearing a flat cap on his head and a red bandanna over his mouth and nose walked into the Omaha branch of the First Agricultural Bank, pointed a gun at a pretty young teller named Rhoda Penmark, and demanded all the money in her drawer. She passed over about 200 dollars, mostly in ones and fives – the grimy kind farmers carry rolled up in the pockets of their bib overalls.

As he left, stuffing the money into his pants with one hand (clearly nervous, he dropped several bills on the floor), the portly guard – a retired policeman – said: 'Son, you don't want to do this.'

The young man fired his .32 into the air. Several people screamed. 'I don't want to shoot you, either,' the young man said from behind his bandanna, 'but I will if I have to. Fall back against that post, sir, and stay there if you know what's good for you. I've got a friend outside watching the door.'

The young man ran out, already stripping the bandanna from his face. The guard waited for a minute or so, then went out with his hands raised (he had no sidearm), just in case there really was a friend. There wasn't, of course. Hank James had no friends in Omaha except for the one with his baby growing in her belly.

I took 200 dollars of my mortgage money in cash and left the rest in Mr Stoppenhauser's bank. I went shopping at the hardware, the lumberyard, and the grocery store where Henry might have gotten a letter from his mother . . . if she were still alive to write one. I drove out of town in a drizzle that had turned to slashing rain by the time I got home. I unloaded my newly purchased lumber and shingles, did the feeding and milking, then put away my groceries – mostly dry goods and staples that were running low without Arlette to ride herd on the kitchen. With that chore done, I put water on the woodstove to heat for a bath and stripped off my damp clothes. I pulled the wad of money out of the right front pocket of my crumpled biballs, counted it, and saw I still had just shy of 160 dollars. Why had I taken so much in cash? Because my mind had been elsewhere. *Where* else-where, pray? On Arlette and Henry, of course. Not to mention Henry and Arlette. They were pretty much all I thought about on those rainy days.

I knew it wasn't a good idea to have so much cash money around. It would have to go back to the bank, where it could earn a little interest (although not nearly enough to equal the interest on the loan) while I was thinking about how best to put it to work. But in the meantime, I should lay it by someplace safe.

The box with the red whore's hat in it came to mind. It was where she'd stashed her own money, and it had been safe there for God knew how long. There was too much in my wad to fit in the band, so I thought I'd put it in the hat itself. It would only be there until I found an excuse to go back to town.

I went into the bedroom, stark naked, and opened the closet door. I shoved aside the box with her white church-hat in it, then reached for the other one. I'd pushed it all the way to the back of the shelf and had to stand on tiptoe to reach it. There was an elastic cord around it. I hooked my finger under it to pull it forward, was momentarily aware that the hatbox felt much too heavy – as though there were a brick inside it instead of a bonnet – and then there was a strange *freezing* sensation, as though my hand had been doused in icewater. A moment later the freeze turned to fire. It was a pain so intense that it locked all the muscles in my arm. I stumbled backwards, roaring in surprise and agony and dropping money everywhere. My finger was still hooked into the elastic, and the hatbox came tumbling out. Crouched on top of it was a Norway rat that looked all too familiar.

You might say to me, 'Wilf, one rat looks like another,' and ordinarily you'd be right, but I knew this one; hadn't I seen it running away from me with a cow's teat jutting from its mouth like the butt of a cigar?

The hatbox came free of my bleeding hand, and the rat tumbled to the floor. If I had taken time to think, it would have gotten away again, but conscious thinking had been canceled by pain, surprise, and the horror I suppose almost any man feels when he sees blood pouring from a part of his body that was whole only seconds before. I didn't even remember that I was as naked as the day I was born, just brought my right foot down on the rat. I heard its bones crunch and felt its guts squash. Blood and liquefied

intestines squirted from beneath its tail and doused my left
ankle with warmth. It tried to twist around and bite me
again; I could see its large front teeth gnashing, but it couldn't
quite reach me. Not, that was, as long as I kept my foot on
it. So I did. I pushed harder, holding my wounded hand
against my chest, feeling the warm blood mat the thick pelt
that grew there. The rat twisted and flopped. Its tail first
lashed my calf, then wrapped around it like a grass snake.
Blood gushed from its mouth. Its black eyes bulged like
marbles.

I stood there with my foot on the dying rat for a
long time. It was smashed to pieces inside, its innards
reduced to gruel, and still it thrashed and tried to bite.
Finally it stopped moving. I stood on it for another minute,
wanting to make sure it wasn't just playing possum (a rat
playing possum – ha!), and when I was sure it was dead,
I limped into the kitchen, leaving bloody footprints and
thinking in a confused way of the oracle warning Pelias
to beware of a man wearing just one sandal. But I was
no Jason; I was a farmer half-mad with pain and amaze-
ment, a farmer who seemed condemned to foul his
sleeping-place with blood.

As I held my hand under the pump and froze it with
cold water, I could hear someone saying, 'No more, no
more, no more.' It was me, I knew it was, but it sounded
like an old man. One who had been reduced to beggary.

I can remember the rest of that night, but it's like looking
at old photographs in a mildewy album. The rat had
bitten all the way through the webbing between my left
thumb and forefinger – a terrible bite, but in a way, lucky.
If it had seized on the finger I'd hooked under that elastic
cord, it might have bitten the finger entirely off. I realized that when I went back into the bedroom and picked
up my adversary by the tail (using my right hand; the

left was too stiff and painful to flex). It was two feet long, a six-pounder, at least.

Then it wasn't the same rat that escaped into the pipe, I hear you saying. *It couldn't have been.* But it was, I tell you it was. There was no identifying mark – no white patch of fur or conveniently memorable chewed ear – but I knew it was the one that had savaged Achelois. Just as I knew it hadn't been crouched up there by accident.

I carried it into the kitchen by the tail and dumped it in the ash bucket. This I took out to our swill-pit. I was naked in the pouring rain, but hardly aware of it. What I was mostly aware of was my left hand, throbbing with a pain so intense it threatened to obliterate all thought.

I took my duster from the hook in the mudroom (it was all I could manage), shrugged into it, and went out again, this time into the barn. I smeared my wounded hand with Rawleigh Salve. It had kept Achelois's udder from infecting, and might do the same for my hand. I started to leave, then remembered how the rat had escaped me last time. The pipe! I went to it and bent over, expecting to see the cement plug either chewed to pieces or completely gone, but it was intact. Of course it was. Even six-pound rats with oversized teeth can't chew through concrete. That the idea had even crossed my mind shows the state I was in. For a moment I seemed to see myself as if from outside: a man naked except for an unbuttoned duster, his body-hair matted with blood all the way to the groin, his torn left hand glistening under a thick snot-like coating of cow-salve, his eyes bugging out of his head. The way the rat's had bugged out, when I stepped on it.

It wasn't the same rat, I told myself. *The one that bit Achelois is either lying dead in the pipe or in Arlette's lap.*

But I knew it was. I knew it then and I know it now.

It was.

Back in the bedroom, I got down on my knees and picked up the bloodstained money. It was slow work with only one hand. Once I bumped my torn hand on the side of the bed and howled with pain. I could see fresh blood staining the salve, turning it pink. I put the cash on the dresser, not even bothering to cover it with a book or one of Arlette's damned ornamental plates. I couldn't even remember why it had seemed so important to hide the bills in the first place. The red hatbox I kicked into the closet, and then slammed the door. It could stay there until the end of time, for all of me.

Anyone who's ever owned a farm or worked on one will tell you that accidents are commonplace, and precautions must be taken. I had a big roll of bandage in the chest beside the kitchen pump – the chest Arlette had always called the 'hurt-locker.' I started to get the roll out, but then the big pot steaming on the stove caught my eye. The water I'd put on for a bath when I was still whole and when such monstrous pain as that which seemed to be consuming me was only theoretical. It occurred to me that hot soapy water might be just the thing for my hand. The wound couldn't hurt any worse, I reasoned, and the immersion would cleanse it. I was wrong on both counts, but how was I to know? All these years later, it still seems like a reasonable idea. I suppose it might even have worked, if I had been bitten by an ordinary rat.

I used my good right hand to ladle hot water into a basin (the idea of tilting the pot and pouring from it was out of the question), then added a cake of Arlette's coarse brown washing soap. The last cake, as it turned out; there are so many supplies a man neglects to lay in when he's not used to doing it. I added a rag, then went into the bedroom, got down on my knees again, and began mopping up the blood and guts. All the time remembering (of course) the last time I had cleaned blood from the floor in that damned bedroom. That time at least Henry had been with me to share the horror. Doing it alone, and in pain, was a terrible job. My shadow bumped and flitted on the wall, making me think of Quasimodo in Hugo's *Notre-Dame de Paris*.

With the job almost finished, I stopped and cocked my head, breath held, eyes wide, my heart seeming to thud in my bitten left hand. I heard a *scuttering* sound, and it seemed to come from everywhere. The sound of running rats. In that moment I was sure of it. The rats from the well. Her loyal courtiers. They had found another way out. The one crouched on top of the red hatbox had only been the first and the boldest. They had infiltrated the house, they were in the walls, and soon they would come out and overwhelm me. She would have her revenge. I would hear her laughing as they tore me to pieces.

The wind gusted hard enough to shake the house and shriek briefly along the eaves. The scuttering sound intensified, then faded a bit when the wind died. The relief that filled me was so intense it overwhelmed the pain (for a few seconds, at least). It wasn't rats; it was sleet. With the coming of dark, the temperature had fallen and the rain had become semi-solid. I went back to scrubbing away the remains.

When I was done, I dumped the bloody wash-water over the porch rail, then went back to the barn to apply a fresh coating of salve to my hand. With the wound completely cleansed, I could see that the webbing between my thumb and forefinger was torn open in three slashes that looked like a sergeant's stripes. My left thumb hung askew, as if the rat's teeth had severed some important cable between it and the rest of my left hand. I applied the cow-goop and then plodded back to the house, thinking, *It hurts but at least it's clean. Achelois was all right;*

I'll be all right, too. Everything's fine. I tried to imagine my body's defenses mobilizing and arriving at the scene of the bite like tiny firemen in red hats and long canvas coats.

At the bottom of the hurt-locker, wrapped in a torn piece of silk that might once have been part of a lady's slip, I found a bottle of pills from the Hemingford Home Drug Store. Fountain-penned on the label in neat capital letters was **ARLETTE JAMES Take 1 or 2 at Bed-Time for Monthly Pain.** I took three, with a large shot of whiskey. I don't know what was in those pills – morphia, I suppose – but they did the trick. The pain was still there, but it seemed to belong to a Wilfred James currently existing on some other level of reality. My head swam; the ceiling began to turn gently above me; the image of tiny firemen arriving to douse the blaze of infection before it could take hold grew clearer. The wind was strengthening, and to my half-dreaming mind, the constant low rattle of sleet against the house sounded more like rats than ever, but I knew better. I think I even said so aloud: 'I know better, Arlette, you don't fool me.'

As consciousness dwindled and I began to slip away, I realized that I might be going for good: that the combination of shock, booze, and morphine might end my life. I would be found in a cold farmhouse, my skin blue-gray, my torn hand resting on my belly. The idea did not frighten me; on the contrary, it comforted me.

While I slept, the sleet turned to snow.

When I woke at dawn the following morning, the house was as chilly as a tomb and my hand had swelled up to twice its ordinary size. The flesh around the bite was ashy gray but the first three fingers had gone a dull pink that would be red by the end of the day. Touching anywhere on that hand except for the pinky caused excruciating pain. Nevertheless, I wrapped it as tightly as I could, and that reduced the throbbing. I got a fire started in the kitchen stove – one handed it was a long job, but I managed – and then drew up close, trying to get warm. All of me except for the bitten hand, that was; that part of me was warm already. Warm and pulsing like a glove with a rat hiding inside it.

By midafternoon I was feverish, and my hand had swelled so tightly against the bandages that I had to loosen them. Just doing that made me cry out. I needed doctoring, but it was snowing harder than ever, and I wouldn't be able to get as far as Cotteries', let alone all the way to Hemingford Home. Even if the day had been clear and bright and dry, how would I ever have managed to crank the truck or the T with just one hand? I sat in the kitchen, feeding the stove until it roared like a dragon, pouring sweat and shaking with cold, holding my bandaged club of a hand to my chest, and remembering the way kindly Mrs McReady had surveyed my cluttered, not-particularly-prosperous dooryard. *Are you on the exchange, Mr James? I see you are not.*

No. I was not. I was by myself on the farm I had killed for, with no means of summoning help. I could see the flesh beginning to turn red beyond where the bandages stopped: at the wrist, full of veins that would carry the poison all through my body. The firemen had failed. I thought of tying the wrist off with elastics – of killing my left hand in an effort to save the rest of me – and even of amputating it with the hatchet we used to chop up kindling and behead the occasional chicken. Both ideas seemed perfectly plausible, but they also seemed like too much work. In the end I did nothing except hobble back to the hurt-locker for more of Arlette's pills. I took three more, this time with cold water – my throat was burning – and then resumed my seat by the fire. I was going to die of the bite. I was sure of it and resigned to it. Death from bites and infections was as common as dirt on the plains. If the pain became more than I could bear, I would swallow all the remaining pain-pills at once. What kept me from doing it right away – apart from the fear of death, which I suppose afflicts all of us, to a greater or lesser degree – was the possibility that someone might come: Harlan, or Sheriff Jones, or kindly Mrs McReady. It was even possible that Attorney Lester might show up to hector me some more about those God damned 100 acres.

But what I hoped most of all was that Henry might return. He didn't, though.

It was Arlette who came.

You may have wondered how I know about the gun Henry bought in the Dodge Street pawnshop, and the bank robbery in Jefferson Square. If you did, you probably said to yourself, *Well, it's a lot of time between 1922 and 1930; enough to fill in plenty of details at a library stocked with back issues of the* Omaha World-Herald.

I *did* go to the newspapers, of course. And I wrote to people who met my son and his pregnant girlfriend on their short, disastrous course from Nebraska to Nevada. Most of those people wrote back, willing enough to supply details. That sort of investigative work makes sense, and no doubt satisfies you. But those investigations came years later, after I left the farm, and only confirmed what I already knew.

Already? you ask, and I answer simply: *Yes. Already. And I knew it not just as it happened, but at least part of it* before *it happened. The last part of it.*

How? The answer is simple. My dead wife told me.

You disbelieve, of course. I understand that. Any rational person would. All I can do is reiterate that this is my confession, my last words on earth, and I've put nothing in it I don't know to be true.

* * *

I woke from a doze in front of the stove the following night (or the next; as the fever settled in, I lost track of time) and heard the rustling, scuttering sounds again. At first I assumed it had recommenced sleeting, but when I got up to tear a chunk of bread from the hardening loaf on the counter, I saw a thin orange sunset-streak on the horizon and Venus glowing in the sky. The storm was over, but the scuttering sounds were louder than ever. They weren't coming from the walls, however, but from the back porch.

The door-latch began moving. At first it only trembled, as if the hand trying to operate it was too weak to lift it entirely clear of the notch. The movement ceased, and I had just decided I hadn't seen it at all – that it was a delusion born of the fever – when it went all the way up with a little *clack* sound and the door swung open on a cold breath of wind. Standing on the porch was my wife. She was still wearing her burlap snood, now flecked with snow; it must have been a slow and painful journey from what should have been her final resting place. Her face was slack with decay, the lower half slewed to one side, her grin wider than ever. It was a knowing grin, and why not? The dead understand everything.

She was surrounded by her loyal court. It was they that had somehow gotten her out of the well. It was they that were holding her up. Without them, she would have been no more than a ghost, malevolent but helpless. But they had animated her. She was their queen; she was also their puppet. She came into the kitchen, moving with a horribly boneless gait that had nothing to do with walking. The rats scurried all around her, some looking up at her with love, some at me with hate. She swayed all the way around the kitchen, touring what had been her domain as clods fell from the skirt of her dress (there was no sign of the quilt or the counterpane) and her head bobbed and rolled on her cut throat. Once it tilted back all the way to her shoulder blades before snapping forward again with a low and fleshy smacking sound.

When she at last turned her cloudy eyes on me, I backed into the corner where the woodbox stood, now almost empty. 'Leave me alone,' I whispered. 'You aren't even here. You're in the well and you can't get out even if you're not dead.'

She made a gurgling noise – it sounded like someone choking on thick gravy – and kept coming, real enough to cast a shadow. And I could smell her decaying flesh, this woman who had sometimes put her tongue in my mouth during the throes of her passion. She was there. She was real. So was her royal retinue. I could feel them scurrying back and forth over my feet and tickling my ankles with their whiskers as they sniffed at the bottoms of my longjohn trousers.

My heels struck the woodbox, and when I tried to bend away from the approaching corpse, I overbalanced and sat down in it. I banged my swollen and infected hand, but hardly registered the pain. She was bending over me, and her face . . . *dangled*. The flesh had come loose from the bones and her face hung down like a face drawn on a child's balloon. A rat climbed the side of the woodbox, plopped onto my belly, ran up my chest, and sniffed at the underside of my chin. I could feel others scurrying around beneath my bent knees. But they didn't bite me. That particular task had already been accomplished.

She bent closer. The smell of her was overwhelming, and her cocked ear-to-ear grin . . . I can see it now, as I write. I told myself to die, but my heart kept pounding. Her hanging face slid alongside mine. I could feel my beard-stubble pulling off tiny bits of her skin; could hear her broken jaw grinding like a branch with ice on it. Then her cold lips were pressed against the burning, feverish cup of my ear, and she began whispering secrets that only a dead woman could know. I shrieked. I promised to kill myself and take her place in Hell if she would only stop. But she didn't. She wouldn't. The dead don't stop.

That's what I know now.

After fleeing the First Agricultural Bank with 200 dollars stuffed into his pocket (or probably more like 150 dollars; some of it went on the floor, remember), Henry disappeared for a little while. He 'laid low,' in the criminal parlance. I say this with a certain pride. I thought he would be caught almost immediately after he got to the city, but he proved me wrong. He was in love, he was desperate, he was still burning with guilt and horror over the crime he and I had committed . . . but in spite of those distractions (those *infections*), my son demonstrated bravery and cleverness, even a certain sad nobility. The thought of that last is the worst. It still fills me with melancholy for his wasted life (*three* wasted lives; I mustn't forget poor pregnant Shannon Cotterie) and shame for the ruination to which I led him, like a calf with a rope around its neck.

Arlette showed me the shack where he went to ground, and the bicycle stashed out back — that bicycle was the first thing he purchased with his stolen cash. I couldn't have told you then exactly where his hideout was, but in the years since I have located it and even visited it; just a side-o'-the-road lean-to with a fading Royal Crown Cola advertisement painted on the side. It was a few miles beyond Omaha's western outskirts and within sight of Boys Town, which had begun operating the year before. One room, a single glassless window, and no stove. He covered the bicycle with hay and weeds and laid his plans. Then, a week or so after robbing the First Agricultural Bank — by then police interest in a very minor robbery would have died down – he began making bicycle trips into Omaha.

A thick boy would have gone directly to the St Eusebia Catholic Home and been snared by the Omaha cops (as Sheriff Jones had no doubt expected he would be), but Henry Freeman James was smarter than that. He sussed out the Home's location, but didn't approach it. Instead, he looked for the nearest candy store and soda fountain. He correctly assumed that the girls would frequent it whenever they could (which was whenever their behavior merited a free afternoon and they had a little money in their bags), and although the St Eusebia girls weren't required to wear uniforms, they were easy enough to pick out by their dowdy dresses, downcast eyes, and their behavior – alternately flirty and skittish. Those with big bellies and no wedding rings would have been particularly conspicuous.

A thick boy would have attempted to strike up a conversation with one of these unfortunate daughters of Eve right there at the soda fountain, thus attracting attention. Henry took up a position outside, at the mouth of an alley running between the candy store and the notions shoppe next to it, sitting on a crate and reading the newspaper with his bike leaning against the brick next to him. He was waiting for a girl a little more adventurous than those content simply to sip their icecream sodas and then scuttle back to the sisters. That meant a girl who smoked. On his third afternoon in the alley, such a girl arrived.

I have found her since, and talked with her. There wasn't much detective work involved. I'm sure Omaha seemed like a metropolis to Henry and Shannon, but in 1922 it was really just a larger-than-average Midwestern town with city pretensions. Victoria Hallett is a respectable married woman with three children now, but in the fall of 1922, she was Victoria Stevenson: young, curious, rebellious, six months pregnant, and very fond of Sweet Caporals. She was happy enough to take one of Henry's when he offered her the pack.

'Take another couple for later,' he invited.

She laughed. 'I'd have to be a ding-dong to do that! The sisters search our bags and pull our pockets inside-out when we come back. I'll have to chew three sticks of Black Jack just to get the smell of this one fag off my breath.' She patted her bulging tummy with amusement and defiance. 'I'm in trouble, as I guess you can see. Bad girl! And my sweetie ran off. Bad *boy*, but the world don't care about that! So then the dapper stuck me in a jail with penguins for guards—'

'I don't get you.'

'Jeez! The dapper's my dad! And penguins is what we call the sisters!' She laughed. 'You're some country palooka, all right! And how! *Anyway*, the jail where I'm doing time's called—'

'St Eusebia's.'

'*Now* you're cooking with gas, Jackson.' She puffed her cig, narrowed her eyes. 'Say, I bet I know who you are – Shan Cotterie's boyfriend.'

'Give that girl a Kewpie doll,' Hank said.

'Well, I wouldn't get within two blocks of our place, that's my advice. The cops have got your description.' She laughed cheerily. 'Yours and half a dozen other Lonesome Lennies, but none of 'em green-eyed clodhoppers like you, and none with gals as good-looking as Shannon. She's a real Sheba! Yow!'

'Why do you think I'm here instead of there?'

'I'll bite – why *are* you here?'

'I want to get in touch, but I don't want to get caught doing it. I'll give you 2 bucks to take a note to her.'

Victoria's eyes went wide. 'Buddy, for a 2-spot, I'd tuck a bugle under my arm and take a message to Garcia – that's how tapped out I am. Hand it over!'

'And another 2 if you keep your mouth shut about it. Now and later.'

'For that you don't have to pay extra,' she said. 'I love pulling the business on those holier-than-thou bitches. Why, they smack your hand if you try to take an extra dinner roll! It's like *Gulliver Twist*!'

He gave her the note, and Victoria gave it to Shannon. It was in her little bag of things when the police finally caught up with her and Henry in Elko, Nevada, and I have seen a police photograph of it. But Arlette told me what it said long before then, and the actual item matched word for word.

I'll wait from midnight to dawn behind yr place every night for 2 weeks, the note said. *If you don't show up, I'll know it's over between us & go back to Hemingford & never bother you again even tho' I will go on loving you forever. We are young but we could lie about our ages & start a good life in another place (California). I have some money & know how to get more. Victoria knows how to find me if you want to send me a note, but only once. More would not be safe.*

I suppose Harlan and Sallie Cotterie might have that note. If so, they have seen that my son signed his name in a heart. I wonder if that was what convinced Shannon. I wonder if she even needed convincing. It's possible that all she wanted on earth was to keep (and legitimize) a baby she had already fallen in love with. That's a question Arlette's terrible whispering voice never addressed. Probably she didn't care one way or the other.

Henry returned to the mouth of the alley every day after that meeting. I'm sure he knew that the cops might arrive instead of Victoria, but felt he had no choice. On the third day of his vigil, she came. 'Shan wrote back right away, but I couldn't get out any sooner,' she said. 'Some goofy-weed showed up in that hole they have the nerve to call a music room, and the penguins have been on the warpath ever since.'

Henry held out his hand for the note, which Victoria gave over in exchange for a Sweet Caporal. There were only four words: *Tomorrow morning. 2 o'clock.*

Henry threw his arms around Victoria and kissed her. She laughed with excitement, eyes sparkling. 'Gosh! Some girls get all the luck.'

They undoubtedly do. But when you consider that Victoria ended up with a husband, three kids, and a nice home on Maple Street in the best part of Omaha, and Shannon Cotterie didn't live out that curse of a year . . . which of them would *you* say struck lucky?

I have some money & know how to get more, Henry had written, and he did. Only hours after kissing the saucy Victoria (who took the message *He says he'll be there with bells on* back to Shannon), a young man with a flat cap pulled low on his forehead and a bandanna over his mouth and nose robbed the First National Bank of Omaha. This time the robber got 800 dollars, which was a fine haul. But the guard was younger and more enthusiastic about his responsibilities, which was not so fine. The thief had to shoot him in the thigh in order to effect his escape, and although Charles Griner lived, an infection set in (I could sympathize), and he lost the leg. When I met with him at his parents' house in the spring of 1925, Griner was philosophical about it.

'I'm lucky to be alive at all,' he said. 'By the time they got a tourniquet on my leg, I was lying in a pool of blood damn near an inch deep. I bet it took a whole box of Dreft to get *that* mess up.'

When I tried to apologize for my son, he waved it away.

'I never should have approached him. The cap was

pulled low and the bandanna was yanked high, but I could see his eyes all right. I should have known he wasn't going to stop unless he was shot down, and I never had a chance to pull my gun. It was in his eyes, see. But I was young myself. I'm older now. Older's something your son never got a chance to get. I'm sorry for your loss.'

After that job, Henry had more than enough money to buy a car – a nice one, a tourer – but he knew better. (Writing that, I again feel that sense of pride: low but undeniable.) A kid who looked like he only started shaving a week or two before, waving around enough wampum to buy an almost-new Olds? That would have brought John Law down on him for sure.

So instead of buying a car, he stole one. Not a touring car, either; he plumped for a nice, nondescript Ford coupe. That was the car he parked behind St Eusebia's, and that was the one Shannon climbed into, after sneaking out of her room, creeping downstairs with her traveling bag in her hand, and wriggling through the window of the washroom adjacent to the kitchen. They had time to exchange a single kiss – Arlette didn't say so, but I still have my imagination – and then Henry pointed the Ford west. By dawn they were on the Omaha-Lincoln Highway. They must have passed close to his old home – and hers – around 3 that afternoon. They might have looked in that direction, but I doubt if Henry slowed; he would not want to stop for the night in an area where they might be recognized.

Their life as fugitives had begun.

Arlette whispered more about that life than I wished to know, and I don't have the heart to put more than the bare details down here. If you want to know more, write to the Omaha Public Library. For a fee, they will send you hectograph copies of stories having to do with the Sweetheart Bandits, as they became known (and as they called themselves). You may even be able to find stories from your own paper, if you do not live in Omaha; the conclusion of the tale was deemed heartrending enough to warrant national coverage.

Handsome Hank and Sweet Shannon, the *World-Herald* called them. In the photographs, they looked impossibly young. And of course they were. I didn't want to look at those photographs, but I did. There's more than one way to be bitten by rats, isn't there?

The stolen car blew a tire in Nebraska's sandhill country. Two men came walking up just as Henry was mounting the spare. One drew a shotgun from a sling setup he had under his coat – what was called a bandit hammerclaw back in the Wild West days – and pointed it at the runaway lovers. Henry had no chance at all to get his own gun; it was in his coat pocket, and if he'd tried for it, he almost certainly would have been killed. So the robber was robbed. Henry and Shannon walked hand-in-hand to a nearby farmer's house under a cold autumn sky, and when the farmer came to the door to ask how he could help, Henry pointed his gun at the man's chest and said he wanted his car and all his cash.

The girl with him, the farmer told a reporter, stood on the porch looking away. The farmer said he thought she was crying. He said he felt sorry for her, because she was no bigger than a minute, just as pregnant as the old woman who lived in a shoe, and traveling with a young desperado bound for a bad end.

Did she try to stop him? the reporter asked. Try to talk him out of it?

No, the farmer said. Just stood with her back turned, like she thought that if she didn't see it, it wasn't happening. The farmer's old rattletrap Reo was found abandoned near the McCook train depot, with a note on the seat: *Here is your car back, we will send the money we stole when*

*we can. We only took from you because we were in a scrape.
Very truly yours, 'The Sweetheart Bandits.'* Whose idea was
that name? Shannon's, probably; the note was in her
handwriting. They only used it because they didn't want
to give their names, but of such things legends are made.

A day or two later, there was a hold-up in the tiny
Frontier Bank of Arapahoe, Colorado. The thief – wearing
a flat cap yanked low and a bandanna yanked high – was
alone. He got less than 100 dollars and drove off in a
Hupmobile that had been reported stolen in McCook.
The next day, in The First Bank of Cheyenne Wells (which
was the only bank of Cheyenne Wells), the young man
was joined by a young woman. She disguised her face
with a bandanna of her own, but it was impossible to
disguise her pregnant state. They made off with 400 dollars
and drove out of town at high speed, headed west. A
roadblock was set up on the road to Denver, but Henry
played it smart and stayed lucky. They turned south not
long after leaving Cheyenne Wells, picking their way along
dirt roads and cattle tracks.

A week later, a young couple calling themselves Harry
and Susan Freeman boarded the train for San Francisco in
Colorado Springs. Why they suddenly got off in Grand
Junction I don't know and Arlette didn't say – saw something
that put their wind up, I suppose. All I know is that they
robbed a bank there, and another in Ogden, Utah. Their
version of saving up money for their new life, maybe. And
in Ogden, when a man tried to stop Henry outside the
bank, Henry shot him in the chest. The man grappled with
Henry anyway, and Shannon pushed him down the granite
steps. They got away. The man Henry shot died in the
hospital two days later. The Sweetheart Bandits had become
murderers. In Utah, convicted murderers got the rope.

By then it was near Thanksgiving, although which
side of it I don't know. The police west of the Rockies

had their descriptions and were on the lookout. I had been bitten by the rat hiding in the closet – I think – or was about to be. Arlette told me they were dead, but they weren't; not when she and her royal court came to visit me, that was. She either lied or prophesied. To me they are both the same.

Their next-to-last stop was Deeth, Nevada. It was a bitterly cold day in late November or early December, the sky white and beginning to spit snow. They only wanted eggs and coffee at the town's only diner, but their luck was almost all gone. The counterman was from Elkhorn, Nebraska, and although he hadn't been home in years, his mother still faithfully sent him issues of the *World-Herald* in large bundles. He had received just such a bundle a few days before, and he recognized the Omaha Sweetheart Bandits sitting in one of the booths.

Instead of ringing the police (or pit security at the nearby copper mine, which would have been quicker and more efficient), he decided to make a citizen's arrest. He took a rusty old cowboy pistol from under the counter, pointed it at them, and told them – in the finest Western tradition – to throw up their hands. Henry did no such thing. He slid out of the booth and walked toward the fellow, saying: 'Don't do that, my friend, we mean you no harm, we'll just pay up and go.'

The counterman pulled the trigger and the old pistol misfired. Henry took it out of his hand, broke it, looked at the cylinder, and laughed. 'Good news!' he told Shannon. 'These bullets have been in there so long they're green.'

He put 2 dollars on the counter – for their food – and then made a terrible mistake. To this day I believe things would have ended badly for them no matter what, yet still I wish I could call to him across the years: *Don't put that gun down still loaded. Don't do that, Son! Green or not, put those bullets in your pocket!* But only the dead can call across time; I know that now, and from personal experience.

As they were leaving (*hand-in-hand*, Arlette whispered in my burning ear), the counterman snatched that old horse-pistol off the counter, held it in both hands, and pulled the trigger again. This time it fired, and although he probably thought he was aiming at Henry, the bullet struck Shannon Cotterie in the lower back. She screamed and stumbled forward out the door into the blowing snow. Henry caught her before she could fall and helped her into their last stolen car, another Ford. The counterman tried to shoot him through the window, and that time the old gun blew up in his hands. A piece of metal took out his left eye. I have never been sorry. I am not as forgiving as Charles Griner.

Seriously wounded – perhaps dying already – Shannon went into labor as Henry drove through thickening snow toward Elko, thirty miles to the southwest, perhaps thinking he might find a doctor there. I don't know if there was a doctor or not, but there was certainly a police station, and the counterman rang it with the remains of his eyeball still drying on his cheek. Two local cops and four members of the Nevada State Patrol were waiting for Henry and Shannon at the edge of town, but Henry and Shannon never saw them. It's 30 miles between Deeth and Elko, and Henry made only 28 of them.

Just inside the town limits (but still well beyond the edge of the village), the last of Henry's luck let go. With Shannon screaming and holding her belly as she bled all over the seat, he must have been driving fast – too fast. Or maybe he just hit a pothole in the road. However it was, the Ford skidded into the ditch and stalled. There they sat in that high-desert emptiness while a strengthening wind blew snow all around them, and what was Henry thinking? That what he and I had done in Nebraska had led him and the girl he loved to that place in Nevada. Arlette didn't tell me that, but she didn't have to. I knew.

He spied the ghost of a building through the thickening snow, and got Shannon out of the car. She managed a few steps into the wind, then could manage no more. The girl who could do triggeronomy and might have been the first female graduate of the normal school in Omaha laid her head on her young man's shoulder and said, 'I can't go any farther, honey, put me on the ground.'

'What about the baby?' he asked her.

'The baby is dead, and I want to die, too,' she said. 'I can't stand the pain. It's terrible. I love you, honey, but put me on the ground.'

He carried her to that ghost of a building instead, which turned out to be a line shack not much different from the shanty near Boys Town, the one with the faded bottle of Royal Crown Cola painted on the side. There was a stove, but no wood. He went out and scrounged a few pieces of scrap lumber before the snow could cover them, and when he went back inside, Shannon was unconscious. Henry lit the stove, then put her head on his lap. Shannon Cotterie was dead before the little fire he'd made burned down to embers, and then there was only Henry, sitting on a mean lineshack cot where a dozen dirty cowboys had lain themselves down before him, drunk more often than sober. He sat there and stroked Shannon's hair while the wind shrieked outside and the shack's tin roof shivered.

All these things Arlette told me on a day when those two doomed children were still alive. All these things she told me while the rats crawled around me and her stink filled my nose and my infected, swollen hand ached like fire.

I begged her to kill me, to open my throat as I had opened hers, and she wouldn't.

That was her revenge.

It might have been two days later when my visitor arrived at the farm, or even three, but I don't think so. I think it was only one. I don't believe I could have lasted two or three more days without help. I had stopped eating and almost stopped drinking. Still, I managed to get out of bed and stagger to the door when the hammering on it commenced. Part of me thought it might be Henry, because part of me still dared hope that Arlette's visit had been a delusion hatched in delirium . . . and even if it had been real, that she had lied.

It was Sheriff Jones. My knees loosened when I saw him, and I pitched forward. If he hadn't caught me, I would have gone tumbling out onto the porch. I tried to tell him about Henry and Shannon – that Shannon was going to be shot, that they were going to end up in a line shack on the outskirts of Elko, that he, Sheriff Jones, had to call somebody and stop it before it happened. All that came out was a garble, but he caught the names.

'He's run off with her, all right,' Jones said. 'But if Harl came down and told you that, why'd he leave you like *this*? What bit you?'

'Rat,' I managed.

He got an arm around me and half-carried me down the porch steps and toward his car. George the rooster was lying frozen to the ground beside the woodpile, and the cows were lowing. When had I last fed them? I couldn't remember.

'Sheriff, you have to—'

But he cut me off. He thought I was raving, and why not? He could feel the fever baking off me and see it glowing in my face. It must have been like carrying an oven. 'You need to save your strength. And you need to be grateful to Arlette, because I never would have come out here if not for her.'

'Dead,' I managed.

'Yes. She's dead, all right.'

So then I told him I'd killed her, and oh, the relief. A plugged pipe inside my head had magically opened, and the infected ghost which had been trapped in there was finally gone.

He slung me into his car like a bag of meal. 'We'll talk about Arlette, but right now I'm taking you to Angels of Mercy, and I'll thank you not to upchuck in my car.'

As he drove out of the dooryard, leaving the dead rooster and lowing cows behind (and the rats! don't forget them! Ha!), I tried to tell him again that it might not be too late for Henry and Shannon, that it still might be possible to save them. I heard myself saying *these are things that may be*, as if I were the Spirit of Christmas Yet to Come in the Dickens story. Then I passed out. When I woke up, it was the second of December, and the Western newspapers were reporting 'SWEETHEART BANDITS' ELUDE ELKO POLICE, ESCAPE AGAIN. They hadn't, but no one knew that yet. Except Arlette, of course. And me.

The doctor thought the gangrene hadn't advanced up my forearm, and gambled my life by amputating only my left hand. That was a gamble he won. Five days after being carried into Hemingford City's Angels of Mercy Hospital by Sheriff Jones, I lay wan and ghostly in a hospital bed, 25 pounds lighter and minus my left hand, but alive.

Jones came to see me, his face grave. I waited for him to tell me he was arresting me for the murder of my wife, and then handcuff my remaining hand to the hospital bedpost. But that never happened. Instead, he told me

how sorry he was for my loss. My loss! What did that
idiot know about loss?

Why am I sitting in this mean hotel room (but not alone!)
instead of lying in a murderer's grave? I'll tell you in two
words: my mother.

Like Sheriff Jones, she had a habit of peppering her
conversation with rhetorical questions. With him it was a
conversational device he'd picked up during a lifetime in
law enforcement – he asked his silly little questions, then
observed the person he was talking to for any guilty reaction: a wince, a frown, a small shift of the eyes. With my
mother, it was only a habit of speech she had picked up
from her own mother, who was English, and passed on to
me. I've lost any faint British accent I might once have
had, but never lost my mother's way of turning statements
into questions. *You'd better come in now, hadn't you?* she'd
say. Or *Your father forgot his lunch again; you'll have to take
it to him, won't you?* Even observations about the weather
came couched as questions: *Another rainy day, isn't it?*

Although I was feverish and very ill when Sheriff
Jones came to the door on that late November day, I
wasn't delirious. I remember our conversation clearly, the
way a man or woman may remember images from a
particularly vivid nightmare.

*You need to be grateful to Arlette, because I never would
have come out here if not for her,* he said.

Dead, I replied.

Sheriff Jones: *She's dead, all right.*

And then, speaking as I had learned to speak at my
mother's knee: *I killed her, didn't I?*

Sheriff Jones took my mother's rhetorical device (and
his own, don't forget) as a real question. Years later – it was
in the factory where I found work after I lost the farm
– I heard a foreman berating a clerk for sending an order

to Des Moines instead of Davenport before the clerk had gotten the shipping form from the front office. *But we always send the Wednesday orders to Des Moines*, the soon-to-be-fired clerk protested. *I simply assumed—*

Assume makes an ass out of you and *me*, the foreman replied. An old saying, I suppose, but that was the first time I heard it. And is it any wonder that I thought of Sheriff Frank Jones when I did? My mother's habit of turning statements into questions saved me from the electric chair. I was never tried by a jury for the murder of my wife.

Until now, that is.

They're here with me, a lot more than twelve, lined up along the baseboard all the way around the room, watching me with their oily eyes. If a maid came in with fresh sheets and saw those furry jurors, she would run, shrieking, but no maid will come; I hung the DO NOT DISTURB sign on the door two days ago, and it's been there ever since. I haven't been out. I could order food sent up from the restaurant down the street, I suppose, but I suspect food would set them off. I'm not hungry, anyway, so it's no great sacrifice. They have been patient so far, my jurors, but I suspect they won't be for much longer. Like any jury, they're anxious for the testimony to be done so they can render a verdict, receive their token fee (in this case to be paid in flesh), and go home to their families. So I must finish. It won't take long. The hard work is done.

What Sheriff Jones said when he sat down beside my hospital bed was, 'You saw it in my eyes, I guess. Isn't that right?'

I was still a very sick man, but enough recovered to be cautious. 'Saw what, Sheriff?'

'What I'd come to tell you. You don't remember, do you? Well, I'm not surprised. You were one sick American, Wilf. I was pretty sure you were going to die, and I thought you might do it before I got you back to town. I guess God's not done with you yet, is he?'

Something wasn't done with me, but I doubted if it was God.

'Was it Henry? Did you come out to tell me something about Henry?'

'No,' he said, 'it was Arlette I came about. It's bad news, the worst, but you can't blame yourself. It's not like you beat her out of the house with a stick.' He leaned forward. 'You might have got the idea that I don't like you, Wilf, but that's not true. There's some in these parts who don't – and we know who they are, don't we? – but don't put me in with them just because I have to take their interests into account. You've irritated me a time or two, and I believe that you'd still be friends with Harl Cotterie if you'd kept your boy on a tighter rein, but I've always respected you.'

I doubted it, but kept my lip buttoned.

'As for what happened to Arlette, I'll say it again, because it bears repeating: you can't blame yourself.'

I couldn't? I thought *that* was an odd conclusion to draw even for a lawman who would never be confused with Sherlock Holmes.

'Henry's in trouble, if some of the reports I'm getting are true,' he said heavily, 'and he's dragged Shan Cotterie into the hot water with him. They'll likely boil in it. That's enough for you to handle without claiming responsibility for your wife's death, as well. You don't have to—'

'Just tell me,' I said.

Two days previous to his visit – perhaps the day the rat bit me, perhaps not, but around that time – a farmer headed into Lyme Biska with the last of his produce had spied a trio of coydogs fighting over something about twenty yards north of the road. He might have gone on if he hadn't also spied a scuffed ladies' patent leather shoe and a pair of pink step-ins lying in the ditch. He stopped, fired his rifle to scare off the coys, and advanced into the field to inspect their prize. What he found was a woman's skeleton with the rags of a dress and a few bits of flesh still hanging from it. What remained of her hair was a listless brown, the color to which Arlette's rich auburn might have gone after months out in the elements.

'Two of the back teeth were gone,' Jones said. 'Was Arlette missing a couple of back teeth?'

'Yes,' I lied. 'Lost them from a gum infection.'

'When I came out that day just after she ran off, your boy said she took her good jewelry.'

'Yes.' The jewelry that was now in the well.

'When I asked if she could have laid her hands on any money, you mentioned 200 dollars. Isn't that right?'

Ah yes. The fictional money Arlette had supposedly taken from my dresser. 'That's right.'

He was nodding. 'Well, there you go, there you go. Some jewelry and some money. That explains everything, wouldn't you say?'

'I don't see—'

'Because you're not looking at it from a lawman's point of view. She was robbed on the road, that's all. Some bad egg spied a woman hitchhiking between Hemingford and Lyme Biska, picked her up, killed her, robbed her of her money and her jewelry, then carried her body far enough into the nearest field so it couldn't be seen from the road.' From his long face I could see he was thinking she had probably been raped as well as robbed, and that it was probably a good thing that there wasn't enough of her left to tell for sure.

'That's probably it, then,' I said, and somehow I was able to keep a straight face until he was gone. Then I turned over, and although I thumped my stump in doing so, I began to laugh. I buried my face in my pillow, but not even that would stifle the sound. When the nurse — an ugly old battle axe — came in and saw the tears streaking my face, she assumed (which makes an ass out of you *and* me) that I had been crying. She softened, a thing I would have thought impossible, and gave me an extra morphine pill. I was, after all, the grieving husband and bereft father. I deserved comfort.

And do you know why I was laughing? Was it Jones's well-meaning stupidity? The fortuitous appearance of a dead female hobo who might have been killed by her male traveling companion while they were drunk? It was both of those things, but mostly it was the shoe. The farmer had only stopped to investigate what the coydogs were fighting over because he'd seen a ladies' patent leather shoe in the ditch. But when Sheriff Jones had asked about footwear that day at the house the previous summer, I'd told him Arlette's *canvas* shoes were the ones that were gone. The idiot had forgotten.

And he never remembered.

When I got back to the farm, almost all my livestock was dead. The only survivor was Achelois, who looked at me with reproachful, starveling eyes and lowed plaintively. I fed her as lovingly as you might feed a pet, and really, that was all she was. What else would you call an animal that can no longer contribute to a family's livelihood?

There was a time when Harlan, assisted by his wife, would have taken care of my place while I was in the hospital; it's how we neighbored out in the middle. But even after the mournful blat of my dying cows started drifting across the fields to him while he sat down to his supper, he stayed away. If I'd been in his place, I might have done the same. In Harl Cotterie's view (and the world's), my son hadn't been content just to ruin his daughter; he'd followed her to what should have been a place of refuge, stolen her away, and forced her into a life of crime. How that 'Sweetheart Bandits' stuff must have eaten into her father! Like acid! Ha!

The following week – around the time the Christmas decorations were going up in farmhouses and along Main Street in Hemingford Home – Sheriff Jones came out to the farm again. One look at his face told me what his news was, and I began to shake my head. 'No. No more. I won't have it. I can't have it. Go away.'

I went back in the house and tried to bar the door against him, but I was both weak and one-handed, and he forced his way in easily enough. 'Take hold, Wilf,' he said. 'You'll get through this.' As if he knew what he was talking about.

He looked in the cabinet with the decorative ceramic beer stein on top of it, found my sadly depleted bottle of whiskey, poured the last finger into the stein, and handed it to me. 'Doctor wouldn't approve,' he said, 'but he's not here and you're going to need it.'

The Sweetheart Bandits had been discovered in their final hideout, Shannon dead of the counterman's bullet, Henry of one he had put into his own brain. The bodies had been taken to the Elko mortuary, pending instructions. Harlan Cotterie would see to his daughter, but would have nothing to do with my son. Of course not. I did that myself. Henry arrived in Hemingford by train on the eighteenth of December, and I was at the depot, along with a black funeral hack from Castings Brothers. My picture was taken repeatedly. I was asked questions which I didn't even try to answer. The headlines in both the *World-Herald* and the much humbler *Hemingford Weekly* featured the phrase GRIEVING FATHER.

If the reporters had seen me at the funeral home, however, when the cheap pine box was opened, they would have seen real grief; they could have featured the phrase SCREAMING FATHER. The bullet my son fired into his temple as he sat with Shannon's head on his lap had mushroomed as it crossed his brain and taken out a large chunk of his skull on the left side. But that wasn't the worst. His eyes were gone. His lower lip was chewed away so that his teeth jutted in a grim grin. All that remained of his nose was a red stub. Before some cop or sheriff's deputy had discovered the bodies, the rats had made a merry meal of my son and his dear love.

'Fix him up,' I told Herbert Castings when I could talk rationally again.

'Mr James . . . sir . . . the damage is . . .'

'I see what the damage is. Fix him up. And get him out of that shitting box. Put him in the finest coffin you have. I don't care what it costs. I have money.' I bent and kissed his torn cheek. No father should have to kiss his son for the last time, but if any father ever deserved such a fate, it was I.

Shannon and Henry were both buried out of the Hemingford Glory of God Methodist Church, Shannon on the twenty-second and Henry on Christmas Eve. The church was full for Shannon, and the weeping was almost loud enough to raise the roof. I know, because I was there, at least for a little while. I stood in the back, unnoticed, then slunk out halfway through Reverend Thursby's eulogy. Rev. Thursby also presided at Henry's funeral, but I hardly need tell you that the attendance was much smaller. Thursby saw only one, but there was another. Arlette was there, too, sitting next to me, unseen and smiling. Whispering in my ear.

Do you like how things have turned out, Wilf? Was it worth it?

Adding in the funeral cost, the burial expenses, the mortuary expenses, and the cost of shipping the body home, the disposal of my son's earthly remains cost just over 300 dollars. I paid out of the mortgage money. What else did I have? When the funeral was finished, I went home to an empty house. But first I bought a fresh bottle of whiskey.

1922 had one more trick left in its bag. The day after Christmas, a huge blizzard roared out of the Rockies, socking us with a foot of snow and gale-force winds. As dark came down, the snow turned first to sleet and then to driving rain. Around midnight, as I sat in the darkened parlor, doctoring my bellowing stump with little sips of whiskey, a grinding, rending sound came from the back of the house. It was the roof coming down on that side – the part I'd taken out the mortgage, at least in part, to fix. I toasted it with my glass, then had another sip. When the cold wind began to blow in around my shoulders, I took my coat from its hook in the mudroom, put it on, then sat back down and drank a little more whiskey. At some point I dozed. Another of those grinding crashes woke me around three o'clock. This time it was the front half of the barn that had collapsed. Achelois survived yet again, and the next night I took her into the house with me. Why? you might ask me, and my answer would be, Why not? Just why the hell not? We were the survivors. We were the survivors.

On Christmas morning (which I spent sipping whiskey in my cold sitting room, with my surviving cow for company), I counted what was left of the mortgage money, and realized it would not begin to cover the damage done by the storm. I didn't much care, because I had lost my taste for the farming life, but the thought of the Farrington Company putting up a hog-butchery and polluting the stream still made me grind my teeth in rage. Especially after the high cost I had paid for keeping those triple-goddamned 100 acres out of the company's hands.

It suddenly struck home to me that, with Arlette officially dead instead of missing, those acres were mine. So two days later I swallowed my pride and went to see Harlan Cotterie.

The man who answered my knock had fared better than I, but that year's shocks had taken their toll, just the same. He had lost weight, he had lost hair, and his shirt was wrinkled — although not as wrinkled as his face, and the shirt, at least, would iron out. He looked sixty-five instead of forty-five.

'Don't hit me,' I said when I saw him ball his fists. 'Hear me out.'

'I wouldn't hit a man with only one hand,' he said, 'but I'll thank you to keep it short. And we'll have to talk out here on the stoop, because you are never going to set foot inside my house again.'

'That's fine,' I said. I had lost weight myself — plenty — and I was shivering, but the cold air felt good on my stump, and on the invisible hand that still seemed to exist below it. 'I want to sell you 100 acres of good land, Harl. The hundred Arlette was so determined to sell to the Farrington Company.'

He smiled at that, and his eyes sparkled in their new deep hollows. 'Fallen on hard times, haven't you? Half your house and half your barn caved in. Hermie Gordon says you've got a cow living in there with you.' Hermie Gordon was the rural route mailman, and a notorious gossip.

I named a price so low that Harl's mouth fell open and his eyebrows shot up. It was then that I noticed a smell wafting out of the neat and well-appointed Cotterie farmhouse that seemed entirely alien to that place: burned fried food. Sallie Cotterie was apparently not doing the cooking. Once I might have been interested in such a thing, but that time had passed. All I cared about right then was getting shed of the 100 acres.

It only seemed right to sell them cheap, since they had cost me so dear.

'That's pennies on the dollar,' he said. Then, with evident satisfaction: 'Arlette would roll in her grave.'

She's done more than just roll in it, I thought.

'What are you smiling about, Wilf?'

'Nothing. Except for one thing, I don't care about that land anymore. The one thing I *do* care about is keeping that God damned Farrington slaughter-mill off it.'

'Even if you lose your own place?' He nodded as if I'd asked a question. 'I know about the mortgage you took out. No secrets in a small town.'

'Even if I do,' I agreed. 'Take the offer, Harl. You'd be crazy not to. That stream they'll be filling up with blood and hair and hog intestines – that's your stream, too.'

'No,' he said.

I stared at him, too surprised to say anything. But again he nodded as if I'd asked a question.

'You think you know what you've done to me, but you don't know all of it. Sallie's left me. She's gone to stay with her folks down McCook. She says she may be back, says she'll think things over, but I don't think she will be. So that puts you and me in the same old broke wagon, doesn't it? We're two men who started the year with wives and are ending it without them. We're two men who started the year with living children and are ending it with dead ones. The only difference I can see is that I didn't lose half my house and most of my barn in a storm.' He thought about it. 'And I've still got both hands. There's that, I suppose. When it comes to pulling my peter – should I ever feel the urge to – I'd have a choice of which one to use.'

'What . . . why would she—'

'Oh, use your head. She blames me as well as you

for Shannon's death. She said that if I hadn't gotten on my high horse and sent Shan away, she'd still be alive and living with Henry at your farm just down the road instead of lying frozen in a box underground. She says she'd have a grandchild. She called me a self-righteous fool, and she's right.'

I reached for him with my remaining hand. He slapped it away.

'Don't touch me, Wilf. A single warning on that is all you get.'

I put my hand back at my side.

'One thing I know for sure,' he said. 'If I took you up on that offer, tasty as it is, I'd regret it. Because that land is cursed. We may not agree on everything, but I bet we would on that. If you want to sell it, sell it to the bank. You'll get your mortgage paper back, and some cash besides.'

'They'd just turn around and sell it to Farrington!'

'Tough titty said the kitty' was his final word on it as he closed the door in my face.

On the last day of the year, I drove to Hemingford Home and saw Mr Stoppenhauser at the bank. I told him that I'd decided I could no longer live on the farm. I told him I would like to sell Arlette's acreage to the bank and use the balance of the proceeds to retire the mortgage. Like Harlan Cotterie, he said no. For a moment or two I just sat in the chair facing his desk, not able to believe what I had heard.

'Why not? That's good land!'

He told me that he worked for a bank, and a bank was not a real estate agency. He addressed me as Mr James. My days of being Wilf in that office were over.

'That's just . . .' *Ridiculous* was the word that came to mind, but I didn't want to risk offending him if there was even a chance he might change his mind. Once I had made the decision to sell the land (and the cow, I would have to find a buyer for Achelois, too, possibly a stranger with a bag of magic beans to trade), the idea had taken hold of me with the force of an obsession. So I kept my voice low and spoke calmly.

'That's not exactly true, Mr Stoppenhauser. The bank bought the Rideout place last summer when it came up for auction. The Triple M, as well.'

'Those were different situations. We hold a mortgage on your original 80, and we're content with that. What you do with that hundred acres of pasturage is of no interest to us.'

'Who's been in to see you?' I asked, then realized I didn't have to. 'It was Lester, wasn't it? Cole Farrington's dogsbody.'

'I have no idea what you're talking about,' Stoppenhauser said, but I saw the flicker in his eyes. 'I think your grief and your . . . your injury . . . have temporarily damaged your ability to think clearly.'

'Oh no,' I said, and began to laugh. It was a dangerously unbalanced sound, even to my own ears, 'I've never thought more clearly in my life, sir. He came to see you – him or another, I'm sure Cole Farrington can afford to retain all the shysters he wants – and you made a deal. You *c-c-colluded*!' I was laughing harder than ever.

'Mr James, I'm afraid I'll have to ask you to leave.'

'Maybe you had it all planned out beforehand,' I said. 'Maybe that's why you were so anxious to talk me into the God damned mortgage in the first place. Or maybe when Lester heard about my son, he saw a golden opportunity to take advantage of my misfortune and came running to you. Maybe he sat right in this chair and said, "This is going to work out for both of us, Stoppie – you get the farm, my client gets the land by the crick, and Wilf James can go to Hell." Isn't that pretty much how it went?'

He had pushed a button on his desk, and now the door opened. It was just a little bank, too small to employ a security guard, but the teller who leaned in was a beefy lad. One of the Rohrbacher family, from the look of him; I'd gone to school with his father, and Henry would have gone with his younger sister, Mandy.

'Is there a problem, Mr Stoppenhauser?' he asked.

'Not if Mr James leaves now,' he said. 'Won't you see him out, Kevin?'

Kevin came in, and when I was slow to rise, he clamped a hand just above my left elbow. He was dressed like a banker, right down to the suspenders and the bow tie, but it was a farmer's hand, hard and calloused. My still-healing stump gave a warning throb.

'Come along, sir,' he said.

'Don't pull me,' I said. 'It hurts where my hand used to be.'

'Then come along.'

'I went to school with your father. He sat beside me and used to cheat off my paper during Spring Testing Week.'

He pulled me out of the chair where I had once been addressed as Wilf. Good old Wilf, who would be a fool not to take out a mortgage. The chair almost fell over.

'Happy New Year, Mr James,' Stoppenhauser said.

'And to you, you cozening fuck,' I replied. Seeing the shocked expression on his face may have been the last good thing to happen to me in my life. I have sat here for five minutes, chewing on the end of my pen and trying to think of one since – a good book, a good meal, a pleasant afternoon in the park – and I can't.

Kevin Rohrbacher accompanied me across the lobby. I suppose that is the correct verb; it wasn't quite dragging.

The floor was marble, and our footfalls echoed. The walls were dark oak. At the high tellers' windows, two women served a little group of year-end customers. One of the tellers was young and one was old, but their big-eyed expressions were identical. Yet it wasn't their horrified, almost prurient interest that took my own eye; it was captivated by something else entirely. A burled oak rail three inches wide ran above the tellers' windows, and scurrying busily along it—

'Ware that rat!' I cried, and pointed.

The young teller voiced a little scream, looked up, then exchanged a glance with her older counterpart. There was no rat, only the passing shadow of the ceiling fan. And now everyone was looking at me.

'Stare all you want!' I told them. 'Look your fill! Look until your God damned eyes fall out!'

Then I was in the street, and puffing out cold winter air that looked like cigarette smoke. 'Don't come back unless you have business to do,' Kevin said. 'And unless you can keep a civil tongue.'

'Your father was the biggest God damned cheater I ever went to school with,' I told him. I wanted him to hit me, but he only went back inside and left me alone on the sidewalk, standing in front of my saggy old truck. And that was how Wilfred Leland James spent his visit to town on the last day of 1922.

When I got home, Achelois was no longer in the house. She was in the yard, lying on her side and puffing her own clouds of white vapor. I could see the snow-scuffs where she'd gone galloping off the porch, and the bigger one where she had landed badly and broken both front legs. Not even a blameless cow could survive around me, it seemed.

I went into the mudroom to get my gun, then into the house, wanting to see – if I could – what had frightened her so badly that she'd left her new shelter at a full gallop. It was rats, of course. Three of them sitting on Arlette's treasured sideboard, looking at me with their black and solemn eyes.

'Go back and tell her to leave me alone,' I told them. 'Tell her she's done damage enough. For God's sake tell her to let me be.'

They only sat looking at me with their tails curled around their plump black-gray bodies. So I lifted my varmint rifle and shot the one in the middle. The bullet tore it apart and splattered its leavings all over the wallpaper Arlette had picked out with such care 9 or 10 years before. When Henry was still just a little 'un and things among the three of us were fine.

The other two fled. Back to their secret way underground, I have no doubt. Back to their rotting queen. What they left behind on my dead wife's sideboard were little piles of rat-shit and three or four bits of the burlap sack Henry fetched from the barn on that early summer night in 1922. The rats had come to kill my last cow and bring me little pieces of Arlette's *snood*.

I went outside and patted Achelois on the head. She stretched her neck up and lowed plaintively. *Make it stop. You're the master, you're the god of my world, so make it stop.*

I did.

Happy New Year.

That was the end of 1922, and that is the end of my story; all the rest is epilogue. The emissaries crowded around this room – how the manager of this fine old hotel would scream if he saw them! – will not have to wait much longer to render their verdict. She is the judge, they are the jury, but I'll be my own executioner.

I lost the farm, of course. Nobody, including the Farrington Company, would buy those 100 acres until the home place was gone, and when the hog-butchers finally swooped in, I was forced to sell at an insanely low price. Lester's plan worked perfectly. I'm sure it was his, and I'm sure he got a bonus.

Oh, well; I would have lost my little toehold in Hemingford County even if I'd had financial resources to fall back on, and there is a perverse sort of comfort in that. They say this depression we are in started on Black Friday of last year, but people in states like Kansas, Iowa, and Nebraska, know it started in 1923, when the crops that survived the terrible storms that spring were killed in the drought that followed, a drought that lasted for 2 years. The few crops that did find their way to the big city markets and the small city agricultural exchanges brought a beggar's price. Harlan Cotterie hung on until 1925 or so, and then the bank took his farm. I happened on that news while perusing the Bank Sales items in the *World-Herald*. By 1925, such items sometimes took up whole pages in the newspaper. The small farms had begun to go, and I believe that in a hundred years – maybe only 75 – they'll all be gone. Come 2030 (if there is such a year), all Nebraska west of Omaha will be one big farm. Probably it will be owned by the Farrington Company, and those unfortunate enough to live on that land will pass their existence under dirty yellow skies and wear gas masks to keep from choking on the stench of dead hogs. And *every* stream will run red with the blood of slaughter.

Come 2030, only the rats will be happy.

That's pennies on the dollar, Harlan said on the day I offered to sell him Arlette's land, and eventually I was forced to sell to Cole Farrington for even fewer on the dollar. Andrew Lester, attorney-at-law, brought the papers to the Hemingford City rooming house where I was then living, and he smiled as I signed them. Of course he did. The big boys always win. I was a fool to think it could ever be any different. I was a fool, and everyone I ever loved paid the price. I sometimes wonder if Sallie Cotterie ever came back to Harlan, or if he went to her in McCook after he lost the farm. I don't know, but I think Shannon's death probably ended that previously happy marriage. Poison spreads like ink in water.

Meanwhile, the rats have begun to move in from the baseboards of this room. What was a square has become a closing circle. They know that this is just the *after*, and nothing that comes after an irrevocable act matters much. Yet I will finish. And they won't have me while I'm alive; the final small victory will be mine. My old brown jacket is hung on the back of the chair I'm sitting in. The pistol is in the pocket. When I've finished the last few pages of this confession, I'll use it. They say suicides and murderers go to Hell. If so, I will know my way around, because I've been there for the last eight years.

I went to Omaha, and if it is indeed a city of fools, as I used to claim, then I was at first a model citizen. I set to work drinking up Arlette's 100 acres, and even at pennies on the dollar, it took 2 years. When I wasn't drinking, I visited the places Henry had been during the last months of his life: the grocery and gasoline station in Lyme Biska with the Blue Bonnet Girl on the roof (by then closed with a sign on the boarded-up door reading FOR SALE BY BANK), the pawnshop on Dodge Street (where I emulated my son and bought the pistol now in my jacket pocket), the Omaha branch of the First Agricultural. The pretty young teller still worked there, although her last name was no longer Penmark.

'When I passed him the money, he said thank you,' she told me. 'Maybe he went wrong, but somebody raised him right. Did you know him?'

'No,' I said, 'but I knew his family.'

Of course I went to St Eusebia's, but made no attempt to go in and inquire about Shannon Cotterie to the governess or matron or whatever her title may have been. It was a cold and forbidding hulk of a building, its thick stone and slit windows expressing perfectly how the papist hierarchy seems to feel in their hearts about women. Watching the few pregnant girls who slunk out with downcast eyes and hunched shoulders told me everything I needed to know about why Shan had been so willing to leave it.

Oddly enough, I felt closest to my son in an alley. It was the one next to the Gallatin Street Drug Store & Soda Fountain (Schrafft's Candy & Best Homemade Fudge Our Specialty), two blocks from St Eusebia's. There was a crate there, probably too new to be the one Henry sat on while waiting for a girl adventurous enough to trade information for cigarettes, but I could pretend, and I did. Such pretense was easier when I was drunk, and most days when I turned up on Gallatin Street, I was very drunk indeed. Sometimes I pretended it was 1922 again and it was I who was waiting for Victoria Stevenson. If she came, I would trade her a whole carton of cigarettes to take one message: *When a young man who calls himself Hank turns up here, asking about Shan Cotterie, tell him to get lost. To take his jazz elsewhere. Tell him his father needs him back on the farm, that maybe with two of them working together, they can save it.*

But that girl was beyond my reach. The only Victoria I met was the later version, the one with the three comely children and the respectable title of Mrs Hallett. I had stopped drinking by then, I had a job at the Bilt-Rite Clothing factory, and had reacquainted myself with razor blade and shaving soap. Given this veneer of respectability, she received me willingly enough. I told her who I was only because – if I am to be honest to the end – lying was not an option. I could see in the slight widening of her eyes that she had noted the resemblance.

'Gee, but he was sweet,' she said. 'And so crazy in love. I'm sorry for Shan, too. She was a great gal. It's like a tragedy out of Shakespeare, isn't it?'

Only she said it *trad a-gee*, and after that I didn't go back to the Gallatin Street alley anymore, because for me Arlette's murder had poisoned even this blameless young Omaha matron's attempt at kindness. She thought Henry and Shannon's deaths were like a trad-a-gee out of Shakespeare. She thought it was romantic. Would she still have thought so, I wonder, if she had heard my wife screaming her last from inside a blood-sodden burlap sack? Or glimpsed my son's eyeless, lipless face?

I held two jobs during my years in the Gateway City, also known as the City of Fools. You will say of *course* I held jobs; I would have been living on the street otherwise. But men more honest than I have continued drinking even when they want to stop, and men more decent than I have ended up sleeping in doorways. I suppose I could say that after my lost years, I made one more effort to live an actual life. There were times when I actually believed that, but lying in bed at night (and listening to the rats scampering in the walls — they have been my constant companions), I always knew the truth: I was still trying to win. Even after Henry and Shannon's deaths, even after losing the farm, I was trying to beat the corpse in the well. She and her *minions*.

John Hanrahan was the storage foreman at the Bilt-Rite factory. He didn't want to hire a man with only one hand, but I begged for a trial, and when I proved to him that I could pull a pallet fully loaded with shirts or overalls as well as any man on his payroll, he took me on. I hauled those pallets for 14 months, and often limped

back to the boardinghouse where I was staying with
my back and stump on fire. But I never complained, and
I even found time to learn sewing. This I did on my
lunch hour (which was actually 15 minutes long), and
during my afternoon break. While the other men were
out back on the loading dock, smoking and telling dirty
jokes, I was teaching myself to sew seams, first in the
burlap shipping bags we used, and then in the overalls
that were the company's main stock-in-trade. I turned
out to have a knack for it; I could even lay in a zipper,
which is no mean skill on a garment assembly line. I'd
press my stump on the garment to hold it in place as
my foot ran the electric treadle.

Sewing paid better than hauling, and it was easier
on my back, but the Sewing Floor was dark and
cavernous, and after four months or so I began to see
rats on the mountains of freshly blued denim and
hunkering in the shadows beneath the hand-trucks that
first brought in the piecework and then rolled it out again.

On several occasions I called the attention of my
co-workers to these vermin. They claimed not to see
them. Perhaps they really did not. I think it far more
likely that they were afraid the Sewing Floor might be
temporarily closed down so the ratcatchers could come
in and do their work. The sewing crew might have lost
three days' wages, or even a week. For men and women
with families, that would have been catastrophic. It was
easier for them to tell Mr Hanrahan that I was seeing
things. I understood. And when they began to call me
Crazy Wilf? I understood that, too. It wasn't why I quit.

I quit because the rats kept moving in.

I had been putting a little money away, and was prepared
to live on it while I looked for another job, but I didn't
have to. Only three days after leaving Bilt-Rite, I saw an

ad in the paper for a librarian at the Omaha Public Library
– must have references or a degree. I had no degree, but
I have been a reader my whole life, and if the events of
1922 taught me anything, it was how to deceive. I forged
references from public libraries in Kansas City and
Springfield, Missouri, and got the job. I felt sure Mr
Quarles would check the references and discover they
were false, so I worked at becoming the best librarian in
America, and I worked fast. When my new boss confronted
me with my deception, I would simply throw myself on
his mercy and hope for the best. But there was no confron-
tation. I held my job at the Omaha Public Library for
four years. Technically speaking, I suppose I still hold it
now, although I haven't been there in a week and have
not phoned in sick.

The rats, you see. They found me there, too. I began
to see them crouched on piles of old books in the
Binding Room, or scuttering along the highest shelves
in the stacks, peering down at me knowingly. Last week,
in the Reference Room, I pulled out a volume of the
Encyclopaedia Britannica for an elderly patron (it was
Ra-St, which no doubt contains an entry for *Rattus
norvegicus*, not to mention *slaughterhouse*) and saw a
hungry gray-black face staring out at me from the vacant
slot. It was the rat that bit off poor Achelois's teat. I
don't know how that could be – I'm sure I killed it
– but there was no doubt. I recognized it. How could
I not? There was a scrap of burlap, *bloodstained* burlap,
caught in its whiskers.

Snood!

I brought the volume of *Britannica* to the old lady
who had requested it (she wore an ermine stole, and the
thing's little black eyes regarded me bleakly). Then I simply
walked out. I wandered the streets for hours, and eventually came here, to the Magnolia Hotel. And here I have

been ever since, spending the money I have saved as a librarian – which doesn't matter any longer – and writing my confession, which does. I—

One of them just nipped me on the ankle. As if to say *Get on with it, time's almost up.* A little blood has begun to stain my sock. It doesn't disturb me, not in the slightest. I have seen more blood in my time; in 1922 there was a room filled with it.

And now I think I hear . . . is it my imagination?

No.

Someone has come visiting.

I plugged the pipe, but the rats still escaped. I filled in the well, but *she* also found her way out. And this time I don't think she's alone. I think I hear two sets of shuffling feet, not just one. Or—

Three? Is it three? Is the girl who would have been my daughter-in-law in a better world with them as well?

I think she is. Three corpses shuffling up the hall, their faces (what remains of them) disfigured by rat-bites, Arlette's cocked to one side as well . . . by the kick of a dying cow.

Another bite on the ankle.

And another!

How the management would—

Ow! Another. But they won't have me. And my visitors won't, either, although now I can see the doorknob turning and I can smell them, the remaining flesh hanging on their bones giving off the stench of slaughtered

slaught

The gun

god where is the

stop

OH MAKE THEM STOP BITING M

*   *   *

From the Omaha *World-Herald*, April 14, 1930

LIBRARIAN COMMITS SUICIDE IN LOCAL HOTEL
Bizarre Scene Greets Hotel Security Man

The body of Wilfred James, a librarian at the Omaha Public Library, was found in a local hotel on Sunday when efforts by hotel staff to contact him met with no response. The resident of a nearby room had complained of 'a smell like bad meat,' and a hotel chambermaid reported hearing 'muffled shouting or crying, like a man in pain' late Friday afternoon.

After knocking repeatedly and receiving no response, the hotel's Chief of Security used his pass-key and discovered the body of Mr James, slumped over the room's writing desk. 'I saw a pistol and assumed he had shot himself,' the security man said, 'but no one had reported a gunshot, and there was no smell of expended powder. When I checked the gun, I determined it was a badly maintained .25, and not loaded.

'By then, of course, I had seen the blood. I have never seen anything like that before, and never want to again. He

had bitten himself all over – arms, legs, ankles, even his toes. Nor was that all. It was clear he had been busy with some sort of writing project, but he had chewed up the paper, as well. It was all over the floor. It looked like paper does when rats chew it up to make their nests. In the end, he chewed his own wrists open. I believe that's what killed him. He certainly must have been deranged.'

Little is known of Mr James at this writing. Ronald Quarles, the head librarian at the Omaha Public Library, took Mr James on in late 1926. 'He was obviously down on his luck, and handicapped by the loss of a hand, but he knew his books and his references were good,' Quarles said. 'He was collegial but distant. I believe he had been doing factory work before applying for a position here, and he told people that before losing his hand, he had owned a small farm in Hemingford County.'

The *World-Herald* is interested in the unfortunate Mr James, and solicits information from any readers who may have known him. The body is being held at the Omaha County Morgue, pending disposition by next of kin. 'If no next of kin appears,' said Dr Tattersall, the Morgue's Chief Medical Officer, 'I suppose he will be buried in public ground.'

BIG DRIVER

1

Tess accepted twelve compensated speaking engagements a year, if she could get them. At twelve hundred dollars each, that came to over fourteen thousand dollars. It was her retirement fund. She was still happy enough with the Willow Grove Knitting Society after twelve books, but didn't kid herself that she could go on writing them until she was in her seventies. If she did, what would she find at the bottom of the barrel? *The Willow Grove Knitting Society Goes to Terre Haute? The Willow Grove Knitting Society Visits the International Space Station*? No. Not even if the ladies' book societies who were her mainstay read them (and they probably would). No.

So she was a good little squirrel, living well on the money her books brought in . . . but putting away acorns for the winter. Each year for the last ten she had put between twelve and sixteen thousand dollars into her money market fund. The total wasn't as high as she might have wished, thanks to the gyrations of the stock market, but she told herself that if she kept on plugging, she'd probably be all right; she was the little engine that could. And she did at least three events each year gratis to salve her conscience. That often annoying organ should not have troubled her about taking honest money for honest work but sometimes it did. Probably because running her gums and signing her name didn't fit the concept of work as she had been raised to understand it.

Other than an honorarium of at least twelve hundred dollars, she had one other requirement: that she be able to drive to the location of her lecture, with not more than one overnight stop on the way to or from. This meant she rarely went farther south than Richmond or farther west than Cleveland. One night in a motel was tiring but acceptable; two made her useless for a week. And Fritzy, her cat, hated keeping house by himself. This he made clear when she came home, twining between her feet on the stairs and often making promiscuous use of his claws when he sat in her lap. And although Patsy McClain from next door was very good about feeding him, he rarely ate much until Tess came home.

It wasn't that she was afraid of flying, or hesitant about billing the organizations that engaged her for travel expenses just as she billed them for her motel rooms (always nice, never elegant). She just hated it: the crowding, the indignity of the full-body scans, the way the airlines now had their hands out for what used to be free, the delays . . . and the inescapable fact that you were not in charge. That was the worst. Once you went through the interminable security checkpoints and were allowed to board, you had put your most valuable possession – your life – into the hands of strangers.

Of course that was also true on the turnpikes and interstates she almost always used when she traveled, a drunk could lose control, jump the median strip, and end your life in a head-on collision (*they* would live; the drunks, it seemed, always did), but at least when she was behind the wheel of her car, she had the *illusion* of control. And she liked to drive. It was soothing. She had some of her best ideas when she was on cruise control with the radio off.

'I bet you were a long-haul trucker in your last incarnation,' Patsy McClain told her once.

Tess didn't believe in past lifetimes, or future ones for that matter – in metaphysical terms, she thought what you saw was pretty much what you got – but she liked the idea of a life where she was not a small woman with an elfin face, a shy smile, and a job writing cozy mysteries, but a big guy with a big hat shading his sunburned brow

and grizzled cheeks, letting a bulldog hood ornament lead
him along the million roads that crisscrossed the country.
No need to carefully match her clothes before public
appearances in that life; faded jeans and boots with side-
buckles would do. She liked to write, and she didn't mind
public speaking, but what she really liked to do was drive.
After her Chicopee appearance, this struck her as
funny . . . but not funny in a way that made you laugh.
No, not that kind of funny at all.

2

The invitation from Books & Brown Baggers filled her
requirements perfectly. Chicopee was hardly more than
sixty miles from Stoke Village, the engagement was to
be a daytime affair, and the Three Bs were offering an
honorarium of not twelve but fifteen hundred dollars. Plus
expenses, of course, but those would be minimal – not
even a stay at a Courtyard Suites or a Hampton Inn. The
query letter came from one Ramona Norville, who
explained that, although she was the head librarian at the
Chicopee Public Library, she was writing in her capacity
as President of Books & Brown Baggers, which put on a
noon lecture each month. People were encouraged to bring
their lunches, and the events were very popular. Janet
Evanovich had been scheduled for October 12, but had
been forced to cancel because of a family matter – a
wedding or a funeral, Ramona Norville wasn't sure which.

'I know this is short notice,' Ms Norville said in her
slightly wheedling final paragraph, 'but Wikipedia says you
live in neighboring Connecticut, and our readers here in
Chicopee are *such* fans of the Knitting Society gals. You
would have our undying gratitude as well as the above-
mentioned honorarium.'

Tess doubted that the gratitude would last much longer

than a day or two, and she already had a speaking engagement lined up for October (Literary Cavalcade Week in
the Hamptons), but I-84 would take her to I-90, and from
90, Chicopee was a straight shot. Easy in, easy out; Fritzy
would hardly know she was gone.

Ramona Norville had of course included her email
address, and Tess wrote her immediately, accepting the
date and the honorarium amount. She also specified – as
was her wont – that she would sign autographs for no
more than an hour. 'I have a cat who bullies me if I'm
not home to feed him his supper personally,' she wrote.
She asked for any further details, although she already
knew most of what would be expected of her; she had
been doing similar events since she was thirty. Still, organ-
izational types like Ramona Norville expected to be asked,
and if you didn't, they got nervous and started to wonder
if that day's hired writer was going to show up braless
and tipsy.

It crossed Tess's mind to suggest that perhaps two
thousand dollars would be more appropriate for what was,
in effect, a triage mission, but she dismissed the idea. It
would be taking advantage. Also, she doubted if all the
Knitting Society books put together (there were an even
dozen) had sold as many copies as any one of Stephanie
Plum's adventures. Like it or not – and in truth, Tess didn't
mind much one way or the other – she was Ramona
Norville's Plan B. A surcharge would be close to blackmail.
Fifteen hundred was more than fair. Of course when she
was lying in a culvert, coughing out blood from her
swollen mouth and nose, it didn't seem fair at all. But
would two thousand have been any fairer? Or two million?

Whether or not you could put a price tag on pain,
rape, and terror was a question the Knitting Society ladies
had never taken up. The crimes they solved were really
not much more than the *ideas* of crimes. But when Tess

was forced to consider it, she thought the answer was no. It seemed to her that only one thing could possibly constitute payback for such a crime. Both Tom and Fritzy agreed.

3

Ramona Norville turned out to be a broad-shouldered, heavy-breasted, jovial woman of sixty or so with flushed cheeks, a Marine haircut, and a take-no-prisoners handshake. She was waiting for Tess outside the library, in the middle of the parking space reserved for Today's Author of Note. Instead of wishing Tess a very good morning (it was quarter to eleven), or complimenting her on her earrings (diamond drops, an extravagance reserved for her few dinners out and engagements like this), she asked a man's question: had Tess come by the 84?

When Tess said she had, Ms Norville widened her eyes and blew out her cheeks. 'Glad you got here safe. 84's the worst highway in America, in my humble opinion. Also the long way around. We can improve the situation going back, if the Internet's right and you live in Stoke Village.'

Tess agreed that she did, although she wasn't sure she liked strangers – even a pleasant librarian – knowing where she went to lay down her weary head. But it did no good to complain; everything was on the Internet these days.

'I can save you ten miles,' Ms Norville said as they mounted the library steps. 'Have you got a GPS? That makes things easier than directions written on the back of an envelope. Wonderful gadgets.'

Tess, who had indeed added a GPS to her Expedition's dashboard array (it was called a TomTom and plugged into the cigarette lighter), said that ten miles off her return journey would be very nice.

'Better a straight shot through Robin Hood's barn

than all the way around it,' Ms Norville said, and clapped Tess lightly on the back. 'Am I right or am I right?'

'Absolutely,' Tess agreed, and her fate was decided as simply as that. She had always been a sucker for a shortcut.

4

Les affaires du livre usually had four well-defined acts, and Tess's appearance at the monthly convocation of Books & Brown Baggers could have been a template for the general case. The only diversion from the norm was Ramona Norville's introduction, which was succinct to the point of terseness. She carried no disheartening pile of file cards to the podium, felt no need to rehash Tess's Nebraska farmgirl childhood, and did not bother producing bouquets of critical praise for the Willow Grove Knitting Society books. (This was good, because they were rarely reviewed, and when they were, the name of Miss Marple was usually invoked, not always in a good way.) Ms Norville simply said that the books were hugely popular (a forgivable overstatement), and that the author had been extremely generous in donating her time on short notice (although, at fifteen hundred dollars, it was hardly a donation). Then she yielded the podium, to the enthusiastic applause of the four hundred or so in the library's small but adequate auditorium. Most were ladies of the sort who do not attend public occasions without first donning hats.

But the introduction was more of an *entr'acte*. Act One was the eleven o'clock reception, where the higher rollers got to meet Tess in person over cheese, crackers, and cups of lousy coffee (evening events featured plastic glasses of lousy wine). Some asked for autographs; many more requested pictures, which they usually took with their cell phones. She was asked where she got her ideas and made the usual polite and humorous noises in response. Half a dozen people asked her how you got an agent, the glint in their eyes suggesting they had paid the extra twenty dollars just to ask this question. Tess said you kept writing letters until one of the hungrier ones agreed to look at your stuff. It wasn't the whole truth − when it came to agents, there *was* no whole truth − but it was close.

Act Two was the speech itself, which lasted about forty-five minutes. This consisted chiefly of anecdotes (none too personal) and a description of how she worked out her stories (back to front). It was important to insert at least three mentions of the current book's title, which that fall happened to be *The Willow Grove Knitting Society Goes Spelunking* (she explained what that was for those who didn't already know).

Act Three was Question Time, during which she was asked where she got her ideas (humorous, vague response), if she drew her characters from real life ('my aunts'), and how one got an agent to look at one's work. Today she was also asked where she got her scrunchie (JCPenney, an answer which brought inexplicable applause).

The last act was Autograph Time, during which she dutifully fulfilled requests to inscribe happy birthday wishes, happy anniversary wishes, *To Janet, a fan of all my books*, and *To Leah − Hope to see you at Lake Toxaway again this summer!* (a slightly odd request, since Tess had never been there, but presumably the autograph-seeker had).

When all the books had been signed and the last few lingerers had been satisfied with more cell-phone pictures, Ramona Norville escorted Tess into her office for a cup of real coffee. Ms Norville took hers black, which didn't surprise Tess at all. Her hostess was a black-coffee type of chick if one had ever strode the surface of the earth (prob-ably in Doc Martens on her day off). The only surprising thing in the office was the framed signed picture on the wall. The face was familiar, and after a moment, Tess was able to retrieve the name from the junkheap of memory that is every writer's most valuable asset.

'Richard Widmark?'

Ms Norville laughed in an embarrassed but pleased sort of way. 'My favorite actor. Had sort of a crush on him when I was a girl, if you want the whole truth. I got him to sign that for me ten years before he died. He was very old, even then, but it's a real signature, not a stamp. This is yours.' For one crazed moment, Tess thought Ms Norville meant the signed photo. Then she saw the envelope in those blunt fingers. The kind of envelope with a window, so you could peek at the check inside.

'Thank you,' Tess said, taking it.

'No thanks necessary. You earned every penny.'

Tess did not demur.

'Now. About that shortcut.'

Tess leaned forward attentively. In one of the Knitting Society books, Doreen Marquis had said, *The two best things in life are warm croissants and a quick way home.* This was a case of the writer using her own dearly held beliefs to enliven her fiction.

'Can you program intersections in your GPS?'

'Yes, Tom's very canny.'

Ms Norville smiled. 'Input Stagg Road and US 47, then. Stagg Road is very little used in this modern age – almost forgotten since that damn 84 – but it's scenic. You'll ramble along it for, oh, sixteen miles or so. Patched asphalt, but not too bumpy, or wasn't the last time I took it, and that was in the spring, when the worst bumps show up. At least that's my experience.'

'Mine, too,' Tess said.

'When you get to 47, you'll see a sign pointing you to I-84, but you'll only need to take the turnpike for twelve miles or so, that's the beauty part. And you'll save tons of time and aggravation.'

'That's also the beauty part,' Tess said, and they laughed together, two women of the same mind watched over by a smiling Richard Widmark. The abandoned store with the ticking sign was then still ninety minutes away, tucked snugly into the future like a snake in its hole. And the culvert, of course.

5

Tess not only had a GPS; she had spent extra for a customized one. She liked toys. After she had input the intersection (Ramona Norville leaned in the window as she did it, watching with manly interest), the gadget thought for a moment or two, then said, 'Tess, I am calculating your route.'

'Whoa-ho, how about that!' Norville said, and laughed the way that people do at some amiable peculiarity.

Tess smiled, although she privately thought programing your GPS to call you by name was no more peculiar than keeping a fan foto of a dead actor on your office wall. 'Thank you for everything, Ramona. It was all very professional.'

'We do our best at Three Bs. Now off you go. With my thanks.'

'Off I go,' Tess agreed. 'And you're very welcome. I enjoyed it.' This was true; she usually did enjoy such occasions, in an all-right-let's-get-this-taken-care-of fashion. And her retirement fund would certainly enjoy the unexpected infusion of cash.

'Have a safe trip home,' Norville said, and Tess gave her a thumbs-up.

When she pulled away, the GPS said, 'Hello, Tess. I see we're taking a trip.'

'Yes indeed,' she said. 'And a good day for it, wouldn't you say?'

Unlike the computers in science fiction movies, Tom was poorly equipped for light conversation, although Tess sometimes helped him. He told her to make a right turn four hundred yards ahead, then take her first left. The map on the TomTom's screen displayed green arrows and street names, sucking the information down from some whirling metal ball of technology high above.

She was soon on the outskirts of Chicopee, but Tom sent her past the turn for I-84 without comment and into countryside that was flaming with October color and smoky with the scent of burning leaves. After ten miles or so on something called Old County Road, and just as she was wondering if her GPS had made a mistake (as if), Tom spoke up again.

'In one mile, right turn.'

Sure enough, she soon saw a green Stagg Road sign so pocked with shotgun pellets it was almost unreadable. But of course, Tom didn't need signs; in the words of the sociologists (Tess had been a major before discovering her talent for writing about old lady detectives), he was other-directed.

You'll ramble along for sixteen miles or so, Ramona Norville had said, but Tess rambled for only a dozen. She came around a curve, spied an old dilapidated building ahead on her left (the faded sign over the pumpless service island still read ESSO), and then saw – too late – several large, splintered pieces of wood scattered across the road. There were rusty nails jutting from many of them. She jounced across the pothole that had probably dislodged them from some country bumpkin's carelessly packed load, then veered for the soft shoulder in an effort to get around the litter, knowing she probably wasn't going to make it; why else would she hear herself saying *Oh-oh*?

There was a *clack-thump-thud* beneath her as chunks of wood flew up against the undercarriage, and then her trusty Expedition began pogoing up and down and pulling to the left, like a horse that's gone lame. She wrestled it into the weedy yard of the deserted store, wanting to get it off the road so someone who happened to come tearing around that last curve wouldn't rear-end her. She hadn't seen much traffic on Stagg Road, but there'd been some, including a couple of large trucks.

'Goddam you, Ramona,' she said. She knew it wasn't really the librarian's fault; the head (and probably only member) of The Richard Widmark Fan Appreciation Society, Chicopee Branch, had only been trying to be helpful, but Tess didn't know the name of the dummocks who had dropped his nail-studded shit on the road and then gone gaily on his way, so Ramona had to do.

'Would you like me to recalculate your route, Tess?' Tom asked, making her jump.

She turned the GPS off, then killed the engine, as well. She wasn't going anywhere for awhile. It was very quiet out here. She heard birdsong, a metallic ticking sound like an old wind-up clock, and nothing else. The good news was that the Expedition seemed to be leaning to the left front instead of just leaning. Perhaps it was only the one tire. She wouldn't need a tow, if that was the case; just a little help from Triple-A.

When she got out and looked at the left front tire, she saw a splintered piece of wood impaled on it by a large, rusty spike. Tess uttered a one-syllable expletive that had never crossed the lips of a Knitting Society member, and got her cell phone out of the little storage compartment between the bucket seats. She would now be lucky to get home before dark, and Fritzy would have to be content with his bowl of dry food in the pantry. So much for Ramona Norville's shortcut . . . although to be fair, Tess supposed the same thing could have happened to her on the interstate; certainly she had avoided her share of potentially car-crippling crap on many thruways, not just I-84.

The conventions of horror tales and mysteries – even mysteries of the bloodless, one-corpse variety enjoyed by her fans – were surprisingly similar, and as she flipped open her phone she thought, *In a story, it wouldn't work.* This was a case of life imitating art, because when she powered up her Nokia the words NO SERVICE appeared in the window. Of course. Being able to use her phone would be too simple.

She heard an indifferently muffled engine approaching, turned, and saw an old white van come around the curve that had done her in. On the side was a cartoon skeleton pounding a drum kit that appeared to be made out of cupcakes. Written in drippy horror-movie script above this apparition (*much* more peculiar than a fan foto of Richard Widmark on a librarian's office wall) were the words ZOMBIE BAKERS. For a moment Tess was too bemused to wave, and when she did, the driver of the Zombie Bakers truck was busy trying to avoid the mess on the road and didn't notice her.

He was quicker to the shoulder than Tess had been, but the van had a higher center of gravity than the Expedition, and for a moment she was sure it was going to roll and land on its side in the ditch. It stayed up – barely – and regained the road beyond the spilled chunks of wood. The van disappeared around the next curve, leaving behind a blue cloud of exhaust and a smell of hot oil.

'*Damn you, Zombie Bakers!*' Tess yelled, then began to laugh. Sometimes it was all you could do.

She clipped her phone to the waistband of her dress

slacks, went out to the road, and began picking up the mess herself. She did it slowly and carefully, because up close it became obvious that all the pieces of wood (which were painted white and looked as if they had been stripped away by someone in the throes of a home renovation project) had nails in them. Big ugly ones. She worked slowly because she didn't want to cut herself, but she also hoped to be out here, observably doing A Good Work of Christian Charity, when the next car came along. But by the time she'd finished picking up everything but a few harmless splinters and casting the big pieces into the ditch below the shoulder of the road, no other cars had come along. *Perhaps*, she thought, *the Zombie Bakers had eaten everyone in this immediate vicinity and were now hurrying back to their kitchen to put the leftovers into the always-popular People Pies.*

She walked back to the defunct store's weedy parking lot and looked moodily at her leaning car. Thirty thousand dollars' worth of rolling iron, four-wheel drive, independent disc brakes, Tom the Talking TomTom . . . and all it took to leave you stranded was a piece of wood with a nail in it.

But of course they all had nails, she thought. *In a mystery – or a horror movie – that wouldn't constitute carelessness; that would constitute a plan. A trap, in fact.*

'Too much imagination, Tessa Jean,' she said, quoting her mother . . . and that was ironic, of course, since it was her imagination that had ended up providing her with her daily bread. Not to mention the Daytona Beach home where her mother had spent the last six years of her life.

In the big silence she again became aware of that tinny ticking sound. The abandoned store was of a kind you didn't see much in the twenty-first century: it had a porch. The lefthand corner had collapsed and the railing was broken in a couple of places, but yes, it was an actual porch, charming even in its dilapidation. Maybe *because* of its dilapidation. Tess supposed general store porches had become obsolete because they encouraged you to sit a spell and chat about baseball or the weather instead of just paying up and hustling your credit cards on down the road to some other place where you could swipe them at the checkout. A tin sign hung askew from the porch roof. It was more faded than the Esso sign. She took a few steps closer, raising a hand to her forehead to shade her eyes. YOU LIKE IT IT LIKES YOU. Which was a slogan for what, exactly?

She had almost plucked the answer from her mental junkheap when her thoughts were interrupted by the sound of an engine. As she turned toward it, sure that the Zombie Bakers had come back after all, the sound of the motor was joined by the scream of ancient brakes. It wasn't the white van but an old Ford-150 pickup with a bad blue paintjob and Bondo around the headlights. A man in bib overalls and a gimme cap sat behind the wheel. He was looking at the litter of wood scraps in the ditch.

'Hello?' Tess called. 'Pardon me, sir?'

He turned his head, saw her standing in the overgrown parking lot, flicked a hand in salute, pulled in beside her Expedition, and turned off his engine. Given the sound of it, Tess thought that an act tantamount to mercy killing.

'Hey, there,' he said. 'Did you pick that happy crappy up off the road?'

'Yes, all but the piece that got my left front tire. And—' *And my phone doesn't work out here*, she almost added, then didn't. She was a woman in her late thirties who went one-twenty soaking wet, and this was a strange man. A big one. '—and here I am,' she finished, a bit lamely.

'I'll change it forya if you got a spare,' he said, working his way out of his truck. 'Do you?'

For a moment she couldn't reply. The guy wasn't big, she'd been wrong about that. The guy was a giant. He had to go six-six, but head-to-foot was only part of it. He was deep in the belly, thick in the thighs, and as wide as a doorway. She knew it was impolite to stare (another of the world's facts learned at her mother's knee), but it was hard not to. Ramona Norville had been a healthy chunk of woman, but standing next to this guy, she would have looked like a ballerina.

'I know, I know,' he said, sounding amused. 'You didn't think you were going to meet the Jolly Green Giant out here in the williwags, didja?' Only he wasn't green; he was tanned a deep brown. His eyes were also brown. Even his cap was brown, although faded almost white in several places, as if it had been splattered with bleach at some point in its long life.

'I'm sorry,' she said. 'It's just that I was thinking you don't ride in that truck of yours, you wear it.'

He put his hands on his hips and guffawed at the sky. 'Never heard it put like that before, but you're sort of right. When I win the lottery, I'm going to buy myself a Hummer.'

'Well, I can't buy you one of those, but if you change my tire, I'd be happy to pay you fifty dollars.'

'You kiddin? I'll do it for free. You saved me a mess of my own when you picked up that scrapwood.'

'Someone went past in a funny truck with a skeleton on the side, but he missed it.'

The big guy had been heading for Tess's flat front tire, but now he turned back to her, frowning. 'Someone went by and didn't offer to help you out?'

'I don't think he saw me.'

'Didn't stop to pick up that mess for the next fellow, either, did he?'

'No. He didn't.'

'Just went on his way?'

'Yes.' There was something about these questions she didn't quite like. Then the big guy smiled and Tess told herself she was being silly.

'Spare under the cargo compartment floor, I suppose?'

'Yes. That is, I think so. All you have to do is—'

'Pull up on the handle, yep, yep. Been there, done that.'

As he ambled around to the back of her Expedition with his hands tucked deep into the pockets of his overalls, Tess saw that the door of his truck hadn't shut all the way and the dome light was on. Thinking that the F-150's battery might be as battered as the truck it was powering, she opened the door (the hinge screamed almost as loudly as the brakes) and then slammed it closed. As she did, she looked through the cab's back window and into the pickup's bed. There were several pieces of wood scattered across the ribbed and rusty metal. They were painted white and had nails sticking out of them.

For a moment, Tess felt as if she were having an out-of-body experience. The ticking sign, YOU LIKE IT IT LIKES YOU, now sounded not like an old-fashioned alarm clock but a ticking bomb.

She tried to tell herself the scraps of wood meant nothing, stuff like that only meant something in the kind of books she didn't write and the kind of movies she rarely watched: the nasty, bloody kind. It didn't work. Which left her with two choices. She could either go on trying to pretend because to do otherwise was terrifying, or she could take off running for the woods on the other side of the road.

Before she could decide, she smelled the whopping aroma of mansweat. She turned and he was there, towering over her with his hands in the side pockets of his overalls. 'Instead of changing your tire,' he said pleasantly, 'how about I fuck you? How would that be?'

Then Tess ran, but only in her mind. What she did in the real world was to stand pressed against his truck, looking up at him, a man so tall he blocked out the sun and put her in his shadow. She was thinking that not two hours ago four hundred people – mostly ladies in hats – had been applauding her in a small but entirely adequate auditorium. And somewhere south of here, Fritzy was waiting for her. It dawned on her – laboriously, like lifting something heavy – that she might never see her cat again.

'Please don't kill me,' some woman said in a very small and very humble voice.

'You bitch,' he said. He spoke in the tone of a man reflecting on the weather. The sign went on ticking against the eave of the porch. 'You whiny whore bitch. Gosh sakes.'

His right hand came out of his pocket. It was a very big hand. On the pinky finger was a ring with a red stone in it. It looked like a ruby, but it was too big to be a ruby. Tess thought it was probably just glass. The sign ticked. YOU LIKE IT IT LIKES YOU. Then the hand turned into a fist and came speeding toward her, growing until everything else was blotted out.

There was a muffled metallic bang from somewhere. She thought it was her head colliding with the side of the pickup truck's cab. Tess thought: *Zombie Bakers*. Then for a little while it was dark.

6

She came to in a large shadowy room that smelled of damp wood, ancient coffee, and prehistoric pickles. An old paddle fan hung crookedly from the ceiling just above her. It looked like the broken merry-go-round in that Hitchcock movie, *Strangers on a Train*. She was on the floor, naked from the waist down, and he was raping her. The rape seemed secondary to the weight: he was also crushing her. She could barely draw a breath. It had to be a dream. But her nose was swollen, a lump that felt the size of a small mountain had grown at the base of her skull, and splinters were digging into her buttocks. You didn't notice those sorts of details in dreams. And you didn't feel actual pain in dreams; you always woke up before the real pain started. This was happening. He was raping her. He had taken her inside the old store and he was raping her while golden dust motes twirled lazily in the slanting afternoon sun. Somewhere people were listening to music and buying products online and taking naps and talking on phones, but in here a woman was being raped and she was that woman. He had taken her underpants; she could see them frothing from the pocket in the bib of his overalls. That made her think of *Deliverance*, which she had watched at a college film retrospective, back in the days when she had been slightly more adventurous in her moviegoing. *Get them panties down*, one of the hillbillies had said before commencing to rape the fat townie. It was funny what crossed your mind when you were lying under three hundred pounds of country meat with a rapist's cock creaking back and forth inside you like an unoiled hinge.

'Please,' she said. 'Oh please, no more.'

'Lots more,' he said, and here came that fist again, filling her field of vision. The side of her face went hot, there was a click in the middle of her head, and she blacked out.

7

The next time she came to, he was dancing around her in his overalls, tossing his hands from side to side and singing 'Brown Sugar' in a squalling, atonal voice. The sun was going down, and the abandoned store's two west-facing windows — the glass dusty but miraculously unbroken by vandals – were filled with fire. His shadow danced behind him, capering down the board floor and up the wall, which was marked with light squares where advertising signs had once hung. The sound of his cludding workboots was apocalyptic.

She could see her dress slacks crumpled under the counter where the cash register must once have stood (probably next to a jar of boiled eggs and another of pickled pigs' feet). She could smell mold. And oh God she hurt. Her face, her chest, most of all down below, where she felt torn open.

Pretend you're dead. It's your only chance.

She closed her eyes. The singing stopped and she smelled approaching mansweat. Sharper now.

Because he's been exercising, she thought. She forgot about playing dead and tried to scream. Before she could, his huge hands gripped her throat and began to choke. She thought: *It's over. I'm over.* They were calm thoughts, full of relief. At least there would be no more pain, no more waking to watch the monster-man dance in the burning sunset light.

She passed out.

8

When Tess swam back to consciousness the third time, the world had turned black and silver and she was floating.

This is what it's like to be dead.

Then she registered hands beneath her – big hands, *his* hands – and the barbwire circlet of pain around her throat. He hadn't choked her quite enough to kill her, but she was wearing the shape of his hands like a necklace, palms in front, fingers on the sides and the nape of her neck.

It was night. The moon was up. A full moon. He was carrying her across the parking lot of the deserted store. He was carrying her past his truck. She didn't see her Expedition. Her Expedition was gone.

Wherefore art thou, Tom?

He stopped at the edge of the road. She could smell his sweat and feel the rise and fall of his chest. She could feel the night air, cool on her bare legs. She could hear the sign ticking behind her, YOU LIKE IT IT LIKES YOU.

Does he think I'm dead? He can't think I'm dead. I'm still bleeding.

Or was she? It was hard to tell for sure. She lay limp in his arms, feeling like a girl in a horror movie, the one who's carried away by Jason or Michael or Freddy or whatever his name was after all the other ones are slaughtered. Carried to some slumpy deep-woods lair where she would be chained to a hook in the ceiling. In those movies there were always chains and hooks in the ceiling.

He got moving again. She could hear his workshoes on the patched tar of Stagg Road: *clud-clump-clud*. Then, on the far side, scraping noises and clattering sounds. He was kicking away the chunks of wood she had so carefully cleaned up and thrown down here in the ditch. She could no longer hear the ticking sign, but she could hear running water. Not much, not a gush, only a trickle. He knelt down. A soft grunt escaped him.

Now he'll kill me for sure. And at least I won't have to listen to anymore of his awful singing. It's the beauty part, Ramona Norville would say.

'Hey girl,' he said in a kindly voice.

She didn't reply, but she could see him bending over her, looking into her half-lidded eyes. She took great care to keep them still. If he saw them move, even a little . . . or a gleam of tears . . .

'Hey.' He popped the flat of his hand against her cheek. She let her head roll to the side.

'Hey!' This time he outright slapped her, but on the other cheek. Tess let her head roll back the other way.

He pinched her nipple, but he hadn't bothered to take off her blouse and bra and it didn't hurt too badly. She lay limp.

'I'm sorry I called you a bitch,' he said, still using the kindly voice. 'You was a good fuck. And I like em a little older.'

Tess realized he really *might* think she was dead. It was amazing, but could be true. And all at once she wanted very badly to live.

He picked her up again. The mansweat smell was suddenly overwhelming. Beard bristles tickled the side of her face, and it was all she could do not to twitch away from them. He kissed the corner of her mouth.

'Sorry I was a little rough.'

Then he was moving her again. The sound of the running water got louder. The moonlight was blotted out. There was a smell – no, a stench – of rotting leaves. He put her down in four or five inches of water. It was very cold, and she almost cried out. He pushed on her feet and she let her knees go up. *Boneless*, she thought. *Have to stay boneless.* They didn't go far before bumping against a corrugated metal surface.

'Fuck,' he said, speaking in a reflective tone. Then he shoved her.

Tess remained limp even when something – a branch – scrawled a line of hurt down the center of her back. Her knees bumped along the corrugations above her. Her buttocks pushed a spongy mass, and the smell of rotting vegetable matter intensified. It was as thick as meat. She felt a terrible urge to cough the smell away. She could feel a mat of wet leaves gathering in the small of her back, like a throw-pillow soaked with water.

If he figures it out now, I'll fight him. I'll kick him and kick him and kick him—

But nothing happened. For a long time she was afraid to open her eyes any wider or move them in the slightest. She imagined him crouching there, looking into the pipe where he'd stashed her, head to one side, tilting a question, waiting for just such a move. How could he not know she was alive? Surely he'd felt the thump of her heart. And what good would kicking be against the giant from the pickup? He'd grab her bare feet in one hand, haul her out, and recommence choking her. Only this time he wouldn't stop.

She lay in the rotting leaves and sluggish water, looking up at nothing from her half-lidded eyes, concentrating on playing dead. She passed into a gray fugue that was not quite unconsciousness, and there she stayed for a length of time that felt long but probably wasn't. When she heard a motor – his truck, surely his truck – Tess thought: *I'm imagining that sound. Or dreaming it. He's still here.*

But the irregular thump of the motor first swelled, then faded off down Stagg Road.

It's a trick.

That was almost certainly hysteria. Even if it wasn't, she couldn't stay here all night. And when she raised her head (wincing at the stab of pain in her abused throat) and looked toward the mouth of the pipe, she saw only an unimpeded silver circle of moonlight. Tess started wriggling toward it, then stopped.

It's a trick. I don't care what you heard, he's still here.

This time the idea was more powerful. Seeing nothing at the mouth of the culvert *made* it more powerful. In a suspense novel, this would be the moment of false relaxation before the big climax. Or in a scary movie. The white hand emerging from the lake in *Deliverance*. Alan Arkin springing out at Audrey Hepburn in *Wait Until Dark*.

She didn't like scary books and movies, but being raped and almost murdered seemed to have unlocked a whole vault of scary-movie memories, all the same. As if they were just there, in the air.

He *could* be waiting. If, for instance, he'd had an accomplice drive his truck away. He could be squatting on his hunkers beyond the mouth of the pipe in that patient way country men had.

'Get those panties down,' she whispered, then covered her mouth. What if he heard her?

Five minutes passed. It might have been five. The water was cold and she began to shiver. Soon her teeth would begin to chatter. If he was out there, he would hear.

He drove away. You heard him.

Maybe. Maybe not.

And maybe she didn't need to leave the pipe the way she'd gone in. It was a culvert, it would go all the way under the road, and since she could feel water running under her, it wasn't blocked. She could crawl the length of it and look out into the deserted store's parking lot. Make sure his old truck was gone. She still wouldn't be safe if there was an accomplice, but Tess felt sure, deep down where her rational mind had gone to hide, that there was no accomplice. An accomplice would have insisted on taking his turn at her. Besides, giants worked alone.

And if he is gone? What then?

She didn't know. She couldn't imagine her life after her afternoon in the deserted store and her evening in the pipe with rotting leaves smooshed up into the hollow of her back, but maybe she didn't have to. Maybe she could concentrate on getting home to Fritzy and feeding him a packet of Fancy Feast. She could see the Fancy Feast box very clearly. It was sitting on a shelf in her peaceful pantry.

She turned over on her belly and started to get up on her elbows, meaning to crawl the length of the pipe. Then she saw what was sharing the culvert with her. One of the corpses was not much more than a skeleton (stretching out bony hands as if in supplication), but there was still enough hair left on its head to make Tess all but certain it was the corpse of a woman. The other might have been a badly defaced department store mannequin, except for the bulging eyes and protruding tongue. This body was fresher, but the animals had been at it and even in the dark Tess could see the grin of the dead woman's teeth.

A beetle came lumbering out of the mannequin's hair and trundled down the bridge of her nose.

Screaming hoarsely, Tess backed out of the culvert and bolted to her feet, her clothes soaked to her body from the waist up. She was naked from the waist down. And although she did not pass out (at least she didn't think she did), for a little while her consciousness was a queerly broken thing. Looking back on it, she would think of the next hour as a darkened stage lit by occasional spotlights. Every now and then a battered woman with a broken nose and blood on her thighs would walk into one of these spotlights. Then she would disappear back into darkness again.

9

She was in the store, in the big empty central room that had once been divided into aisles, with a frozen food case (maybe) at the back, and a beer cooler (for sure) running the length of the far wall. She was in the smell of departed coffee and pickles. He had either forgotten her dress slacks or meant to come back for them later – perhaps when he picked up the nail-studded scrapwood. She was fishing them out from under the counter. Beneath them were her shoes and her phone – smashed. Yes, at some point he would be back. Her scrunchie was gone. She remembered (vaguely, the way one remembers certain things from one's earliest childhood) some woman asking earlier today where she'd gotten it, and the inexplicable applause when she'd said JCPenney. She thought of the giant singing 'Brown Sugar' – that squalling monotonous childish voice – and she went away again.

10

She was walking behind the store in the moonlight. She had a carpet remnant wrapped around her shivering shoulders, but couldn't remember where she had gotten it. It was filthy but it was warm, and she pulled it tighter. It came to her that she was actually *circling* the store, and this might be her second, third, or even fourth go-round. It came to her that she was looking for her Expedition, but each time she didn't find it behind the store, she forgot that she had looked and went around again. She forgot because she had been thumped on the head and raped and choked and was in shock. It came to her that her brain might be bleeding – how could you know, unless you woke up with the angels and they told you? The afternoon's light breeze had gotten a little stronger, and the ticking of the tin sign was a little louder. YOU LIKE IT IT LIKES YOU.

'7Up,' she said. Her voice was hoarse but serviceable. 'That's what it is. You like it and it likes you.' She heard herself raising her own voice in song. She had a good singing voice, and being choked had given it a surprisingly pleasant rasp. It was like listening to Bonnie Tyler sing out here in the moonlight. '7Up tastes good . . . like a cigarette should!' It came to her that that wasn't right, and even if it was, she should be singing something better than fucked-up advertising jingles while she had that pleasing rasp in her voice; if you were going to be raped and left for dead in a pipe with two rotting corpses, something good should come out of it.

I'll sing Bonnie Tyler's hit record. I'll sing 'It's a Heartache.' I'm sure I know the words, I'm sure they're in the junkheap every writer has in the back of her . . .

But then she went away again.

11

She was sitting on a rock and crying her eyes out. The filthy carpet remnant was still around her shoulders. Her crotch ached and burned. The sour taste in her mouth suggested to her that she had vomited at some point between walking around the store and sitting on this rock, but she couldn't remember doing it. What she remembered—

I was raped, I was raped, I was raped!

'You're not the first and you won't be the last,' she said, but this tough-love sentiment, coming out as it did in a series of choked sobs, was not very helpful.

He tried to kill me, he almost did kill me!

Yes, yes. And at this moment his failure did not seem like much consolation. She looked to her left and saw the store fifty or sixty yards down the road.

He killed others! They're in the pipe! Bugs are crawling on them and they don't care!

'Yes, yes,' she said in her raspy Bonnie Tyler voice, then went away again.

12

She was walking down the center of Stagg Road and singing 'It's a Heartache' when she heard an approaching motor from behind her. She whirled around, almost falling, and saw headlights brightening the top of a hill she must have just come over. It was him. The giant. He had come back, had investigated the culvert after finding her clothes gone, and seen she was no longer in it. He was looking for her.

Tess bolted down into the ditch, stumbled to one knee, lost hold of her makeshift shawl, got up, and blundered into the bushes. A branch drew blood from her cheek. She heard a woman sobbing with fear. She dropped down on her hands and knees with her hair hanging in her eyes. The road brightened as the headlights cleared the hill. She saw the dropped piece of carpeting very clearly, and knew the giant would see it too. He would stop and get out. She would try to run but he would catch her. She would scream, but no one would hear her. In stories like this, they never did. He would kill her, but first he would rape her some more.

The car – it *was* a car, not a pickup truck – went by without slowing. From inside came the sound of Bachman-Turner Overdrive, turned up loud: 'B–B–B–Baby, you just ain't seen n–n–nuthin yet.' She watched the taillights wink out of sight. She felt herself getting ready to go away again and slapped her cheeks with both hands.

'*No!*' she growled in her Bonnie Tyler voice. 'No.'

She came back a little. She felt a strong urge to stay crouched in the bushes, but that was no good. It wasn't just a long time until daylight, it was probably still a long time until midnight. The moon was low in the sky. She couldn't stay here, and she couldn't just keep . . . blinking out. She had to think.

Tess picked the piece of carpeting out of the ditch, started to wrap it around her shoulders again, then touched her ears, knowing what she'd find. The diamond drop earrings, one of her few real extravagances, were gone. She burst into tears again, but this crying fit was shorter, and when it ended she felt more like herself. More *in* herself, a resident of her head and body instead of a specter floating around it.

Think, Tessa Jean!

All right, she would try. But she would walk while she did it. And no more singing. The sound of her changed voice was creepy. It was as if by raping her, the giant had created a new woman. She didn't *want* to be a new woman. She had liked the old one.

Walking. Walking in the moonlight with her shadow walking on the road beside her. What road? Stagg Road. According to Tom, she had been a little less than four miles from the intersection of Stagg Road and US 47 when she'd run into the giant's trap. That wasn't so bad; she walked at least three miles a day to keep in shape, treadmilling on days when it rained or snowed. Of course this was her first walk as the New Tess, she of the aching, bleeding snatch and the raspy voice. But there was an upside: she was warming up, her top half was drying out, and she was in flat shoes. She had almost worn her three-quarter heels, and that would have made this evening stroll very unpleasant, indeed. Not that it would have been fun under any circumstances, no no n—

Think!

But before she could start doing that, the road brightened ahead of her. Tess darted into the underbrush again, this time managing to hold onto the carpet remnant. It was another car, thank God, not his truck, and it didn't slow.

It could still be him. Maybe he switched to a car. He could have driven back to his house, his lair, *and switched to a car. Thinking, she'll see it's a car and come out of wherever she's hiding. She'll wave me down and then I'll have her.*

Yes, yes. That was what would happen in a horror movie, wasn't it? *Screaming Victims 4* or *Stagg Road Horror 2*, or—

She was trying to go away again, so she slapped her

cheeks some more. Once she was home, once Fritzy was fed and she was in her own bed (with all the doors locked and all the lights on), she could go away all she wanted. But not now. No no no. Now she had to keep walking, and hiding when cars came. If she could do those two things, she'd eventually reach US 47, and there might be a store. A *real* store, one with a pay phone, if she was lucky . . . and she deserved some good luck. She didn't have her purse, her purse was still in her Expedition (wherever *that* was), but she knew her AT&T calling-card number by heart; it was her home phone number plus 9712. Easy-as-can-beezy.

Here was a sign at the side of the road. Tess read it easily enough in the moonlight:

YOU ARE NOW ENTERING COLEWICH
TOWNSHIP
WELCOME, FRIEND!

'You like Colewich, it likes you,' she whispered.

She knew the town, which the locals pronounced 'Collitch.' It was actually a small city, one of many in New England that had been prosperous back in the textile-mill days and continued to struggle along somehow in the new free-trade era, when America's pants and jackets were made in Asia or Central America, probably by children who couldn't read or write. She was on the outskirts, but surely she could walk to a phone.

Then what?

Then she would . . . would . . .

'Call a limousine,' she said. The idea burst on her like a sunrise. Yes, that was exactly what she'd do. If this was Colewich, then her own Connecticut town was thirty miles away, maybe less. The limo service she used when she wanted to go to Bradley International or into Hartford or New York (Tess did not do city driving if she could help it) was based in the neighboring town of Woodfield. Royal Limousine boasted round-the-clock service. Even better, they would have her credit card on file.

Tess felt better and began to walk a little faster. Then headlights brightened the road and she once more hurried into the bushes and crouched down, as terrified as any hunted thing: doe fox rabbit. This vehicle *was* a truck, and she began to tremble. She went on trembling even when she saw it was a little white Toyota, nothing at all like the giant's old Ford. When it was gone, she tried to force herself to walk back to the road, but at first she couldn't. She was crying again, the tears warm on her chilly face. She felt herself getting ready to step out of the spotlight of awareness once more. She couldn't let that happen. If she allowed herself to go into that waking blackness too many times, she might eventually lose her way back.

She made herself think of thanking the limo driver and adding a tip to the credit card form before making her way slowly up the flower-lined walk to her front door. Tilting up her mailbox and taking the extra key from the hook behind it. Listening to Fritzy meow anxiously.

The thought of Fritzy turned the trick. She worked her way out of the bushes and resumed walking, ready to dart back into cover the second she saw more headlights. The very second. Because he was out there somewhere. She realized that from now on he would always be out there. Unless the police caught him, that was, and put him in jail. But for that to occur, she would have to report what had happened, and the moment this idea came into her mind, she saw a glaring black *New York Post*-style headline:

'WILLOW GROVE' SCRIBE RAPED AFTER LECTURE

Tabloids like the *Post* would undoubtedly run a picture of her from ten years ago, when her first *Knitting Society* book had been published. Back then she'd been in her late twenties, with long dark blond hair cascading down her back and good legs she liked to showcase in short skirts. Plus – in the evening – the kind of high-heeled slingbacks some men (the giant for one, almost certainly) referred to as fuck-me shoes. They wouldn't mention that she was now ten years older, twenty pounds heavier, and had been dressed in sensible – almost dowdy – business attire when she was assaulted; those details didn't fit the kind of story the tabloids liked to tell. The copy would be respectful enough (if panting a trifle between the lines), but the picture of her old self would tell the real story, one that probably pre-dated the invention of the wheel: *She asked for it . . . and she got it.*

Was that realistic, or only her shame and badly battered sense of self-worth imagining the worst-case scenario? The part of her that might want to go on hiding in the bushes even if she managed to get off this awful road and out of this awful state of Massachusetts and back to her safe little house in Stoke Village? She didn't know, and guessed that the true answer lay somewhere in between. One thing she *did* know was that she would get the sort of nationwide coverage every writer would like when she publishes a book and no writer wants when she has been raped and robbed and left for dead. She could visualize someone raising a hand during Question Time and asking, 'Did you in any way encourage him?'

That was ridiculous, and even in her current state Tess knew it . . . but she also knew that if this came out, someone *would* raise his or her hand to ask, 'Are you going to write about this?'

And what would she say? What *could* she say?

Nothing, Tess thought. *I would run off the stage with my hands over my ears.*

But no.

No no no.

The truth was she wouldn't be there in the first place. How could she ever do another reading, lecture, or autographing, knowing that *he* might turn up, smiling at her from the back row? Smiling from beneath that weird brown cap with the bleach spots on it? Maybe with her earrings in his pocket. Fondling them.

The thought of telling the police made her skin burn, and she could feel her face literally wincing in shame, even out here, alone in the dark. Maybe she wasn't Sue Grafton or Janet Evanovich, but neither was she, strictly speaking, a private person. She would even be on CNN for a day or two. The world would know a crazy, grinning giant had shot his load inside of the Willow Grove Scribe. Even the fact that he had taken her underwear as a souvenir might come out. CNN wouldn't report that part, but *The National Enquirer* or *Inside View* would have no such compunctions.

Sources inside the investigation say they found a pair of the Scribe's panties in the accused rapist's drawer: blue Victoria's Secret hip-huggers, trimmed with lace.

'I can't tell,' she said. 'I won't tell.'

But there were others before you, there could be others after y—

She pushed this thought away. She was too tired to consider what might or might not be her moral responsibility. She'd work on that part later, if God meant to grant her a later . . . and it seemed He might. But not on this deserted road where any set of approaching lights might have her rapist behind it.

Hers. He was hers now.

13

A mile or so after passing the Colewich sign, Tess began to hear a low, rhythmic thudding that seemed to come up from the road through her feet. Her first thought was of H. G. Wells's mutant Morlocks, tending their machinery deep in the bowels of the earth, but another five minutes clarified the sound. It was coming through the air, not from the ground, and it was one she knew: the heartbeat of a bass guitar. The rest of the band coalesced around it as she walked. She began to see light on the horizon, not headlights but the white of arc sodiums and the red gleam of neon. The band was playing 'Mustang Sally,' and she could hear laughter. It was drunken and beautiful, punctu-ated by happy party-down whoops. The sound made her feel like crying some more.

The roadhouse, a big old honkytonk barn with a huge dirt parking lot that looked full to capacity, was called The Stagger Inn. She stood at the edge of the glare cast by the parking lot lights, frowning. Why so many cars? Then she remembered it was Friday night. Apparently The Stagger Inn was the place to go on Friday nights if you were from Colewich or any of the surrounding towns. They would have a phone, but there were too many people. They would see her bruised face and leaning nose. They would want to know what had happened to her, and she was in no shape to make up a story. At least not yet. Even a pay phone outside was no good, because she could see people out there, too. Lots of them. Of course. These days you had to go outside if you wanted to smoke a cigarette. Also . . .

He could be there. Hadn't he been capering around her at one point, singing a Rolling Stones song in his awful tuneless voice? Tess supposed she might have dreamed that part – or hallucinated it – but she didn't think so. Wasn't it possible that after hiding her car, he'd come right here to The Stagger Inn, pipes all cleaned and ready to party the night away?

The band launched into a perfectly adequate cover of an old Cramps song: 'Can Your Pussy Do the Dog?' *No*, Tess thought, *but today a dog certainly did my pussy.* The Old Tess would not have approved of such a joke, but the New Tess thought it was pretty goddam funny. She barked a hoarse laugh and got walking again, moving to the other side of the road, where the lights from the roadhouse parking lot did not quite reach.

As she passed the far side of the building, she saw an old white van backed up to the loading dock. There were no arc sodiums on this side of The Stagger Inn, but the moonlight was enough to show her the skeleton pounding its cupcake drums. No wonder the van hadn't stopped to pick up the nail-studded road litter. The Zombie Bakers had been late for the load-in, and that wasn't good, because on Friday nights, The Stagger Inn was hopping with the bopping, rolling with the strolling, and reeling with the feeling.

'Can your pussy do the dog?' Tess asked, and pulled the filthy carpet remnant a little tighter around her neck. It was no mink stole, but on a cool October night, it was better than nothing.

14

When Tess got to the intersection of Stagg Road and Route 47, she saw something beautiful: a Gas & Dash with two pay telephones on the cinder-block wall between the restrooms.

She used the Women's first, and had to put a hand over her mouth to stifle a cry when her urine started to flow; it was as if someone had lit a book of matches in there. When she got up from the toilet, fresh tears were rolling down her cheeks. The water in the bowl was a pastel pink. She blotted herself – very gently – with a pad of toilet paper, then flushed. She would have taken another wad to fold into the crotch of her underwear, but of course she couldn't do that. The giant had taken her underpants as a souvenir.

'You bastard,' she said.

She paused with her hand on the doorknob, looking at the bruised, wide-eyed woman in the water-spotted metal mirror over the washbasin. Then she went out.

15

She discovered that using a pay telephone in this modern age had grown strangely difficult, even if you had your calling-card number memorized. The first phone she tried worked only one-way: she could hear the directory assistance operator, but the directory assistance operator couldn't hear her, and broke such connection as there was. The other phone was tilted askew on the cinder-block wall – not encouraging – but it worked. There was a steady annoying underwhine, but at least she and the operator could communicate. Only Tess had no pen or pencil. There were several writing implements in her purse, but of course her purse was gone.

'Can't you just connect me?' she asked the operator.

'No, ma'am, you have to dial it yourself in order to utilize your credit card.' The operator spoke in the voice of someone explaining the obvious to a stupid child. This didn't make Tess angry; she *felt* like a stupid child. Then she saw how dirty the cinder-block wall was. She told the operator to give her the number, and when it came, she wrote it in the dust with her finger.

Before she could start dialing, a truck pulled into the

parking lot. Her heart launched itself into her throat with dizzying, acrobatic ease, and when two laughing boys in high school jackets got out and whipped into the store, she was glad it was up there. It blocked the scream that surely would have come out otherwise.

She felt the world trying to go away and leaned her head against the wall for a moment, gasping for breath. She closed her eyes. She saw the giant towering over her, hands in the pockets of his biballs, and opened her eyes again. She dialed the number written in dust on the wall.

She braced herself for an answering machine, or for a bored dispatcher telling her that they had no cars, of course they didn't, it was Friday night, were you born stupid, lady, or did you just grow that way? But the phone was answered on the second ring by a businesslike woman who identified herself as Andrea. She listened to Tess, and said they would send a car right out, her driver would be Manuel. Yes, she knew exactly where Tess was calling from, because they ran cars out to The Stagger Inn all the time.

'Okay, but I'm not there,' Tess said. 'I'm at the intersection about half a mile down from th—'

'Yes, ma'am, I have that,' Andrea said. 'The Gas & Dash. Sometimes we go there, too. People often walk down and call if they've had a little too much to drink. It'll probably be forty-five minutes, maybe even an hour.'

'That's fine,' Tess said. The tears were falling again. Tears of gratitude this time, although she told herself not to relax, because in stories like this the heroine's hopes so often turned out to be false. 'That's absolutely fine. I'll be around the corner by the pay telephones. And I'll be watching.'

Now she'll ask me if I had a little too much to drink. Because I probably sound that way.

But Andrea only wanted to know if she would be paying with cash or credit.

'American Express. I should be in your computer.'

'Yes, ma'am, you are. Thank you for calling Royal Limousine, where every customer is treated like royalty.' Andrea clicked off before Tess could say she was very welcome.

She started to hang up the phone, and then a man – *him, it's him* – ran around the corner of the store and right at her. This time there was no chance of screaming; she was paralyzed with terror.

It was one of the teenage boys. He went past without looking at her and hooked a left into the Men's. The door slammed. A moment later she heard the enthusiastic, horselike sound of a young man voiding an awesomely healthy bladder.

Tess went down the side of the building and around back. There she stood beside a reeking Dumpster (*no*, she thought, *I'm not standing, I'm lurking*), waiting for the young man to finish and be gone. When he was, she walked back to the pay phones to watch the road. In spite of all the places where she hurt, her belly was rumbling with hunger. She had missed her dinner, had been too busy being raped and almost killed to eat. She would have been glad to have any of the snacks they sold in places like this – even some of those little nasty peanut butter crackers, so weirdly yellow, would have been a treat – but she had no money. Even if she had, she wouldn't have gone in there. She knew what kind of lights they had in roadside convenience stores like Gas & Dash, those bright and heartless fluorescents that made even healthy people look like they were suffering from pancreatic cancer. The clerk behind the counter would look at her bruised cheeks and forehead, her broken nose and her swollen lips, and he or she might not say anything, but Tess would see the widening of the eyes. And maybe a quickly suppressed twitch of the lips. Because, face it, people could think a beat-up woman was funny. Especially on a Friday night.

Who turned up on you, lady, and what did you do to deserve it? Wouldn't you come across after some guy spent his overtime on you?

That reminded her of an old joke she'd heard somewhere: *Why are there three hundred thousand battered women each year in America? Because they won't . . . fuckin . . .* listen.

'Never mind,' she whispered. 'I'll have something to eat when I get home. Tuna salad, maybe.'

It sounded good, but part of her was convinced that her days of eating tuna salad – or nasty yellow convenience-store peanut butter crackers, for that matter – were all over. The idea of a limo pulling up and driving her out of this nightmare was an insane mirage.

From somewhere to her left, Tess could hear cars rushing by on I-84 – the road she would have taken if she hadn't been so pleased to be offered a shorter way home. Over there on the turnpike, people who had never been raped or stuffed in pipes were going places. Tess thought the sound of their blithe travel was the loneliest she'd ever heard.

16

The limo came. It was a Lincoln Town Car. The man behind the wheel got out and looked around. Tess observed him closely from the corner of the store. He was wearing a dark suit. He was a small, bespectacled fellow who didn't look like a rapist . . . but of course not all giants were rapists and not all rapists were giants. She had to trust him, though. If she were to get home and feed Fritzy, there was no other option. So she dropped her filthy makeshift stole beside the pay phone that actually worked and walked slowly and steadily toward the car. The light shining through the store windows seemed blindingly bright after the shadows at the side of the building, and she knew what her face looked like.

He'll ask what happened to me and then he'll ask if I want to go to the hospital.

But Manuel (who might have seen worse, it wasn't impossible) only held the door for her and said, 'Welcome to Royal Limousine, ma'am.' He had a soft Hispanic accent to go with his olive skin and dark eyes.

'Where I'm treated like royalty,' Tess said. She tried to smile. It hurt her swollen lips.

'Yes, ma'am.' Nothing else. God bless Manuel, who might have seen worse – perhaps back where he'd come from, perhaps in the back of this very car. Who knew what secrets limo drivers kept? It was a question that might have a good book hidden in it. Not the kind she wrote, of course . . . only who knew what kind of books she might write after this? Or if she would write anymore at all? Tonight's adventure might have turned that solitary joy out of her for awhile. Maybe even forever. It was impossible to tell.

She got into the back of the car, moving like an old woman with advanced osteoporosis. When she was seated and he had closed the door, she wrapped her fingers around the handle and watched closely, wanting to make sure it was Manuel who got in behind the wheel and not the giant in the bib overalls. In *Stagg Road Horror 2* it would have been the giant: one more turn of the screw before the credits. *Have some irony, it's good for your blood.*

But it was Manuel who got in. Of course it was. She relaxed.

'The address I have is 19 Primrose Lane, in Stoke Village. Is that correct?'

For a moment she couldn't remember; she had punched her calling-card number into the pay phone without a pause, but she was blanking on her own address.

Relax, she told herself. *It's over. This isn't a horror movie, it's your life. You've had a terrible experience, but it's over. So relax.*

'Yes, Manuel, that's right.'

'Will you want to be making any stops, or are we going right to your home?' It was the closest he came to mentioning what the lights of the Gas & Dash must have shown him when she walked to the Town Car.

It was only luck that she was still taking her oral contraceptive pills – luck and perhaps optimism, she hadn't had so much as a one-night stand for three years, unless you counted tonight – but luck had been in short supply today, and she was grateful for this short stroke of it. She was sure Manuel could find an all-night pharmacy some-where along the way, limo drivers seem to know all that stuff, but she didn't think she would have been able to walk into a drugstore and ask for the morning-after pill. Her face would have made it all too obvious why she needed one. And of course there was the money problem.

'No other stops, just take me home, please.'

Soon they were on I-84, which was busy with Friday-night traffic. Stagg Road and the deserted store were behind her. What was ahead of her was her own house, with a security system and a lock for every door. And that was good.

17

It all went exactly as she had visualized: the arrival, the tip added to the credit card slip, the walk up the flower-lined path (she asked Manuel to stay, illuminating her with his headlights, until she was inside), the sound of Fritzy meowing as she tilted the mailbox and fished the emergency key off its hook. Then she was inside and Fritzy was twining anxiously around her feet, wanting to be picked up and stroked, wanting to be fed. Tess did those things, but first she locked the front door behind her, then set the burglar alarm for the first time in months. When she saw ARMED flash in the little green window above the keypad, she at last began to feel something like her true self. She looked at the kitchen clock and was astounded to see it was only quarter past eleven.

While Fritzy was eating his Fancy Feast, she checked the doors to the backyard and the side patio, making sure they were both locked. Then the windows. The alarm's command-box was supposed to tell you if something was open, but she didn't trust it. When she was positive everything was secure, she went to the front-hall closet and took down a box that had been on the top shelf so long there was a scrim of dust on the top.

Five years ago there had been a rash of burglaries and home invasions in northern Connecticut and southern Massachusetts. The bad boys were mostly drug addicts hooked on eighties, which was what its many New England fans called OxyContin. Residents were warned to be particularly careful and 'take reasonable precautions.' Tess had no strong feelings about handguns pro or con, nor had she felt especially worried about strange men breaking in at night (not then), but a gun seemed to come under the heading of reasonable precautions, and she had been meaning to educate herself about pistols for the next Willow Grove book, anyway. The burglary scare had seemed like the perfect opportunity.

She went to the Hartford gun store that rated best on the Internet, and the clerk had recommended a Smith & Wesson .38 model he called a Lemon Squeezer. She bought it mostly because she liked that name. He also told her about a good shooting range on the outskirts of Stoke Village. Tess had dutifully taken her gun there once the forty-eight-hour waiting period was up and she was actually able to obtain it. She had fired off four hundred rounds or so over the course of a week, enjoying the thrill of banging away at first but quickly becoming bored. The gun had been in the closet ever since, stored in its box along with fifty rounds of ammunition and her carry permit.

She loaded it, feeling better – *safer* – with each filled chamber. She put it on the kitchen counter, then checked the answering machine. There was one message. It was from Patsy McClain next door. 'I didn't see any lights this evening, so I guess you decided to stay over in Chicopee. Or maybe you went to Boston? Anyway, I used the key behind the mailbox and fed Fritzy. Oh, and I put your mail on the hall table. All adverts, sorry. Call me tomorrow before I go to work, if you're back. Just want to know you got in safe.'

'Hey, Fritz,' Tess said, bending over to stroke him. 'I guess you got double rations tonight. Pretty clever of y—'

Wings of grayness came over her vision, and if she hadn't caught hold of the kitchen table, she would have gone sprawling full length on the linoleum. She uttered a cry of surprise that sounded faint and faraway. Fritzy twitched his ears back, gave her a narrow, assessing look, seemed to decide she wasn't going to fall over (at least not on him), and went back to his second supper.

Tess straightened up slowly, holding onto the table for safety's sake, and opened the fridge. There was no tuna salad, but there was cottage cheese with strawberry jam. She ate it eagerly, scraping the plastic container with her spoon to get every last curd. It was cool and smooth on her hurt throat. She wasn't sure she could have eaten flesh, anyway. Not even tuna out of a can.

She drank apple juice straight from the bottle, belched, then trudged to the downstairs bathroom. She took the gun along, curling her fingers outside the trigger guard, as she had been taught.

There was an oval magnifying mirror standing on the shelf above the washbasin, a Christmas gift from her brother in New Mexico. Written in gold-gilt script above it were the words PRETTY ME. The Old Tess had used it for tweezing her eyebrows and doing quick fixes to her makeup. The new one used it to examine her eyes. They were bloodshot, of course, but the pupils looked the same size. She turned off the bathroom light, counted to twenty, then turned it back on and watched her pupils contract. That looked okay, too. So, probably no skull fracture. Maybe a concussion, a *light* concussion, but—

As if I'd know. I've got a Bachelor of Arts from the University of Connecticut and an advanced degree in old lady detectives who spend at least a quarter of each book exchanging recipes I crib from the Internet and then change just enough so I won't get sued for plagiarism. I could go into a coma or die of a brain hemorrhage in the night. Patsy would find me the next time she came in to feed the cat. You need to see a doctor, Tessa Jean. And you know it.

What she knew was that if she went to her doctor, her misfortune really could become public property. Doctors guaranteed confidentiality, it was a part of their oath, and a woman who made her living as a lawyer or a cleaning woman or a realtor could probably count on getting it. Tess might get it herself, it was certainly possible. Probable, even. On the other hand, look what had happened to Farrah Fawcett: tabloid-fodder when some hospital employee blabbed. Tess herself had heard rumors about the psychiatric misadventures of a male novelist who had been a chart staple for years with his tales of lusty derring-do. Her own agent had passed the juiciest of these rumors on to Tess over lunch not two months ago . . . and Tess had listened.

I did more than listen, she thought as she looked at her magnified, beaten self. *I passed that puppy on just as soon as I could.*

Even if the doctor and his staff kept mum about the lady mystery writer who had been beaten, raped, and robbed on her way home from a public appearance, what about the other patients who might see her in the waiting room? To some of them she wouldn't be just another woman with a bruised face that practically screamed beating; she would be Stoke Village's resident novelist, you know the one, they made a TV movie about her old lady detectives a year or two ago, it was on Lifetime Channel, and my God, you should have *seen* her.

Her nose wasn't broken, after all. It was hard to believe anything could hurt that badly and *not* be broken, but it wasn't. Swollen (of course, poor thing), and it hurt, but she could breathe through it and she had some Vicodin upstairs that would manage the pain tonight. But she had a couple of blooming shiners, a bruised and swollen cheek, and a ring of bruises around her throat. That was the worst, the sort of necklace people got in only one way. There were also assorted bumps, bruises, and scratches on her back, legs, and tushie. But clothes and hose would hide the worst of those.

Great. I'm a poet and I don't know it.

'The throat . . . I could wear a turtleneck . . .'

Absolutely. October was turtleneck weather. As for Patsy, she could say she'd fallen downstairs and hit her face in the night. Say that—

'That I thought I heard a noise and Fritzy got between my feet when I went downstairs to check.'

Fritzy heard his name and meowed from the bathroom door.

'Say I hit my stupid face on the newel post at the bottom. I could even . . .'

Even put a little mark on the post, of course she could. Possibly with the meat-tenderizing hammer she had in one of her kitchen drawers. Nothing gaudy, just a tap or two to chip the paint. Such a story wouldn't fool a doctor (or a sharp old lady detective like Doreen Marquis, doyenne of the Knitting Society), but it would fool sweet Patsy McC, whose husband had surely never raised a hand to her a single time in the twenty years they'd been together.

'It's not that I have anything to be ashamed about,' she whispered at the woman in the mirror. The New Woman with the crooked nose and the puffy lips. 'It's not that.' True, but public exposure would *make* her ashamed. She would be naked. A naked victim.

But what about the women, Tessa Jean? The women in the pipe?

She would have to think about them, but not tonight. Tonight she was tired, in pain, and harrowed to the bottom of her soul.

Deep inside her (in her harrowed soul) she felt a glowing ember of fury at the man responsible for this. The man who had put her in this position. She looked at the pistol lying beside the basin, and knew that if he were here, she would use it on him without a moment's hesitation. Knowing that made her feel confused about herself. It also made her feel a little stronger.

18

She chipped at the newel post with the meat-tenderizing hammer, by then so tired she felt like a dream in some other woman's head. She examined the mark, decided it looked too deliberate, and gave several more light taps around the edges of the blow. When she thought it looked like something she might have done with the side of her face – where the worst bruise was – she went slowly up the stairs and down the hall, holding her gun in one hand.

For a moment she hesitated outside her bedroom

door, which was standing ajar. What if *he* was in there? If he had her purse, he had her address. The burglar alarm had not been set until she got back (so sloppy). He could have parked his old F-150 around the corner. He could have forced the kitchen door lock. It probably wouldn't have taken much more than a chisel.

If he was here, I'd smell him. That mansweat. And I'd shoot him. No 'Lie down on the floor,' no 'Keep your hands up while I dial 911,' no horror-movie bullshit. I'd just shoot him. But you know what I'd say first?

'You like it, it likes you,' she said in her low rasp of a voice. Yes. That was it exactly. He wouldn't understand, but *she* would.

She discovered she sort of *wanted* him in her room. That probably meant the New Woman was more than a little crazy, but so what? If it all came out then, it would be worth it. Shooting him would make public humiliation bearable. And look at the bright side! It would probably help sales!

I'd like to see the terror in his eyes when he realized I really meant to do it. That might make at least some of this right.

It seemed to take her groping hand an age to find the bedroom light-switch, and of course she kept expecting her fingers to be grabbed while she fumbled. She took off her clothes slowly, uttering one watery, miserable sob when she unzipped her pants and saw dried blood in her pubic hair.

She ran the shower as hot as she could stand it, washing the places that could bear to be washed, letting the water rinse the rest. The clean hot water. She wanted his smell off her, and the mildewy smell of the carpet remnant, too. Afterward, she sat on the toilet. This time peeing hurt less, but the bolt of pain that went through her head when she tried − very tentatively − to straighten her leaning nose made her cry out. Well, so what? Nell Gwynn, the famous

Elizabethan actress, had had a bent nose. Tess was sure she had read that somewhere.

She put on flannel pajamas and shuffled to bed, where she lay with all the lights on and the Lemon Squeezer .38 on the night table, thinking she would never sleep, that her inflamed imagination would turn every sound from the street into the approach of the giant. But then Fritzy jumped up on the bed, curled himself beside her, and began to purr. That was better.

I'm home, she thought. *I'm home, I'm home, I'm home.*

19

When she woke up, the inarguably sane light of six AM was streaming through the windows. There were things that needed to be done and decisions that needed to be made, but for the moment it was enough to be alive and in her own bed instead of stuffed into a culvert.

This time peeing felt almost normal, and there was no blood. She got into the shower again, once more running the water as hot as she could stand it, closing her eyes and letting it beat on her throbbing face. When she'd had all of that she could take, she worked shampoo into her hair, doing it slowly and methodically, using her fingers to massage her scalp, skipping the painful spot where he must have hit her. At first the deep scratch on her back stung, but that passed and she felt a kind of bliss. She hardly thought of the shower scene in *Psycho* at all.

The shower was always where she had done her best thinking, a womblike environment, and if she had ever needed to think both hard and well, it was now.

I don't want to see Dr Hedstrom, and I don't need to see Dr Hedstrom. That decision's been made, although later – a couple of weeks from now, maybe, when my face looks more or less normal again – I'll have to get checked out for STDs . . .

'Don't forget the AIDS test,' she said, and the thought made her grimace hard enough to hurt her mouth. It was a scary thought. Nevertheless, the test would have to be taken. For her own peace of mind. And none of that addressed what she now recognized as this morning's central issue. What she did or didn't do about her own violation was her own business, but that was not true of the women in the pipe. They had lost far more than she. And what about the next woman the giant attacked? That there would be another she had no doubt. Maybe not for a month or a year, but there would be. As she turned off the shower Tess realized (again) that it might even be her, if he went back to check the culvert and found her gone. And her clothes gone from the store, of course. If he'd looked through her purse, and surely he had, then he *did* have her address.

'Also my diamond earrings,' she said.

'Fucking pervert sonofabitch stole my earrings.'

Even if he steered clear of the store and the culvert for awhile, those women belonged to her now. They were her responsibility, and she couldn't shirk it just because her picture might appear on the cover of *Inside View*.

In the calm morning light of a suburban Connecticut morning, the answer was ridiculously simple: an anonymous call to the police. The fact that a professional novelist with ten years' experience hadn't thought of it right away almost deserved a yellow penalty card. She would give them the location – the deserted YOU LIKE IT IT LIKES YOU store on Stagg Road – and she would describe the giant. How hard could it be to locate a man like that? Or a blue F-150 Ford pickup with Bondo around the headlights?

Easy-as-can-beezy.

But while she was drying her hair, her eyes fell on her

Lemon Squeezer .38 and she thought, *Too easy-as-can-beezy. Because . . .*

'What's in it for me?' she asked Fritzy, who was sitting in the doorway and looking at her with his luminous green eyes. 'Just what's in that for me?'

20

Standing in the kitchen an hour and a half later. Her cereal bowl soaking in the sink. Her second cup of coffee growing cold on the counter. Talking on the phone.

'Oh my God!' Patsy exclaimed. 'I'm coming right over!'

'No, no, I'm fine, Pats. And you'll be late for work.'

'Saturday mornings are strictly optional, and you should go to the doctor! What if you're concussed, or something?'

'I'm not concussed, just colorful. And I'd be ashamed to go to the doctor, because I was three drinks over the limit. At least three. The only sensible thing I did all night was call a limo to bring me home.'

'You're sure your nose isn't broken?'

'Positive.' Well . . . *almost* positive.

'Is Fritzy all right?'

Tess burst into perfectly genuine laughter. 'I go downstairs half-shot in the middle of the night because the smoke detector's beeping, trip over the cat and almost kill myself, and your sympathies are with the cat. Nice.'

'Honey, no—'

'I'm just teasing,' Tess said. 'Go on to work and stop worrying. I just didn't want you to scream when you saw me. I've got a couple of absolutely beautiful shiners. If I had an ex-husband, you'd probably think he'd paid me a visit.'

'Nobody would dare to put a hand on you,' Patsy said. 'You're feisty, girl.'

'That's right,' Tess said. 'I take no shit.'

'You sound hoarse.'

'On top of everything else, I'm getting a cold.'

'Well . . . if you need something tonight . . . chicken soup . . . a couple of old Percocets . . . a Johnny Depp DVD . . .'

'I'll call if I do. Now go on. Fashion-conscious women seeking the elusive size six Ann Taylor are depending on you.'

'Piss off, woman,' Patsy said, and hung up, laughing.

Tess took her coffee to the kitchen table. The gun was sitting on it, next to the sugar bowl: not quite a Dalí image, but damn close. Then the image doubled as she burst into tears. It was the memory of her own cheery voice that did it. The sound of the lie she would now live until it felt like the truth. 'You bastard!' she shouted. 'You fuck-bastard! *I hate you!*'

She had showered twice in less than seven hours and still felt dirty. She had douched, but she thought she could still feel him in there, his . . .

'His cockslime.'

She bolted to her feet, from the corner of her eye glimpsed her alarmed cat racing down the front hall, and arrived at the sink just in time to avoid making a mess on the floor. Her coffee and Cheerios came up in a single hard contraction. When she was sure she was done, she collected her pistol and went upstairs to take another shower.

21

When she was done and wrapped in a comforting terry-cloth robe, she lay down on her bed to think about where she should go to make her anonymous call. Someplace big and busy would be best. Someplace with a parking lot so she could hang up and then scat. Stoke Village Mall sounded right. There was also the question of which authorities to call. Colewich, or would that be too Deputy Dawg? Maybe the State Police would be better. And she should write down what she meant to say . . . the call would go quicker . . . she'd be less likely to forget anyth . . .

Tess drifted off, lying on her bed in a bar of sunlight.

22

The telephone was ringing far away, in some adjacent universe. Then it stopped and Tess heard her own voice, the pleasantly impersonal recording that started *You have reached* . . . This was followed by someone leaving a message. A woman. By the time Tess struggled back to wakefulness, the caller had clicked off.

She looked at the clock on the night table and saw it was quarter to ten. She'd slept another two hours. For a moment she was alarmed: maybe she'd suffered a concussion or a fracture after all. Then she relaxed. She'd had a lot of exercise the previous night. Much of it had been extremely unpleasant, but exercise was exercise. Falling asleep again was natural. She might even take another nap this afternoon (another shower for sure), but she had an errand to run first. A responsibility to fulfill.

She put on a long tweed skirt and a turtleneck that was actually too big for her; it lapped the underside of her chin. That was fine with Tess. She had applied concealer to the bruise on her cheek. It didn't cover it completely, nor would even her biggest pair of sunglasses completely obscure her black eyes (the swollen lips were a lost cause), but the makeup helped, just the same. The very act of applying it made her feel more anchored in her life. More in charge.

Downstairs, she pushed the Play button on her answering machine, thinking the call had probably been from Ramona Norville, doing the obligatory day-after follow-up: we had fun, hope you had fun, the feedback was great, please come again (not bloody likely), blah-blah-blah. But it wasn't Ramona. The message was from a woman who identified herself as Betsy Neal. She said she was calling from The Stagger Inn.

'As part of our effort to discourage drinking and driving, our policy is to courtesy-call people who leave their cars in our lot after closing,' Betsy Neal said. 'Your Ford Expedition, Connecticut license plate 775 NSD, will be available for pickup until five PM this evening. After five it will be towed to Excellent Auto Repair, 1500 John Higgins Road, North Colewich, at your expense. Please note that we don't have your keys, ma'am. You must have taken them with you.' Betsy Neal paused. 'We have other property of yours, so please come to the office. Remember that I'll need to see some ID. Thank you and have a nice day.'

Tess sat down on her sofa and laughed. Before listening to the Neal woman's canned speech, she had been planning to drive her Expedition to the mall. She didn't have her purse, she didn't have her keyring, she didn't have her damn *car*, but she had still planned to just walk out to the driveway, climb in, and—

She sat back against the cushion, whooping and pounding a fist on her thigh. Fritzy was under the easy chair on the other side of the room, looking at her as if she were mad. *We're all mad here, so have another cup of tea*, she thought, and laughed harder than ever.

When she finally stopped (only it felt more like running down), she played the message again. This time what she focused on was the Neal woman saying they had other property of hers. Her purse? Perhaps even her diamond earrings? But that would be too good to be true. Wouldn't it?

Arriving at The Stagger Inn in a black car from Royal Limo might be a little too memorable, so she called Stoke Village Taxi. The dispatcher said they'd be glad to run her out to what he called 'The Stagger' for a flat fifty-dollar fee. 'Sorry to charge you so much,' he said, 'but the driver's got to come back empty.'

'How do you know that?' Tess asked, bemused.

'Left your car, right? Happens all the time, specially on weekends. Although we also get calls after karaoke nights. Your cab'll be there in fifteen minutes or less.'

Tess ate a Pop-Tart (swallowing hurt, but she had lost her first try at breakfast and was hungry), then stood at the living-room window, watching for the taxi and bouncing her spare Expedition key on her palm. She decided on a change of plan. Never mind Stoke Village Mall; once she'd collected her car (and whatever other property Betsy Neal was holding), she would drive the half a mile or so to the Gas & Dash and call the police from there.

It seemed only fitting.

23

When her cab turned onto Stagg Road, Tess's pulse began to rise. By the time they reached The Stagger Inn, it was flying along at what felt like a hundred and thirty beats a minute. The cabbie must have seen something in his rearview mirror . . . or maybe it was just the visible signs of the beating that prompted his question.

'Everything okay, ma'am?'

'Peachy,' she said. 'It's just that I didn't plan on coming back here this morning.'

'Few do,' the cabbie said. He was sucking on a

toothpick, which made a slow and philosophical journey from one side of his mouth to the other. 'They got your keys, I suppose? Left em with the bartender?'

'Oh, no trouble there,' she said brightly. 'But they're holding other property for me – the lady who called wouldn't say what, and I can't for the life of me think what it could be.' *Good God, I sound like one of my old lady detectives.*

The cabbie rolled his toothpick back to its starting point. It was his only reply.

'I'll pay you an extra ten dollars to wait until I come out,' Tess said, nodding at the roadhouse. 'I want to make sure my car starts.'

'No problem-o,' the cabbie said.

And if I scream because he's in there, waiting for me, come on the run, okay?

But she wouldn't have said that even if she could have done so without sounding absolutely bonkers. The cabdriver was fat, fifty, and wheezy. He'd be no match for the giant if this was a setup . . . in a horror movie, which it would be.

Lured back, Tess thought dismally. *Lured back by a phone call from the giant's girlfriend, who's just as crazy as he is.*

Foolish, paranoid idea, but the walk to The Stagger Inn's door seemed long, and the hard-packed dirt made her walking shoes seem very loud: *clump-clud-clump.* The parking lot that had been a sea of cars last night was now deserted save for four automotive islands, one of which was her Expedition. It was at the very back of the lot – sure, he would not have wanted to be observed putting it there – and she could see the left front tire. It was a plain old blackwall that didn't match the other three, but otherwise it looked fine. He had changed her tire. Of course he had. How else could he have moved it away from his . . . his . . .

His recreational facility. His kill-zone. He drove it down here, parked, walked back to the deserted store, and then off he went in his old F-150. Good thing I didn't come to sooner; he'd have found me wandering around in a daze and I wouldn't be here now.

She looked back over her shoulder. In one of the movies she now could not stop thinking about, she surely would have seen the cab speeding away (*leaving me to my fate*), but it was still right there. She lifted a hand to the driver, and he lifted his in return. She was fine. Her car was here and the giant wasn't. The giant was at his house (his *lair*), quite possibly still sleeping off the previous evening's exertions.

The sign on the door said WE ARE CLOSED. Tess knocked and got no response. She tried the knob and when it turned, sinister movie plots returned to her mind. The really stupid plots where the knob always turns and the heroine calls out (in a tremulous voice), 'Is anybody there?' Everyone knows she's crazy to go in, but she does anyway.

Tess looked back at the cab again, saw it was still right there, reminded herself that she was carrying a loaded gun in her spare purse, and went in anyway.

24

She entered a foyer that ran the length of the building on the parking lot side. The walls were decorated with publicity stills: bands in leather, bands in jeans, an all-girl band in miniskirts. An auxiliary bar stretched out beyond the coatracks; no stools, just a rail where you could have a drink while you waited for someone or because the bar inside was too packed. A single red sign glowed above the ranked bottles: BUDWEISER.

You like Bud, Bud likes you, Tess thought.

She took off her dark glasses so she could walk without stumbling into something and crossed the foyer to peep into the main room. It was vast and redolent of beer. There was a disco ball, now dark and still. The wooden floor reminded her of the roller-skating rink where she and her girlfriends had all but lived during the summer between eighth grade and high school. The instruments were still up on the bandstand, suggesting that the Zombie Bakers would be back tonight for another heaping bowl of rock n roll.

'Hello?' Her voice echoed.

'I'm right here,' a voice replied softly from behind her.

25

If it had been a man's voice, Tess would have shrieked. She managed to avoid that, but she still whirled around so quickly that she stumbled a little. The woman standing in the coat alcove – a skinny breath of a thing, no more than five feet three – blinked in surprise and took a step back. 'Whoa, easy.'

'You startled me,' Tess said.

'I see I did.' The woman's tiny, perfect oval of a face was surrounded by a cloud of teased black hair. A pencil peeked from it. She had piquant blue eyes that didn't quite match. *A Picasso girl*, Tess thought. 'I was in the office. Are you the Expedition lady or the Honda lady?'

'Expedition.'

'Have ID?'

'Yes, two pieces, but only one with my picture on it. My passport. The other stuff was in my purse. My other purse. I thought that was what you might have.'

'No, sorry. Maybe you stashed it under the seat, or something? We only look in the glove compartments, and of course we can't even do that if the car is locked. Yours wasn't, and your phone number was on the insurance card. But probably you know that. Maybe you'll find your purse at home.' Neal's voice suggested that this wasn't likely. 'One photo ID will be okay if it looks like you, I guess.'

Neal led Tess to a door at the back of the coat area, then down a narrow curving corridor that skirted the main room. There were more band photos on the walls. At one point they passed through a fume of chlorine that stung Tess's eyes and tender throat.

'If you think the johns smell now, you should be here when the joint is going full tilt,' Neal said, then added, 'Oh, I forgot – you were.'

Tess made no comment.

At the end of the hallway was a door marked OFFICE STAFF ONLY. The room beyond was large, pleasant, and filled with morning sunshine. A framed picture of Barack Obama hung on the wall, above a bumper sticker bearing the YES WE CAN slogan. Tess couldn't see her cab – the building was in the way – but she could see its shadow.

That's good. Stay right there and get your ten bucks. And if I don't come out, don't come in. Just call the police.

Neal went to the desk in the corner and sat down. 'Let's see your ID.'

Tess opened her purse, fumbled past the .38, and brought out her passport and her Author's Guild card. Neal gave the passport photo only a cursory glance, but when she saw the Guild card, her eyes widened. 'You're the Willow Grove lady!'

Tess smiled gamely. It hurt her lips. 'Guilty as charged.' Her voice sounded foggy, as though she were getting over a bad cold.

'My gran loves those books!'

'Many grans do,' Tess said. 'When the affection finally

filters down to the next generation – the one not currently living on fixed incomes – I'm going to buy myself a château in France.'

Sometimes this earned her a smile. Not from Ms Neal, however. 'I hope that didn't happen here.' She wasn't more specific and didn't have to be. Tess knew what she was talking about, and Betsy Neal knew she knew.

Tess thought of revisiting the story she'd already told Patsy – the beeping smoke detector alarm, the cat under her feet, the collision with the newel post – and didn't bother. This woman had a look of daytime efficiency about her and probably visited The Stagger Inn as infrequently as possible during its hours of operation, but she was clearly under no illusions about what sometimes happened here when the hour grew late and the guests grew drunk. She was, after all, the one who came in early on Saturday mornings to make the courtesy calls. She had probably heard her share of morning-after stories featuring midnight stumbles, slips in the shower, etc., etc.

'Not here,' Tess said. 'Don't worry.'

'Not even in the parking lot? If you ran into trouble there, I'll have to have Mr Rumble talk with the security staff. Mr Rumble's the boss, and security's supposed to check the video monitors regularly on busy nights.'

'It happened after I left.'

I really do *have to make the report anonymously now, if I mean to report it at all. Because I'm lying, and she'll remember.*

If she meant to report it at all? Of course she did. Right?

'I'm very sorry.' Neal paused, seeming to debate with herself. Then she said, 'I don't mean to offend you, but you probably don't have any business in a place like this to begin with. It didn't turn out so well for you, and if it got into the papers . . . well, my gran would be very disappointed.'

Tess agreed. And because she could embellish convincingly (it was the talent that paid the bills, after all), she did. 'A bad boyfriend is sharper than a serpent's tooth. I think the Bible says that. Or maybe it's Dr Phil. In any case, I've broken up with him.'

'A lot of women say that, then weaken. And a guy who does it once—'

'Will do it again. Yes, I know, I was very foolish. If you don't have my purse, what property of mine *do* you have?'

Ms Neal turned in her swivel chair (the sun licked across her face, momentarily highlighting those unusual blue eyes), opened one of her file cabinets, and brought out Tom the TomTom. Tess was delighted to see her old traveling buddy. It didn't make things all better, but it was a step in the right direction.

'We're not supposed to remove anything from patrons' cars, just get the address and the phone number if we can, then lock it up, but I didn't like to leave this. Thieves don't mind breaking a window to get a particularly tasty item, and it was sitting right there on your dashboard.'

'Thank you.' Tess felt tears springing into her eyes behind her dark glasses and willed them back. 'That was very thoughtful.'

Betsy Neal smiled, which transformed her stern Ms Taking Care of Business face to radiant in an instant. 'Very welcome. And when that boyfriend of yours comes crawling back, asking for a second chance, think of my gran and all your other loyal readers and tell him no way Jose.' She considered. 'But do it with the chain on your door. Because a bad boyfriend really *is* sharper than a serpent's tooth.'

'That's good advice. Listen, I have to go. I told the cab to wait while I made sure I was really going to get my car.'

And that might have been all – it really might have been – but then Neal asked, with becoming diffidence, if Tess would mind signing an autograph for her grandmother. Tess told her of course not, and in spite of all that had happened, watched with real amusement as Neal found a piece of business stationery and used a ruler to tear off The Stagger Inn logo at the top before handing it across the desk.

'Make it "To Mary, a true fan." Can you do that?'

Tess could. And as she was adding the date, a fresh confabulation came to mind. 'A man helped me when my boyfriend and I were . . . you know, tussling. If not for him, I might have been hurt a lot worse.' *Yes! Raped, even!* 'I'd like to thank him, but I don't know his name.'

'I doubt if I could do you much good there. I'm just the office help.'

'But you're local, right?'

'Yes . . .'

'I met him at the little store down the road.'

'The Gas & Dash?'

'I think that's the name. It's where my boyfriend and I had our argument. It was about the car. I didn't want to drive and I wouldn't let him. We were arguing about it all the time we walked down the road . . . staggered down the road . . . staggered down Stagg Road . . .'

Neal smiled as people do when they've heard a joke many times before.

'Anyway, this guy came along in an old blue pickup truck with that plastic stuff for rust around the headlights—'

'Bondo?'

'I think that's what it's called.' Knowing damn well that was what it was called. Her father had supported the company almost singlehanded. 'Anyway, I remember thinking when he got out that he wasn't really riding in that truck, he was wearing it.'

When she handed the signed sheet of paper back across the desk, she saw that Betsy Neal was now actually grinning. 'Oh my God, I might actually know who he was.'

'Really?'

'Was he big or was he *real* big?'

'Real big,' Tess said. She felt a peculiar watchful happiness that seemed located not in her head but in the center of her chest. It was the way she felt when the strings of some outlandish plot actually started to come together, pulling tight like the top of a nicely crafted tote-bag. She always felt both surprised and not surprised when this happened. There was no satisfaction like it.

'Did you happen to notice if he was wearing a ring on his little finger? Red stone?'

'Yes! Like a ruby! Only too big to be real. And a brown hat—'

Neal was nodding. 'With white splatters on it. He's been wearing the damn thing for ten years. That's Big Driver you're talking about. I don't know where he lives, but he's local, either Colewich or Nestor Falls. I see him around — supermarket, hardware store, Walmart, places like that. And once you see him, you don't forget him. His real name is Al Something-Polish. You know, one of those hard-to-pronounce names. Strelkowicz, Stancowitz, something like that. I bet I could find him in the phone book, because he and his brother own a trucking company. Hawkline, I think it's called. Or maybe Eagle Line. Something with a bird in it, anyway. Want me to look him up?'

'No, thanks,' Tess said pleasantly. 'You've been helpful enough, and my cabdriver's waiting.'

'Okay. Just do yourself a favor and stay away from that boyfriend of yours. And stay away from The Stagger.

Of course, if you tell anyone I said that, I'll have to find you and kill you.'

'Fair enough,' Tess said, smiling. 'I'd deserve it.' At the doorway, she turned back. 'A favor?'

'If I can.'

'If you happen to see Al Something-Polish around town, don't mention that you talked to me.' She smiled more widely. It hurt her lips, but she did it. 'I want to surprise him. Give him a little gift, or something.'

'Not a problem.'

Tess lingered a bit longer. 'I love your eyes.'

Neal shrugged and smiled. 'Thanks. They don't quite match, do they? It used to make me self-conscious, but now . . .'

'Now it works for you,' Tess said. 'You grew into them.'

'I guess I did. I even picked up some work modeling in my twenties. But sometimes, you know what? It's better to grow out of things. Like a taste for bad-tempered men.'

To that there seemed to be nothing to say.

26

She made sure her Expedition would start, then tipped the cabdriver twenty instead of ten. He thanked her with feeling, then drove away toward the I-84. Tess followed, but not until she'd plugged Tom back into the cigarette lighter receptacle and powered him up.

'Hello, Tess,' Tom said. 'I see we're taking a trip.'

'Just home, Tommy-boy,' she said, and pulled out of the parking lot, very aware she was riding on a tire that had been mounted by the man who had almost killed her. Al Something-Polish. A truck-driving son of a gun. 'One stop on the way.'

'I don't know what you're thinking, Tess, but you should be careful.'

If she had been home instead of in her car, Fritzy would have been the one to say this, and Tess would have been equally unsurprised. She had been making up voices and conversations since childhood, although at the age of eight or nine, she'd quit doing it around other people, unless it was for comic effect.

'I don't know what I'm thinking, either,' she said, but this was not quite true.

Up ahead was the US 47 intersection, and the Gas & Dash. She signaled, turned in, and parked with the Expedition's nose centered between the two pay phones on the side of the building. She saw the number for Royal Limousine on the dusty cinder block between them. The numbers were crooked, straggling, written by a finger that hadn't been able to stay steady. A chill shivered its way up her back, and she wrapped her arms around herself, hugging hard. Then she got out and went to the pay phone that still worked.

The instruction card had been defaced, maybe by a drunk with a car key, but she could still read the salient information: no charge for 911 calls, just lift the handset and punch in the numbers. Easy-as-can-beezy.

She punched 9, hesitated, punched 1, then hesitated again. She visualized a piñata, and a woman poised to hit it with a stick. Soon everything inside would come tumbling out. Her friend and associates would know she had been raped. Patsy McClain would know the story about stumbling over Fritzy in the dark was a shame-driven lie . . . and that Tess hadn't trusted her enough to tell the truth. But really, those weren't the main things. She supposed she could stand up to a little public scrutiny, especially if it kept the man Betsy Neal had called Big Driver from raping and killing another woman. Tess realized that she might even be perceived as a heroine, a thing that had been impossible to even consider last night; when urinating hurt enough to make her cry and her mind kept returning to the image of her stolen panties in the center pocket of the giant's bib overalls.

Only . . .

'What's in it for me?' she asked again. She spoke very quietly, while looking at the telephone number she'd written in the dust. 'What's in that for me?'

And thought: *I have a gun and I know how to use it.*

She hung up the phone and went back to her car. She looked at Tom's screen, which was showing the intersection of Stagg Road and Route 47. 'I need to think about this some more,' she said.

'What's to think about?' Tom asked. 'If you were to kill him and then get caught, you'd go to jail. Raped or not.'

'That's what I need to think about,' she said, and turned onto US 47, which would take her to I-84.

Traffic on the big highway was Saturday-morning light, and being behind the wheel of her Expedition was good. Soothing. Normal. Tom was quiet until she passed the sign reading EXIT 9 STOKE VILLAGE 2 MILES. Then he said, 'Are you sure it was an accident?'

'What?' Tess jumped, startled. She had heard Tom's words coming out of her mouth, spoken in the deeper voice she always used for the make-believe half of her make-believe conversations (it was a voice very little like Tom the TomTom's actual robo-voice), but it didn't feel like her *thought*. 'Are you saying the bastard raped me by *accident*?'

'No,' Tom replied. 'I'm saying that if it had been up to you, you would have gone back the way you came. *This* way. I-84. But somebody had a better idea, didn't they? Somebody knew a shortcut.'

'Yes,' she agreed. 'Ramona Norville did.' She considered

it, then shook her head. 'That's pretty far-fetched, my friend.'

To this Tom made no reply.

27

Leaving the Gas & Dash, she had planned to go online and see if she could locate a trucking company, maybe a small independent, that operated out of Colewich or one of the surrounding towns. A company with a bird name, probably hawk or eagle. It was what the Willow Grove ladies would have done; they loved their computers and were always texting each other like teenagers. Other considerations aside, it would be interesting to see if her version of amateur sleuthing worked in real life.

Driving up the I-84 exit ramp a mile and a half from her house, she decided that she would do a little research on Ramona Norville first. Who knew, she might discover that, besides presiding over Books & Brown Baggers, Ramona was president of the Chicopee Rape Prevention Society. It was even plausible. Tess's hostess had pretty clearly been not just a lesbian but a *dyke* lesbian, and women of that persuasion were often not fond of men who were *non*-rapists.

'Many arsonists belong to their local volunteer fire departments,' Tom observed as she turned onto her street.

'What's *that* supposed to mean?' Tess asked.

'That you shouldn't eliminate anyone based on their public affiliations. The Knitting Society ladies would never do that. But by all means check her out online.' Tom spoke in a be-my-guest tone that Tess hadn't quite expected. It was mildly irritating.

'How kind of you to give me permission, Thomas,' she said.

28

But when she was in her office with her computer booted up, she only stared at the Apple welcome screen for the first five minutes, wondering if she was really thinking of finding the giant and using her gun, or if that was just the sort of fantasy to which liars-for-profit such as herself were prone. A revenge fantasy, in this case. She avoided those kinds of movies, too, but she knew they were out there; you couldn't avoid the vibe of your culture unless you were a total recluse, and Tess wasn't. In the revenge movies, admirably muscular fellows like Charles Bronson and Sylvester Stallone didn't bother with the police, they got the baddies on their own. Frontier justice. Do you feel lucky, punk. She believed that even Jodie Foster, one of Yale's more famous graduates, had made a movie of this type. Tess couldn't quite remember the title. *The Courageous Woman*, maybe? It was something like that, anyway.

Her computer flipped to the word-of-the-day screen-saver. Today's word was *cormorant*, which just happened to be a bird.

'When you send your goodies by Cormorant Trucking, you'll think you're flying,' Tess said in her deep pretending-to-be-Tom voice. Then she tapped a key and the screen-saver disappeared. She went online, but not to one of the search engines, at least not to begin with. First she went to YouTube and typed in RICHARD WIDMARK, with no idea at all why she was doing it. No conscious one, anyway.

Maybe I want to find out if the guy's really worthy of fanship, she thought. *Ramona certainly thinks so.*

There were lots of clips. The top-rated one was a six-minute compilation titled **HE'S BAD, HE'S REALLY BAD**. Several hundred thousand people had viewed it. There were scenes from three movies, but the one that transfixed her was the first. It was black-and-white, it looked on the cheap side . . . but it was definitely one of *those* movies. Even the title told you so: *Kiss of Death*.

Tess watched the entire video, then returned to the *Kiss of Death* segment twice. Widmark played a giggling hood menacing an old lady in a wheelchair. He wanted information: 'Where's that squealin' son of yours?' And when the old lady wouldn't tell him: 'You know what I do to squealers? I let em have it in the belly, so they can roll around for a long time, thinkin' it over.'

He didn't shoot the old lady in the belly, though. He tied her into her wheelchair with a lamp cord and pushed her down the stairs.

Tess exited YouTube, Binged Richard Widmark, and found what she expected, given the power of that brief clip. Although he had played in many subsequent movies, more and more often as the hero, he was best known for *Kiss of Death*, and the giggling, psychotic Tommy Udo.

'Big deal,' Tess said. 'Sometimes a cigar is just a cigar.'

'Meaning what?' Fritzy asked from the windowsill where he was sunning himself.

'Meaning Ramona probably fell in love with him after seeing him play a heroic sheriff or a courageous battleship commander, or something like that.'

'She must have,' Fritzy agreed, 'because if you're right about her sexual orientation, she probably doesn't idolize men who murder old ladies in wheelchairs.'

Of course that was true. Good thinking, Fritzy.

The cat regarded Tess with a skeptical eye and said, 'But maybe you're not right about that.'

'Even if I'm not,' Tess said, '*nobody* roots for psycho bad guys.'

She recognized this for the stupidity it was as soon as it was out of her mouth. If people didn't root for psychos, they wouldn't still be making movies about the nut in the hockey mask and the burn victim with scissors for fingers. But Fritzy did her the courtesy of not laughing.

'You better not,' Tess said. 'If you're tempted, remember who fills your food dish.'

She googled *Ramona Norville*, got forty-four thousand hits, added *Chicopee*, and got a more manageable twelve hundred (although even most of those, she knew, would be coincidental dreck). The first relevant one was from the Chicopee *Weekly Reminder*, and concerned Tess herself: LIBRARIAN RAMONA NORVILLE ANNOUNCES 'WILLOW GROVE FRIDAY.'

'There I am, the starring attraction,' Tess murmured. 'Hooray for Tessa Jean. Now let's see my supporting actress.' But when she pulled up the clipping, the only photo Tess saw was her own. It was the bare-shoulders publicity shot her part-time assistant routinely sent out. She wrinkled her nose and went back to Google, not sure why she wanted to look at Ramona again, only knowing that she did. When she finally found a photo of the librarian, she saw what her subconscious might already have suspected, at least judging by Tom's comments on the ride back to her house.

It was in a story from the August 3 issue of the *Weekly Reminder*. BROWN BAGGERS ANNOUNCE SPEAKING SCHEDULE FOR FALL, the headline read. Below it, Ramona Norville stood on the library steps, smiling and squinting into the sun. A bad photograph, taken by a part-timer without much talent, and a bad (but probably typical) choice of clothes on Norville's part. The man-tailored blazer made her look as wide in the chest as a pro football tackle. Her shoes were ugly brown flatboats. A pair of too-tight gray slacks showcased what Tess and her friends back in middle school had called 'thunder thighs.'

'Holy fucking shit, Fritzy,' she said. Her voice was watery with dismay. 'Look at this.' Fritzy didn't come over to look and didn't reply – how could he, when she was too upset to make his voice?

Make sure of what you're seeing, she told herself. *You've had a terrible shock, Tessa Jean, maybe the biggest shock a woman can have, short of a mortal diagnosis in a doctor's office. So make sure.*

She closed her eyes and summoned the image of the man from the old Ford pickup truck with the Bondo around the headlights. He had seemed so friendly at first. *Didn't think you were going to meet the Jolly Green Giant out here in the williwags, didja?*

Only he *hadn't* been green, he'd been a tanned hulk of a man who didn't ride in his pickup but wore it.

Ramona Norville, not a Big Driver but certainly a Big Librarian, was too old to be his sister. And if she was a lesbian now, she hadn't always been one, because the resemblance was unmistakable.

Unless I'm badly mistaken, I'm looking at a picture of my rapist's mother.

29

She went to the kitchen and had a drink of water, but water wasn't getting it. An old half-filled bottle of tequila had been brooding in a back corner of a kitchen cabinet for donkey's years. She took it out, considered a glass, then nipped directly from the bottle. It stung her mouth and throat, but had a positive effect otherwise. She helped herself to more – a sip rather than a nip – and then put the bottle back. She had no intention of getting drunk. If she had ever needed her wits about her, she needed them about her today.

Rage – the biggest, truest rage of her adult life – had

invaded her like a fever, but it wasn't like any fever she had known previously. It circulated like weird serum, cold on the right side of her body, then hot on the left, where her heart was. It seemed to come nowhere near her head, which remained clear. Clearer since she'd had the tequila, actually.

She paced a series of rapid circles around the kitchen, head down, one hand massaging the ring of bruises around her throat. It did not occur to her that she was circling her kitchen as she had circled the deserted store after crawling out of the pipe Big Driver had meant for her tomb. Did she really think Ramona Norville had sent her, Tess, to her psychotic son like some kind of sacrifice? Was that likely? It was not. Could she even be sure that the two of them were mother and son, based on one bad photograph and her own memory?

But my memory's good. Especially my memory for faces.

Well, so she thought, but probably everyone did. Right?

Yes, and the whole idea's crazy. You have to admit it is.

She did admit it, but she had seen crazier things on true-crime programs (which she *did* watch). The ladies with the apartment house in San Francisco who had spent years killing their elderly tenants for their Social Security checks and burying them in the backyard. The airline pilot who murdered his wife, then froze the body so he could run her through the woodchipper behind the garage. The man who had doused his own children with gasoline and cooked them like Cornish game hens to make sure his wife never got the custody the courts had awarded her. A woman sending victims to her own son was shocking and unlikely . . . but not impossible. When it came to the dark fuckery of the human heart, there seemed to be no limit.

'Oh boy,' she heard herself saying in a voice that combined dismay and anger. 'Oh boy, oh boy, oh boy.'

Find out. Find out for sure. If you can.

She went back to her trusty computer. Her hands were trembling badly, and it took her three tries to enter COLEWICH TRUCKING FIRMS in the search field at the top of the Google page. Finally she got it right, hit enter, and there it was, at the top of the list: RED HAWK TRUCKING. The entry took her to the Red Hawk website, which featured a badly animated big rig with what she assumed was a red hawk on the side and a bizarre smiley-head man behind the wheel. The truck crossed the screen from right to left, flipped and came back left to right, then flipped again. An endless crisscross journey. The company's motto flashed red, white, and blue above the animated truck: THE SMILES COME WITH THE SERVICE!

For those wishing to journey beyond the welcome screen, there were four or five choices, including phone numbers, rates, and testimonials from satisfied customers. Tess skipped these and clicked on the last one, which read CHECK OUT THE NEWEST ADDITION TO OUR FLEET! And when the picture came up, the final piece fell into place.

It was a much better photograph than the one of Ramona Norville standing on the library steps. In it, Tess's rapist was sitting behind the wheel of a shiny cab-over Pete with RED HAWK TRUCKING COLEWICH, MASSACHUSETTS written on the door in fancy script. He wasn't wearing his bleach-splattered brown cap, and the bristly blond crewcut revealed by its absence made him look even more like his mother, almost eerily so. His cheerful, you-can-trust-me grin was the one Tess had seen yesterday afternoon. The one he'd still been wearing when he said *Instead of changing your tire, how about I fuck you? How would that be?*

Looking at the photo made the weird rage-serum

cycle faster through her system. There was a pounding in her temples that wasn't exactly a headache; in fact, it was almost pleasant.

He was wearing the red glass ring.

The caption below the picture read: 'Al Strehlke, President of Red Hawk Trucking, seen here behind the wheel of the company's newest acquisition, a 2008 Peterbilt 389. This horse of a hauler is now available to our customers, who are THE FINEST IN ALL THE LAND. Say! Doesn't Al look like a Proud Papa?'

She heard him calling her a bitch, a whiny whore bitch, and clenched her hands into fists. She felt her fingernails sinking into her palms and clenched them even tighter, relishing the pain.

Proud Papa. That was what her eyes kept returning to. *Proud Papa.* The rage moved faster and faster, circling through her body the way she had circled her kitchen. The way she had circled the store last night, moving in and out of consciousness like an actress through a series of spotlights.

You're going to pay, Al. And never mind the cops, I'm the one coming to collect.

And then there was Ramona Norville. The proud papa's proud mama. Although Tess was still not sure of her. Partly it was not wanting to believe that a woman could allow something so horrible to happen to another woman, but she could also see an innocent explanation. Chicopee wasn't that far from Colewich, and Ramona would have used the Stagg Road shortcut all the time when she went there.

'To visit her son,' Tess said, nodding. 'To visit the proud papa with the new cab-over Pete. For all I know, she might be the one who took the picture of him behind the wheel.' And why wouldn't she recommend her favorite route to that day's speaker?

But why didn't she say, 'I go that way all the time to visit my son?' Wouldn't that be natural?

'Maybe she doesn't talk to strangers about the Strehlke phase of her life,' Tess said. 'The phase before she discovered short hair and comfortable shoes.' It was possible, but there was the scatter of nailstudded boards to think about. The trap. Norville had sent her that way, and the trap had been set ahead of time. Because she had called him? Called him and said *I'm sending you a juicy one, don't miss out?*

It still doesn't mean she was involved . . . or not knowingly *involved. The proud papa could keep track of her guest speakers, how hard would that be?*

'Not hard at all,' Fritzy said after leaping up on her filing cabinet. He began to lick one of his paws.

'And if he saw a photo of one he liked . . . a reasonably attractive one . . . I suppose he'd know his mother would send her back by . . .' She stopped. 'No, that doesn't scan. Without some input from Ma, how would he know I wasn't driving to my home in Boston? Or flying back to my home in New York City?'

'You googled *him*,' Fritzy said. 'Maybe he googled *you*. Just like she did. Everything's on the Internet these days; you said so yourself.'

That hung together, if only by a thread.

She thought there was one way to find out for sure, and that was to pay Ms Norville a surprise visit. Look in her eyes when she saw Tess. If there was nothing in them but surprise and curiosity at the Return of the Willow Grove Scribe . . . to Ramona's home rather than her library . . . that would be one thing. But if there was fear in them as well, the kind that might be prompted by the thought, *Why are you here instead of in a rusty culvert on the Stagg Road?* . . . well . . .

'That would be different, Fritzy. Wouldn't it?'

Fritzy looked at her with his cunning green eyes, still licking his paw. It looked harmless, that paw, but there were claws hidden inside it. Tess had seen them, and on occasion felt them.

She found out where I lived; let's see if I can return the favor.

Tess went back to her computer, this time searching for a Books & Brown Baggers website. She was quite sure she'd find one – everybody had websites these days, there were prisoners doing life for murder who had websites – and she did. The Brown Baggers posted newsy notes about their members, book reviews, and informal summaries – not quite minutes – of their meetings. Tess chose the latter and began scrolling. It did not take her long to discover that the June 10 meeting had been held at Ramona Norville's home in Brewster. Tess had never been to this town, but knew where it was, had passed a green turnpike sign pointing to it while on her way to yesterday's gig. It was only two or three exits south of Chicopee.

Next she went to the Brewster Township tax records and scrolled down until she found Ramona's name. She had paid $913.06 in property taxes the year before; said property at 75 Lacemaker Lane.

'Found you, dear,' Tess murmured.

'You need to think about how you're going to handle this,' Fritzy said. 'And about how far you're willing to go.'

'If I'm right,' Tess said, 'maybe quite far.'

She started to turn off her computer, then thought of one more thing worth checking out, although she knew it might come to nothing. She went to the *Weekly Reminder*'s home page and clicked on OBITUARIES. There was a place to enter the name you were interested in, and Tess typed STREHLKE. There was a single hit, for a man named Roscoe Strehlke. According to the 1999 obit, he had died suddenly in his home, at the age of forty-eight. Survived by his wife, Ramona, and two sons: Alvin (23) and Lester (17). For a mystery writer, even of the bloodless sort known as 'cozies,' *died suddenly* was a red flag. She searched the *Reminder*'s general database and found nothing more.

She sat still for a moment, drumming her fingers restlessly against the arms of her chair as she did when she was working and found herself stuck for a word, a phrase, or a way of describing something. Then she looked for a list of newspapers in western and southern Massachusetts, and found the Springfield *Republican*. When she typed the name of Ramona Norville's husband, the headline that came up was stark and to the point: CHICOPEE BUSINESSMAN COMMITS SUICIDE.

Strehlke had been discovered in his garage, hanging from a rafter. There was no note and Ramona wasn't quoted, but a neighbor said that Mr Strehlke had been distraught over 'some trouble his older boy had been in.'

'What kind of trouble was Al in that got you so upset?' Tess asked the computer screen. 'Was it something to do with a girl? Assault, maybe? Sexual battery? Was he working up to bigger things, even then? If that's why you hung yourself, you were one chickenshit daddy.'

'Maybe Roscoe had help,' Fritzy said. 'From Ramona. Big strong woman, you know. You *ought* to know; you saw her.'

Again, that didn't sound like the voice she made when she was essentially talking to herself. She looked at Fritzy, startled. Fritzy looked back: green eyes asking *who, me*?

What Tess wanted to do was drive directly to Lacemaker Lane with her gun in her purse. What she *ought* to do was stop playing detective and call the police. Let them handle it. It was what the Old Tess would have done, but she was no longer that woman. That woman now seemed to her like a distant relative, the kind you sent a card to at Christmas and forgot for the rest of the year.

Because she couldn't decide — and because she hurt all over — she went upstairs and back to bed. She slept for four hours and got up almost too stiff to walk. She took two extra-strength Tylenol, waited until they improved matters, then drove down to Blockbuster video. She carried the Lemon Squeezer in her purse. She thought she would always carry it now while she was riding alone.

She got to Blockbuster just before closing and asked for a Jodie Foster movie called *The Courageous Woman*. The clerk (who had green hair, a safety pin in one ear, and looked all of eighteen years old) smiled indulgently and told her the film was actually called *The Brave One*. Mr Retro Punk told her that for an extra fifty cents, she could get a bag of microwave popcorn to go with. Tess almost said no, then reconsidered. 'Why the fuck not?' she asked Mr Retro Punk. 'You only live once, right?'

He gave her a startled, reconsidering look, then smiled and agreed that it was a case of one life to a customer.

At home, she popped the corn, inserted the DVD, and plopped onto the couch with a pillow at the small of her back to cushion the scrape there. Fritzy joined her and they watched Jodie Foster go after the men (the *punks*, as in *do you feel lucky, punk*) who had killed her boyfriend. Foster got assorted other punks along the way, and used a pistol to do it. *The Brave One* was very much *that* kind of a movie, but Tess enjoyed it just the same. She thought it made perfect sense. She also thought that she had been missing something all these years: the low but authentic catharsis movies like *The Brave One* offered. When it was over, she turned to Fritzy and said, 'I wish Richard Widmark had met Jodie Foster instead of the old lady in the wheelchair, don't you?'

Fritzy agreed one thousand percent.

30

Lying in bed that night with an October wind getting up to dickens around the house and Fritzy beside her, curled up nose to tail, Tess made an agreement with herself: if she woke up tomorrow feeling as she did now, she would go to see Ramona Norville, and perhaps after Ramona – depending on how things turned out on Lacemaker Lane – she would pay a visit to Alvin 'Big Driver' Strehlke. More likely she'd wake up with some semblance of sanity restored and call the police. No anonymous call, either; she'd face the music and dance. Proving actual rape forty hours and God knew how many showers after the fact might be difficult, but the signs of sexual battery were written all over her body.

And the women in the pipe: she was their advocate, like it or not.

Tomorrow all these revenge ideas will seem silly to me. Like the kind of delusions people have when they're sick with a high fever.

But when she woke up on Sunday, she was still in full New Tess mode. She looked at the gun on the night table and thought, *I want to use it. I want to take care of this myself, and given what I've been through, I* deserve *to take care of it myself.*

'But I need to make sure, and I don't want to get caught,' she said to Fritzy, who was now on his feet and stretching, getting ready for another exhausting day of lying around and snacking from his bowl.

Tess showered, dressed, then took a yellow legal pad out to the sunporch. She stared at her back lawn for almost fifteen minutes, occasionally sipping at a cooling cup of tea. Finally she wrote DON'T GET CAUGHT at the top of the first sheet. She considered this soberly, and then began making notes. As with each day's work when she was writing a book, she started slowly, but picked up speed.

31

By ten o'clock she was ravenous. She cooked herself a huge brunch and ate every bite. Then she took her movie back to Blockbuster and asked if they had *Kiss of Death*. They didn't, but after ten minutes of browsing, she settled on a substitute called *Last House on the Left*. She took it home and watched closely. In the movie, men raped a young girl and left her for dead. It was so much like what had happened to her that Tess burst into tears, crying so loudly that Fritzy ran from the room. But she stuck with it and was rewarded with a happy ending: the parents of the young girl murdered the rapists.

She returned the disc to its case, which she left on the table in the hall. She would return it tomorrow, if she were still alive tomorrow. She planned to be, but nothing was certain; there were many strange twists and devious turns as one hopped down the overgrown bunnytrail of life. Tess had found this out for herself.

With time to kill – the daylight hours seemed to move so slowly – she went back online, searching for information about the trouble Al Strehlke had been in before his father committed suicide. She found nothing. Possibly the neighbor was full of shit (neighbors so often were), but Tess could think of another scenario: the trouble might have occurred while Strehlke was still a minor. In cases like that, names weren't released to the press and the court records (assuming the case had even gone to court) were sealed.

'But maybe he got worse,' she told Fritzy.

'Those guys often do get worse,' Fritzy agreed. (This was rare; Tom was usually the agreeable one. Fritzy's role tended to be devil's advocate.)

'Then, a few years later, something else happened. Something worse. Say Mom helped him to cover it up—'

'Don't forget the younger brother,' Fritzy said. 'Lester. He might have been in on it, too.'

'Don't confuse me with too many characters, Fritz. All I know is that Al Fucking Big Driver raped me, and his mother may have been an accessory. That's enough for me.'

'Maybe Ramona's his aunt,' Fritzy speculated.

'Oh, shut up,' Tess said, and Fritzy did.

32

She lay down at four o'clock, not expecting to sleep a wink, but her healing body had its own priorities. She went under almost instantly, and when she woke to the insistent *dah-dah-dah* of her bedside clock, she was glad she had set the alarm. Outside, a gusty October breeze was combing leaves from the trees and sending them across her backyard in colorful skitters. The light had gone that strange and depthless gold which seems the exclusive property of late-fall afternoons in New England.

Her nose was better — the pain there down to a dull throb — but her throat was still sore and she hobbled rather than walked to the bathroom. She got into the shower and stayed in the stall until the bathroom was as foggy as an English moor in a Sherlock Holmes story. The shower helped. A couple of Tylenol from the medicine cabinet would help even more.

She dried her hair, then swiped a clear place on the mirror. The woman in the glass looked back from eyes haunted by rage and sanity. The glass didn't stay clear for long, but it was long enough for Tess to realize that she really meant to do this, no matter the consequences.

She dressed in a black turtleneck sweater and black

cargo pants with big flap pockets. She tied her hair up in a bun and then yanked on a big black gimme cap. The bun made the cap bulge a little behind, but at least no potential witness would be able to say, *I didn't get a good look at her face, but she had long blond hair. It was tied back in one of those scrunchie things. You know, the kind you can buy at JCPenney.*

She went down to the basement where her kayak had been stored since Labor Day and took the reel of yellow boat-line from the shelf above it. She used the hedge clippers to cut off four feet, wound it around her forearm, then slipped the coil into one of her big pants pockets. Upstairs again in the kitchen, she tucked her Swiss Army knife into the same pocket – the left. The right pocket was for the Lemon Squeezer .38 . . . and one other item, which she took from the drawer next to the stove. Then she spooned out double rations for Fritzy, but before she let him start eating, she hugged him and kissed the top of his head. The old cat flattened his ears (more in surprise than distaste, probably; she wasn't ordinarily a kissy mistress) and hurried to his dish as soon as she put him down.

'Make that last,' Tess told him. 'Patsy will check on you eventually if I don't come back, but it could be a couple of days.' She smiled a little and added, 'I love you, you scruffy old thing.'

'Right, right,' Fritzy said, then got busy eating.

Tess checked her DON'T GET CAUGHT memo one more time, mentally inventorying her supplies as she did so and going over the steps she intended to take once she got to Lacemaker Lane. She thought the most important thing to keep in mind was that things wouldn't go as she hoped they would. When it came to things like this, there were always jokers in the deck. Ramona might not be at home. Or she might be home but with her rapist-murderer son, the two of them cozied up in the living room and watching something uplifting from Blockbuster. *Saw*, maybe. The younger brother – no doubt known in Colewich as Little Driver – might be there, as well. For all Tess knew, Ramona might be hosting a Tupperware party or a reading circle tonight. The important thing was not to get flummoxed by unexpected developments. If she couldn't improvise, Tess thought it very likely that she really was leaving her house in Stoke Village for the last time.

She burned the DON'T GET CAUGHT memo in the fireplace, stirred the ashes apart with the poker, then put on her leather jacket and a pair of thin leather gloves. The jacket had a deep pocket in the lining. Tess slipped one of her butcher knives into it, just for good luck, then told herself not to forget it was there. The last thing she needed this weekend was an accidental mastectomy.

Just before stepping out the door, she set the burglar alarm.

The wind surrounded her immediately, flapping the collar of her jacket and the legs of her cargo pants. Leaves swirled in mini-cyclones. In the not-quite-dark sky above her tasteful little piece of Connecticut suburbia, clouds scudded across the face of a three-quarter moon. Tess thought it was a fine night for a horror movie.

She got into her Expedition and closed the door. A leaf spun down on the windshield, then dashed away. 'I've lost my mind,' she said matter-of-factly. 'It fell out and died in that culvert, or when I was walking around the store. It's the only explanation for this.'

She started the engine. Tom the TomTom lit up and said, 'Hello, Tess. I see we're taking a trip.'

'That's right, my friend.' Tess leaned forward and

programed 75 Lacemaker Lane into Tom's tidy little mechanical head.

33

She had checked out Ramona's neighborhood on Google Earth, and it looked the same when she got there. So far, so good. Brewster was a small New England town, Lacemaker Lane was on the outskirts, and the houses were far apart. Tess cruised past number 75 at a sedately suburban twenty miles an hour, determining that the lights were on and only a single car – a late-model Subaru that almost screamed librarian – was in the driveway. There was no sign of a cab-over Pete or any other big rig. No old Bondo-patched pickup, either.

The street ended in a turnaround. Tess took it, came back, and turned into Norville's driveway without giving herself a chance to hesitate. She killed the lights and the motor, then took a long, deep breath.

'Come back safe, Tess,' Tom said from his place on the dashboard. 'Come back safe and I'll take you to your next stop.'

'I'll do my best.' She grabbed her yellow legal pad (there was now nothing written on it) and got out of her car. She held the pad to the front of her jacket as she walked to Ramona Norville's door. Her moonshadow – perhaps all that was left of the Old Tess – walked beside her.

34

Norville's front door had beveled glass strips on either side. They were thick and warped the view, but Tess could make out nice wallpaper and a hallway floored with polished wood. There was an end table with a couple of magazines on it. Or maybe they were catalogues. There

was a big room at the end of the hall. The sound of a
TV came from there. She heard singing, so Ramona
probably wasn't watching *Saw*. In fact – if Tess was right
and the song was 'Climb Ev'ry Mountain' – Ramona was
watching *The Sound of Music*.

Tess rang the doorbell. From inside came a run of
chimes that sounded like the opening notes of 'Dixie' – a
strange choice for New England, but then, if Tess was
right about her, Ramona Norville was a strange woman.

Tess heard the clump of big feet and made a half-
turn, so the light from the beveled glass would catch only
a bit of her face. She lowered her blank pad from her
chest and made writing motions with one gloved hand.
She let her shoulders slump a little. She was a woman
taking some kind of survey. It was Sunday evening, she
was tired, all she wanted was to discover the name of this
woman's favorite toothpaste (or maybe if she had Prince
Albert in a can) and then go home.

*Don't worry, Ramona, you can open the door, anybody
can see that I'm harmless, the kind of woman who wouldn't
say boo to a goose.*

From the corner of her eye she glimpsed a distorted
fish-face swim into view behind the beveled glass. There
was a pause that seemed to last a very long time, then
Ramona Norville opened the door. 'Yes? Can I help
y—'

Tess turned back. The light from the open door fell
on her face. And the shock she saw on Norville's face,
the utter drop-jaw shock, told her everything she needed
to know.

'*You?* What are *you* doing h—'

Tess pulled the Lemon Squeezer .38 from her right
front pocket. On the drive from Stoke Village she had
imagined it getting stuck in there – had imagined it with
nightmarish clarity – but it came out smoothly.

'Move back from the door. If you try to shut it, I'll shoot you.'

'You won't,' Norville said. She didn't move back, but she didn't shut the door, either. 'Are you crazy?'

'Get inside.'

Norville was wearing a big blue housecoat, and when Tess saw the front of it rise precipitously, she raised the gun. 'If you even start to yell, I'll shoot. You better believe me, bitch, because I'm not even close to kidding.'

Norville's large bosom deflated. Her lips were drawn back from her teeth and her eyes were shifting from side to side in their sockets. She didn't look like a librarian now, and she didn't look jovial and welcoming. To Tess she looked like a rat caught outside its hole.

'If you fire that gun, the whole neighborhood will hear.'

Tess doubted that, but didn't argue. 'It won't matter to you, because you'll be dead. Get inside. If you behave yourself and answer my questions, you might still be alive tomorrow morning.'

Norville backed up, and Tess came in through the open door with the gun held stiffly out in front of her. As soon as she closed the door – she did it with her foot – Norville stopped moving. She was standing by the little table with the catalogues on it.

'No grabbing, no throwing,' Tess said, and saw by the twitch of the other woman's mouth that grabbing and throwing had indeed been in Ramona's mind. 'I can read you like a book. Why else would I be here? Keep backing up. All the way down to the living room. I just love the Trapp Family when they're really rocking.'

'You're crazy,' Ramona said, but she began to back up again. She was wearing shoes. Even in her housecoat she was wearing big ugly shoes. Men's laceups. 'I have no idea what you're doing here, but—'

'Don't bullshit me, Mommy. Don't you *dare*. It was all on your face when you opened the door. Every bit of it. You thought I was dead, didn't you?'

'I don't know what you're—'

'It's just us girls, honey, so why not fess up?'

They were in the living room now. There were sentimental paintings on the walls – clowns, waifs with big eyes — and lots of shelves and tables cluttered with knickknacks: snowglobes, troll babies, Hummel figures, Care Bears, a ceramic candy house à la Hansel and Gretel. Although Norville was a librarian, there were no books in evidence. Facing the TV was a La-Z-Boy with a hassock in front of it. There was a TV tray beside the chair. On it was a bag of Cheez Doodles, a large bottle of Diet Coke, the remote control, and a *TV Guide*. On top of the television was a framed photograph of Ramona and another woman with their arms around each other and their cheeks pressed together. It looked as if it had been taken at an amusement park or a county fair. In front of the photo was a glass candy dish that gleamed with sparkle-points of light beneath the over-head fixture.

'How long have you been doing it?'

'I don't know what you're talking about.'

'How long have you been pimping for your homi-cidal rapist of a son?'

Norville's eyes flickered, but again she denied it . . . which presented Tess with a problem. When she had come here, killing Ramona Norville had seemed not just an option but the most likely outcome. Tess had been almost positive she could do it, and that the boat-rope in the left front pocket of her cargo pants would go unused. Now, however, she discovered she couldn't go ahead unless the woman admitted her complicity. Because what had been written on her face when she'd seen Tess standing at her door, bruised but otherwise very much alive, wasn't enough.

Not quite enough.

'When did it start? How old was he? Fifteen? Did he claim he was "just foolin around"? That's what a lot of them claim when they first start.'

'I have no idea what you mean. You come to the library and put on a perfectly acceptable presentation — lackluster, obviously you were only there for the money, but at least it filled the open date on our calendar — and the next thing I know you're on my doorstep, pointing a gun and making all sorts of wild—'

'It's no good, Ramona. I saw his picture on the Red Hawk website. Ring and all. He raped me and tried to kill me. He thought he *did* kill me. *And you sent me to him.*'

Norville's mouth dropped open in a gruesome combination of shock, dismay, and guilt. '*That's not true! You stupid cunt, you don't know what you're talking about.*' She started forward.

Tess raised the gun. 'Nuh-uh, don't do that. No.'

Norville stopped, but Tess didn't think she would stay stopped for long. She was nerving herself up for either fight or flight. And because she had to know Tess would follow her if she tried to run deeper into the house, it would probably be fight.

The Trapp Family was singing again. Given the situation Tess was in — that she had put herself in — all that happy choral crap was maddening. Keeping the Lemon Squeezer trained on Norville with her right hand, Tess picked up the remote with her left and muted the TV. She started to put the remote down again, then froze. There were two things on top of the TV, but at first she had only registered the picture of Ramona and her girlfriend; the candy dish had just earned a glance.

Now she saw that the sparkles she had assumed were coming from the cut-glass sides of the dish weren't coming from the sides at all. They were coming from something inside. Her earrings were in the dish. Her diamond earrings.

Norville grabbed the Hansel and Gretel candy house from its shelf and threw it. She threw it hard. Tess ducked and the candy house went an inch over her head, shattering on the wall behind her. She stepped backward, tripped over the hassock, and went sprawling. The gun flew from her hand.

They both went for it, Norville dropping to her knees and slamming her shoulder against Tess's arm and shoulder like a football tackle intent on sacking the quarterback. She grabbed the gun, at first juggling it and then securing her grip. Tess reached inside her jacket and closed her hand around the handle of the butcher knife that was her backup, aware that she was going to be too late. Norville was too big . . . and too maternal. Yes, that was it. She had protected that rogue son of hers for years, and was intent on protecting him now. Tess should have shot her in the hall, the moment the door was shut behind her.

But I couldn't, she thought, and even at this moment, knowing it was the truth brought some comfort. She got up on her knees, hand still inside the jacket, facing Ramona Norville.

'You're a shitty writer and you were a shitty guest speaker,' Norville said. She was smiling, speaking faster and faster. Her voice had a nasal auctioneer's lilt. 'You phoned in your talk the same way you phone in your stupid books. You were perfect for him and he was going to do someone, I know the signs. I sent you that way and it worked out right and I'm glad he fucked you. I don't know what you thought you were going to do, coming here, but this is what you get.'

She pulled the trigger and there was nothing but a dry click. Tess had taken lessons when she bought the gun, and the most important had been not to put a bullet in the chamber that would first fall under the hammer. Just in case the trigger was pulled by accident.

An expression of almost comical surprise came over Norville's face. It made her young again. She looked down at the gun, and when she did, Tess drew the knife from the inside pocket of the jacket, stumbled forward, and jammed it up to the hilt in Norville's belly.

The woman made a glassy 'OOO-OOOO' sound that tried to be a scream and failed. Tess's pistol dropped and Ramona staggered back against the wall, looking down at the handle of the knife. One flailing arm struck a rank of Hummel figures. They tumbled from the shelf and shattered on the floor. She made that 'OOO-OOOO' sound again. The front of the housecoat was still unstained, but blood began to patter from beneath its hem, onto Ramona Norville's manshoes. She put her hands on the haft of the knife, tried to tug it free, and made the 'OOO-OOOO' for the third time.

She looked up at Tess, unbelieving. Tess looked back. She was remembering something that had happened on her tenth birthday. Her father had given her a slingshot, and she had gone out looking for things to shoot with it. At some point, five or six blocks from her house, she had seen a raggedy-eared stray dog rooting in a garbage can. She had put a small rock in her slingshot and fired at it, only meaning to scare the dog away (or so she told herself), but hitting it in the rump instead. The dog had made a miserable *ike-ike-ike* sound and run away, but before it did, it gave Tess a look of reproach she had never forgotten. She would have given anything to take that casual shot back, and she had never fired her slingshot at another living thing. She understood that killing was a part of life – she felt no compunction about swatting mosquitoes, put down traps when she saw mouse-droppings in the cellar, and had eaten her fair share of Mickey D's Quarter Pounders – but then she had believed she would never again be able to hurt something that way without feeling remorse or regret. She suffered neither in the living room of the house on Lacemaker Lane. Perhaps because, in the end, it had been self-defense. Or perhaps that wasn't it at all.

'Ramona,' she said, 'I'm feeling a certain kinship to Richard Widmark right now. This is what we do to squealers, honey.'

Norville was standing in a puddle of her own blood and her housecoat was at last blooming with blood-poppies. Her face was pale. Her dark eyes were huge and glittery with shock. Her tongue came out and swiped slowly across her lower lip.

'Now you can roll around for a long time, thinkin' it over – how would that be?'

Norville began to slide. Her manshoes made squittering sounds in the blood. She groped for one of the other shelves and pulled it off the wall. A platoon of Care Bears tilted forward and committed suicide.

Although she still felt no regret or remorse, Tess found that, in spite of her big talk, she had very little inner Tommy Udo; she had no urge to watch or prolong Norville's suffering. She bent and picked up the .38. From the right front pocket of her cargo pants she removed the item she had taken from the kitchen drawer beside her stove. It was a quilted oven glove. It would silence a single pistol shot quite effectively, as long as the caliber wasn't too big. She had learned this while writing *The Willow Grove Knitting Society Goes on a Mystery Cruise*.

'You don't understand.' Norville's voice was a harsh whisper. 'You can't do this. It's a mistake. Take me . . . hospital.'

'The mistake was yours.' Tess pulled the oven glove over the pistol, which was in her right hand. 'It was not having your son castrated as soon as you found out what he was.' She put the oven glove against Ramona Norville's temple, turned her head slightly to one side, and pulled the trigger. There was a low, emphatic *pluh* sound, like a big man clearing his throat.

That was all.

35

She hadn't googled Al Strehlke's home address; she had been expecting to get that from Norville. But, as she had already reminded herself, things like this never went according to plan. What she had to do now was keep her wits about her and carry the job through to the end.

Norville's home office was upstairs, in what had probably been meant as a spare bedroom. There were more Care Bears and Hummels here. There were also half a dozen framed pictures, but none of her sons, her main squeeze, or the late great Roscoe Strehlke; these were autographed photos of writers who had spoken to the Brown Baggers. The room reminded Tess of The Stagger Inn's foyer, with its band photos.

She didn't ask for an autograph on my *photo,* Tess thought. *Of course not, why would she want to be reminded of a shitty writer like me? I was basically just a talking head to fill a hole in her schedule. Not to mention meat for her son's meatgrinder. How lucky for them that I came along at the right time.*

On Norville's desk, below a bulletin board buried in circulars and library correspondence, was a desktop Mac very much like Tess's. The screen was dark, but the glowing light on the CPU told her it was only sleeping. She pushed one of the keys with a gloved fingertip. The screen refreshed and she was looking at Norville's electronic desktop. No need for those pesky passwords, how nice.

Tess clicked the address book icon, scrolled down to the R's, and found Red Hawk Trucking. The address was 7 Transport Plaza, Township Road, Colewich. She scrolled further, to the S's, and found both her overgrown acquaintance from Friday night and her acquaintance's brother, Lester. Big Driver and Little Driver. They both lived on Township Road, near the company they must have inherited from their father: Alvin at number 23, Lester at number 101.

If there was a third brother, she thought, *they'd be The Three Little Truckers. One in a house of straw, one in a house of sticks, one in a house of bricks. Alas, there are only two.*

Downstairs again, she plucked her earrings from the glass dish and put them in her coat pocket. She looked at the dead woman sitting against the wall as she did it. There was no pity in the glance, only the sort of parting acknowledgment anyone may give to a piece of hard work that has now been finished. There was no need to worry about trace evidence; Tess was confident she had left none, not so much as a single strand of hair. The oven glove – now with a hole blown in it – was back in her pocket. The knife was a common item sold in department stores all over America. For all she knew (or cared), it matched Ramona's own set. So far she was clean, but the hard part might still be ahead. She left the house, got in her car, and drove away. Fifteen minutes later she pulled into the lot of a deserted strip mall long enough to program 23 Township Road, Colewich, into her GPS.

36

With Tom's guidance, Tess found herself near her destination not long after nine o'clock. The three-quarter moon was still low in the sky. The wind was blowing harder than ever.

Township Road branched off US 47, but at least seven miles from The Stagger Inn and even farther from Colewich's downtown. Transport Plaza was at the intersection of the two roads. According to the signage, three trucking firms and a moving company were based here. The buildings that housed them had an ugly prefab look. The smallest belonged to Red Hawk Trucking. All were dark on this Sunday night. Beyond them were acres of parking lot surrounded by Cyclone fence and lit with high-intensity arc lights. The depot lot was full of parked cabs and freight haulers. At least one of the cab-overs had RED HAWK TRUCKING on the side, but Tess didn't think it was the one pictured on the website, the one with the Proud Papa behind the wheel.

There was a truck stop adjacent to the depot area. The pumps – over a dozen – were lit by the same high-intensity arcs. Bright white fluorescents spilled out from the right side of the main building; the left side was dark. There was another building, this one U-shaped, to the rear. A scattering of cars and trucks was parked there. The sign out by the road was a huge digital job, loaded with bright red information.

RICHIE'S TOWNSHIP ROAD TRUCK STOP
'YOU DRIVE 'EM, WE FILL 'EM'
REG $2.99 GAL
DIESEL $2.69 GAL
NEWEST LOTTERY TIX ALWAYS AVAILABLE
RESTAURANT CLOSED SUN. NITE
SORRY NO SHOWERS SUN. NITE
STORE & MOTEL 'ALWAYS OPEN'
RVS 'ALWAYS WELCOME'

And at the bottom, badly spelled but fervent:

SUPPORT OUR TROOPS! WIN IN AFGANDISTAN!

With truckers coming and going, fueling up both their rigs and themselves (even with its lights off, Tess could tell that, when open, the restaurant was of the sort where chicken-fried steak, meatloaf, and Mom's Bread Pudding would always be on the menu), the place would probably be a beehive of activity during the week, but on Sunday night it was a graveyard because there was nothing out here, not even a roadhouse like The Stagger.

There was only a single vehicle parked at the pumps, facing out toward the road with a pump nozzle stuck in its gas hatch. It was an old Ford F-150 pickup with Bondo around the headlights. It was impossible to read the color in the harsh lighting, but Tess didn't have to. She had seen that truck close up, and knew the color. The cab was empty.

'You don't seem surprised, Tess,' Tom said as she slowed to a stop on the shoulder of the road and squinted at the store. She could make out a couple of people in there in spite of the glare from the harsh outside lighting, and she could see that one of them was big. *Was he big or real big?* Betsy Neal had asked.

'I'm not surprised at all,' she said. 'He lives out here. Where else would he go to gas up?'

'Maybe he's getting ready to take a trip.'

'This late on Sunday night? I don't think so. I think he was at home, watching *The Sound of Music*. I think he drank up all of his beer and came down here for more. He decided to top off his tank while he was at it.'

'You could be wrong, though. Hadn't you better pull in behind the store and follow him when he leaves?'

But Tess didn't want to do that. The front of the truck-stop store was all glass. He might look out and see her when she drove in. Even if the bright lighting above the pump islands made it hard for him to see her face, he might recognize the vehicle. There were lots of Ford SUVs on the road, but after Friday night, Al Strehlke had to be particularly sensitized to black Ford Expeditions. And there was her license plate – surely he would have noticed her Connecticut license plate on Friday, when he pulled up beside her in the gone-to-weeds parking lot of the deserted store.

There was something else. Something even more important. She got rolling again, putting Richie's Township Road Truck Stop in the rearview.

'I don't want to be behind him,' she said. 'I want to be ahead of him. I want to be waiting for him.'

'What if he's married, Tess?' Tom asked. 'What if he's got a wife waiting for him?'

The idea startled her for a moment. Then she smiled, and not just because the only ring he'd been wearing was the one too big to be a ruby. 'Guys like him don't have wives,' she said. 'Not ones that stick around, anyway. There was only one woman in Al's life, and she's dead.'

37

Unlike Lacemaker Lane, there was nothing suburban about Township Road; it was as country as Travis Tritt. The houses were glimmering islands of electric light beneath the glow of the rising moon.

'Tess, you are approaching your destination,' Tom said in his non-imaginary voice.

She breasted a rise, and there on her left was a mailbox marked STREHLKE and 23. The driveway was long, rising on a curve, paved with asphalt, smooth as black ice. Tess turned in without hesitation, but apprehension dropped over her as soon as Township Road was behind her. She had to fight to keep from jamming on the brakes and backing out again. Because if she kept going, she had no choice. She'd be like a bug in a bottle. And even if he *wasn't* married, what if someone else was up there at the house? Brother Les, for instance? What if Big Driver had been at Tommy's buying beer and snacks not for one but for two?

Tess killed her headlights and drove on by moonlight.

In her keyed-up state, the driveway seemed to go on forever, but it could have been no more than an eighth of a mile before she saw the lights of Strehlke's house. It was at the top of the hill, a tidy-looking place that was bigger than a cottage but smaller than a farmhouse. Not a house of bricks, but not a humble house of straw, either. In the story of the three little pigs and the big bad wolf, Tess reckoned this would have been the house of sticks.

Parked on the left side of the house was a long trailer-box with RED HAWK TRUCKING on the side. Parked at the end of the driveway, in front of the garage, was the cab-over Pete from the website. It looked haunted in the moonlight. Tess slowed as she approached it, and then she was flooded with a white glare that dazzled her eyes and lit the lawn and the driveway. It was a motion-activated pole light, and if Strehlke came back while it was on, he would be able to see its glow at the foot of his driveway. Maybe even while he was still approaching on Township Road.

She jammed on the brakes, feeling as she had when, as a teenager, she'd dreamed of finding herself in school with no clothes on. She heard a woman groaning. She supposed it was her, but it didn't sound or feel like her.

'This isn't good, Tess.'

'Shut up, Tom.'

'He could come back any minute, and you don't know how long the timer on that thing is. You had trouble with the mother. He's *much* bigger than her.'

'I said shut *up!*'

She tried to think, but that blaring light made it hard. Shadows from the parked cab-over and the long-box to her left seemed to reach for her with sharp black fingers – boogeyman fingers. Goddam pole light! Of *course* a man like him would have a pole light! She ought to go right now, just turn around on his lawn and drive back down to the road as fast as she could, but she would meet him if she did. She knew it. And with the element of surprise gone, she would die.

Think, Tessa Jean, think!

And oh God, just to make things a little worse, a dog started barking. There was a dog in the house. She imagined a pit bull with a headful of jutting teeth.

'If you're going to stay, you need to get out of sight,' Tom said . . . and no, that didn't sound like her voice. Or not *exactly* like her voice. Perhaps it was the one that belonged to her deepest self, the survivor. And the killer – her, too. How many unsuspected selves could a person have, hiding deep inside? She was beginning to think the number might be infinite.

She glanced into her rearview mirror, chewing at her still-swollen lower lip. No approaching headlights yet. But would she even be able to tell, given the combined brilliance of the moon and that Christing pole light?

'It's on a timer,' Tom said, 'but I'd do something before it goes out, Tess. If you move the car after it does, you'll only trip it again.'

She threw the Expedition into four-wheel, started to swing around the cab-over, then stopped. There was high grass on that side. In the pitiless glare of the pole light, he couldn't help but see the tracks she would leave.

Even if the Christing light went out, it would come back on again when he drove up and then he would see them.

Inside, the dog continued to weigh in: *Yark! Yark! YarkYarkYark!*

'Drive across the lawn and put it behind the long-box,' Tom said.

'The tracks, though! The *tracks*!'

'You have to hide it somewhere,' Tom returned. He spoke apologetically but firmly. 'At least the grass is mown on that side. Most people are pretty unobservant, you know. Doreen Marquis says that all the time.'

'Strehlke's not a Knitting Society lady, he's a fucking lunatic.'

But because there was really no choice – not now that she was up here – Tess drove onto the lawn and toward the parked silver long-box through a glare that seemed as bright as a summer noonday. She did it with her bottom slightly raised off the seat, as if by doing that she could somehow magically render the tracks of the Expedition's passage less visible.

'Even if the motion light is still on when he comes back, he may not be suspicious,' Tom said. 'I'll bet deer trip it all the time. He might even have a light like that to scare them out of his vegetable garden.'

This made sense (and it sounded like her special Tom-voice again), but it did not comfort her much.

Yark! Yark! YarkYark! Whatever it was, it sounded like it was shitting nickels in there.

The ground behind the silver box was bumpy and bald – other freight-boxes had no doubt been parked on it from time to time – but solid enough. She drove the Expedition as deep into the long-box's shadow as she could, then killed the engine. She was sweating heavily, producing a rank aroma no deodorant would be able to defeat.

She got out, and the motion light went out when she slammed the door. For one superstitious moment Tess thought she had done it herself, then realized the scary fucking thing had just timed out. She leaned over the warm hood of the Expedition, pulling in deep breaths and letting them out like a runner in the last quarter-mile of a marathon. It might come in handy to know how long it had been on, but that was a question she couldn't answer. She'd been too scared. It had seemed like hours.

When she had herself under control again, she took inventory, forcing herself to move slowly and methodically. Pistol and oven glove. Both present and accounted for. She didn't think the oven glove would muffle another shot, not with a hole in it; she'd have to count on the isolation of the little hilltop house. It was okay that she'd left the knife in Ramona's belly; if she were reduced to trying to take out Big Driver with a butcher knife, she'd be in serious trouble.

And there are only four shots left in the gun, you better not forget that and just start spraying him. Why didn't you bring anymore bullets, Tessa Jean? You thought you were planning, but I don't think you did a very good job.

'Shut up,' she whispered. 'Tom or Fritzy or whoever you are, just shut up.'

The scolding voice ceased, and when it did, Tess realized the real world had also gone silent. The dog had ceased its mad barking when the pole light went off. Now the only sound was the wind and the only light was the moon.

38

With that terrible glare gone, the long-box provided excellent cover, but she couldn't stay there. Not if she meant to do what she had come here to do. Tess scurried around the back of the house, terrified of tripping another motion light, but feeling she had no choice. There was no light to trip, but the moon went behind a cloud and she stumbled over the cellar bulkhead, almost hitting her head on a wheelbarrow when she went to her knees. For a moment as she lay there, she wondered again what she had turned into. She was a member of the Authors Guild who had shot a woman in the head not long ago. After stabbing her in the stomach. *I've gone entirely off the reservation.* Then she thought of him calling her a bitch, a whiny whore bitch, and quit caring about whether she was on or off the reservation. It was a stupid saying, anyway. And racist in the bargain.

Strehlke *did* have a garden behind his house, but it was small and apparently not worth protecting from the depredations of the deer with a motion light. There was nothing left in it anyway except for a few pumpkins, most now rotting on the vine. She stepped over the rows, rounded the far corner of the house, and there was the cab-over. The moon had come out again and turned its chrome to the liquid silver of sword blades in fantasy novels.

Tess came up behind it, walked along the left side, and knelt by the chin-high (to her, at least) front wheel. She took the Lemon Squeezer out of her pocket. He couldn't drive into his garage because the cab-over was in the way. Even if it hadn't been, the garage was probably full of bachelor rickrack: tools, fishing gear, camping gear, truck parts, cases of discount soda.

That's just guessing. It's dangerous to guess. Doreen would scold you for it.

Of course she would, no one knew the Knitting Society ladies better than Tess did, but those dessert-loving babies rarely took chances. When you did take them, you were forced to make a certain number of guesses.

Tess looked at her watch and was astounded to see it was only twenty-five to ten. It seemed that she had fed Fritzy double rations and left the house four years ago. Maybe five. She thought she heard an approaching engine, then decided she didn't. She wished the wind wasn't blowing so hard, but wish in one hand and shit in the other, see which one fills up first. It was a saying no Knitting Society lady had ever voiced — Doreen Marquis and her friends were more into things like *soonest begun, soonest done* — but it was a true saying, just the same.

Maybe he really *was* going on a trip, Sunday night or not. Maybe she was still going to be here when the sun came up, chilled to her already aching bones by the constant wind combing this lonely hilltop where she was crazy to be.

No, he's the crazy one. Remember how he danced? His shadow dancing on the wall behind him? Remember how he sang? His squalling voice? You wait for him, Tessa Jean. You wait until hell freezes over. You've come too far to turn back.

She was afraid of that, actually.

It can't be a decorous drawing-room murder. You understand that, don't you?

She did. This particular killing — if she was able to bring it off — would be more *Death Wish* than *The Willow Grove Knitting Society Goes Backstage*. He would pull in, hopefully right up to the cab-over she was hiding behind. He would douse the lights of the pickup, and before his eyes could adjust—

It wasn't the wind this time. She recognized the badly tuned thump of the engine even before the head-lights splashed up the curve of the drive. Tess got on one knee and yanked the brim of her cap down so the wind wouldn't blow it off. She would have to approach, and that meant her timing would have to be exquisite. If she tried to shoot him from ambush, she would quite likely miss, even at close range; the gun instructor had told her she could only count on the Lemon Squeezer at ten feet or less. He had recommended she buy a more reliable handgun, but she never had. And getting close enough to make sure of killing him wasn't all. She had to make sure it was Strehlke in the truck, and not the brother or some friend.

I have no plan.

But it was too late to plan, because it was the truck and when the pole light came on, she saw the brown cap with the bleach-splatters on it. She also saw him wince against the glare, as she had, and knew he was momentarily blinded. It was now or not at all.

I am the Courageous Woman.

With no plan, without even thinking, she walked around the back of the cab-over, not running but taking big, calm strides. The wind gusted around her, flapping her cargo pants. She opened the passenger door and saw the ring with the red stone on his hand. He was grabbing a paper bag with the shape of a square box inside it. Beer, probably a twelve-pack. He turned toward her and something terrible happened: she divided in two. The Courageous Woman saw the animal that had raped her, choked her, and put her in a pipe with two other rotting bodies. Tess saw the slightly broader face and lines around the mouth and eyes that hadn't been there on Friday afternoon. But even as she was registering these things, the Lemon Squeezer barked twice in her hand. The first bullet punctured Strehlke's throat, just below the chin. The second opened a black hole above his bushy right eyebrow and shattered the driver's side window. He fell backward against the door, the hand that had been grasping the top of the paper bag dropping away. He gave a monstrous whole-body twitch, and the hand with the ring on it thudded against the middle of the steering wheel, honking the horn. Inside the house, the dog began to bark again.

'No, it's him!' She stood at the open door with the gun in her hand, staring in. '*It's got to be him.*'

She rushed around the front of the pickup, lost her balance, went to one knee, got up, and yanked open the driver's side door. Strehlke fell out and hit his dead head on the smooth asphalt of his driveway. His hat fell off. His right eye, pulled out of true by the bullet that had entered his head just above it, stared up at the moon. The left one stared at Tess. And it wasn't the face that finally convinced her – the face with lines on it she was seeing for the very first time, the face pitted with old acne scars that hadn't been there on Friday afternoon.

Was he big or real *big?* Betsy Neal had asked.

Real big, Tess had replied, and he had been . . . but not as big as this man. Her rapist had been six-six, she had thought when he got out of the truck (*this* truck, she was in no doubt about that). Deep in the belly, thick in the thighs, and as wide as a doorway. But this man had to be at least six-*nine*. She had come hunting a giant and killed a leviathan.

'Oh my God,' Tess said, and the wind whipped her words away. 'Oh my dear God, what have I done?'

'You killed me, Tess,' the man on the ground said . . . and that certainly made sense, given the hole in his head and the one in his throat. 'You went and killed Big Driver, just like you meant to.'

The strength left her muscles. She went to her knees beside him. Overhead, the moon beamed down from the roaring sky.

'The ring,' she whispered. 'The hat. The *truck.*'

'He wears the ring and the hat when he goes hunting,' Big Driver said. 'And he drives the pickup. When he goes hunting, I'm on the road in a Red Hawk cab-over and if anyone sees him – especially if he's sitting down – they think they're seeing me.'

'Why would he do that?' Tess asked the dead man. 'You're his *brother*.'

'Because he's crazy,' Big Driver said patiently.

'And because it worked before,' Doreen Marquis said. 'When they were younger and Lester got in trouble with the police. The question is whether Roscoe Strehlke committed suicide because of that first trouble, or because Ramona made big brother Al take the blame for it. Or maybe Roscoe was going to tell and Ramona killed him. Made it look like suicide. Which way was it, Al?'

But on this subject Al was quiet. Dead quiet, in fact.

'I'll tell you how I think it was,' Doreen said in the moonlight. 'I think Ramona knew that if your little brother wound up in an interrogation room with an even half-smart policeman, he might confess to something a lot worse than touching a girl on the schoolbus or peeking into cars on the local lovers' lane or whatever ten-cent crime it was he'd been accused of. I think she talked *you* into taking the blame, and she talked her husband into dummying up. Or browbeat him into it, that's more like it. And either because the police never asked the girl to make a positive identification or because she wouldn't press charges, they got away with it.'

Al said nothing.

Tess thought, *I'm kneeling here talking in imaginary voices. I've lost my mind.*

Yet part of her knew she was trying to *keep* her mind. The only way to do it was to understand, and she thought the story she was telling in Doreen's voice was either true or close to true. It was based on guesswork and slopped-on deduction, but it made sense. It fit in with what Ramona had said in her last moments.

You stupid cunt, you don't know what you're talking about.

And: *You don't understand. It's a mistake.*

It was a mistake, all right. Everything she'd done tonight had been a mistake.

No, not everything. She was in on it. She knew.

'Did *you* know?' Tess asked the man she had killed. She reached out to grab Strehlke's arm, then drew away. It would be still warm under his sleeve. Still thinking it was alive. '*Did* you?'

He didn't answer.

'Let me try,' Doreen said. And in her kindliest, you-can-tell-me-everything old lady voice, the one that always worked in the books, she asked: 'How *much* did you know, Mr Driver?'

'I sometimes suspected,' he said. 'Mostly I didn't think about it. I had a business to run.'

'Did you ever ask your mother?'

'I might have,' he said, and Tess thought his strangely cocked right eye evasive. But in that wild moonlight, who could tell about such things? Who could tell for sure?

'When girls disappeared? Is that when you asked?'

To this Big Driver made no reply, perhaps because Doreen had begun to sound like Fritzy. And like Tom the TomTom, of course.

'But there was never any proof, was there?' This time it was Tess herself. She wasn't sure he would answer her voice, but he did.

'No. No proof.'

'And you didn't *want* proof, did you?'

No answer this time, so Tess got up and walked unsteadily to the bleach-spattered brown hat, which had blown across the driveway and onto the lawn. Just as she picked it up, the pole light went off again. Inside, the dog stopped barking. This made her think of Sherlock Holmes, and standing there in the windy moonlight, Tess heard herself voicing the saddest chuckle to ever come from a human throat. She took off her hat, stuffed it into her jacket pocket, and put his on in its place. It was too big for her, so she took it off again long enough to adjust the strap in back. She returned to the man she had killed, the one she judged perhaps not quite innocent . . . but surely too innocent to deserve the punishment the Courageous Woman had meted out.

She tapped the brim of the brown hat and asked, 'Is this the one you wear when you go on the road?' Knowing it wasn't.

Strehlke didn't answer, but Doreen Marquis, doyenne of the Knitting Society, did. 'Of course not. When you're driving for Red Hawk, you wear a Red Hawk cap, don't you, dear?'

'Yes,' Strehlke said.

'And you don't wear your ring, either, do you?'

'No. Too gaudy for customers. Not businesslike. And what if someone at one of those skanky truck-stops – someone too drunk or stoned to know better – saw it and thought it was real? No one would risk mugging me, I'm too big and strong for that – at least I was until tonight – but someone might shoot me. And I don't deserve to be shot. Not for a fake ring, and not for the terrible things my brother might have done.'

'And you and your brother never drive for the company at the same time, do you, dear?'

'No. When he's out on the road, I mind the office. When I'm out on the road, he . . . well. I guess you know what he does when I'm out on the road.'

'You should have *told*!' Tess screamed down at him. 'Even if you only suspected, you should have *told*!'

'He was scared,' Doreen said in her kindly voice. 'Weren't you, dear?'

'Yes,' Al said. 'I was scared.'

'Of your brother?' Tess asked, either unbelieving or not wanting to believe. 'Scared of your *kid brother*?'

'Not him,' Al Strehlke said. 'Her.'

39

When Tess got back in her car and started the motor, Tom said: 'There was no way you could know, Tess. And it all happened so fast.'

That was true, but it ignored the central looming fact: by going after her rapist like a vigilante in a movie, she had sent herself to hell.

She raised the gun to her temple, then lowered it again. She couldn't, not now. She still had an obligation to the women in the pipe, and any other women who might join them if Lester Strehlke escaped. And after what she had just done, it was more important than ever that he not escape.

She had one more stop to make. But not in her Expedition.

40

The driveway at 101 Township Road wasn't long, and it wasn't paved. It was just a pair of ruts with bushes growing close enough to scrape the sides of the blue F-150 pickup truck as she drove it up to the little house. Nothing neat about this one; this one was a huddled old creep-manse that could have been straight out of *The Texas Chainsaw Massacre*. How life did imitate art, sometimes. And the cruder the art, the closer the imitation.

Tess made no attempt at stealth – why bother to kill the headlights when Lester Strehlke would know the sound of his brother's truck almost as well as the sound of his brother's voice?

She was still wearing the bleach-splattered brown cap Big Driver wore when he wasn't on the road, the lucky cap that turned out to be unlucky in the end. The ring with the fake ruby stone was far too big for any of her fingers, so she had put it into the left front pocket of her cargo pants. Little Driver had dressed and driven as his big brother when he went out hunting, and while he might never have time enough (or brains enough) to appreciate the irony of his last victim coming to him with the same accessories, Tess did.

She parked by the back door, turned off the engine, and got out. She carried the gun in one hand. The door was unlocked. She stepped into a shed that smelled of beer and spoiled food. A single sixty-watt bulb hung from the ceiling on a length of dirty cord. Straight ahead were four overflowing plastic garbage cans, the thirty-two-gallon kind you could buy at Walmart. Behind them, stacked against the shed wall, were what looked like five years' worth of *Uncle Henry's* swap guide. To the left was another door, up a single step. It would lead to the kitchen. It had an old-fashioned latch rather than a knob. The door squalled on unoiled hinges when she depressed the latch and pushed it open. An hour ago, such a squall would have terrified her into immobility. Now it didn't bother her in the slightest. She had work to do. That was all it came down to, and it was a relief to be free of all that emotional baggage. She stepped into the smell of whatever greasy meat Little Driver had fried for his supper. She could hear a TV laugh-track. Some sitcom. *Seinfeld*, she thought.

'What the hell are you doing here?' Lester Strehlke called from the vicinity of the laugh track. 'I ain't got but a beer and a half left, if that's what you came for. I'm gonna drink up and then go to bed.' She followed the sound of his voice. 'If you'da called, I coulda saved you the tr—'

She came into the room. He saw her. Tess hadn't speculated on what his reaction might be to the reappearance of his last victim, carrying a gun and wearing the hat Lester himself wore when his urges came over him. Even if she had, she could never have predicted the extremity of the one she saw. His mouth dropped open, and then his entire face froze. The can of beer he was holding dropped from his hand and fell into his lap, spraying foam onto his only article of clothing, a pair of yellowing Jockey shorts.

He's seeing a ghost, she thought as she walked toward him, raising the gun. *Good*.

There was time to see that, although the living room was a bachelor mess and there were no snowglobes or cutie-poo figurines, the TV-watching setup was the same as the one at his mother's house on Lacemaker Lane: the La-Z-Boy, the TV tray (here holding a final unopened can of Pabst Blue Ribbon and a bag of Doritos instead of Diet Coke and Cheez Doodles), the same *TV Guide*, the one with Simon Cowell on it.

'You're dead,' he whispered.

'No,' Tess replied. She put the barrel of the Lemon Squeezer against the side of his head. He made one feeble effort to grab her wrist, but it was far too little and much too late. 'That's you.'

She pulled the trigger. Blood came out of his ear and his head snapped briskly to the side. He looked like a man trying to free up a kink in his neck. On the TV, George Costanza said, 'I was in the pool, I was in the pool.' The audience laughed.

41

It was almost midnight, and the wind was blowing harder than ever. When it gusted, Lester Strehlke's whole house shook, and each time Tess thought of the little pig who had built his house out of sticks.

The little piggy who had lived in this one would never have to worry about his shitty house blowing away, because he was dead in his La-Z-Boy. *And he wasn't a little piggy, anyway*, Tess thought. *He was a big bad wolf.*

She was sitting in the kitchen, writing on the pages of a grimy Blue Horse tablet she had found in Strehlke's upstairs bedroom. There were four rooms on the second floor, but the bedroom was the only one not stuffed with junk, everything from iron bedsteads to an Evinrude boat-motor that looked as if it might have been dropped from the top of a five-story building. Because it would take weeks or months to go through those caches of the useless, the worthless, and the pointless, Tess turned all her attention on Strehlke's bedroom and searched it carefully. The Blue Horse tablet was a bonus. She had found what she was looking for in an old travel-tote pushed to the very back of the closet shelf, where it had been camouflaged – not very successfully – with old issues of *National Geographic*. In it was a tangle of women's underwear. Her own panties were on top. Tess put them in her pocket and, packrat-like, replaced them with the coil of yellow boatline. Nobody would be surprised to find rope in a rapist-killer's suitcase of trophy lingerie. Besides, she would not be needing it.

'Tonto,' said the Lone Ranger, *'our work here is done.'*

What she wrote, as *Seinfeld* gave way to *Frasier* and *Frasier* gave way to the local news (one Chicopee resident had won the lottery and another had suffered a broken back after falling from a scaffolding, so *that* balanced out), was a confession in the form of a letter. As she reached page five, the TV news gave way to an apparently endless commercial for Almighty Cleanse. Danny Vierra was saying, 'Some Americans have a bowel movement only

once every two or three *days*, and because this has gone
on for years, *they believe it's normal!* Any doctor worth his
salt will tell you *it's not!*'

The letter was headed *TO THE PROPER
AUTHORITIES*, and the first four pages consisted of a
single paragraph. In her head it sounded like a scream.
Her hand was tired, and the ballpoint pen she'd found in
a kitchen drawer (RED HAWK TRUCKING printed in
fading gilt on the barrel) was showing signs of drying up,
but she was, thank God, almost done. While Little Driver
went on not watching TV from where he sat in his
La-Z-Boy, she at last started a new paragraph at the top
of page five.

> *I will not make excuses for what I have done. Nor
> can I say that I did it while of unsound mind. I was
> furious and I made a mistake. It's that simple. Under
> other circumstances — those less terrible, I mean — I
> might say, 'It was a natural mistake, the two of them
> look almost enough alike to be twins.' But these are
> not other circumstances.*
>
> *I have thought of atonement as I sat here, writing
> these pages and listening to his television and to the
> wind — not because I hope for forgiveness, but because
> it seems wrong to do wrong without at least trying
> to balance it out with something right.* (Here Tess
> thought of how the lottery winner and the man
> with the broken back evened out, but the
> concept would be difficult to express when she
> was so tired, and she wasn't sure it was germane,
> anyway.) *I thought of going to Africa and working
> with AIDS victims. I thought about going down to
> New Orleans and volunteering at a homeless shelter
> or a food bank. I thought about going to the Gulf
> to clean oil off birds. I thought of donating the million*

*dollars or so I have put away for my retirement to
some group that works to end violence against women.
There must be such a society in Connecticut, perhaps
even several of them.*

*But then I thought of Doreen Marquis, from the
Knitting Society, and what she says once in every
book . . .*

What Doreen said at least once in every book was
*murderers always overlook the obvious. You may depend on it,
dears.* And even as Tess wrote about atonement, she realized it would be impossible. Because Doreen was absolutely
right.

Tess had worn a cap so that she wouldn't leave hair
that could be analyzed for DNA. She had worn gloves
which she had never taken off, even while driving Alvin
Strehlke's pickup. It was not too late to burn this confession in Lester's kitchen woodstove, drive to Brother Alvin's
considerably nicer house (house of bricks instead of house
of sticks), get into her Expedition, and head back to
Connecticut. She could go home, where Fritzy was
waiting. At first glance she looked clear, and it might take
the police a few days to get to her, but get to her they
would. Because while she had been concentrating on the
forensic molehills, she had overlooked the obvious mountain, exactly like the killers in the Knitting Society books.

The obvious mountain had a name: Betsy Neal. A
pretty woman with an oval face, mismatched Picasso eyes,
and a cloud of dark hair. She had recognized Tess, had even
gotten her autograph, but that wasn't the clincher. The
clincher was going to be the bruises on her face (*I hope that
didn't happen here*, Neal had said), and the fact that Tess had
asked about Alvin Strehlke, describing his truck and recog-
nizing the ring when Neal mentioned it. *Like a ruby*, Tess
had agreed.

Neal would see the story on TV or read it in the newspaper — with three dead from the same family, how could she avoid it? — and she would go to the police. The police would come to Tess. They would check the Connecticut gun-registration records as a matter of course and discover that Tess owned a .38 Smith & Wesson revolver known as a Lemon Squeezer. They would ask her to produce it so they could test-fire it and do comparisons to the bullets found in the three victims. And what was she going to say? Was she going to look at them from her blackened eyes and say (in a voice still hoarse from the choking Lester Strehlke had given her) that she lost it? Would she continue to stick to that story even after the dead women were found in the culvert pipe?

Tess picked up her borrowed pen and began writing again.

> . . . what she says once in every book: murderers always overlook the obvious. Doreen also once took a leaf from Dorothy Sayers's book and left a murderer with a loaded gun, telling him to take the honorable way out. I have a gun. My brother Mike is my only surviving close relative. He lives in Taos, New Mexico. I suppose he may inherit my estate. It depends on the legal ramifications of my crimes. If he does, I hope the authorities who find this letter will show it to him, and convey my wish that he donate the bulk to some charitable organization that works with women who have been sexually abused.
>
> I am sorry about Big Driver — Alvin Strehlke. He was not the man who raped me, and Doreen is sure he didn't rape and kill those other women, either.

Doreen? No, *her*. Doreen wasn't real. But Tess was too tired to go back and change it. And what the hell — she was near the end, anyway.

> *For Ramona and that piece of garbage in the other*
> *room, I make no apologies. They are better off dead.*
> *So, of course, am I.*

She paused long enough to look back over the pages and see if there was anything she had forgotten. There didn't appear to be, so she signed her name — her final autograph. The pen ran dry on the last letter and she put it aside.

'Got anything to say, Lester?' she asked.

Only the wind replied, gusting hard enough to make the little house groan in its joints and puff drafts of cold air.

She went back into the living room. She put the hat on his head and the ring on his finger. That was the way she wanted them to find him. There was a framed photo on the TV. In it, Lester and his mother stood with their arms around each other. They were smiling. Just a boy and his mum. She looked at it for awhile, then left.

42

She felt that she should go back to the deserted store where it had happened and finish her business there. She could sit for awhile in the weedy lot, listen to the wind ticking the old sign (YOU LIKE IT IT LIKES YOU), thinking about whatever people think about in the final moments of a life. In her case that would probably be Fritzy. She guessed Patsy would take him, and that would be fine. Cats were survivors. They didn't much care who fed them, as long as the bowl was full.

It wouldn't take long to get to the store at this hour, but it still seemed too far. She was very tired. She decided she would get into Al Strehlke's old truck and do it there. But she didn't want to splatter her painfully written confession with her blood, that seemed very wrong considering all the bloodshed detailed within it, and so—

She took the pages from the Blue Horse tablet into the living room, where the TV played on (a young man who looked like a criminal was now selling a robot floor-washer), and dropped them in Strehlke's lap. 'Hold that for me, Les,' she said.

'No problem,' he replied. She noted that a portion of his diseased brains was now drying on his bony naked shoulder. That was all right.

Tess went out into the windy dark and slowly climbed behind the wheel of the pickup truck. The scream of the hinge when the driver's door swung shut was oddly familiar. But no, not so odd; hadn't she heard it at the store? Yes. She had been trying to do him a favor, because he was going to do her one – he was going to change her tire so she could go home and feed her cat. 'I didn't want his battery to run down,' she said, and laughed.

She put the short barrel of the .38 against her temple, then reconsidered. A shot like that wasn't always effective. She wanted her money to help women who had been hurt, not to pay for her care as she lay unconscious year after year in some home for human vegetables.

The mouth, that was better. Surer.

The barrel was oily against her tongue, and she could feel the small nub of the sight digging into the roof of her mouth.

I've had a good life – pretty good, anyway – and although I made a terrible mistake at the end of it, maybe that won't be held against me if there's something after this.

Ah, but the night wind was very sweet. So were the

fragile fragrances it carried through the half-open driver's side window. It was a shame to leave, but what choice? It was time to go.

Tess closed her eyes, tightened her finger on the trigger, and that was when Tom spoke up. It was strange that he could do that, because Tom was in her Expedition, and the Expedition was at the other brother's house, almost a mile down the road from here. Also, the voice she heard was nothing like the one she usually manufactured for Tom. Nor did it sound like her own. It was a cold voice. And she – she had a gun in her mouth. She couldn't talk at all.

'She was never a very good detective, was she?'

She took it out. 'Who? Doreen?'

In spite of everything, she was shocked.

'Who else, Tessa Jean? And why *would* she be a good one? She came from the old you. Didn't she?'

Tess supposed that was true.

'Doreen believes Big Driver didn't rape and kill those other women. Isn't that what you wrote?'

'*Me*,' Tess said. '*I'm* sure. That's what I meant to write. I was just tired, that's all. And shocked, I suppose.'

'Also guilty.'

'Yes. Also guilty.'

'Do guilty people make good deductions, do you think?'

No. Perhaps they didn't.

'What are you trying to tell me?'

'That you only solved part of the mystery. Before you could solve all of it – *you*, not some cliché-ridden old lady detective – something admittedly unfortunate happened.'

'Unfortunate? Is that what you call it?' From a great distance, Tess heard herself laugh. Somewhere the wind was making a loose gutter click against an eave. It sounded like the 7Up sign at the deserted store.

'Before you *shoot* yourself,' the new, strange Tom said (he was sounding more female all the time), 'why don't you *think* for yourself? But not here.'

'Where, then?'

Tom didn't answer this question, and didn't have to. What he said was, 'And take that fucking confession with you.'

Tess got out of the truck and went back inside Lester Strehlke's house. She stood in the dead man's kitchen, thinking. She did it aloud, in Tom's voice (which sounded more like her own all the time). Doreen seemed to have taken a hike.

'Al's housekey will be on the ring with his ignition key,' Tom said, 'but there's the dog. You don't want to forget the dog.'

No, that would be bad. Tess went to Lester's refrigerator. After a little rummaging, she found a package of hamburger at the back of the bottom shelf. She used an issue of *Uncle Henry's* to double-wrap it, then went back into the living room. She plucked the confession from Strehlke's lap doing it gingerly, very aware that the part of him that had hurt her – the part that had gotten three people killed tonight – lay just beneath the pages. 'I'm taking your ground chuck, but don't hold it against me. I'm doing you a favor. It smells spunky-going-on-rotten.'

'A thief as well as a murderer,' Little Driver said in his droning deadvoice. 'Isn't that nice.'

'Shut up, Les,' she said, and left.

43

Before you shoot *yourself, why don't you* think *for yourself?*

As she drove the old pickup back down the windy road to Alvin Strehlke's house, she tried to do that. She was starting to think Tom, even when he wasn't in the vehicle with her, was a better detective than Doreen Marquis on her best day.

'I'll keep it short,' Tom said. 'If you don't think Al Strehlke was part of it – and I mean a *big* part – you're crazy.'

'Of course I'm crazy,' she replied. 'Why else would I be trying to convince myself that I didn't shoot the wrong man when I know I *did*?'

'That's guilt talking, not logic,' Tom replied. He sounded maddeningly smug. 'He was no innocent little lamb, not even a half-black sheep. Wake up, Tessa Jean. They weren't just brothers, they were partners.'

'*Business* partners.'

'Brothers are never just business partners. It's always more complicated than that. Especially when you've got a woman like Ramona for a mother.'

Tess turned up Al Strehlke's smoothly paved driveway. She supposed Tom could be right about that. She knew one thing: Doreen and her Knitting Society friends had never met a woman like Ramona Norville.

The pole light went on. The dog started up: *yark-yark, yarkyarkyark*. Tess waited for the light to go out and the dog to quiet down.

'There's no way I'll ever know for sure, Tom.'

'You can't be certain of that unless you look.'

'Even if he knew, *he wasn't the one who raped me*.'

Tom was silent for a moment. She thought he'd given up. Then he said, 'When a person does a bad thing and another person knows but doesn't stop it, they're equally guilty.'

'In the eyes of the law?'

'Also in the eyes of *me*. Say it was just Lester who did the hunting, the raping, and the killing. I don't think so, but say it was. If big brother knew and said nothing, that makes him worth killing. In fact, I'd say bullets were too good for him. Impaling on a hot poker would be closer to justice.'

Tess shook her head wearily and touched the gun on the seat. One bullet left. If she had to use it on the dog (and really, what was one more killing among friends), she would have to hunt for another gun, unless she meant to try and hang herself, or something. But guys like the Strehlkes usually had firearms. That was the beauty part, as Ramona would have said.

'If he knew, yes. But an if that big didn't deserve a bullet in the head. The mother, yes — on that score, the earrings were all the proof I needed. But there's no proof here.'

'Really?' Tom's voice was so low Tess could barely hear it. 'Go see.'

44

The dog didn't bark when she clumped up the steps, but she could picture it standing just inside the door with its head down and its teeth bared.

'Goober?' What the hell, it was as good a name for a country dog as any. 'My name's Tess. I have some hamburger for you. I also have a gun with one bullet in it. I'm going to open the door now. If I were you, I'd choose the meat. Okay? Is it a deal?'

Still no barking. Maybe it took the pole light to set him off. Or a juicy female burglar. Tess tried one key, then another. No good. Those two were probably for the trucking office. The third one turned in the lock, and she opened the door before she could lose her courage. She had been visualizing a bulldog or a Rottweiler or a pit bull with red eyes and slavering jaws. What she saw was a Jack Russell terrier who was looking at her hopefully and thumping its tail.

Tess put the gun in her jacket pocket and stroked the dog's head. 'Good God,' she said. 'To think I was *terrified* of you.'

'No need to be,' Goober said. 'Say, where's Al?'

'Don't ask,' she said. 'Want some hamburger? I warn you, it may have gone off.'

'Give it to me, baby,' Goober said.

Tess fed him a chunk of the hamburger, then came in, closed the door, and turned on the lights. Why not? It was only her and Goober, after all.

Alvin Strehlke had kept a neater house than his younger brother. The floors and walls were clean, there were no stacks of *Uncle Henry's* swap guide, and she actually saw a few books on the shelves. There were also several clusters of Hummel figures, and a large framed photo of Momzilla on the wall. Tess found that a touch suggestive, but it was hardly proof positive. Of anything. *If there was a photo of Richard Widmark in his famous Tommy Udo role, that might be different.*

'What are you smiling about?' Goober asked. 'Want to share?'

'Actually, no,' Tess said. 'Where should we start?'

'I don't know,' Goober said. 'I'm just the dog. How about some more of that tasty cow?'

Tess fed him some more meat. Goober got up on his hind legs and turned around twice. Tess wondered if she were going insane.

'Tom? Anything to say?'

'You found your underpants at the other brother's house, right?'

'Yes, and I took them. They're torn . . . and I'd never want to wear them again even if they weren't . . . but they're *mine*.'

'And what else did you find besides a bunch of undies?'

'What do you mean, what else?'

But Tom didn't need to tell her that. It wasn't a question of what she had found; it was a question of what she hadn't: no purse and no keys. Lester Strehlke had probably thrown the keys into the woods. It was what Tess herself would have done in his place. The bag was a different matter. It had been a Kate Spade, very pricey, and inside was a sewn-in strip of silk with her name on it. If the bag – and the stuff in the bag – wasn't at Lester's house, and if he didn't throw it into the woods with her keys, where is it?

'I vote for here,' Tom said. 'Let's look around.'

'Meat!' Goober cried, and did another pirouette.

45

Where should she start?

'Come on,' Tom said. 'Men keep most of their secrets in one of two places: the study or the bedroom. Doreen might not know that, but you do. And this house doesn't have a study.'

She went into Al Strehlke's bedroom (trailed by Goober), where she found an extra-long double bed made up in no-nonsense military style. Tess looked under it. Nada. She started to turn toward the closet, paused, then pivoted back to the bed. She lifted the mattress. Looked. After five seconds – maybe ten – she uttered a single word in a dry flat voice.

'Jackpot.'

Lying on the box spring were three ladies' handbags. The one in the middle was a cream-colored clutch that Tess would have recognized anywhere. She flipped it open. There was nothing inside but some Kleenex and an eyebrow pencil with a cunning little lash-comb hidden in the top half. She looked for the silk strip with her

name on it, but it was gone. It had been removed carefully, but she saw one tiny cut in the fine Italian leather
where the stitches had been unpicked.

'Yours?' Tom asked.

'You know it is.'

'What about the eyebrow pencil?'

'They sell those things by the thousands in drugstores
all over Amer—'

'*Is it yours?*'

'Yes. It is.'

'Are you convinced yet?'

'I . . .' Tess swallowed. She was feeling something, but
she wasn't sure what it was. Relief? Horror? 'I guess I
am. But *why*? Why *both* of them?'

Tom didn't say. He didn't need to. Doreen might not
know (or want to admit it if she did, because the old
ladies who followed her adventures didn't like the ooky
stuff), but Tess supposed she did. Because Mommy fucked
both of them up. That's what a psychiatrist would say.
Lester was the rapist; Al was the fetishist who participated
vicariously: Maybe he even helped with one or both of
the women in the pipe. She'd never know for sure.

'It would probably take until dawn to search the
whole house,' Tom said, 'but you can search the rest of
this room, Tessa Jean. He probably destroyed everything
from the purse – cut up the credit cards and tossed them
in the Colewich River, would be my guess – but you
have to make sure, because anything with your name on
it would lead the police right to your door. Start with
the closet.'

Tess didn't find her credit cards or anything else
belonging to her in the closet, but she did find something.
It was on the top shelf. She got off the chair she'd been
standing on and studied it with growing dismay: a stuffed
duck that might have been some child's favorite toy. One

of its eyes was missing and its synthetic fur was matted. That fur was actually gone in places, as if the duck had been petted half to death.

On the faded yellow beak was a dark maroon splash. 'Is that what I think it is?' Tom asked.

'Oh Tom, I think so.'

'The bodies you saw in the culvert . . . could one of them have been a child's body?'

No, neither of them had been that small. But maybe the culvert running beneath Stagg Road hadn't been the Strehlke brothers' only body dump.

'Put it back on the shelf. Leave it for the police to find. You need to make sure he doesn't have a computer with stuff on it about you. Then you need to get the hell out of here.'

Something cold and wet nuzzled Tess's hand. She almost screamed. It was Goober, looking up at her with bright eyes.

'More meat!' Goober said, and Tess gave him some.

'If Al Strehlke has a computer,' Tess said, 'you can be sure it's password-protected. And his probably won't be open for me to poke around in.'

'Then take it and throw it in the goddam river when you go home. Let it sleep with the fishes.'

But there was no computer.

At the door, Tess fed Goober the rest of the hamburger. He would probably puke it all up on the rug, but that wasn't going to bother Big Driver.

Tom said, 'Are you satisfied, Tessa Jean? Are you satisfied you didn't kill an innocent man?'

She supposed she must be, because suicide no longer seemed like an option. 'What about Betsy Neal, Tom? What about her?'

Tom didn't answer . . . and once again didn't need to. Because, after all, he was she.

Wasn't she?

Tess wasn't entirely sure about that. And did it matter, as long as she knew what to do next? As for tomorrow, it was another day. Scarlett O'Hara had been right about that much.

What mattered most was that the police had to know about the bodies in the culvert. If only because somewhere there were friends and relatives who were still wondering. Also because . . .

'Because the stuffed duck says there might be more.'

That was her own voice.

And that was all right.

46

At seven-thirty the next morning, after less than three hours of broken, nightmare-haunted sleep, Tess booted up her office computer. But not to write. Writing was the farthest thing from her mind.

Was Betsy Neal single? Tess thought so. She had seen no wedding ring that day in Neal's office, and while she might have missed that, there had been no family pictures, either. The only picture she could remember seeing was a framed photo of Barack Obama . . . and *he* was already married. So yes — Betsy Neal was probably divorced or single. And probably unlisted. In which case, a computer search would do her no good at all. Tess supposed she could go to The Stagger Inn and find her there . . . but she didn't *want* to go back to The Stagger. Ever again.

'Why are you buying trouble?' Fritzy said from the windowsill. 'At least check the telephone listings for Colewich. And what's that I smell on you? Is that *dog*?'

'Yes. That's Goober.'

'Traitor,' Fritzy said contemptuously.

Her search turned up an even dozen Neals. One

was an E Neal. E for Elizabeth? There was one way to
find out.

With no hesitation – that would almost certainly
have caused her to lose her courage – Tess punched in
the number. She was sweating, and her heart was beating
rapidly.

The phone rang once. Twice.

*It's probably not her. It could be an Edith Neal. An Edwina
Neal. Even an Elvira Neal.*

Three times.

*If it is Betsy Neal's phone, she's probably not even there.
She's probably on vacation in the Catskills—*

Four times.

*—or shacked up with one of the Zombie Bakers, how
about that? The lead guitarist. They probably sing 'Can Your
Pussy Do the Dog?' together in the shower after they—*

The phone was picked up, and Tess recognized the
voice in her ear at once.

'Hello, you've reached Betsy, but I can't come to the
phone right now. There's a beep coming, and you know
what to do when you hear it. Have a nice day.'

I had a bad day, thanks, and last night was ever so much w—

The beep came, and Tess heard herself talking before
she was even aware she meant to. 'Hello, Ms Neal, this
is Tessa Jean calling – the Willow Grove Lady? We met
at The Stagger Inn. You gave me back my TomTom and
I signed an autograph for your gran. You saw how
marked up I was and I told you some lies. It wasn't a
boyfriend, Ms Neal.' Tess began to speak faster, afraid
that the message tape would run out before she
finished . . . and she discovered she badly wanted to
finish. 'I was raped and that was bad, but then I tried
to make it right and . . . I . . . I have to talk to you
about it because—'

There was a click on the line and then Betsy Neal

herself was in Tess's ear. 'Start again,' she said, 'but go slow.
I just woke up and I'm still half asleep.'

47

They met for lunch on the Colewich town common.
They sat on a bench near the bandstand. Tess didn't think
she was hungry, but Betsy Neal forced a sandwich on her,
and Tess found herself eating it in large bites that made
her think of Goober snarfing up Lester Strehlke's
hamburger.

'Start at the beginning,' Betsy said. She was calm,
Tess thought – almost preternaturally so. 'Start from the
beginning and tell me everything.'

Tess began with the invitation from Books & Brown
Baggers. Betsy Neal said little, only occasionally adding
an 'Uh-huh' or 'Okay' to let Tess know she was still
following the story. Telling it was thirsty work. Luckily,
Betsy had also brought two cans of Dr Brown's cream
soda. Tess took one and drank it greedily.

When she finished, it was past one in the afternoon.
The few people who had come to the common to eat
their lunches were gone. There were two women walking
babies in strollers, but they were a good distance away.

'Let me get this straight,' Betsy Neal said. 'You were
going to kill yourself, and then some phantom voice told
you to go back to Alvin Strehlke's house, instead.'

'Yes,' Tess replied. 'Where I found my purse. And the
duck with the blood on it.'

'Your panties you found in the younger brother's
house.'

'Little Driver's, yes. They're in my Expedition. And
the purse. Do you want to see them?'

'No. What about the gun?'

'That's in the car, too. With one bullet left in it.' She

looked at Neal curiously, thinking: *The girl with the Picasso eyes*. 'Aren't you afraid of me? You're the one loose end. The only one I can think of, anyway.'

'We're in a public park, Tess. Also, I've got quite the confession on my answering machine at home.'

Tess blinked. Something else she hadn't thought of.

'Even if you somehow managed to kill me without those two young mothers over there noticing—'

'I'm not up for killing anyone else. Here or anywhere.'

'Good to know. Because even if you took care of me and my answering machine tape, sooner or later someone would find the cabdriver who brought you out to The Stagger on Saturday morning. And when the police got to you, they'd find you wearing a load of incriminating bruises.'

'Yes,' Tess said, touching the worst of them. 'That's true. So what now?'

'For one thing, I think you'd be wise to stay out of sight as much as you can until your pretty face looks pretty again.'

'I think I'm covered there,' Tess said, and told Betsy the tale she had confabulated for Patsy McClain's benefit.

'That's pretty good.'

'Ms Neal . . . Betsy . . . do you believe me?'

'Oh yes,' she said, almost absently. 'Now listen. Are you listening?'

Tess nodded.

'We're a couple of women having a little picnic in the park, and that's fine. But after today, we're not going to see each other again. Right?'

'If you say so,' Tess said. Her brain felt the way her jaw did after the dentist gave her a healthy shot of novocaine.

'I do. And you need to have another story made up and ready, just in case the cops talk to either the limo driver who took you home—'

'Manuel. His name was Manuel.'

'—or the taxi driver who took you out to The Stagger on Saturday morning. I don't think anybody will make the connection between you and the Strehlkes as long as none of your ID shows up, but when the story breaks, this is going to be big news and we can't assume the investigation won't touch you.' She leaned forward and tapped Tess once above the left breast. 'I'm counting on you to make sure that it never touches *me*. Because I don't deserve that.'

No. She absolutely didn't.

'What story could you tell the cops, hon? Something good without me in it. Come on, you're the writer.'

Tess thought for a full minute. Betsy let her.

'I'd say Ramona Norville told me about the Stagg Road shortcut after my appearance – which is true – and that I saw The Stagger Inn when I drove by. I'd say I stopped for dinner a few miles down the road, then decided to go back and have a few drinks. Listen to the band.'

'That's good. They're called—'

'I know what they're called,'Tess said. Maybe the novocaine was wearing off. 'I'd say I met some guys, drank a bunch, and decided I was too blitzed to drive. You're not in this story, because you don't work nights. I could also say—'

'Never mind, that's enough. You're pretty good at this stuff once you get cooking. Just don't embellish too much.'

'I won't,'Tess said. 'And this is one story I might not ever have to tell. Once they have the Strehlkes and the Strehlkes' victims, they'll be looking for a killer a lot different than a little book-writing lady like me.'

Betsy Neal smiled. 'Little book-writing lady, my ass. You're one bad bitch.' Then she saw the look of startled alarm on Tess's face. 'What? What *now*?'

'They *will* be able to tie the women in the pipe to the Strehlkes, won't they? At least to Lester?'

'Did he put on a rubber before he raped you?'

'No. God, no. His stuff was still on my thighs when I got home. And inside me.' She shuddered.

'Then he'll have gone in bareback with the others. Plenty of evidence. They'll put it together. As long as those bad boys really got rid of your ID, you should be home and dry. And there's no sense worrying about what you can't control, is there?'

'No.'

'As for you . . . not planning on going home and cutting your wrists in the bathtub, are you? Or using that last bullet?'

'No.' Tess thought of how sweet the night air had smelled as she sat in the truck with the short barrel of the Lemon Squeezer in her mouth. 'No, I'm good.'

'Then it's time for you to leave. I'll sit here a little longer.'

Tess started to get off the bench, then sat down again. 'There's something I need to know. You're making yourself an accessory after the fact. Why would you do that for a woman you don't even know? A woman you only met once?'

'Would you believe because my gran loves your books and would be very disappointed if you went to jail for a triple murder?'

'Not a bit,' Tess said.

Betsy said nothing for a moment. She picked up her can of Dr Brown's, then put it back down again. 'Lots of women get raped, wouldn't you say? I mean, you're not unique in that respect, are you?'

No, Tess knew she was not unique in that respect, but knowing it did not make the pain and shame any less. Nor would it help with her nerves while she waited for the results of the AIDS test she'd soon be taking.

Betsy smiled. There was nothing pleasant about it.

Or pretty. 'Women all over the world are being raped as we speak. Girls, too. Some who undoubtedly have favorite stuffed toys. Some are killed, and some survive. Of the survivors, how many do you think report what happened to them?'

Tess shook her head.

'I don't know, either,' Betsy said, 'but I know what the National Crime Victimization Survey says, because I googled it. Sixty percent of rapes go unreported, according to them. Three in every five. I think that might be low, but who can say for sure? Outside of math classes, it's hard to prove a negative. Impossible, really.'

'Who raped you?' Tess asked.

'My stepfather. I was twelve. He held a butter knife to my face while he did it. I kept still — I was scared — but the knife slipped when he came. Probably not on purpose, but who can say?'

Betsy pulled down the lower lid of her left eye with her left hand. The right she cupped beneath it, and the glass eye rolled neatly into that palm. The empty socket was mildly red and uptilted, seeming to stare out at the world with surprise.

'The pain was . . . well, there's no way to describe pain like that, not really. It seemed like the end of the world to me. There was blood, too. Lots. My mother took me to the doctor. She said I was to tell him I was running in my stocking feet and slipped on the kitchen linoleum because she'd just waxed it. That I pitched forward and put out my eye on the corner of the kitchen counter. She said the doctor would want to speak to me alone, and she was depending on me. "I know he did a terrible thing to you," she said, "but if people find out, they'll blame me. Please, baby, do this one thing for me and I'll make sure nothing bad ever happens to you again." So that's what I did.'

'And did it happen again?'

'Three or four more times. And I always kept still, because I only had one eye left to donate to the cause. Listen, are we done here or not?'

Tess moved to embrace her, but Betsy cringed back — *like a vampire who sees a crucifix*, Tess thought.

'Don't do that,' Betsy said.

'But—'

'I know, I know, mucho thanks, solidarity, sisterhood forever, blah-blah-blah. I don't like to be hugged, that's all. Are we done here, or not?'

'We're done.'

'Then go. And I'd throw that gun of yours in the river on your way back home. Did you burn the confession?'

'Yes. You bet.'

Betsy nodded. 'And I'll erase the message you left on my answering machine.'

Tess walked away. She looked back once. Betsy Neal was still sitting on the bench. She had put her eye back in.

48

In her Expedition, Tess realized it might be an extremely good idea to delete her last few journeys from her GPS. She pushed the power button, and the screen brightened. Tom said: 'Hello, Tess. I see we're taking a trip.'

Tess finished making her deletions, then turned the GPS unit off again. No trip, not really; she was only going home. And she thought she could find the way by herself.

FAIR EXTENSION

Streeter only saw the sign because he had to pull over and puke. He puked a lot now, and there was very little warning – sometimes a flutter of nausea, sometimes a brassy taste in the back of his mouth, and sometimes nothing at all; just *urk* and out it came, howdy-do. It made driving a risky proposition, yet he also drove a lot now, partly because he wouldn't be able to by late fall and partly because he had a lot to think about. He had always done his best thinking behind the wheel.

He was out on the Harris Avenue Extension, a broad thoroughfare that ran for two miles beside the Derry County Airport and the attendant businesses: mostly motels and warehouses. The Extension was busy during the daytime, because it connected Derry's west and east sides as well as servicing the airport, but in the evening it was nearly deserted. Streeter pulled over into the bike lane, snatched one of his plastic barf-bags from the pile of them on the passenger seat, dropped his face into it, and let fly. Dinner made an encore appearance. Or would have, if he'd had his eyes open. He didn't. Once you'd seen one bellyful of puke, you'd seen them all.

When the puking phase started, there hadn't been pain. Dr Henderson had warned him that would change, and over the last week, it had. Not agony as yet; just a quick lightning-stroke up from the gut and into the throat, like acid indigestion. It came, then faded. But it would get worse. Dr Henderson had told him that, too.

He raised his head from the bag, opened the glove compartment, took out a wire bread-tie, and secured his dinner before the smell could permeate the car. He looked to his right and saw a providential litter basket with a cheerful lop-eared hound on the side and a stenciled message reading **DERRY DAWG SEZ 'PUT LITTER IN ITS PLACE!'**

Streeter got out, went to the Dawg Basket, and disposed of the latest ejecta from his failing body. The summer sun was setting red over the airport's flat (and currently deserted) acreage, and the shadow tacked to his heels was long and grotesquely thin. It was as if it were four months ahead of his body, and already fully ravaged by the cancer that would soon be eating him alive.

He turned back to his car and saw the sign across the road. At first – probably because his eyes were still watering – he thought it said HAIR EXTENSION. Then he blinked and saw it actually said FAIR EXTENSION. Below that, in smaller letters: FAIR PRICE.

Fair extension, fair price. It sounded good, and almost made sense.

There was a gravel area on the far side of the Extension, outside the Cyclone fence marking the county airport's property. Lots of people set up roadside stands there during the busy hours of the day, because it was possible for customers to pull in without getting tailgated (if you were quick and remembered to use your blinker, that was). Streeter had lived his whole life in the little Maine city of Derry, and over the years he'd seen people selling fresh fiddleheads there in the spring, fresh berries and corn on the cob in the summer, and lobsters almost year-round. In mud season, a crazy old guy known as the Snowman took over the spot, selling scavenged knick-knacks that had been lost in the winter and were revealed by the melting snow. Many years ago Streeter had bought a good-looking rag dolly from this man, intending to give it to his daughter May, who had been two or three back then. He made the mistake of telling Janet that he'd gotten it from the Snowman, and she made him throw it away.

'Do you think we can boil a rag doll to kill the germs?' she asked. 'Sometimes I wonder how a smart man like you can be so stupid.'

Well, cancer didn't discriminate when it came to brains. Smart or stupid, he was about ready to leave the game and take off his uniform.

There was a card table set up where the Snowman had once displayed his wares. The pudgy man sitting behind it was shaded from the red rays of the lowering sun by a large yellow umbrella that was cocked at a rakish angle.

Streeter stood in front of his car for a minute, almost got in (the pudgy man had taken no notice of him; he appeared to be watching a small portable TV), and then curiosity got the better of him. He checked for traffic, saw none – the Extension was predictably dead at this hour, all the commuters at home eating dinner and taking their non-cancerous states for granted – and crossed the four empty lanes. His scrawny shadow, the Ghost of Streeter Yet to Come, trailed out behind him.

The pudgy man looked up. 'Hello there,' he said. Before he turned the TV off, Streeter had time to see the guy was watching *Inside Edition*. 'How are we tonight?'

'Well, I don't know about you, but I've been better,' Streeter said. 'Kind of late to be selling, isn't it? Very little traffic out here after rush hour. It's the backside of the airport, you know. Nothing but freight deliveries. Passengers go in on Witcham Street.'

'Yes,' the pudgy man said, 'but unfortunately, the zoning goes against little roadside businesses like mine on the busy side of the airport.' He shook his head at the unfairness of the world. 'I was going to close up and go home at seven, but I had a feeling one more prospect might come by.'

Streeter looked at the table, saw no items for sale

(unless the TV was), and smiled. 'I can't really be a prospect, Mr—?'

'George Elvid,' the pudgy man said, standing and extending an equally pudgy hand.

Streeter shook with him. 'Dave Streeter. And I can't really be a prospect, because I have no idea what you're selling. At first I thought the sign said *hair* extension.'

'Do you *want* a hair extension?' Elvid asked, giving him a critical once-over. 'I ask because yours seems to be thinning.'

'And will soon be gone,' Streeter said. 'I'm on chemo.'

'Oh my. Sorry.'

'Thanks. Although what the point of chemo can be . . .' He shrugged. He marveled at how easy it was to say these things to a stranger. He hadn't even told his kids, although Janet knew, of course.

'Not much chance?' Elvid asked. There was simple sympathy in his voice – no more and no less – and Streeter felt his eyes fill with tears. Crying in front of Janet embarrassed him terribly, and he'd done it only twice. Here, with this stranger, it seemed all right. Nonetheless, he took his handkerchief from his back pocket and swiped his eyes with it. A small plane was coming in for a landing. Silhouetted against the red sun, it looked like a moving crucifix.

'No chance is what I'm hearing,' Streeter said. 'So I guess the chemo is just . . . I don't know . . .'

'Knee-jerk triage?'

Streeter laughed. 'That's it exactly.'

'Maybe you ought to consider trading the chemo for extra painkillers. Or, you could do a little business with me.'

'As I started to say, I can't really be a prospect until I know what you're selling.'

'Oh, well, most people would call it snake-oil,' Elvid

said, smiling and bouncing on the balls of his feet behind his table. Streeter noted with some fascination that, although George Elvid was pudgy, his shadow was as thin and sick-looking as Streeter's own. He supposed everyone's shadow started to look sick as sunset approached, especially in August, when the end of the day was long and lingering and somehow not quite pleasant.

'I don't see the bottles,' Streeter said.

Elvid tented his fingers on the table and leaned over them, looking suddenly businesslike. 'I sell extensions,' he said.

'Which makes the name of this particular road fortuitous.'

'Never thought of it that way, but I suppose you're right. Although sometimes a cigar is just a smoke and a coincidence is just a coincidence. Everyone wants an extension, Mr Streeter. If you were a young woman with a love of shopping, I'd offer you a credit extension. If you were a man with a small penis – genetics can be so cruel – I'd offer you a dick extension.'

Streeter was amazed and amused by the baldness of it. For the first time in a month – since the diagnosis – he forgot he was suffering from an aggressive and extremely fast-moving form of cancer. 'You're kidding.'

'Oh, I'm a great kidder, but I never joke about business. I've sold dozens of dick extensions in my time, and was for awhile known in Arizona as *El Pene Grande*. I'm being totally honest, but, fortunately for me, I neither require nor expect you to believe it. Short men frequently want a height extension. If you *did* want more hair, Mr Streeter, I'd be *happy* to sell you a hair extension.'

'Could a man with a big nose – you know, like Jimmy Durante – get a smaller one?'

Elvid shook his head, smiling. 'Now you're the one who's kidding. The answer is no. If you need a reduction, you have to go somewhere else. I specialize only in extensions, a very American product. I've sold love extensions, sometimes called *potions*, to the lovelorn, loan extensions to the cash-strapped – plenty of those in this economy – time extensions to those under some sort of deadline, and once an eye extension to a fellow who wanted to become an Air Force pilot and knew he couldn't pass the vision test.'

Streeter was grinning, having fun. He would have said having fun was now out of reach, but life was full of surprises.

Elvid was also grinning, as if they were sharing an excellent joke. 'And once,' he said, 'I swung a *reality* extension for a painter – very talented man – who was slipping into paranoid schizophrenia. *That* was expensive.'

'How much? Dare I ask?'

'One of the fellow's paintings, which now graces my home. You'd know the name; famous in the Italian Renaissance. You probably studied him if you took an art appreciation course in college.'

Streeter continued to grin, but he took a step back, just to be on the safe side. He had accepted the fact that he was going to die, but that didn't mean he wanted to do so today, at the hands of a possible escapee from the Juniper Hill asylum for the criminally insane in Augusta. 'So what are we saying? That you're kind of . . . I don't know . . . immortal?'

'Very long-lived, certainly,' Elvid said. 'Which brings us to what I can do for you, I believe. You'd probably like a *life* extension.'

'Can't be done, I suppose?' Streeter asked. Mentally he was calculating the distance back to his car, and how long it would take him to get there.

'Of course it can . . . for a price.'

Streeter, who had played his share of Scrabble in his

time, had already imagined the letters of Elvid's name on tiles and rearranged them. 'Money? Or are we talking about my soul?'

Elvid flapped his hand and accompanied the gesture with a roguish roll of his eyes. 'I wouldn't, as the saying goes, know a soul if it bit me on the buttocks. No, money's the answer, as it usually is. Fifteen percent of your income over the next fifteen years should do it. An agenting fee, you could call it.'

'That's the length of my extension?' Streeter contemplated the idea of fifteen years with wistful greed. It seemed like a very long time, especially when he stacked it next to what actually lay ahead: six months of vomiting, increasing pain, coma, death. Plus an obituary that would undoubtedly include the phrase 'after a long and courageous battle with cancer.' Yada-yada, as they said on *Seinfeld*.

Elvid lifted his hands to his shoulders in an expansive who-knows gesture. 'Might be twenty. Can't say for sure; this is not rocket science. But if you're expecting immortality, fuggeddaboudit. All I sell is fair extension. Best I can do.'

'Works for me,' Streeter said. The guy had cheered him up, and if he needed a straight man, Streeter was willing to oblige. Up to a point, anyway. Still smiling, he extended his hand across the card table. 'Fifteen percent, fifteen years. Although I have to tell you, fifteen percent of an assistant bank manager's salary won't exactly put you behind the wheel of a Rolls-Royce. A Geo, maybe, but—'

'That's not quite all,' Elvid said.

'Of course it isn't,' Streeter said. He sighed and withdrew his hand. 'Mr Elvid, it's been very nice talking to you, you've put a shine on my evening, which I would have thought was impossible, and I hope you get help with your mental prob—'

'Hush, you stupid man,' Elvid said, and although he was still smiling, there was nothing pleasant about it now. He suddenly seemed taller — at least three inches taller — and not so pudgy.

It's the light, Streeter thought. *Sunset light is tricky.* And the unpleasant smell he suddenly noticed was probably nothing but burned aviation fuel, carried to this little graveled square outside the Cyclone fence by an errant puff of wind. It all made sense . . . but he hushed as instructed.

'Why does a man or woman need an extension? Have you ever asked yourself that?'

'Of course I have,' Streeter said with a touch of asperity. 'I work in a bank, Mr Elvid — Derry Savings. People ask me for loan extensions all the time.'

'Then you know that people need *extensions* to compensate for *shortfalls* — short credit, short dick, short sight, et cetera.'

'Yeah, it's a short-ass world,' Streeter said.

'Just so. But even things not there have weight. *Negative* weight, which is the worst kind. Weight lifted from you must go somewhere else. It's simple physics. *Psychic* physics, we could say.'

Streeter studied Elvid with fascination. That momentary impression that the man was taller (and that there were too many teeth inside his smile) had gone. This was just a short, rotund fellow who probably had a green outpatient card in his wallet — if not from Juniper Hill, then from Acadia Mental Health in Bangor. If he *had* a wallet. He certainly had an extremely well-developed delusional geography, and that made him a fascinating study.

'Can I cut to the chase, Mr Streeter?'

'Please.'

'You have to transfer the weight. In words of one

syllable, you have to do the dirty to someone else if the dirty is to be lifted from you.'

'I see.' And he did. Elvid was back on message, and the message was a classic.

'But it can't be just anyone. The old anonymous sacrifice has been tried, and it doesn't work. It has to be someone you hate. Is there someone you hate, Mr Streeter?'

'I'm not too crazy about Kim Jong-il,' Streeter said. 'And I think jail's *way* too good for the evil bastards who blew up the USS *Cole*, but I don't suppose they'll ever—'

'Be serious or begone,' Elvid said, and once again he seemed taller. Streeter wondered if this could be some peculiar side-effect of the medications he was taking.

'If you mean in my personal life, I don't hate anyone. There are people I don't *like* – Mrs Denbrough next door puts out her garbage cans without the lids, and if a wind is blowing, crap ends up all over my law—'

'If I may misquote the late Dino Martino, Mr Streeter, everybody hates somebody sometime.'

'Will Rogers said—'

'He was a rope-twirling fabricator who wore his hat down around his eyes like a little kid playing cowboy. Besides, if you really hate nobody, we can't do business.'

Streeter thought it over. He looked down at his shoes and spoke in a small voice he hardly recognized as his own. 'I suppose I hate Tom Goodhugh.'

'Who is he in your life?'

Streeter sighed. 'My best friend since grammar school.'

There was a moment of silence before Elvid began bellowing laughter. He strode around his card table, clapped Streeter on the back (with a hand that felt cold and fingers that felt long and thin rather than short and pudgy), then strode back to his folding chair. He collapsed into it, still snorting and roaring. His face was red, and the tears streaming down his face also looked red – bloody, actually – in the sunset light.

'*Your best . . . since grammar . . . oh, that's . . .*'

Elvid could manage no more. He went into gales and howls and gut-shaking spasms, his chin (strangely sharp for such a chubby face) nodding and dipping at the innocent (but darkening) summer sky. At last he got himself under control. Streeter thought about offering his handkerchief, and decided he didn't want it on the extension salesman's skin.

'This is excellent, Mr Streeter,' he said. 'We can do business.'

'Gee, that's great,' Streeter said, taking another step back. 'I'm enjoying my extra fifteen years already. But I'm parked in the bike lane, and that's a traffic violation. I could get a ticket.'

'I wouldn't worry about that,' Elvid said. 'As you may have noticed, not even a single *civilian* car has come along since we started dickering, let alone a minion of the Derry PD. Traffic never interferes when I get down to serious dealing with a serious man or woman; I see to it.'

Streeter looked around uneasily. It was true. He could hear traffic over on Witcham Street, headed for Upmile Hill, but here, Derry was utterly deserted. *Of course*, he reminded himself, *traffic's always light over here when the working day is done.*

But *absent*? Completely *absent*? You might expect that at midnight, but not at seven-thirty PM.

'Tell me why you hate your best friend,' Elvid invited.

Streeter reminded himself again that this man was crazy. Anything Elvid passed on wouldn't be believed. It was a liberating idea.

'Tom was better-looking when we were kids, and he's *far* better-looking now. He lettered in three sports; the only one I'm even halfway good at is miniature golf.'

'I don't think they have a cheerleading squad for that one,' Elvid said.

Streeter smiled grimly, warming to his subject. 'Tom's plenty smart, but he lazed his way through Derry High. His college ambitions were nil. But when his grades fell enough to put his athletic eligibility at risk, he'd panic. And then who got the call?'

'You did!' Elvid cried. 'Old Mr Responsible! Tutored him, did you? Maybe wrote a few papers as well? Making sure to misspell the words Tom's teachers got used to him misspelling?'

'Guilty as charged. In fact, when we were seniors – the year Tom got the State of Maine Sportsman award – I was really *two* students: Dave Streeter and Tom Goodhugh.'

'Tough.'

'Do you know what's tougher? I had a girlfriend. Beautiful girl named Norma Witten. Dark brown hair and eyes, flawless skin, beautiful cheekbones—'

'Tits that wouldn't quit—'

'Yes indeed. But, sex appeal aside—'

'Not that you ever *did* put it aside—'

'—I loved that girl. Do you know what Tom did?'

'Stole her from you!' Elvid said indignantly.

'Correct. The two of them came to me, you know. Made a clean breast of it.'

'Noble!'

'Claimed they couldn't help it.'

'Claimed they were in *love*, L–U–V.'

'Yes. Force of nature. This thing is bigger than both of us. And so on.'

'Let me guess. He knocked her up.'

'Indeed he did.' Streeter was looking at his shoes again, remembering a certain skirt Norma had worn when she was a sophomore or a junior. It was cut to show just a flirt of the slip beneath. That had been almost thirty years ago, but sometimes he still summoned that image to mind when he and Janet made love. He had never made love with Norma – not the Full Monty sort, anyway; she wouldn't allow it. Although she had been eager enough to drop her pants for Tom Goodhugh. *Probably the first time he asked her.*

'And left her with a bun in the oven.'

'No.' Streeter sighed. 'He married her.'

'Then divorced her! Possibly after beating her silly?'

'Worse still. They're still married. Three kids. When you see them walking in Bassey Park, they're usually holding hands.'

'That's about the crappiest thing I've ever heard. Not much could make it worse. Unless . . .' Elvid looked shrewdly at Streeter from beneath bushy brows. 'Unless *you're* the one who finds himself frozen in the iceberg of a loveless marriage.'

'Not at all,' Streeter said, surprised by the idea. 'I love Janet very much, and she loves me. The way she's stood by me during this cancer thing has been just extraordinary. If there's such a thing as harmony in the universe, then Tom and I ended up with the right partners. Absolutely. But . . .'

'But?' Elvid looked at him with delighted eagerness.

Streeter became aware that his fingernails were sinking into his palms. Instead of easing up, he bore down harder. Bore down until he felt trickles of blood. 'But he *fucking stole her*!' This had been eating him for years, and it felt good to shout the news.

'Indeed he did, and we never cease wanting what we want, whether it's good for us or not. Wouldn't you say so, Mr Streeter?'

Streeter made no reply. He was breathing hard, like a man who has just dashed fifty yards or engaged in a street scuffle. Hard little balls of color had surfaced in his formerly pale cheeks.

'And is that all?' Elvid spoke in the tones of a kindly parish priest.

'No.'

'Get it all out, then. Drain that blister.'

'He's a millionaire. He shouldn't be, but he is. In the late eighties — not long after the flood that damn near wiped this town out — he started up a garbage company . . . only he called it Derry Waste Removal and Recycling. Nicer name, you know.'

'Less germy.'

'He came to me for the loan, and although the proposition looked shaky to everyone at the bank, I pushed it through. Do you know *why* I pushed it through, Elvid?'

'Of course! Because he's your friend!'

'Guess again.'

'Because you thought he'd crash and burn.'

'Right. He sank all his savings into four garbage trucks, and mortgaged his house to buy a piece of land out by the Newport town line. For a landfill. The kind of thing New Jersey gangsters own to wash their dope-and-whore money and use as body-dumps. I thought it was crazy and I couldn't wait to write the loan. He still loves me like a brother for it. Never fails to tell people how I stood up to the bank and put my job on the line. "Dave carried me, just like in high school," he says. Do you know what the kids in town call his landfill now?'

'Tell me!'

'Mount Trashmore! It's huge! I wouldn't be surprised if it was radioactive! It's covered with sod, but there are KEEP OUT signs all around it, and there's probably a Rat Manhattan under that nice green grass! *They're* probably radioactive, as well!'

He stopped, aware that he sounded ridiculous, not

caring. Elvid was insane, but – surprise! Streeter had turned out to be insane, too! At least on the subject of his old friend. Plus . . .

In cancer veritas, Streeter thought.

'So let's recap.' Elvid began ticking off the points on his fingers, which were not long at all but as short, pudgy, and inoffensive as the rest of him. 'Tom Goodhugh was better-looking than you, even when you were children. He was gifted with athletic skills you could only dream of. The girl who kept her smooth white thighs closed in the backseat of your car opened them for Tom. He married her. They are still in love. Children okay, I suppose?'

'Healthy and beautiful!' Streeter spat. 'One getting married, one in college, one in high school! *That* one's captain of the football team! Chip off the old fucking block!'

'Right. And – the cherry on the chocolate sundae – he's rich and you're knocking on through life at a salary of sixty thousand or so a year.'

'I got a bonus for writing his loan,' Streeter muttered. 'For showing *vision*.'

'But what you actually wanted was a promotion.'

'How do you know that?'

'I'm a businessman now, but at one time I was a humble salaryman. Got fired before striking out on my own. Best thing that ever happened to me. I know how these things go. Anything else? Might as well get it all off your chest.'

'He drinks Spotted Hen Microbrew!' Streeter shouted. 'Nobody in Derry drinks that pretentious shit! Just him! Just Tom Goodhugh, the Garbage King!'

'Does he have a sports car?' Elvid spoke quietly, the words lined with silk.

'No. If he did, I could at least joke with Janet about sports car menopause. He drives a goddam *Range Rover*.'

'I think there might be one more thing,' Elvid said. 'If so, you might as well get that off your chest, too.'

'He doesn't have cancer.' Streeter almost whispered it. 'He's fifty-one, just like me, and he's as healthy . . . as a fucking . . . *horse*.'

'So are you,' Elvid said.

'*What?*'

'It's done, Mr Streeter. Or, since I've cured your cancer, at least temporarily, may I call you Dave?'

'You're a very crazy man,' Streeter said, not without admiration.

'No, sir. I'm as sane as a straight line. But notice I said *temporarily*. We are now in the "try it, you'll buy it" stage of our relationship. It will last a week at least, maybe ten days. I urge you to visit your doctor. I think he'll find remarkable improvement in your condition. But it won't last. Unless . . .'

'Unless?'

Elvid leaned forward, smiling chummily. His teeth again seemed too many (and too big) for his inoffensive mouth. 'I come out here from time to time,' he said. 'Usually at this time of day.'

'Just before sunset.'

'Exactly. Most people don't notice me – they look through me as if I wasn't there – but you'll be looking. Won't you?'

'If I'm better, I certainly will,' Streeter said.

'And you'll bring me something.'

Elvid's smile widened, and Streeter saw a wonderful, terrible thing: the man's teeth weren't just too big or too many. They were *sharp*.

Janet was folding clothes in the laundry room when he got back. 'There you are,' she said. 'I was starting to worry. Did you have a nice drive?'

'Yes,' he said. He surveyed his kitchen. It looked different. It looked like a kitchen in a dream. Then he turned on a light, and that was better. Elvid was the dream. Elvid and his promises. Just a loony on a day pass from Acadia Mental.

She came to him and kissed his cheek. She was flushed from the heat of the dryer and very pretty. She was fifty herself, but looked years younger. Streeter thought she would probably have a fine life after he died. He guessed May and Justin might have a stepdaddy in their future.

'You look good,' she said. 'You've actually got some color.'

'Do I?'

'You do.' She gave him an encouraging smile that was troubled just beneath. 'Come talk to me while I fold the rest of these things. It's so boring.'

He followed her and stood in the door of the laundry room. He knew better than to offer help; she said he even folded dish-wipers the wrong way.

'Justin called,' she said. 'He and Carl are in Venice. At a youth hostel. He said their cabdriver spoke very good English. He's having a ball.'

'Great.'

'You were right to keep the diagnosis to yourself,' she said. 'You were right and I was wrong.'

'A first in our marriage.'

She wrinkled her nose at him. 'Jus has so looked forward to this trip. But you'll have to fess up when he gets back. May's coming up from Searsport for Gracie's wedding, and that would be the right time.' Gracie was Gracie Goodhugh, Tom and Norma's oldest child. Carl Goodhugh, Justin's traveling companion, was the one in the middle.

'We'll see,' Streeter said. He had one of his puke-bags

in his back pocket, but he had never felt less like upchucking. Something he *did* feel like was eating. For the first time in days.

Nothing happened out there — you know that, right? This is just a little psychosomatic elevation. It'll recede.

'Like my hairline,' he said.

'What, honey?'

'Nothing.'

'Oh, and speaking of Gracie, Norma called. She reminded me it was their turn to have us to dinner at their place Thursday night. I said I'd ask you, but that you were awfully busy at the bank, working late hours, all this bad-mortgage stuff. I didn't think you'd want to see them.'

Her voice was as normal and as calm as ever, but all at once she began crying big storybook tears that welled in her eyes and then went rolling down her cheeks. Love grew humdrum in the later years of a marriage, but now his swelled up as fresh as it had been in the early days, the two of them living in a crappy apartment on Kossuth Street and sometimes making love on the living-room rug. He stepped into the laundry room, took the shirt she was folding out of her hands, and hugged her. She hugged him back, fiercely.

'This is just so hard and unfair,' she said. 'We'll get through it. I don't know how, but we will.'

'That's right. And we'll start by having dinner on Thursday night with Tom and Norma, just like we always do.'

She drew back, looking at him with her wet eyes. 'Are you going to tell them?'

'And spoil dinner? Nope.'

'Will you even be able to eat? Without . . .' She put two fingers to her closed lips, puffed her cheeks, and crossed her eyes: a comic pantomime that made Streeter grin.

'I don't know about Thursday, but I could eat some-thing now,' he said. 'Would you mind if I rustled myself up a hamburger? Or I could go out to McDonald's . . . maybe bring you back a chocolate shake . . .'

'My God,' she said, and wiped her eyes. 'It's a miracle.'

'I wouldn't call it a miracle, exactly,' Dr Henderson told Streeter on Wednesday afternoon. 'But . . .'

It was two days since Streeter had discussed matters of life and death under Mr Elvid's yellow umbrella, and a day before the Streeters' weekly dinner with the Goodhughs, this time to take place at the sprawling resi-dence Streeter sometimes thought of as The House That Trash Built. The conversation was taking place not in Dr Henderson's office, but in a small consultation room at Derry Home Hospital. Henderson had tried to discourage the MRI, telling Streeter that his insurance wouldn't cover it and the results were sure to be disappointing. Streeter had insisted.

'But what, Roddy?'

'The tumors appear to have shrunk, and your lungs seem clear. I've never seen such a result, and neither have the two other docs I brought in to look at the images. More important – this is just between you and me – the MRI tech has never seen anything like it, and those are the guys I really trust. He thinks it's probably a computer malfunction in the machine itself.'

'I feel good, though,' Streeter said, 'which is why I asked for the test. Is that a malfunction?'

'Are you vomiting?'

'I have a couple of times,' Streeter admitted, 'but I think that's the chemo. I'm calling a halt to it, by the way.'

Roddy Henderson frowned. 'That's very unwise.'

'The unwise thing was starting it in the first place, my friend. You say, "Sorry, Dave, the chances of you dying before you get a chance to say Happy Valentine's Day are in the ninetieth percentile, so we're going to fuck up the time you have left by filling you full of poison. You might feel worse if I injected you with sludge from Tom Goodhugh's landfill, but probably not." And like a fool, I said okay.'

Henderson looked offended. 'Chemo is the last best hope for—'

'Don't bullshit a bullshitter,' Streeter said with a goodnatured grin. He drew a deep breath that went all the way down to the bottom of his lungs. It felt *wonderful*. 'When the cancer's aggressive, chemo isn't for the patient. It's just an agony surcharge the patient pays so that when he's dead, the doctors and relatives can hug each other over the coffin and say "We did everything we could."'

'That's harsh,' Henderson said. 'You know you're apt to relapse, don't you?'

'Tell that to the tumors,' Streeter said. 'The ones that are no longer there.'

Henderson looked at the images of Deepest Darkest Streeter that were still flicking past at twenty-second intervals on the conference room's monitor and sighed. They were good pictures, even Streeter knew that, but they seemed to make his doctor unhappy.

'Relax, Roddy.' Streeter spoke gently, as he might once have spoken to May or Justin when a favorite toy got lost or broken. 'Shit happens; sometimes miracles happen, too. I read it in the *Reader's Digest*.'

'In my experience, one has never happened in an MRI tube.' Henderson picked up a pen and tapped it against Streeter's file, which had fattened considerably over the last three months.

'There's a first time for everything,' Streeter said.

*   *   *

Thursday evening in Derry; dusk of a summer night. The declining sun casting its red and dreamy rays over the three perfectly clipped, watered, and landscaped acres Tom Goodhugh had the temerity to call 'the old backyard.' Streeter sat in a lawn chair on the patio, listening to the rattle of plates and the laughter of Janet and Norma as they loaded the dishwasher.

Yard? It's not a yard, it's a Shopping Channel fan's idea of heaven.

There was even a fountain with a marble child standing in the middle of it. Somehow it was the bare-ass cherub (pissing, of course) that offended Streeter the most. He was sure it had been Norma's idea — she had gone back to college to get a liberal arts degree, and had half-assed Classical pretensions — but still, to see such a thing here in the dying glow of a perfect Maine evening and know its presence was a result of Tom's garbage monopoly . . .

And, speak of the devil (*or the Elvid, if you like that better*, Streeter thought), enter the Garbage King himself, with the necks of two sweating bottles of Spotted Hen Microbrew caught between the fingers of his left hand. Slim and erect in his open-throated Oxford shirt and faded jeans, his lean face perfectly lit by the sunset glow, Tom Goodhugh looked like a model in a magazine beer ad. Streeter could even see the copy: *Live the good life, reach for a Spotted Hen.*

'Thought you might like a fresh one, since your beautiful wife says she's driving.'

'Thanks.' Streeter took one of the bottles, tipped it to his lips, and drank. Pretentious or not, it was good.

As Goodhugh sat down, Jacob the football player came out with a plate of cheese and crackers. He was as broad-shouldered and handsome as Tom had been back in the day. *Probably has cheerleaders crawling all over him,*

Streeter thought. *Probably has to beat them off with a damn stick.*

'Mom thought you might like these,' Jacob said.

'Thanks, Jake. You going out?'

'Just for a little while. Throw the Frisbee with some guys down in the Barrens until it gets dark, then study.'

'Stay on this side. There's poison ivy down there since the crap grew back.'

'Yeah, we know. Denny caught it when we were in junior high, and it was so bad his mother thought he had cancer.'

'Ouch!' Streeter said.

'Drive home carefully, son. No hot-dogging.'

'You bet.' The boy put an arm around his father and kissed his cheek with a lack of self-consciousness that Streeter found depressing. Tom not only had his health, a still-gorgeous wife, and a ridiculous pissing cherub; he had a handsome eighteen-year-old son who still felt all right about kissing his dad goodbye before going out with his best buds.

'He's a good boy,' Goodhugh said fondly, watching Jacob mount the stairs to the house and disappear inside. 'Studies hard and makes his grades, unlike his old man. Luckily for me, I had you.'

'Lucky for both of us,' Streeter said, smiling and putting a goo of Brie on a Triscuit. He popped it into his mouth.

'Does me good to see you eating, chum,' Goodhugh said. 'Me n Norma were starting to wonder if there was something wrong with you.'

'Never better,' Streeter said, and drank some more of the tasty (and no doubt expensive) beer. 'I've been losing my hair in front, though. Jan says it makes me look thinner.'

'That's one thing the ladies don't have to worry

about,' Goodhugh said, and stroked a hand back through his own locks, which were as full and rich as they had been at eighteen. Not a touch of gray in them, either. Janet Streeter could still look forty on a good day, but in the red light of the declining sun, the Garbage King looked thirty-five. He didn't smoke, he didn't drink to excess, and he worked out at a health club that did business with Streeter's bank but which Streeter could not afford himself. His middle child, Carl, was currently doing the European thing with Justin Streeter, the two of them traveling on Carl Goodhugh's dime. Which was, of course, actually the Garbage King's dime.

O man who has everything, thy name is Goodhugh, Streeter thought, and smiled at his old friend.

His old friend smiled back, and touched the neck of his beer bottle to Streeter's. 'Life is good, wouldn't you say?'

'Very good,' Streeter agreed. 'Long days and pleasant nights.'

Goodhugh raised his eyebrows. 'Where'd you get that?'

'Made it up, I guess,' Streeter said. 'But it's true, isn't it?'

'If it is, I owe a lot of my pleasant nights to you,' Goodhugh said. 'It has crossed my mind, old buddy, that I owe you my life.' He toasted his insane backyard. 'The tenderloin part of it, anyway.'

'Nah, you're a self-made man.'

Goodhugh lowered his voice and spoke confidentially. 'Want the truth? The woman made this man. The Bible says "Who can find a good woman? For her price is above rubies." Something like that, anyway. And you introduced us. Don't know if you remember that.'

Streeter felt a sudden and almost irresistible urge to smash his beer bottle on the patio bricks and shove the jagged and still foaming neck into his old friend's eyes. He smiled instead, sipped a little more beer, then stood up. 'Think I need to pay a little visit to the facility.'

'You don't buy beer, you only rent it,' Goodhugh said, then burst out laughing. As if he had invented this himself, right on the spot.

'Truer words, et cetera,' Streeter said. 'Excuse me.'

'You really are looking better,' Goodhugh called after him as Streeter mounted the steps.

'Thanks,' Streeter said. 'Old buddy.'

He closed the bathroom door, pushed in the locking button, turned on the lights, and – for the first time in his life – swung open the medicine cabinet door in another person's house. The first thing his eye lighted on cheered him immensely: a tube of Just For Men shampoo. There were also a few prescription bottles.

Streeter thought, *People who leave their drugs in a bathroom the guests use are just asking for trouble*. Not that there was anything sensational: Norma had asthma medicine; Tom was taking blood pressure medicine – Atenolol – and using some sort of skin cream.

The Atenolol bottle was half full. Streeter took one of the tablets, tucked it into the watch-pocket of his jeans, and flushed the toilet. Then he left the bathroom, feeling like a man who has just snuck across the border of a strange country.

The following evening was overcast, but George Elvid was still sitting beneath the yellow umbrella and once again watching *Inside Edition* on his portable TV. The lead story had to do with Whitney Houston, who had lost a suspicious amount of weight shortly after signing a huge new recording contract. Elvid disposed of this rumor with a twist of his pudgy fingers and regarded Streeter with a smile.

'How have you been feeling, Dave?'

'Better.'

'Yes?'

'Yes.'

'Vomiting?'

'Not today.'

'Eating?'

'Like a horse.'

'And I'll bet you've had some medical tests.'

'How did you know?'

'I'd expect no less of a successful bank official. Did you bring me something?'

For a moment Streeter considered walking away. He really did. Then he reached into the pocket of the light jacket he was wearing (the evening was chilly for August, and he was still on the thin side) and brought out a tiny square of Kleenex. He hesitated, then handed it across the table to Elvid, who unwrapped it.

'Ah, Atenolol,' Elvid said. He popped the pill into his mouth and swallowed.

Streeter's mouth opened, then closed slowly.

'Don't look so shocked,' Elvid said. 'If you had a high-stress job like mine, you'd have blood pressure problems, too. And the reflux I suffer from, oy. You don't want to know.'

'What happens now?' Streeter asked. Even in the jacket, he felt cold.

'Now?' Elvid looked surprised. 'Now you start enjoying your fifteen years of good health. Possibly twenty or even twenty-five. Who knows?'

'And happiness?'

Elvid favored him with the roguish look. It would have been amusing if not for the coldness Streeter saw just beneath. And the *age*. In that moment he felt certain that George Elvid had been doing business for a very long time, reflux or no reflux. 'The happiness part is up to you, Dave. And your family, of course – Janet, May, and Justin.'

Had he told Elvid their names? Streeter couldn't remember.

'Perhaps the children most of all. There's an old saying to the effect that children are our hostages to fortune, but in fact it's the children who take the *parents* hostage, that's what I think. One of them could have a fatal or disabling accident on a deserted country road . . . fall prey to a debilitating disease . . .'

'Are you saying—'

'No, no, no! This isn't some half-assed morality tale. I'm a *businessman*, not a character out of "The Devil and Daniel Webster." All I'm saying is that your happiness is in your hands and those of your nearest and dearest And if you think I'm going to show up two decades or so down the line to collect your soul in my moldy old pocketbook, you'd better think again. The souls of humans have become poor and transparent things.'

He spoke, Streeter thought, as the fox might have done after repeated leaps had proved to it that the grapes were really and truly out of reach. But Streeter had no intention of saying such a thing. Now that the deal was done, all he wanted to do was get out of here.

But still he lingered, not wanting to ask the question that was on his mind but knowing he had to. Because there was no gift-giving going on here; Streeter had been making deals in the bank for most of his life, and he knew a horse-trade when he saw one. Or when he smelled it: a faint, unpleasant stink like burned aviation fuel.

In words of one syllable, you have to do the dirty to someone else if the dirty is to be lifted from you.

But stealing a single hypertension pill wasn't exactly doing the dirty. Was it?

Elvid, meanwhile, was yanking his big umbrella closed. And when it was furled, Streeter observed an amazing and disheartening fact: it wasn't yellow at all. It was as gray as the sky. Summer was almost over.

'Most of my clients are perfectly satisfied, perfectly happy. Is that what you want to hear?'

It was . . . and wasn't.

'I sense you have a more pertinent question,' Elvid said. 'If you want an answer, quit beating around the bush and ask it. It's going to rain, and I want to get undercover before it does. The last thing I need at my age is bronchitis.'

'Where's your car?'

'Oh, was that your question?' Elvid sneered openly at him. His cheeks were lean, not in the least pudgy, and his eyes turned up at the corners, where the whites shaded to an unpleasant and – yes, it was true – cancerous black. He looked like the world's least pleasant clown, with half his makeup removed.

'Your teeth,' Streeter said stupidly. 'They have *points*.'

'*Your question, Mr Streeter!*'

'Is Tom Goodhugh going to get cancer?'

Elvid gaped for a moment, then started to giggle. The sound was wheezy, dusty, and unpleasant – like a dying calliope.

'No, Dave,' he said. 'Tom Goodhugh isn't going to get cancer. Not *him*.'

'What, then? What?'

The contempt with which Elvid surveyed him made Streeter's bones feel weak – as if holes had been eaten in them by some painless but terribly corrosive acid. 'Why would you care? You hate him, you said so yourself.'

'But—'

'Watch. Wait. *Enjoy*. And take this.' He handed Streeter a business card. Written on it was THE NON-SECTARIAN

CHILDREN'S FUND and the address of a bank in the Cayman Islands.

'Tax haven,' Elvid said. 'You'll send my fifteen percent there. If you short me, I'll know. And then woe is you, kiddo.'

'What if my wife finds out and asks questions?'

'Your wife has a personal checkbook. Beyond that, she never looks at a thing. She trusts you. Am I right?'

'Well . . .' Streeter observed with no surprise that the raindrops striking Elvid's hands and arms smoked and sizzled. 'Yes.'

'Of course I am. Our dealing is done. Get out of here and go back to your wife. I'm sure she'll welcome you with open arms. Take her to bed. Stick your mortal penis in her and pretend she's your best friend's wife. You don't deserve her, but lucky you.'

'What if I want to take it back,' Streeter whispered.

Elvid favored him with a stony smile that revealed a jutting ring of cannibal teeth. 'You can't,' he said.

That was in August of 2001, less than a month before the fall of the Towers.

In December (on the same day Winona Ryder was busted for shoplifting, in fact), Dr Roderick Henderson proclaimed Dave Streeter cancer-free – and, in addition, a bona fide miracle of the modern age.

'I have no explanation for this,' Henderson said.

Streeter did, but kept his silence.

Their consultation took place in Henderson's office. At Derry Home Hospital, in the conference room where Streeter had looked at the first pictures of his miraculously cured body, Norma Goodhugh sat in the same chair where Streeter had sat, looking at less pleasant MRI scans. She listened numbly as her doctor told her – as gently as possible – that the lump in her left breast was indeed cancer, and it had spread to her lymph nodes.

'The situation is bad, but not hopeless,' the doctor said, reaching across the table to take Norma's cold hand. He smiled. 'We'll want to start you on chemotherapy immediately.'

In June of the following year, Streeter finally got his promotion. May Streeter was admitted to the Columbia School of Journalism grad school. Streeter and his wife took a long-deferred Hawaii vacation to celebrate. They made love many times. On their last day in Maui, Tom Goodhugh called. The connection was bad and he could hardly talk, but the message got through: Norma had died.

'We'll be there for you,' Streeter promised.

When he told Janet the news, she collapsed on the hotel bed, weeping with her hands over her face. Streeter lay down beside her, held her close, and thought: *Well, we were going home, anyway.* And although he felt bad about Norma (and sort of bad for Tom), there was an upside: they had missed bug season, which could be a bitch in Derry.

In December, Streeter sent a check for just over fifteen thousand dollars to The Non-Sectarian Children's Fund. He took it as a deduction on his tax return.

In 2003, Justin Streeter made the Dean's List at Brown and – as a lark – invented a video game called Walk Fido Home. The object of the game was to get your leashed dog back from the mall while avoiding bad drivers, objects falling from tenth-story balconies, and a pack of crazed old ladies who called themselves the Canine-Killing Grannies. To Streeter it sounded like a joke (and Justin assured them it *was* meant as a satire), but Games, Inc. took one look and paid their handsome, good-humored son seven hundred and fifty thousand dollars for the rights. Plus royalties. Jus bought his parents matching Toyota

Pathfinder SUVs, pink for the lady, blue for the gentleman. Janet wept and hugged him and called him a foolish, impetuous, generous, and altogether splendid boy. Streeter took him to Roxie's Tavern and bought him a Spotted Hen Microbrew.

In October, Carl Goodhugh's roommate at Emerson came back from class to find Carl facedown on the kitchen floor of their apartment with the grilled cheese sandwich he'd been making for himself still smoking in the frypan. Although only twenty-two years of age, Carl had suffered a heart attack. The doctors attending the case pinpointed a congenital heart defect – something about a thin atrial wall – that had gone undetected. Carl didn't die; his roommate got to him just in time and knew CPR. But he suffered oxygen deprivation, and the bright, handsome, physically agile young man who had not long before toured Europe with Justin Streeter became a shuffling shadow of his former self. He was not always continent, he got lost if he wandered more than a block or two from home (he had moved back with his still-grieving father), and his speech had become a blurred blare that only Tom could understand. Goodhugh hired a companion for him. The companion administered physical therapy and saw that Carl changed his clothes. He also took Carl on biweekly 'outings.' The most common 'outing' was to Wishful Dishful Ice Cream, where Carl would always get a pistachio cone and smear it all over his face. Afterward the companion would clean him up, patiently, with Wet Naps.

Janet stopped going with Streeter to dinner at Tom's. 'I can't bear it,' she confessed. 'It's not the way Carl shuffles, or how he sometimes wets his pants – it's the look in his eyes, as if he remembers how he was, and can't quite remember how he got to where he is now. And . . . I don't know . . . there's always something *hopeful* in his face that makes me feel like everything in life is a joke.'

Streeter knew what she meant, and often considered the idea during his dinners with his old friend (without Norma to cook, it was now mostly takeout). He enjoyed watching Tom feed his damaged son, and he enjoyed the hopeful look on Carl's face. The one that said, 'This is all a dream I'm having, and soon I'll wake up.' Jan was right, it was a joke, but it was sort of a good joke.

If you really thought about it.

In 2004, May Streeter got a job with the *Boston Globe* and declared herself the happiest girl in the USA. Justin Streeter created Rock the House, which would be a perennial bestseller until the advent of Guitar Hero made it obsolete. By then Jus had moved on to a music composition computer program called You Moog Me, Baby. Streeter himself was appointed manager of his bank branch, and there were rumors of a regional post in his future. He took Janet to Cancún, and they had a fabulous time. She began calling him 'my nuzzle-bunny.'

Tom's accountant at Goodhugh Waste Removal embezzled two million dollars and departed for parts unknown. The subsequent accounting review revealed that the business was on very shaky ground; that bad old accountant had been nibbling away for years, it seemed.

Nibbling? Streeter thought, reading the story in *The Derry News. Taking it a chomp at a time is more like it.*

Tom no longer looked thirty-five; he looked sixty. And must have known it, because he stopped dying his hair. Streeter was delighted to see that it hadn't gone white underneath the artificial color; Goodhugh's hair was the dull and listless gray of Elvid's umbrella when he had furled it. The hair-color, Streeter decided, of the old

men you see sitting on park benches and feeding the
pigeons. Call it Just For Losers.

In 2005, Jacob the football player, who had gone to work
in his father's dying company instead of to college (which
he could have attended on a full-boat athletic scholarship),
met a girl and got married. Bubbly little brunette named
Cammy Dorrington. Streeter and his wife agreed it was
a beautiful ceremony, even though Carl Goodhugh hooted,
gurgled, and burbled all the way through it, and even
though Goodhugh's oldest child – Gracie – tripped over
the hem of her dress on the church steps as she was
leaving, fell down, and broke her leg in two places. Until
that happened, Tom Goodhugh had looked almost like
his former self. Happy, in other words. Streeter did not
begrudge him a little happiness. He supposed that even
in hell, people got an occasional sip of water, if only so
they could appreciate the full horror of unrequited thirst
when it set in again.

The honeymooning couple went to Belize. *I'll bet it
rains the whole time*, Streeter thought. It didn't, but Jacob
spent most of the week in a run-down hospital, suffering
from violent gastroenteritis and pooping into paper didies.
He had only drunk bottled water, but then forgot and
brushed his teeth from the tap. 'My own darn fault,' he
said.

Over eight hundred US troops died in Iraq. Bad luck
for those boys and girls.

Tom Goodhugh began to suffer from gout, developed
a limp, started using a cane.

That year's check to The Non-Sectarian Children's
Fund was of an extremely good size, but Streeter didn't
begrudge it. It was more blessed to give than to receive.
All the best people said so.

*   *   *

In 2006, Tom's daughter Gracie fell victim to pyorrhea and lost all her teeth. She also lost her sense of smell. One night shortly thereafter, at Goodhugh and Streeter's weekly dinner (it was just the two men; Carl's attendant had taken Carl on an 'outing'), Tom Goodhugh broke down in tears. He had given up microbrews in favor of Bombay Sapphire gin, and he was very drunk. 'I don't understand what's happened to me!' he sobbed. 'I feel like . . . I don't know . . . *fucking Job!*'

Streeter took him in his arms and comforted him. He told his old friend that clouds always roll in, and sooner or later they always roll out.

'Well, these clouds have been here a fuck of a long time!' Goodhugh cried, and thumped Streeter on the back with a closed fist. Streeter didn't mind. His old friend wasn't as strong as he used to be.

Charlie Sheen, Tori Spelling, and David Hasselhoff got divorces, but in Derry, David and Janet Streeter celebrated their thirtieth wedding anniversary. There was a party. Toward the end of it, Streeter escorted his wife out back. He had arranged fireworks. Everybody applauded except for Carl Goodhugh. He tried, but kept missing his hands. Finally the former Emerson student gave up on the clapping thing and pointed at the sky, hooting.

In 2007, Kiefer Sutherland went to jail (not for the first time) on DUI charges, and Gracie Goodhugh Dickerson's husband was killed in a car crash. A drunk driver veered into his lane while Andy Dickerson was on his way home from work. The good news was that the drunk wasn't Kiefer Sutherland. The bad news was that Gracie Dickerson was four months pregnant and broke. Her husband had let his life insurance lapse to save on expenses. Gracie moved back in with her father and her brother Carl.

'With their luck, that baby will be born deformed,'

Streeter said one night as he and his wife lay in bed after making love.

'Hush!' Janet cried, shocked.

'If you say it, it won't come true,' Streeter explained, and soon the two nuzzle-bunnies were asleep in each other's arms.

That year's check to the Children's Fund was for thirty thousand dollars. Streeter wrote it without a qualm.

Gracie's baby came at the height of a February snowstorm in 2008. The good news was that it wasn't deformed. The bad news was that it was born dead. That damned family heart defect. Gracie — toothless, husbandless, and unable to smell anything — dropped into a deep depression. Streeter thought that demonstrated her basic sanity. If she had gone around whistling 'Don't Worry, Be Happy,' he would have advised Tom to lock up all the sharp objects in the house.

A plane carrying two members of the rock band Blink 182 crashed. Bad news, four people died. Good news, the rockers actually survived for a change . . . although one of them would die not much later.

'I have offended God,' Tom said at one of the dinners the two men now called their 'bachelor nights.' Streeter had brought spaghetti from Cara Mama, and cleaned his plate. Tom Goodhugh barely touched his. In the other room, Gracie and Carl were watching *American Idol*, Gracie in silence, the former Emerson student hooting and gabbling. 'I don't know how, but I have.'

'Don't say that, because it isn't true.'

'You don't know that.'

'I *do*,' Streeter said emphatically. 'It's foolish talk.'

'If you say so, buddy.' Tom's eyes filled with tears. They rolled down his cheeks. One clung to the line of his unshaven jaw, dangled there for a moment, then plinked into his uneaten spaghetti. 'Thank God for Jacob. *He's* all right. Working for a TV station in Boston these days, and his wife's in accounting at Brigham and Women's. They see May once in awhile.'

'Great news,' Streeter said heartily, hoping Jake wouldn't somehow contaminate his daughter with his company.

'And you still come and see me. I understand why Jan doesn't, and I don't hold it against her, but . . . I look forward to these nights. They're like a link to the old days.'

Yes, Streeter thought, *the old days when you had everything and I had cancer.*

'You'll always have me,' he said, and clasped one of Goodhugh's slightly trembling hands in both of his own. 'Friends to the end.'

2008, what a year! Holy fuck! China hosted the Olympics! Chris Brown and Rihanna became nuzzle-bunnies! Banks collapsed! The stock market tanked! And in November, the EPA closed Mount Trashmore, Tom Goodhugh's last source of income. The government stated its intention to bring suit in matters having to do with groundwater pollution and illegal dumping of medical wastes. *The Derry News* hinted that there might even be criminal action.

Streeter often drove out along the Harris Avenue Extension in the evenings, looking for a certain yellow umbrella. He didn't want to dicker; he only wanted to shoot the shit. But he never saw the umbrella or its owner. He was disappointed but not surprised. Dealmakers were like sharks; they had to keep moving or they'd die.

He wrote a check and sent it to the bank in the Caymans.

In 2009, Chris Brown beat the hell out of his Number One Nuzzle-Bunny after the Grammy Awards, and a few

weeks later, Jacob Goodhugh the ex-football player beat
the hell out of his bubbly wife Cammy after Cammy
found a certain lady's undergarment and half a gram of
cocaine in Jacob's jacket pocket. Lying on the floor, crying,
she called him a son of a bitch. Jacob responded by stabbing her in the abdomen with a meat fork. He regretted
it at once and called 911, but the damage was done; he'd
punctured her stomach in two places. He told the police
later that he remembered none of this. He was in a
blackout, he said. His court-appointed lawyer was too
dumb to get a bail reduction. Jake Goodhugh appealed
to his father, who was hardly able to pay his heating bills,
let alone provide high-priced Boston legal talent for his
spouse-abusing son. Goodhugh turned to Streeter, who
didn't let his old friend get a dozen words into his painfully rehearsed speech before saying *you bet*. He still
remembered the way Jacob had so unselfconsciously kissed
his old man's cheek. Also, paying the legal fees allowed
him to question the lawyer about Jake's mental state, which
wasn't good; he was racked with guilt and deeply depressed.
The lawyer told Streeter that the boy would probably get
five years, hopefully with three of them suspended.

When he gets out, he can go home, Streeter thought.
He can watch American Idol *with Gracie and Carl, if it's still
on. It probably will be.*

'I've got my insurance,' Tom Goodhugh said one
night. He had lost a lot of weight, and his clothes bagged
on him. His eyes were bleary. He had developed psoriasis,
and scratched restlessly at his arms, leaving long red marks
on the white skin. 'I'd kill myself if I thought I could get
away with making it look like an accident.'

'I don't want to hear talk like that,' Streeter said.
'Things will turn around.'

In June, Michael Jackson kicked the bucket. In August,
Carl Goodhugh went and did likewise, choking to death

on a piece of apple. The companion might have performed the Heimlich maneuver and saved him, but the companion had been let go due to lack of funds sixteen months before. Gracie heard Carl gurgling but said she thought 'it was just his usual bullshit.' The good news was Carl also had life insurance. Just a small policy, but enough to bury him.

After the funeral (Tom Goodhugh sobbed all the way through it, holding onto his old friend for support), Streeter had a generous impulse. He found Kiefer Sutherland's studio address and sent him an AA Big Book. It would probably go right in the trash, he knew (along with the countless other Big Books fans had sent him over the years), but you never knew. Sometimes miracles happened.

In early September of 2009, on a hot summer evening, Streeter and Janet rode out to the road that runs along the back end of Derry's airport. No one was doing business on the graveled square outside the Cyclone fence, so he parked his fine blue Pathfinder there and put his arm around his wife, whom he loved more deeply and completely than ever. The sun was going down in a red ball.

He turned to Janet and saw that she was crying. He tilted her chin toward him and solemnly kissed the tears away. That made her smile.

'What is it, honey?'

'I was thinking about the Goodhughs. I've never known a family to have such a run of bad luck. *Bad* luck?' She laughed. '*Black* luck is more like it.'

'I haven't, either,' he said, 'but it happens all the time. One of the women killed in the Mumbai attacks was pregnant, did you know that? Her two-year-old lived, but the kid was beaten within an inch of his life. And—'

She put two fingers to her lips. 'Hush. No more. Life's not fair. We know that.'

'But it *is*!' Streeter spoke earnestly. In the sunset light his face was ruddy and healthy. 'Just look at me. There was a time when you never thought I'd live to see 2009, isn't that true?'

'Yes, but—'

'And the marriage, still as strong as an oak door. Or am I wrong?'

She shook her head. He wasn't wrong.

'You've started selling freelance pieces to *The Derry News*, May's going great guns with the *Globe*, and our son the geek is a media mogul at twenty-five.'

She began to smile again. Streeter was glad. He hated to see her blue.

'Life *is* fair. We all get the same nine-month shake in the box, and then the dice roll. Some people get a run of sevens. Some people, unfortunately, get snake-eyes. It's just how the world is.'

She put her arms around him. 'I love you, sweetie. You always look on the bright side.'

Streeter shrugged modestly. 'The law of averages favors optimists, any banker would tell you that. Things have a way of balancing out in the end.'

Venus came into view above the airport, glimmering against the darkening blue.

'Wish!' Streeter commanded.

Janet laughed and shook her head. 'What would I wish for? I have everything I want.'

'Me too,' Streeter said, and then, with his eyes fixed firmly on Venus, he wished for more.

A GOOD MARRIAGE

1

The one thing nobody asked in casual conversation, Darcy thought in the days after she found what she found in the garage, was this: *How's your marriage?* They asked *how was your weekend* and *how was your trip to Florida* and *how's your health* and *how are the kids*; they even asked *how's life been treatin you, hon?* But nobody asked *how's your marriage?*

Good, she would have answered the question before that night. *Everything's fine.*

She had been born Darcellen Madsen (Darcellen, a name only parents besotted with a freshly purchased book of baby names could love), in the year John F. Kennedy was elected President. She was raised in Freeport, Maine, back when it was a town instead of an adjunct to L.L.Bean, America's first superstore, and half a dozen other oversized retail operations of the sort that are called 'outlets' (as if they were sewer drains rather than shopping locations). She went to Freeport High School, and then to Addison Business School, where she learned secretarial skills. She was hired by Joe Ransome Chevrolet, which by 1984, when she left the company, was the largest car dealership in Portland. She was plain, but, with the help of two marginally more sophisticated girlfriends, learned enough makeup skills to make herself pretty on workdays and downright eye-catching on Friday and Saturday nights, when a bunch of them liked to go out for margaritas at The Lighthouse or Mexican Mike's (where there was live music).

In 1982, Joe Ransome hired a Portland accounting firm to help him figure out his tax situation, which had become complicated ('The kind of problem you want to have,' Darcy overheard him tell one of the senior salesmen).

A pair of briefcase-toting men came out, one old and one young. Both wore glasses and conservative suits; both combed their short hair neatly away from their foreheads in a way that made Darcy think of the photographs in her mother's MEMORIES OF '54 senior yearbook, the one with the image of a boy cheerleader holding a megaphone to his mouth stamped on its faux-leather cover.

The younger accountant was Bob Anderson. She got talking with him on their second day at the dealership, and in the course of their conversation, asked him if he had any hobbies. Yes, he said, he was a numismatist.

He started to tell her what that was and she said, 'I know. My father collects Lady Liberty dimes and buffalo-head nickels. He says they're his numismatical hobby-horse. Do you have a hobby-horse, Mr Anderson?'

He did: wheat pennies. His greatest hope was to some day come across a 1955 double-date, which was—

But she knew that, too. The '55 double-date was a mistake. A valuable mistake.

Young Mr Anderson, he of the thick and carefully combed brown hair, was delighted with this answer. He asked her to call him Bob. Later, during their lunch – which they took on a bench in the sunshine behind the body shop, a tuna on rye for him and a Greek salad in a Tupperware bowl for her – he asked if she would like to go with him on Saturday to a street sale in Castle Rock. He had just rented a new apartment, he said, and was looking for an armchair. Also a TV, if someone was selling a good one at a fair price. *A good one at a fair price* was a phrase with which she would grow comfortably familiar in the years to come.

He was as plain as she was, just another guy you'd pass on the street without noticing, and would never have makeup to make him prettier . . . except that day on the bench, he did. His cheeks flushed when he asked her out, just enough to light him up a little and give him a glow.

'No coin collections?' she teased.

He smiled, revealing even teeth. Small teeth, nicely cared for, and white. It never occurred to her that the thought of those teeth could make her shudder – why would it?

'If I saw a nice set of coins, of course I'd look,' he said.

'Especially wheat pennies?' Teasing, but just a little.

'Especially those. Would you like to come, Darcy?'

She came. And she came on their wedding night, too. Not terribly often after that, but now and then. Often enough to consider herself normal and fulfilled.

In 1986, Bob got a promotion. He also (with Darcy's encouragement and help) started up a small mail-order business in collectible American coins. It was successful from the start, and in 1990, he added baseball trading cards and old movie memorabilia. He kept no stock of posters, one-sheets, or window cards, but when people queried him on such items, he could almost always find them. Actually it was Darcy who found them, using her overstuffed Rolodex in those pre-computer days to call collectors all over the country. The business never got big enough to become full-time, and that was all right. Neither of them wanted such a thing. They agreed on that as they did on the house they eventually bought in Pownal, and on the children when it came time to have them. They agreed. When they didn't agree, they compromised. But mostly they agreed. They saw eye-to-eye.

How's your marriage?

It was good. A good marriage. Donnie was born in 1986 – she quit her job to have him, and except for helping with Anderson Coins & Collectibles never held another one – and Petra was born in 1988. By then, Bob

Anderson's thick brown hair was thinning at the crown, and by 2002, the year Darcy's Macintosh computer finally swallowed her Rolodex whole, he had a large shiny bald spot back there. He experimented with different ways of combing what was left, which only made the bald spot more conspicuous, in her opinion. And he irritated her by trying two of the magical grow-it-all-back formulas, the kind of stuff sold by shifty-looking hucksters on high cable late at night (Bob Anderson became something of a night owl as he slipped into middle age). He didn't tell her he'd done it, but they shared a bedroom and although she wasn't tall enough to see the top shelf of the closet unaided, she sometimes used a stool to put away his 'Saturday shirts,' the tees he wore for puttering in the garden. And there they were: a bottle of liquid in the fall of 2004, a bottle of little green gel capsules a year later. She looked the names up on the Internet, and they weren't cheap. *Of course magic never is*, she remembered thinking.

But, irritated or not, she had held her peace about the magic potions, and also about the used Chevy Suburban he for some reason just had to buy in the same year that gas prices really started to climb. As he had held his, she supposed (as she *knew*, actually), when she had insisted on good summer camps for the kids, an electric guitar for Donnie (he had played for two years, long enough to get surprisingly good, and then had simply stopped), horse rentals for Petra. A successful marriage was a balancing act – that was a thing everyone knew. A successful marriage was also dependent on a high tolerance for irritation – this was a thing *Darcy* knew. As the Stevie Winwood song said, you had to roll widdit, baby.

She rolled with it. So did he.

In 2004, Donnie went off to college in Pennsylvania. In 2006, Petra went to Colby, just up the road in Waterville. By then, Darcy Madsen Anderson was forty-six years old.

Bob was forty-nine, and still doing Cub Scouts with Stan Morin, a construction contractor who lived half a mile down the road. She thought her balding husband looked rather amusing in the khaki shorts and long brown socks he wore for the monthly Wildlife Hikes, but never said so. His bald spot had become well entrenched; his glasses had become bifocals; his weight had spun up from one-eighty into the two-twenty range. He had become a partner in the accounting firm – Benson and Bacon was now Benson, Bacon & Anderson. They had traded the starter home in Pownal for a more expensive one in Yarmouth. Her breasts, formerly small and firm and high (her best feature, she'd always thought; she'd never wanted to look like a Hooters waitress), were now larger, not so firm, and of course they dropped down when she took off her bra at night – what else could you expect when you were closing in on the half-century mark? – but every so often Bob would still come up behind her and cup them. Every so often there was the pleasant interlude in the upstairs bedroom overlooking their peaceful two-acre patch of land, and if he was a little quick on the draw and often left her unsatisfied, often was not always, and the satisfaction of holding him afterwards, feeling his warm man's body as he drowsed away next to her . . . that satisfaction never failed. It was, she supposed, the satisfaction of knowing they were still together when so many others were not; the satisfaction of knowing that as they approached their Silver Anniversary, the course was still steady as she goes.

In 2009, twenty-five years down the road from their I-do's in a small Baptist church that no longer existed (there was now a parking lot where it had stood), Donnie and Petra threw them a surprise party at The Birches on Castle View. There were over fifty guests, champagne (the good stuff), steak tips, a four-tier cake. The honorees danced to Kenny Loggins's 'Footloose,' just as they had at their wedding. The guests applauded Bob's breakaway move, one she had forgotten until she saw it again, and its still-airy execution gave her a pang. Well it should have; he had grown a paunch to go with the embarrassing bald spot (embarrassing to him, at least), but he was still extremely light on his feet for an accountant.

But all of that was just history, the stuff of obituaries, and they were still too young to be thinking of those. It ignored the minutiae of marriage, and such ordinary mysteries, she believed (*firmly* believed), were the stuff that validated the partnership. The time she had eaten bad shrimp and vomited all night long, sitting on the edge of the bed with her sweaty hair clinging to the nape of her neck and tears rolling down her flushed cheeks and Bob sitting beside her, patiently holding the basin and then taking it to the bathroom, where he emptied and rinsed it after each ejection – so the smell of it wouldn't make her even sicker, he said. He had been warming up the car to take her to the Emergency Room at six the next morning when the horrible nausea had finally begun to abate. He had called in sick at B, B & A; he'd also canceled a trip to White River so he could sit with her in case the sickness came back.

That kind of thing worked both ways; one year's sauce for the goose was next year's sauce for the gander. She had sat with him in the waiting room at St Stephen's – back in '94 or '95, this had been – waiting for the biopsy results after he had discovered (in the shower) a suspicious lump in his left armpit. The biopsy had been negative, the diagnosis an infected lymph node. The lump had lingered for another month or so, then went away on its own.

The sight of a crossword book on his knees glimpsed through the half-open bathroom door as he sat on the commode. The smell of cologne on his cheeks, which meant that the Suburban would be gone from the driveway for a day or two and his side of the bed would be empty for a night or two because he had to straighten out someone's accounting in New Hampshire or Vermont (B, B & A now had clients in all the northern New England states). Sometimes the smell meant a trip to look at someone's coin collection at an estate sale, because not all the numismatic buying and selling that went with their side-business could be accomplished by computer, they both understood that. The sight of his old black suitcase, the one he would never give up no matter how much she nagged, in the front hall. His slippers at the end of the bed, one always tucked into the other. The glass of water on his endtable, with the orange vitamin pill next to it, on that month's issue of *Coin & Currency Collecting*. How he always said, 'More room out than there is in' after belching and 'Look out, gas attack!' after he farted. His coat on the first hook in the hall. The reflection of his toothbrush in the mirror (he would still be using the same one he'd had when they got married, Darcy believed, if she didn't regularly replace it). The way he dabbed his lips with his napkin after every second or third bite of food. The careful arrangement of camping gear (always including an extra compass) before he and Stan set out with yet another bunch of nine-year-olds on the hike up Dead Man's Trail – a dangerous and terrifying trek that took them through the woods behind the Golden Grove Mall and came out at Weinberg's Used Car City. The look of his nails, always short and clean. The taste of Dentyne on his breath when they kissed. These things and ten thousand others comprised the secret history of the marriage.

She knew he must have his own history of her, everything from the cinnamon-flavored ChapStick she used on

her lips in the winter to the smell of her shampoo when
he nuzzled the back of her neck (that nuzzle didn't come
so often now, but it still came) to the click of her computer
at two in the morning on those two or three nights a
month when sleep for some reason jilted her.

Now it was twenty-seven years, or — she had amused
herself figuring this one day using the calculator function
on her computer — nine thousand, eight hundred and fifty-
five days. Almost a quarter of a million hours and over
fourteen million minutes. Of course some of that time he'd
been gone on business, and she'd taken a few trips herself
(the saddest to be with her parents in Minneapolis after
her kid sister Brandolyn had died in a freak accident), but
mostly they had been together.

Did she know everything about him? Of course not.
No more than he knew everything about her — how she
sometimes (mostly on rainy days or on those nights when
the insomnia was on her) gobbled Butterfingers or Baby
Ruths, for instance, eating the candybars even after she
no longer wanted them, even after she felt sick to her
stomach. Or how she thought the new mailman was sort
of cute. There was no knowing everything, but she felt
that after twenty-seven years, they knew all the important
things. It was a good marriage, one of the fifty percent
or so that kept working over the long haul. She believed
that in the same unquestioning way she believed that
gravity would hold her to the earth when she walked
down the sidewalk.

Until that night in the garage.

2

The TV controller stopped working, and there were no
double-A batteries in the kitchen cabinet to the left of
the sink. There were D-cells and C-cells, even an unopened

pack of the teeny tiny triple-As, but no goddarn frigging double-As. So she went out to the garage because she knew Bob kept a stash of Duracells there, and that was all it took to change her life. It was as if everyone was in the air, *high* in the air. One lousy little step in the wrong direction and you were falling.

The kitchen and the garage were connected by a breezeway. Darcy went through it in a hurry, clutching her housecoat against her – two days before their run of exceptionally warm Indian summer weather had broken, and now it felt more like November than October. The wind nipped at her ankles. She probably should have put on socks and a pair of slacks, but *Two and a Half Men* was going to come on in less than five minutes, and the goddarn TV was stuck on CNN. If Bob had been here, she would have asked him to change the channel manually – there were buttons for that somewhere, probably on the back where only a man could find them – and then sent him for the batteries. The garage was mostly his domain, after all. She only went there to get her car out, and that only on bad-weather days; otherwise she parked it in the driveway turnaround. But Bob was in Montpelier, evaluating a collection of World War II steel pennies, and she was, at least temporarily, in sole charge of *casa* Anderson.

She fumbled for the trio of switches beside the door and shoved them up with the heel of her hand. The overhead fluorescents buzzed on. The garage was spacious and neat, the tools hung on the pegboards and Bob's workbench in good order. The floor was a concrete slab painted battleship gray. There were no oilstains; Bob said that oilstains on a garage floor either meant the people who owned the garage were running junk or were careless about maintenance. The year-old Prius he used for his weekday commutes into Portland was there; he had taken his high-mileage SUV dinosaur to Vermont. Her Volvo was parked outside.

'It's just as easy to pull it in,' he had said on more than one occasion (when you were married for twenty-seven years, original comments tended to be thin on the ground). 'Just use the door opener on the visor.'

'I like it where I can see it,' she always replied, although the real reason was her fear of clipping the garage bay door while backing out. She hated backing. And she supposed he knew it . . . just as she knew that he had a peculiar fetish about keeping the paper money in his wallet heads-side up and would never leave a book facedown and open when he paused in his reading — because, he said, it broke the spine.

At least the garage was warm; big silver pipes (probably you called them ducts, but Darcy wasn't quite sure) crisscrossed the ceiling. She walked to the bench, where several square tins were lined up, each neatly labeled: BOLTS, SCREWS, HINGES HASPS & L-CLAMPS, PLUMBING, and — she found this rather endearing — ODDS & ENDS. There was a calendar on the wall featuring a *Sports Illustrated* swimsuit girl who looked depressingly young and sexy; to the left of the calendar two photos had been tacked up. One was an old snap of Donnie and Petra on the Yarmouth Little League field, dressed in Boston Red Sox jerseys. Below it, in Magic Marker, Bob had printed **THE HOME TEAM, 1999.** The other, much newer, showed a grown-up and just-short-of-beautiful Petra standing with Michael, her fiancé, in front of a clam shack on Old Orchard Beach with their arms around each other. The Magic Marker caption below this one read **THE HAPPY COUPLE!**

The cabinet with the batteries bore a Dymo tape label reading ELECTRICAL STUFF and was mounted to the left of the photos. Darcy moved in that direction without looking where she was going – trusting to Bob's just-short-of-maniacal neatness – and stumbled over a cardboard box that hadn't been entirely pushed under the workbench. She tottered, then grabbed the workbench at the last possible second. She broke off a fingernail – painful and annoying – but saved herself a potentially nasty fall, which was good. *Very* good, considering there was no one in the house to call 911, had she cracked her skull on the floor – greaseless and clean, but extremely hard.

She could simply have pushed the box back under with the side of her foot – later she would realize this and ponder it carefully, like a mathematician going over an abstruse and complicated equation. She was in a hurry, after all. But she saw a Patternworks knitting catalogue on top of the box, and knelt down to grab it and take it in with the batteries. And when she lifted it out, there was a Brookstone catalogue she had misplaced just underneath. And beneath that Paula Young . . . Talbots . . . For zieri . . . Bloomingdale's . . .

'Bob!' she cried, only it came out in two exasperated syllables (the way it did when he tracked in mud or left his sopping towels on the bathroom floor, as if they were in a fancy hotel with maid service), not *Bob* but *BOH-ub*! Because, really, she could read him like a book. He thought she ordered too much from the mail-order catalogues, had once gone so far as to declare she was addicted to them (which was ridiculous, it was Butterfingers she was addicted to). That little psychological analysis had earned him a two-day cold shoulder. But he knew how her mind worked, and that with things that weren't absolutely vital, she was the original out-of-sight, out-of-mind girl. So he had gathered up her catalogues, the sneak, and stowed them out here. Probably the next stop would have been the recycling bin.

Danskin . . . Express . . . Computer Outlet . . . *Mac world* . . . Monkey Ward . . . Layla Grace . . .

The deeper she went, the more exasperated she became. You'd think they were tottering on the edge of bankruptcy because of her spendthrift ways, which was utter bullshit. She had forgotten all about *Two and a Half Men*; she was already selecting the piece of her mind she intended to give Bob when he called from Montpelier (he always called after he'd had his dinner and was back at the motel). But first, she intended to take all these catalogues right back into the goddarn house, which would take three or possibly four trips, because the stack was at least two feet high, and those slick catalogues were *heavy*. It was really no wonder she'd stumbled over the box.

Death by catalogues, she thought. *Now that* would *be an ironic way to g—*

The thought broke off as clean as a dry branch. She was thumbing as she was thinking, now a quarter of the way down in the stack, and beneath Gooseberry Patch (country décor), she came to something that wasn't a catalogue. No, not a catalogue at all. It was a magazine called *Bondage Bitches*. She almost didn't take it out, and probably wouldn't have if she'd come across it in one of his drawers, or on that high shelf with the magic hair-replacement products. But finding it here, stashed in a pile of what had to be at least two hundred catalogues . . . *her* catalogues . . . there was something about that which went beyond the embarrassment a man might feel about a sexual kink.

The woman on the cover was bound to a chair and naked except for a black hood, but the hood only covered the top half of her face and you could see she was screaming. She was tied with heavy ropes that bit into her breasts and belly. There was fake blood on her chin, neck, and arms. Across the bottom of the page, in screaming yellow type, was this unpleasant come-on:

BAD BITCH BRENDA ASKED FOR IT AND GETS IT ON PAGE 49!

Darcy had no intention of turning to page 49, or to any other page. She was already explaining to herself what this was: a *male investigation*. She knew about male investigations from a *Cosmo* article she'd read in the dentist's office. A woman had written in to one of the magazine's many advisors (this one the on-staff shrink who specialized in the often mysterious bearded sex) about finding a couple of gay magazines in her husband's briefcase. Very explicit stuff, the letter-writer had said, and now she was worried that her husband might be in the closet. Although if he was, she continued, he was certainly hiding it well in the bedroom.

Not to worry, the advice-lady said. Men were adventurous by nature, and many of them liked to investigate sexual behavior that was either alternative – gay sex being number one in that regard, group sex a close second – or fetishistic: water sports, cross-dressing, public sex, latex. And, of course, bondage. She had added that some women were also fascinated by bondage, which had mystified Darcy, but she would have been the first to admit she didn't know everything.

Male investigation, that was all this was. He had maybe seen the magazine on a newsstand somewhere (although when Darcy tried to imagine that particular cover on a newsstand, her mind balked), and had been curious. Or maybe he'd picked it out of a trash can at a convenience store. He had taken it home, looked through it out here in the garage, had been as appalled as she was (the blood on the cover model was obviously fake, but that scream looked all too real), and had stuck it in this gigantic stack of catalogues bound for the recycling bin so she wouldn't come across it and give him a hard time. That was all it was, a one-off. If she looked through the rest of these catalogues, she'd find nothing else like it. Maybe a few *Penthouses* and panty-mags – she knew most men liked silk and lace, and Bob was no exception in this regard – but nothing more in the *Bondage Bitches* genre.

She looked at the cover again, and noticed an odd thing: there was no price on it. No bar code, either. She checked the back cover, curious about what such a magazine might cost, and winced at the picture there: a naked blonde strapped to what looked like a steel operating-room table. This one's expression of terror looked about as real as a three-dollar bill, however, which was sort of comforting. And the portly man standing over her with what appeared to be a Ginsu knife just looked ridiculous in his armlets and leather underpants – more like an accountant than someone about to carve up the Bondage Bitch du jour.

Bob's an accountant, her mind remarked.

A stupid thought launched from her brain's all-too-large Stupid Zone. She pushed it away just as she pushed the remarkably unpleasant magazine back into the pile of catalogues after ascertaining that there was no price or bar code on the back, either. And as she shoved the cardboard box under the workbench – she had changed her mind about carting the catalogues back into the house – the answer to the no-price/no-bar-code mystery came to her. It was one of those magazines they sold in a plastic wrapper, with all the naughty bits covered. The price and the code had been on the wrapper, of course that was it, what else could it be? He had to've bought the goddarn thing somewhere, assuming he hadn't fished it out of the trash.

Maybe he bought it over the Internet. There are probably sites that specialize in that sort of thing. Not to mention young women dressed up to look like twelve-year-olds.

'Never mind,' she said, and gave her head a single

brisk nod. This was a done deal, a dead letter, a closed discussion. If she mentioned it on the phone when he called later tonight, or when he came home, he'd be embarrassed and defensive. He'd probably call her sexually naïve, which she supposed she was, and accuse her of overreacting, which she was determined not to do. What she was determined to do was roll widdit, baby. A marriage was like a house under constant construction, each year seeing the completion of new rooms. A first-year marriage was a cottage; one that had gone on for twenty-seven years was a huge and rambling mansion. There were bound to be crannies and storage spaces, most of them dusty and abandoned, some containing a few unpleasant relics you would just as soon you hadn't found. But that was no biggie. You either threw those relics out or took them to Goodwill.

She liked this thought (which had a conclusive feel) so well that she said it out loud: 'No biggie.' And to prove it, she gave the cardboard box a hard two-handed shove, sending it all the way to the rear wall.

Where there was a clunk. What was that?

I don't want to know, she told herself, and was pretty sure that thought wasn't coming from the Stupid Zone but from the smart one. It was shadowy back there under the worktable, and there might be mice. Even a well-kept garage like this one could have mice, especially once cold weather came, and a scared mouse might bite.

Darcy stood up, brushed off the knees of her housecoat, and left the garage. Halfway across the breezeway, she heard the phone begin to ring.

3

She was back in the kitchen before the answering machine kicked in, but she waited. If it was Bob, she'd let the robot take it. She didn't want to talk to him right this minute. He might hear something in her voice. He would assume she'd gone out to the corner store or maybe to Video Village and call back in an hour. In an hour, after her unpleasant discovery would have had a chance to settle a bit, she'd be fine and they could have a pleasant conversation.

But it wasn't Bob, it was Donnie. 'Oh, shoot, I really wanted to talk to you guys.'

She picked up the phone, leaned back against the counter, and said, 'So talk. I was coming back from the garage.'

Donnie was bubbling over with news. He was living in Cleveland, Ohio, now, and after two years of thankless toiling in an entry-level position with the city's largest ad firm, he and a friend had decided to strike out on their own. Bob had strongly advised against this, telling Donnie that Donnie and his partner would never get the start-up loan they needed to make it through the first year.

'Wake up,' he'd said after Darcy turned the phone over to him. In the early spring this had been, with the last bits of snow still lurking beneath the trees and bushes in the backyard. 'You're twenty-four, Donnie, and so's your pal Ken. You two galoots can't even get collision insurance on your cars for another year, just straight liability. No bank's going to underwrite a seventy-thousand-dollar start-up, especially with the economy the way it is.'

But they *had* gotten the loan, and now had landed two big clients, both on the same day. One was a car dealership looking for a fresh approach that would attract thirtysomething buyers. The other was the very bank that had issued Anderson & Hayward their start-up loan. Darcy shouted with delight, and Donnie yelled right back. They talked for twenty minutes or so. Once during the conversation they were interrupted by the double-beep of an incoming call.

'Do you want to get that?' Donnie asked.

'No, it's just your father. He's in Montpelier, looking at a collection of steel pennies. He'll call back before he turns in.'

'How's he doing?'

Fine, she thought. *Developing new interests.*

'Upright and sniffin the air,' she said. It was one of Bob's favorites, and it made Donnie laugh. She loved to hear him laugh.

'And Pets?'

'Call her yourself and see, Donald.'

'I will, I will. I always get around to it. In the mean-time, thumbnail me.'

'She's great. Full of wedding plans.'

'You'd think it was next week instead of next June.'

'Donnie, if you don't make an effort to understand women, you'll never get married yourself.'

'I'm in no hurry, I'm having too much fun.'

'Just as long as you have fun carefully.'

'I'm very careful and very polite. I've got to run, Ma. I'm meeting Ken for a drink in half an hour. We're going to start brainstorming this car thing.'

She almost told him not to drink too much, then restrained herself. He might still look like a high school junior, and in her clearest memory of him he was a five-year-old in a red corduroy jumper, tirelessly pushing his scooter up and down the concrete paths of Joshua Chamberlain Park in Pownal, but he was neither of those boys anymore. He was a young man, and also, as improbable as it seemed, a young entrepreneur beginning to make his way in the world.

'Okay,' she said. 'Thanks for calling, Donnie. It was a treat.'

'Same here. Say hello to the old feller when he calls back, and give him my love.'

'I will.'

'Upright and sniffin the air,' Donnie said, and snickered. 'How many Cub Scout packs has he taught that one to?'

'All of them.' Darcy opened the refrigerator to see if there was perchance a Butterfinger in there, chilling and awaiting her amorous intentions. Nope. 'It's terrifying.'

'Love you, Mom.'

'Love you, too.'

She hung up, feeling good again. Smiling. But as she stood there, leaning against the counter, the smile faded.

A clunk.

There had been a clunk when she pushed the box of catalogues back under the workbench. Not a clatter, as if the box had struck a dropped tool, but a *clunk*. Sort of hollow-sounding.

I don't care.

Unfortunately, this was not true. The clunk felt like unfinished business. The carton did, too. *Were* there other magazines like *Bondage Bitches* stashed in there?

I don't want to know.

Right, right, but maybe she should find out, just the same. Because if there was just the one, she was right about its being sexual curiosity that had been fully satisfied by a single peek into an unsavory (*and unbalanced*, she added to herself) world. If there were more that might still be all right – he was throwing them out, after all – but maybe she should know.

Mostly . . . that clunk. It lingered on her mind more than the question about the magazines.

She snagged a flashlight from the pantry and went back out to the garage. She pinched the lapels of her housecoat shut immediately and wished she'd put on her jacket. It was really getting cold.

4

Darcy got down on her knees, pushed the box of catalogues to one side, and shone the light under the worktable. For a moment she didn't understand what she was seeing: two lines of darkness interrupting the smooth baseboard, one slightly fatter than the other. Then a thread of disquiet formed in her midsection, stretching from the middle of her breastbone down to the pit of her stomach. It was a hiding place.

Leave this alone, Darcy. It's his business, and for your own peace of mind you should let it stay that way.

Good advice, but she had come too far to take it. She crawled under the worktable with the flashlight in her hand, steeling herself for the brush of cobwebs, but there were none. If she was the original out-of-sight, out-of-mind girl, then her balding, coin-collecting, Cub Scouting husband was the original everything-polished, everything-clean boy.

Also, he's crawled under here himself, so no cobwebs would have a chance to form.

Was that true? She didn't actually know, did she?

But she thought she did.

The cracks were at either end of an eight-inch length of baseboard that appeared to have a dowel or something in the middle so it could pivot. She had struck it with the box just hard enough to jar it open, but that didn't explain the clunk. She pushed one end of the board. It swung in on one end and out on the other, revealing a hidey-hole eight inches long, a foot high, and maybe eighteen inches deep. She thought she might discover more magazines, possibly rolled up, but there were no magazines. There was a little wooden box, one she was pretty sure she recognized. It was the box that had made the clunking sound. It had been standing on end, and the pivoting baseboard had knocked it over.

She reached in, grasped it, and – with a sense of misgiving so strong it almost had a texture – brought it out. It was the little oak box she had given to him at Christmas five years ago, maybe more. Or had it been for his birthday? She didn't remember, just that it had been a good buy at the craft shop in Castle Rock. Hand-carved on the top, in bas-relief, was a chain. Below the chain, also in bas-relief, was the box's stated purpose: **LINKS**. Bob had a clutter of cufflinks, and although he favored button-style shirts for work, some of his wrist-jewelry was quite nice. She remembered thinking the box would help keep them organized. Darcy knew she'd seen it on top of the bureau on his side of the bedroom for awhile after the gift was unwrapped and exclaimed over, but couldn't remember seeing it lately. Of course she hadn't. It was out here, in the hidey-hole under his worktable, and she would have bet the house and lot (another of his sayings) that if she opened it, it wouldn't be cufflinks she found inside.

Don't look, then.

More good advice, but now she had come *much* too far to take it. Feeling like a woman who has wandered into a casino and for some mad reason staked her entire life's savings on a single turn of a single card, she opened the box.

Let it be empty. Please God, if you love me let it be empty.

But it wasn't. There were three plastic oblongs inside, bound with an elastic band. She picked the bundle out, using just the tips of her fingers – as a woman might handle a cast-off rag she fears may be germy as well as dirty. Darcy slipped off the elastic.

They weren't credit cards, which had been her first idea. The top one was a Red Cross blood donor's card belonging to someone named Marjorie Duvall. Her type was A-positive, her region New England. Darcy turned the card over and saw that Marjorie — whoever she was — had last given blood on August sixteenth of 2010. Three months ago.

Who the hell was Marjorie Duvall? How did Bob know her? And why did the name ring a faint but very clear bell?

The next one was Marjorie Duvall's North Conway Library card, and it had an address: 17 Honey Lane, South Gansett, New Hampshire.

The last piece of plastic was Marjorie Duvall's New Hampshire driver's license. She looked like a perfectly ordinary American woman in her mid-thirties, not very pretty (although nobody looked their best in driver's license photographs), but presentable. Darkish blond hair pulled back from her face, either bunned or ponytailed; in the picture you couldn't tell. DOB, January 6, 1974. The address was the same as the one on the library card.

Darcy realized that she was making a desolate mewing sound. It was horrible to hear a sound like that coming from her own throat, but she couldn't stop. And her stomach had been replaced by a ball of lead. It was pulling all of her insides down, stretching them into new and unpleasant shapes. She had seen Marjorie Duvall's face in the newspaper. Also on the six o'clock news.

With hands that had absolutely no feeling, she put the rubber band back around the ID cards, put them back in the box, then put the box back in his hidey-hole. She was getting ready to close it up again when she heard herself saying, 'No, no, no, that isn't right. It can't be.'

Was that the voice of Smart Darcy or Stupid Darcy? It was hard to tell. All she knew for sure was that Stupid

Darcy had been the one to open the box. And thanks to Stupid Darcy, she was falling.

Taking the box back out. Thinking, *It's a mistake, it has to be, we've been married over half our lives, I'd know, I would know.* Opening the box. Thinking, *Does anybody really know anybody?*

Before tonight she certainly would have thought so.

Marjorie Duvall's driver's license was now on the top of the stack. Before, it had been on the bottom. Darcy put it there. But which of the others had been on top, the Red Cross card or the library card? It was simple, it *had* to be simple when there were only two choices, but she was too upset to remember. She put the library card on top and knew at once that was wrong, because the first thing she'd seen when she opened the box was a flash of red, red like blood, of course a blood donor card would be red, and that had been the one on top.

She put it there, and as she was putting the elastic back around the little collection of plastic, the phone in the house started to ring again. It was him. It was Bob, calling from Vermont, and were she in the kitchen to take the call, she'd hear his cheery voice (a voice she knew as well as her own) asking, *Hey, honey, how are you?*

Her fingers jerked and the rubber band snapped. It flew away, and she cried out, whether in frustration or fear she didn't know. But really, why would she be afraid? Twenty-seven years of marriage and he had never laid a hand on her, except to caress. On only a few occasions had he raised his voice to her.

The phone rang again . . . again . . . and then cut off in mid-ring. Now he would be leaving a message. *Missed you again! Damn! Give me a call so I won't worry, okay? The number is . . .*

He'd add the number of his room, too. He left nothing to chance, took nothing for granted.

What she was thinking absolutely couldn't be true. It was like one of those monster delusions that sometimes reared up from the mud at the bottom of a person's mind, sparkling with hideous plausibility: that the acid indigestion was the onset of a heart attack, the headache a brain tumor, and Petra's failure to call on Sunday night meant she had been in a car accident and was lying comatose in some hospital. But those delusions usually came at four in the morning, when the insomnia was in charge. Not at eight o'clock in the evening . . . and where was that damned rubber band?

She found it at last, lying behind the carton of catalogues she never wanted to look in again. She put it in her pocket, started to get up to look for another one without remembering where she was, and thumped her head on the bottom of the table. Darcy began to cry.

There were no rubber bands in any of the worktable's drawers, and that made her cry even harder. She went back through the breezeway, the terrible, inexplicable identity cards in her housecoat pocket, and got an elastic out of the kitchen drawer where she kept all sorts of semi-useful crap: paper clips, bread ties, fridge magnets that had lost most of their pull. One of these latter said DARCY RULES, and had been a stocking-stuffer present from Bob.

On the counter, the light on top of the phone blinked steadily, saying *message, message, message*.

She hurried back to the garage without holding the lapels of her housecoat. She no longer felt the outer chill, because the one inside was greater. And then there was the lead ball pulling down her guts. Elongating them. She was vaguely aware that she needed to move her bowels, and badly.

Never mind. Hold it. Pretend you're on the turnpike and the next rest area's twenty miles ahead. Get this done. Put everything back the way it was. Then you can—

Then she could what? Forget it?

Fat chance of that.

She bound the ID cards with the elastic, realized the driver's license had somehow gotten back on top, and called herself a stupid bitch . . . a pejorative for which she would have slapped Bob's face, had he ever tried to hang it on her. Not that he ever had.

'A stupid bitch but not a bondage bitch,' she muttered, and a cramp knifed her belly. She dropped to her knees and froze that way, waiting for it to pass. If there had been a bathroom out here she would have dashed for it, but there wasn't. When the cramp let go – reluctantly – she rearranged the cards in what she was pretty sure was the right order (blood donor, library, driver's license), then put them back in the **LINKS** box. Box back in hole. Pivoting piece of baseboard closed up tight. Carton of catalogues back where it had been when she tripped on it: sticking out slightly. He would never know the difference.

But was she sure of that? If he was what she was thinking – monstrous that such a thing should even be in her mind, when all she'd wanted just a half an hour ago was fresh batteries for the goddarn remote control – if he *was*, then he'd been careful for a long time. And he *was* careful, he was neat, he was the original everything-polished, everything-clean boy, but if he was what those goddarn (no, *goddamned*) plastic cards seemed to suggest he was, then he must be *supernaturally* careful. Supernaturally watchful. Sly.

It was a word she had never thought of in connection to Bob until tonight.

'No,' she told the garage. She was sweating, her hair was stuck to her face in unlovely spikelets, she was crampy and her hands were trembling like those of a person with Parkinson's, but her voice was weirdly calm, strangely serene. 'No, he's not. It's a mistake. *My husband is not Beadie.*'

She went back into the house.

5

She decided to make tea. Tea was calming. She was filling the kettle when the phone began to ring again. She dropped the kettle into the sink – the *bong* sound made her utter a small scream – then went to the phone, wiping her wet hands on her housecoat.

Calm, calm, she told herself. *If he can keep a secret, so can I. Remember that there's a reasonable explanation for all this—*

Oh, really?

—and I just don't know what it is. I need time to think about it, that's all. So: calm.

She picked up the phone and said brightly, 'If that's you, handsome, come right over. My husband's out of town.'

Bob laughed. 'Hey, honey, how are you?'

'Upright and sniffin the air. You?'

There was a long silence. It felt long, anyway, although it couldn't have been more than a few seconds. In it she heard the somehow terrible whine of the refrigerator, and water dripping from the faucet onto the teakettle she'd dropped in the sink, the beating of her own heart – that last sound seeming to come from her throat and ears rather than her chest. They had been married so long that they had become almost exquisitely attuned to each other. Did that happen in every marriage? She didn't know. She only knew her own. Except now she had to wonder if she even knew that one.

'You sound funny,' he said. 'All thick in the voice. Is everything okay, sweetie?'

She should have been touched. Instead she was terrified.

Marjorie Duvall: the name did not just hang in front of her eyes; it seemed to blink on and off, like a neon bar sign. For a moment she was speechless, and to her horror, the kitchen she knew so well was wavering in front of her as more tears rose in her eyes. That crampy heaviness was back in her bowels, too. Marjorie Duvall. A-positive. 17 Honey Lane. As in *hey, hon, how's life been treatin you, are you upright and sniffin the air?*

'I was thinking about Brandolyn,' she heard herself say.

'Oh, baby,' he said, and the sympathy in his voice was all Bob. She knew it well. Hadn't she leaned on it time after time since 1984? Even before, when they'd still been courting and she came to understand that he was the one? Sure she had. As he had leaned on her. The idea that such sympathy could be nothing but sweet icing on a poison cake was insane. The fact that she was at this moment lying to him was even more insane. If, that was, there were degrees of insanity. Or maybe insane was like unique, and there was no comparative or superlative form. And what was she thinking? In God's name, what?

But he was talking, and she had no idea what he'd just said.

'Run that past me again. I was reaching for the tea.' Another lie, her hands were shaking too badly to reach for anything, but a small plausible one. And her voice wasn't shaking. At least she didn't think it was.

'I said, what got that going?'

'Donnie called and asked after his sister. It got me thinking about mine. I went out and walked around for awhile. I got sniffling, although some of that was just the cold. You probably heard it in my voice.'

'Yep, right away,' he said. 'Listen, I should skip Burlington tomorrow and come back home.'

She almost cried out *No!*, but that would be exactly

the wrong thing to do. That might get him on the road at first light, all solicitude.

'You do and I'll punch you in the eye,' she said, and was relieved when he laughed. 'Charlie Frady told you that estate sale in Burlington was worth going to, and his contacts are good. His instincts are, too. You've always said so.'

'Yeah, but I don't like to hear you sounding so low.'

That he had known (and at once! at *once!*) that something was wrong with her was bad. That she needed to lie about what the trouble was — ah, that was worse. She closed her eyes, saw Bad Bitch Brenda screaming inside the black hood, and opened them again.

'I was low, but I'm not now,' she said. 'It was just a momentary fugue. She was my sister, and I saw my father bring her home. Sometimes I think about it, that's all.'

'I know,' he said. He did, too. Her sister's death wasn't the reason she'd fallen in love with Bob Anderson, but his understanding of her grief had tightened the connection.

Brandolyn Madsen had been struck and killed by a drunk snowmobiler while she was out cross-country skiing. He fled, leaving her body in the woods half a mile from the Madsen house. When Brandi wasn't back by eight o'clock, a pair of Freeport policemen and the local Neighborhood Watch had mounted a search party. It was Darcy's father who found her body and carried it home through half a mile of pine woods. Darcy — stationed in the living room, monitoring the phone and trying to keep her mother calm — had been the first to see him. He came walking up the lawn under the harsh glare of a full winter moon with his breath puffing out in white clouds. Darcy's initial thought (this was still terrible to her) had been of those corny old black-and-white love-movies they sometimes showed on TCM, the ones where some guy carries his new bride across the threshold of their happy honeymoon cottage while fifty violins pour syrup onto the soundtrack.

Bob Anderson, Darcy had discovered, could relate in a way many people could not. He hadn't lost a brother or sister; he had lost his best friend. The boy had darted out into the road to grab an errant throw during a game of pickup baseball (not Bob's throw, at least; no baseball player, he'd been swimming that day), had been struck by a delivery truck, and died in the hospital shortly afterward. This coincidence of old sorrows wasn't the only thing that made their pairing seem special to her, but it was the one that made it feel somehow mystical — not a coincidence but a planned thing.

'Stay in Vermont, Bobby. Go to the estate sale. I love you for being concerned, but if you come running home, I'll feel like a kid. Then I'll be mad.'

'Okay. But I'm going to call you tomorrow at seven-thirty. Fair warning.'

She laughed, and was relieved to hear it was a real one . . . or so close as to make no difference. And why shouldn't she be allowed a real laugh? Just why the heck not? She loved him, and would give him the benefit of the doubt. Of *every* doubt. Nor was this a choice. You could not turn off love — even the rather absent, sometimes taken for granted love of twenty-seven years — the way you'd turn off a faucet. Love ran from the heart, and the heart had its own imperatives.

'Bobby, you always call at seven-thirty.'

'Guilty as charged. Call tonight if you—'

'—need anything, no matter what the hour,' she finished for him. Now she almost felt like herself again. It was really amazing, the number of hard hits from which a mind could recover. 'I will.'

'Love you, honey.' The coda of so many conversations over the years.

'Love you, too,' she said, smiling. Then she hung up, put her forehead against the wall, closed her eyes, and began weeping before the smile could leave her face.

6

Her computer, an iMac now old enough to look fashionably retro, was in her sewing room. She rarely used it for anything but email and eBay, but now she opened Google and typed in Marjorie Duvall's name. She hesitated before adding *Beadie* to the search, but not long. Why prolong the agony? It would come up anyway, she was sure of it. She hit Enter, and as she watched the little wait-circle go around and around at the top of the screen, those cramps struck again. She hurried to the bathroom, sat down on the commode, and took care of her business with her face in her hands. There was a mirror on the back of the door, and she didn't want to see herself in it. Why was it there, anyway? Why had she *allowed* it to be there? Who wanted to watch themselves sitting on the pot? Even at the best of times, which this most certainly wasn't?

She went back to the computer slowly, dragging her feet like a child who knows she is about to be punished for the kind of thing Darcy's mother had called a Big Bad. She saw that Google had provided her with over five million results for her search: o omnipotent Google, so generous and so terrible. But the first one actually made her laugh; it invited her to follow Marjorie Duvall Beadie on Twitter. Darcy felt she could ignore that one. Unless she was wrong (and how wildly grateful that would make her), the Marjorie she was looking for had Twittered her last tweet some time ago.

The second result was from the *Portland Press Herald*, and when Darcy clicked on it, the photograph that greeted her (it felt like a slap, that greeting) was the one she remembered from TV, and probably in this very article, since the *Press Herald* was their paper. The article had been published ten days before, and was the lead story. **NEW HAMPSHIRE WOMAN MAY HAVE BEEN 'BEADIE'S' 11th VICTIM,** the headline screamed. And the subhead: *Police Source: 'We're Ninety Per Cent Sure'*.

Marjorie Duvall looked a lot prettier in the newspaper picture, a studio shot that showed her posed in classic fashion, wearing a swirly black dress. Her hair was down, and looked a much lighter blond in this photo. Darcy wondered if her husband had provided the picture. She supposed he had. She supposed it had been on their mantel at 17 Honey Lane, or perhaps mounted in the hall. The pretty hostess of the house greeting guests with her eternal smile.

Gentlemen prefer blondes because they get tired of squeezin them blackheads.

One of Bob's sayings. She had never much liked that one, and hated having it in her head now.

Marjorie Duvall had been found in a ravine six miles from her house in South Gansett, just over the North Conway town line. The County Sheriff speculated that the death had probably resulted from strangulation, but he couldn't say for sure; that was up to the County Medical Examiner. He refused to speculate further, or answer any other questions, but the reporter's unnamed source (whose information was at least semi-validated by being 'close to the investigation') said that Duvall had been bitten and sexually molested 'in a manner consistent with the other Beadie killings.'

Which was a natural transition to a complete recap of the previous murders. The first had occurred in 1977. There had been two in 1978, another in 1980, and then two more in 1981. Two of the murders had occurred in

New Hampshire, two in Massachusetts, the fifth and sixth in Vermont. After that, there had been a hiatus of sixteen years. The police assumed that one of three things had happened: Beadie had moved to another part of the country and was pursuing his hobby there, Beadie had been arrested for some other, unrelated crime and was in prison, or Beadie had killed himself. The one thing that *wasn't* likely, according to a psychiatrist the reporter had consulted for his story, was that Beadie had just gotten tired of it. 'These guys don't get bored,' the psychiatrist said. 'It's their sport, their compulsion. More than that, it's their secret life.'

Secret life. What a poison bonbon that phrase was.

Beadie's sixth victim had been a woman from Barre, uncovered in a snowdrift by a passing plow just a week before Christmas. *Such a holiday that must have been for her relatives,* Darcy thought. Not that she'd had much of a Christmas herself that year. Lonely away from home (a fact wild horses wouldn't have dragged from her mouth when talking to her mother), working at a job she wasn't sure she was qualified for even after eighteen months and one merit raise, she had felt absolutely no spirit of the season. She had acquaintances (the Margarita Girls), but no real friends. She wasn't good when it came to making friends, never had been. Shy was the kind word for her personality, introverted probably a more accurate one.

Then Bob Anderson had walked into her life with a smile on his face – Bob who had asked her out and wouldn't take no for an answer. Not three months after the plow had uncovered the body of Beadie's last 'early cycle' victim, that must have been. They fell in love. And Beadie stopped for sixteen years.

Because of her? Because he loved her? Because he wanted to stop doing Big Bads?

Or just a coincidence. It could be that.

Nice try, but the IDs she'd found squirreled away in the garage made the idea of coincidence seem a lot less likely.

Beadie's seventh victim, the first of what the paper called 'the new cycle,' had been a woman from Waterville, Maine, named Stacey Moore. Her husband found her in the cellar upon returning from Boston, where he and two friends had taken in a couple of Red Sox games. August of 1997, this had been. Her head had been stuffed into a bin of the sweet corn the Moores sold at their roadside Route 106 farmstand. She was naked, her hands bound behind her back, her buttocks and thighs bitten in a dozen places.

Two days later, Stacey Moore's driver's license and Blue Cross card, bound with a rubber band, had arrived in Augusta, addressed in block printing to BOOB ATTORNEY JENRAL DEPT. OF CRINIMAL INVESTIGATION. There was also a note: *HELLO! I'M BACK! BEADIE!*

This was a packet the detectives in charge of the Moore murder recognized at once. Similar selected bits of ID – and similar cheerful notes – had been delivered following each of the previous killings. He knew when they were alone. He tortured them, principally with his teeth; he raped or sexually molested them; he killed them; he sent their identification to some branch of the police weeks or months later. Taunting them with it.

To make sure he gets the credit, Darcy thought dismally.

There had been another Beadie murder in 2004, the ninth and tenth in 2007. Those two were the worst, because one of the victims had been a child. The woman's ten-year-old son had been excused from school after complaining of a stomachache, and had apparently walked in on Beadie while he was at work. The boy's body had been found with his mother's, in a nearby creek. When the woman's ID – two credit cards and a driver's license – arrived at Massachusetts State Police Barracks #7, the attached card read: *HELLO! THE BOY WAS AN ACCIDENT! SORRY! BUT IT WAS QUICK, HE DID NOT 'SUFFER!' BEADIE!*

There were many other articles she could have accessed (o omnipotent Google), but to what end? The sweet dream of one more ordinary evening in an ordinary life had been swallowed by a nightmare. Would reading more about Beadie dispel the nightmare? The answer to that was obvious.

Her belly clenched. She ran for the bathroom – still smelly in spite of the fan, usually you could ignore what a smelly business life was, but not always – and fell on her knees in front of the toilet, staring into the blue water with her mouth open. For a moment she thought the need to vomit was going to pass, then she thought of Stacey Moore with her black strangled face shoved into the corn and her buttocks covered with blood dried to the color of chocolate milk. That tipped her over and she vomited twice, hard enough to splash her face with Ty-D-Bol and a few flecks of her own effluvium.

Crying and gasping, she flushed the toilet. The porcelain would have to be cleaned, but for now she only lowered the lid and laid her flushed cheek on its cool beige plastic.

What am I going to do?

The obvious step was to call the police, but what if she did that and it all turned out to be a mistake? Bob had always been the most generous and forgiving of men – when she'd run the front of their old van into a tree at the edge of the post office parking lot and shattered the windshield, his only concern had been if she had cut her face – but would he forgive her if she mistakenly fingered him for eleven torture-killings he hadn't committed? And the world would know. Guilty or innocent, his picture would be in the paper. On the front page. Hers, too.

Darcy dragged herself to her feet, got the toilet-scrubbing brush from the bathroom closet, and cleaned up her mess. She did it slowly. Her back hurt. She supposed she had thrown up hard enough to pull a muscle.

Halfway through the job, the next realization thudded down. It wouldn't be just the two of them dragged into newspaper speculation and the filthy rinse-cycle of twenty-four-hour cable news; there were the kids to think about. Donnie and Ken had just landed their first two clients, but the bank and the car dealer-ship looking for a fresh approach would be gone three hours after this shit-bomb exploded. Anderson & Hayward, which had taken its first real breath today, would be dead tomorrow. Darcy didn't know how much Ken Hayward had invested, but Donnie was all in the pot. That didn't amount to such of a much in cash, but there were other things you invested when you were starting out on your own voyage. Your heart, your brains, your sense of self-worth.

Then there were Petra and Michael, probably at this very moment with their heads together making more wedding plans, unaware that a two-ton safe was dangling above them on a badly frayed cord. Pets had always idolized her father. What would it do to her if she found out the hands which had once pushed her on the backyard swing were the same hands that had strangled the life out of eleven women? That the lips which had kissed her goodnight were hiding teeth that had bitten eleven women, in some cases all the way down to the bone?

Sitting at her computer again, a terrible newspaper headline rose in Darcy's mind. It was accompanied by a photograph of Bob in his neckerchief, absurd khaki shorts, and long socks. It was so clear it could already have been printed:

MASS MURDERER 'BEADIE' LED CUB SCOUTS FOR 17 YEARS

Darcy clapped a hand over her mouth. She could feel her eyes pulsing in their sockets. The notion of suicide occurred to her, and for a few moments (long ones) the idea seemed completely rational, the only reasonable solution. She could leave a note saying she'd done it because she was afraid she had cancer. Or early-onset Alzheimer's, that was even better. But suicide cast a deep shadow over families, too, and what if she was wrong? What if Bob had just found that ID packet by the side of the road, or something?

Do you know how unlikely that is? Smart Darcy sneered.

Okay, yes, but unlikely wasn't the same as impossible, was it? There was something else, too, something that made the cage she was in escape-proof: what if she was right? Wouldn't her death free Bob to kill more, because he no longer had to lead so deep a double life? Darcy wasn't sure she believed in a conscious existence after death, but what if there was one? And what if she were confronted there not by Edenic green fields and rivers of plenty but by a ghastly receiving line of strangled women branded by her husband's teeth, all accusing her of causing their deaths by taking the easy way out herself? And by ignoring what she had found (if such a thing were even possible, which she didn't believe for a minute), wouldn't the accusation be true? Did she really think she could condemn more women to horrible deaths just so her daughter could have a nice June wedding?

She thought: *I wish I was dead.*

But she wasn't.

For the first time in years, Darcy Madsen Anderson slipped from her chair onto her knees and began to pray. It did no good. The house was empty except for her.

7

She had never kept a diary, but she had ten years' worth of appointment books stored in the bottom of her capacious sewing chest. And decades' worth of Bob's travel records stuffed in one of the file drawers of the cabinet he kept in his home office. As a tax accountant (and one with his own duly incorporated side-business to boot), he was meticulous when it came to record-keeping, taking every deduction, tax credit, and cent of automotive depreciation he could.

She stacked his files beside her computer along with her appointment books. She opened Google and forced herself to do the research she needed, noting the names and dates of death (some of these were necessarily approximate) of Beadie's victims. Then, as the digital clock on her computer's control strip marched soundlessly past ten PM, she began the laborious work of cross-checking.

She would have given a dozen years of her life to find something that would have indisputably eliminated him from even one of the murders, but her appointment books only made things worse. Kellie Gervais, of Keene, New Hampshire, had been discovered in the woods behind the local landfill on March fifteenth of 2004. According to the medical examiner, she had been dead three to five days. Scrawled across March tenth to twelfth in Darcy's appointment book for 2004 was *Bob to Fitzwilliam, Brat.* George Fitzwilliam was a well-heeled client of Benson, Bacon & Anderson. *Brat* was her abbreviation for Brattleboro, where Fitzwilliam lived. An easy drive from Keene, New Hampshire.

Helen Shaverstone and her son Robert had been discovered in Newrie Creek, in the town of Amesbury, on November eleventh of 2007. They had lived in Tassel Village, some twelve miles away. On the November page of her 2007 address book, she had drawn a line across the eighth to the tenth, scrawling *Bob in Saugus, 2 estate sales plus Boston coin auc.* And did she remember calling his Saugus motel on one of those nights and not getting him? Assuming he was out late with some coin salesman, sniffing for leads, or maybe in the shower? She *seemed* to remember that. If so, had he actually been on the road that night? Perhaps coming back from doing an errand (a little drop-off) in the town of Amesbury? Or, if he *had* been in the shower, what in God's name had he been washing off?

She turned to his travel records and vouchers as the clock on the control strip passed eleven and started climbing toward midnight, the witching hour when grave-yards reputedly yawned. She worked carefully and stopped often to double-check. The stuff from the late seventies was spotty and not much help — he hadn't been much more than your basic office drone in those days — but everything from the eighties was there, and the correla-tions she found for the Beadie murders in 1980 and 1981 were clear and undeniable. He had been traveling at the right times and in the right areas. And, Smart Darcy insisted, if you found enough cat hairs in a person's house, you pretty much had to assume there was a feline on the premises somewhere.

So what do I do now?

The answer seemed to be, carry her confused and frightened head upstairs. She doubted if she could sleep, but at least she could take a hot shower and then lie down. She was exhausted, her back ached from throwing up, and she stank of her own sweat.

She shut off her computer and climbed to the second floor at a slow trudge. The shower eased her back and a couple of Tylenol would probably ease it more by two AM or so; she was sure she'd be awake to find out. When she put the Tylenol back in the medicine cabinet, she took the Ambien bottle out, held it in her hand for almost a full minute, then replaced that, too. It wouldn't put her to sleep, only make her muzzy and – perhaps – more paranoid than she was already.

She lay down and looked at the night table on the other side of the bed. Bob's clock. Bob's spare set of reading glasses. A copy of a book called *The Shack. You ought to read this, Darce, it's a life-changer*, he'd said two or three nights before this latest trip.

She turned off her lamp, saw Stacey Moore stuffed into the cornbin, and turned the lamp back on again. On most nights, the dark was her friend – sleep's kindly harbinger – but not tonight. Tonight the dark was populated by Bob's harem.

You don't know that. Remember that you don't absolutely know that.

But if you find enough cat hairs . . .

Enough with the cat hairs, too.

She lay there, even more wide awake than she'd feared she'd be, her mind going around and around, now thinking of the victims, now thinking of her children, now thinking of herself, even thinking of some long-forgotten Bible story about Jesus praying in the Garden of Gethsemane. She glanced at Bob's clock after what felt like an hour of going around that wretched worry-circle and saw that only twelve minutes had passed. She got up on one elbow and turned the clock's face to the window.

He won't be home until six tomorrow night, she thought . . . although, since it was now quarter past midnight, she supposed it was technically tonight that he'd be home. Still, that gave her eighteen hours. Surely enough time to make some sort of decision. It would help if she could sleep, even a little – sleep had a way of resetting the mind – but it was out of the question. She would drift a little, then think *Marjorie Duvall* or *Stacey Moore* or (this was the worst) *Robert Shaverstone, ten years old. HE DID NOT 'SUFFER!'* And then any possibility of sleep would again be gone. The idea that she might never sleep again came to her. That was impossible, of course, but lying here with the taste of puke still in her mouth in spite of the Scope she had rinsed with, it seemed completely plausible.

At some point she found herself remembering the year in early childhood when she had gone around the house looking in mirrors. She would stand in front of them with her hands cupped to the sides of her face and her nose touching the glass, but holding her breath so she wouldn't fog the surface.

If her mother caught her, she'd swat her away. *That leaves a smudge, and I have to clean it off. Why are you so interested in yourself, anyway? You'll never be hung for your beauty. And why stand so close? You can't see anything worth looking at that way.*

How old had she been? Four? Five? Too young to explain that it wasn't her reflection she was interested in, anyway – or not primarily. She had been convinced that mirrors were doorways to another world, and what she saw reflected in the glass wasn't *their* living room or bath-room, but the living room or bathroom of some other family. The Matsons instead of the Madsens, perhaps. Because it was *similar* on the other side of the glass, but not the *same*, and if you looked long enough, you could begin to pick up on some of the differences: a rug that appeared to be oval over there instead of round like over here, a door that seemed to have a turn-latch instead of a bolt, a light-switch that was on the wrong side of the door. The little girl wasn't the same, either. Darcy was sure they were related – sisters of the mirror? – but no, not the same. Instead of Darcellen Madsen that little girl might be named Jane or Sandra or even Eleanor Rigby, who for some reason (some *scary* reason) picked up the rice at churches where a wedding had been.

Lying in the circle of her bedside lamp, drowsing without realizing it, Darcy supposed that if she *had* been able to tell her mother what she was looking for, if she had explained about the Darker Girl who wasn't quite her, she might have passed some time with a child psychiatrist. But it wasn't the girl who interested her, it had never been the girl. What interested her was the idea that there was a whole other world behind the mirrors, and if you could walk through that other house (the Darker House) and out the door, the rest of that world would be waiting.

Of course this idea had passed and, aided by a new doll (which she had named Mrs Butterworth after the pancake syrup she loved) and a new dollhouse, she had moved on to more acceptable little-girl fantasies: cooking, cleaning, shopping, Scolding The Baby, Changing For Dinner. Now, all these years later, she had found her way through the mirror after all. Only there was no little girl waiting in the Darker House; instead there was a Darker Husband, one who had been living behind the mirror all the time, and doing terrible things there.

A good one at a fair price, Bob liked to say – an accountant's credo if ever there was one.

Upright and sniffin the air – an answer to *how you doin* that every kid in every Cub Scout pack he'd ever taken down Dead Man's Trail knew well. A response some of those boys no doubt still repeated as grown men.

Gentlemen prefer blondes, don't forget that one. Because they get tired of squeezin . . .

But then sleep took Darcy, and although that soft

nurse could not carry her far, the lines on her forehead and at the corners of her reddened, puffy eyes softened a bit. She was close enough to consciousness to stir when her husband pulled into the driveway, but not close enough to come around. She might have if the Suburban's headlights had splashed across the ceiling, but Bob had doused them halfway down the block so as not to wake her.

8

A cat was stroking her cheek with a velvet paw. Very lightly but very insistently.

Darcy tried to brush it away, but her hand seemed to weigh a thousand pounds. And it was a dream, anyway – surely had to be. They had no cat. *Although if there are enough cat hairs in a house, there must be one around somewhere*, her struggling-to-wake mind told her, quite reasonably.

Now the paw was stroking her bangs and the forehead beneath, and it couldn't be a cat because cats don't talk.

'Wake up, Darce. Wake up, hon. We have to talk.'

The voice, as soft and soothing as the touch. Bob's voice. And not a cat's paw but a hand. Bob's hand. Only it couldn't be him, because he was in Montp—

Her eyes flew open and he was there, all right, sitting beside her on the bed, stroking her face and hair as he sometimes did when she was feeling under the weather. He was wearing a three-piece Jos. A. Bank suit (he bought all his suits there, calling it – another of his semi-amusing sayings – 'Joss-Bank'), but the vest was unbuttoned and his collar undone. She could see the end of his tie poking out of his coat pocket like a red tongue. His midsection bulged over his belt and her first coherent thought was *You really have to do something about your weight, Bobby, that isn't good for your heart.*

'Wha—' It came out an almost incomprehensible crow-croak.

He smiled and kept stroking her hair, her cheek, the nape of her neck. She cleared her throat and tried again.

'What are you doing here, Bobby? It must be—' She raised her head to look at his clock, which of course did no good. She had turned its face to the wall.

He glanced down at his watch. He had been smiling as he stroked her awake, and was smiling now. 'Quarter to three. I sat in my stupid old motel room for almost two hours after we talked, trying to convince myself that what I was thinking couldn't be true. Only I didn't get to where I am by dodging the truth. So I jumped in the 'Burban and hit the road. No traffic whatsoever. I don't know why I don't do more traveling late at night. Maybe I will. If I'm not in Shawshank, that is. Or New Hampshire State Prison in Concord. But that's kind of up to you. Isn't it?'

His hand, stroking her face. The feel of it was familiar, even the smell of it was familiar, and she had always loved it. Now she didn't, and it wasn't just the night's wretched discoveries. How could she have never noticed how complacently possessive that stroking touch was? *You're an old bitch, but you're* my *old bitch*, that touch now seemed to say. *Only this time you piddled on the floor while I was gone, and that's bad. In fact, it's a Big Bad.*

She pushed his hand away and sat up. 'What in God's name are you talking about? You come sneaking in, you wake me up—'

'Yes, you were sleeping with the light on – I saw it as soon as I turned up the driveway.' There was no guilt in his smile. Nothing sinister, either. It was the same sweet-natured Bob Anderson smile she'd loved almost from the first. For a moment her memory flickered over how gentle he'd been on their wedding night, not hurrying her. Giving her time to get used to the new thing.

Which he will do now, she thought.

'You never sleep with the light on, Darce. And although you've got your nightgown on, you're wearing your bra under it, and you never do that, either. You just forgot to take it off, didn't you? Poor darlin. Poor tired girl.'

For just a moment he touched her breast, then – thankfully – took his hand away.

'Also, you turned my clock around so you wouldn't have to look at the time. You've been upset, and I'm the cause. I'm sorry, Darce. From the bottom of my heart.'

'I ate something that disagreed with me.' It was all she could think of.

He smiled patiently. 'You found my special hiding place in the garage.'

'I don't know what you're talking about.'

'Oh, you did a good job of putting things back where you found them, but I'm very careful about such things, and the strip of tape I put on above the pivot in the base-board was broken. You didn't notice that, did you? Why would you? It's the kind of tape that's almost invisible once it's on. Also, the box inside was an inch or two to the left of where I put it – where I always put it.'

He reached to stroke her cheek some more, then withdrew his hand (seemingly without rancor) when she turned her face away.

'Bobby, I can see you've got a bee in your bonnet about something, but I honestly don't know what it is. Maybe you've been working too hard.'

His mouth turned down in a *moue* of sadness, and his eyes were moistening with tears. Incredible. She actually had to stop herself from feeling sorry for him. Emotions were only another human habit, it seemed, as conditioned as any other. 'I guess I always knew this day would come.'

'I haven't got the slightest idea what you're talking about.'

He sighed. 'I had a long ride back to think about this, honey. And the longer I thought, the *harder* I thought, the more it seemed like there was really only one question that needed an answer: WWDD.'

'I don't—'

'Hush,' he said, and put a gentle finger on her lips. She could smell soap. He must have showered before he left the motel, a very Bob-like thing to do. 'I'll tell you everything. I'll make a clean breast. I think that, down deep, I've always wanted you to know.'

He'd always wanted her to know? Dear God. There might be worse things waiting, but this was easily the most terrible thing so far. 'I don't *want* to know. Whatever it is you've got stuck in your head, I don't *want* to know.'

'I see something different in your eyes, honey, and I've gotten very good at reading women's eyes. I've become something of an expert. WWDD stands for What Would Darcy Do. In this case, What Would Darcy Do if she found my special hiding place, and what's inside my special box. I've always loved that box, by the way, because you gave it to me.'

He leaned forward and planted a quick kiss between her brows. His lips were moist. For the first time in her life, the touch of them on her skin revolted her, and it occurred to her that she might be dead before the sun came up. Because dead women told no tales. *Although*, she thought, *he'd try to make sure I didn't 'suffer.'*

'First, I asked myself if the name Marjorie Duvall would mean anything to you. I would have liked to answer that question with a big ole no, but sometimes a fellow has to be a realist. You're not the world's number one news junkie, but I've lived with you long enough to know that you follow the main stories on TV and in the newspaper. I thought you'd know the name, and even if you didn't, I thought you'd recognize the picture on the driver's license. Besides, I said to myself, won't she be curious as to why I have those ID cards? Women are always curious. Look at Pandora.'

Or Bluebeard's wife, she thought. *The woman who peeked into the locked room and found the severed heads of all her predecessors in matrimony.*

'Bob, I swear to you I don't have any idea what you're tal— '

'So the first thing I did when I came in was to boot up your computer, open Firefox — that's the search engine you always use — and check the history.'

'The what?'

He chuckled as if she'd gotten off an exceptionally witty line. 'You don't even know. I didn't think you did, because every time I check, everything's there. You *never* clear it!' And he chuckled again, as a man will do when a wife exhibits a trait he finds particularly endearing.

Darcy felt the first thin stirrings of anger. Probably absurd, given the circumstances, but there it was.

'You check my *computer*? You sneak! You dirty sneak!'

'Of *course* I check. I have a very bad friend who does very bad things. A man in a situation like that has to keep current with those closest to him. Since the kids left home, that's you and only you.'

Bad friend? A bad friend who does bad things? Her head was swimming, but one thing seemed all too clear: further denials would be useless. She knew, and he knew she did.

'You haven't just been checking on Marjorie Duvall.' She heard no shame or defensiveness in his voice, only a hideous regret that it should have come to this. 'You've been checking on all of them.' Then he laughed and said, 'Whoops!'

She sat up against the headboard, which pulled her slightly away from him. That was good. Distance was good. All those years she'd lain with him hip to hip and thigh to thigh, and now distance was good.

'What bad friend? What are you talking about?'

He cocked his head to one side, Bob's body language for *I find you dense; but amusingly so.* 'Brian.'

At first she had no idea who he was talking about, and thought it must be someone from work. Possibly an accomplice? It didn't seem likely on the face of it, she would have said Bob was as lousy at making friends as she was, but men who did such things sometimes did have accomplices. Wolves hunted in packs, after all.

'Brian Delahanty,' he said, 'Don't tell me you forgot Brian. I told you all about him after you told me about what happened to Brandolyn.'

Her mouth dropped open. 'Your friend from junior high? Bob, he's dead! He got hit by a truck while he was chasing down a baseball, and he's *dead.*'

'Well . . .' Bob's smile grew apologetic. 'Yes . . . and no. I almost always called him Brian when I talked about him to you, but that's not what I called him back in school, because he hated that name. I called him by his initials. I called him BD.'

She started to ask him what that had to do with the price of tea in China, but then she knew. Of course she knew. BD.

Beadie.

9

He talked for a long time, and the longer he talked, the more horrified she became. All these years she'd been living with a madman, but how could she have known? His insanity was like an underground sea. There was a layer of rock over it, and a layer of soil over the rock; flowers grew there. You could stroll through them and never know the madwater was there . . . but it was. It always had been. He blamed BD (who had become Beadie only years later, in his notes to the police) for everything, but Darcy suspected Bob knew better than that; blaming Brian Delahanty only made it easier to keep his two lives separate.

It had been BD's idea to take guns to school and go on a rampage, for instance. According to Bob, this inspiration had occurred in the summer between their freshman and sophomore years at Castle Rock High School. '1971,' he said, shaking his head goodnaturedly, as a man might do when recalling some harmless childhood peccadillo. 'Long before those Columbine oafs were even a twinkle in their daddies' eyes. There were these girls that snooted us. Diane Ramadge, Laurie Swenson, Gloria Haggerty . . . there were a couple of others, too, but I forget their names. The plan was to get a bunch of guns — Brian's dad had about twenty rifles and pistols in his basement, including a couple of German Lugers from World War II that we were just *fascinated* with — and take them to school. No searches or metal detectors back then, you know.

'We were going to barricade ourselves in the science wing. We'd chain the doors shut, kill some people – mostly teachers, but also some of the guys we didn't like – and then stampede the rest of the kids outside through the fire door at the far end of the hall. Well . . . *most* of the kids. We were going to keep the girls who snooted us as hostages. We planned – *BD* planned – to do all of this before the cops could get there, right? He drew maps, and he kept a list of the steps we'd have to take in his geometry note-book. I think there were maybe twenty steps in all, starting with "Pull fire alarms to create confusion."' He chuckled. 'And after we had the place locked down . . .'

He gave her a slightly shamefaced smile, but she thought what he was mostly ashamed of was how stupid the plan had been in the first place.

'Well, you can probably guess. Couple of teenage boys, hormones so high we got horny when the wind blew. We were going to tell those girls that if they'd, you know, fuck us real good, we'd let them go. If they didn't, we'd have to kill them. And they'd fuck, all right.'

He nodded slowly.

'They'd fuck to live. BD was right about that.'

He was lost in his story. His eyes were hazy with (grotesque but true) nostalgia. For what? The crazy dreams of youth? She was afraid that might actually be it.

'We didn't plan to kill ourselves like those heavy-metal dumbbells in Colorado, either. No way. There was a basement under the science wing, and Brian said there was a tunnel down there. He said it went from the supply room to the old fire station on the other side of Route 119. Brian said that when the high school was just a K-through-eight grammar school back in the fifties, there was a park over there, and the little kids used to play in it at recess. The tunnel was so they could get to the park without having to cross the road.'

Bob laughed, making her jump.

'I took his word for all that, but it turned out he was full of shit. I went down there the next fall to look for myself. The supply room was there, full of paper and stinking of that mimeograph juice they used to use, but if there was a tunnel, I never found it, and even back then I was very thorough. I don't know if he was lying to both of us or just to himself, I only know there was no tunnel. We would have been trapped upstairs, and who knows, we might have killed ourselves after all. You never know what a fourteen-year-old's going to do, do you? They roll around like unexploded bombs.'

You're not unexploded anymore, she thought. *Are you, Bob?*

'We probably would have chickened out, anyway. But maybe not. Maybe we would have tried to go through with it. BD got me all excited, talking about how we were going to feel them up first, then make them take off each other's clothes . . .' He looked at her earnestly. 'Yes, I know how it sounds, just boys' jack-off fantasies, but those girls really *were* snoots. You tried to talk to them, they'd laugh and walk away. Then stand in the corner of the caff, the bunch of them, looking us over and laughing some more. So you really couldn't blame us, could you?'

He looked at his fingers, drumming restlessly on his suit-pants where they stretched tight over his thighs, then back up at Darcy.

'The thing you have to understand – that you really have to see – is how persuasive Brian was. He was lots worse than me. He really *was* crazy. Plus it was a time when the whole country was rioting, don't forget, and that was part of it, too.'

I doubt it, she thought.

The amazing thing was how he made it sound almost normal, as if every adolescent boy's sexual fantasies involved rape and murder. Probably he believed that, just as he had believed in Brian Delahanty's mythical escape tunnel. Or had he? How could she know? She was, after all, listening to the recollections of a lunatic. It was just hard to believe that – still! – because the madman was Bob. Her Bob.

'Anyway,' he said, shrugging, 'it never happened. That was the summer Brian ran into the road and got killed. There was a reception at his house after the funeral, and his mother said I could go up to his room and take something, if I wanted. As a souvenir, you know. And I did want to! You bet I did! I took his geometry notebook, so nobody would go leafing through it and come across his plans for The Great Castle Rock Shoot-Out and Fuck Party. That's what he called it, you know.'

Bob laughed ruefully.

'If I was a religious fella, I'd say God saved me from myself. And who knows if there isn't Something . . . some Fate . . . that has its own plan for us.'

'And this Fate's plan for you was for you to torture and kill women?' Darcy asked. She couldn't help herself.

He looked at her reproachfully. 'They were snoots,' he said, and raised a teacherly finger. 'Also, it wasn't me. It was Beadie who did that stuff – and I say *did* for a reason, Darce. I say *did* instead of *does* because all of that's behind me now.'

'Bob – your friend BD is dead. He's been dead for almost forty years. You must know that. I mean, on some level you *must*.'

He tossed his hands in the air: a gesture of good-natured surrender. 'Do you want to call it guilt-avoidance? That's what a shrink would call it, I suppose, and it's fine if you do. But Darcy, listen!' He leaned forward and pressed a finger to her forehead, between her eyebrows. 'Listen and get this through your head. It *was* Brian. He infected me with . . . well, certain ideas, let's say that. Some ideas, once you get them in your head, you can't unthink them. You can't . . .'

'Put the toothpaste back in the tube?'

He clapped his hands together, almost making her scream. '*That's it exactly!* You can't put the toothpaste back in the tube. Brian was dead, but the ideas were alive. Those ideas – getting women, doing whatever to them, whatever crazy idea came into your head – they became his ghost.'

His eyes shifted upward and to the left when he said this. She had read somewhere that this meant the person who was talking was telling a conscious lie. But did it matter if he was? Or which one of them he was lying to? She thought not.

'I won't go into the details,' he said. 'It's nothing for a sweetheart like you to hear, and like it or not – I know you don't right now – you're still my sweetheart. But you have to know I fought it. For seven years I fought it, but those ideas – *Brian's* ideas – kept growing inside my head. Until finally I said to myself, "I'll try it once, just to get it out of my head. To get *him* out of my head. If I get caught, I get caught – at least I'll stop thinking about it. *Wondering* about it. What it would be like."'

'You're telling me it was a male exploration,' she said dully.

'Well, yes. I suppose you could say that.'

'Or like trying a joint just to see what all the shouting was about.'

He shrugged modestly, boyishly. 'Kinda.'

'It wasn't an exploration, Bobby. It wasn't trying a joint. It was *taking a woman's life.*'

She had seen no guilt or shame, absolutely none – he appeared incapable of those things, it seemed the circuit-breaker that controlled them had been fried, perhaps even before birth – but now he gave her a sulky, put-upon look. A teenager's you-don't-understand-me look.

'Darcy, they were *snoots.*'

She wanted a glass of water, but she was afraid to get up and go into the bathroom. She was afraid he would stop her, and what would come after that? What then?

'Besides,' he resumed, 'I didn't think I'd get caught. Not if I was careful and made a plan. Not a half-baked and horny-fourteen-year-old boy's plan, you know, but a realistic one. And I realized something else, too. I couldn't do it myself. Even if I didn't screw up out of nervousness, I might out of guilt. Because I was one of the good guys.

That's how I saw myself, and believe it or not, I still do. And I have the proof, don't I? A good home, a good wife, two beautiful children who are all grown up and starting their own lives. And I give back to the community. That's why I took the Town Treasurer's job for two years, gratis. That's why I work with Vinnie Eschler every year to put on the Halloween blood drive.'

You should have asked Marjorie Duvall to give, Darcy thought. *She was A-positive.*

Then, puffing out his chest slightly – a man nailing down his argument with one final, irrefutable point – he said: 'That's what the Cub Scouts are about. You thought I'd quit when Donnie went on to Boy Scouts, I know you did. Only I didn't. Because it's not just about him, and never was. It's about the community. It's about giving back.'

'Then give Marjorie Duvall back her life. Or Stacey Moore. Or Robert Shaverstone.'

That last one got through; he winced as if she had struck him. 'The boy was an accident. He wasn't supposed to be there.'

'But you being there wasn't an accident?'

'It wasn't *me*,' he said, then added the ultimate surreal absurdity. 'I'm no adulterer. It was BD. It's always BD. It was his fault for putting those ideas in my head in the first place. I never would have thought of them on my own. I signed my notes to the police with his name just to make that clear. Of course I changed the spelling, because I sometimes called him BD back when I first told you about him. You might not remember that, but I did.'

She was impressed by the obsessive lengths he'd gone to. No wonder he hadn't been caught. If she hadn't stubbed her toe on that damned carton—

'None of them had any relation to me or my business. *Either* of my businesses. That would be very bad. Very dangerous. But I travel a lot, and I keep my eyes open. BD – the BD inside – he does, too. We watch out for the snooty ones. You can always tell. They wear their skirts too high and show their bra straps on purpose. They entice men. That Stacey Moore, for instance. You read about her, I'm sure. Married, but that didn't keep her from brushing her titties against me. She worked as a waitress in a coffee shop – the Sunnyside in Waterville. I used to go up there to Mickleson's Coins, remember? You even went with me a couple of times, when Pets was at Colby. This was before George Mickleson died and his son sold off all the stock so he could go to New Zealand or somewhere. That woman was *all over me*, Darce! Always asking me if I wanted a warm-up on my coffee and saying stuff like how 'bout those Red Sox, bending over, rubbing her titties on my shoulder, trying her best to get me hard. Which she did, I admit it, I'm a man with a man's needs, and although you never turned me away or said no . . . well, rarely . . . I'm a man with a man's needs and I've always been highly sexed. Some women sense that and like to play on it. It gets them off.'

He was looking down at his lap with dark, musing eyes. Then something else occurred to him and his head jerked up. His thinning hair flew, then settled back.

'Always smiling! Red lipstick and always smiling! Well, I recognize smiles like that. Most men do. "Ha-ha, I know you want it, I can smell it on you, but this little rub's all you're going to get, so deal with it." *I* could! I *could* deal with it! But not BD, not him.'

He shook his head slowly.

'There are lots of women like that. It's easy to get their names. Then you can trace them down on the Internet. There's a lot of information if you know how to look for it, and accountants know how. I've done that . . . oh, dozens of times. Maybe even a hundred. You could call it a hobby, I guess. You could say I collect information as well as coins. Usually it comes to nothing. But sometimes BD will say, "She's the one you want to follow through on, Bobby. That one right there. We'll make the plan together, and when the time comes, you just let me take over." And that's what I do.'

He took her hand, and folded her limp and chilly fingers into his.

'You think I'm crazy. I can see it in your eyes. But I'm not, honey. It's BD who's crazy . . . or Beadie, if you like his for-the-public name better. By the way, if you read the stories in the paper, you know I purposely put a lot of misspellings in my notes to the police. I even misspell the addresses. I keep a list of misspellings in my wallet so that I'll always do it the same way. It's misdirection. I want them to think Beadie's dumb – illiterate, anyway – and they do. Because *they're* dumb. I've only been questioned a single time, years ago, and that was as a witness, about two weeks after BD killed the Moore woman. An old guy with a limp, semi-retired. Told me to give him a call if I remembered anything. I said I would. That was pretty rich.'

He chuckled soundlessly, as he sometimes did when they were watching *Modern Family* or *Two and a Half Men*. It was a way of laughing that had, until tonight, always heightened her own amusement.

'You want to know something, Darce? If they caught me dead to rights, I'd admit it – at least I guess I would, I don't think anybody knows a hundred percent for sure what they'd do in a situation like that – but I couldn't give them much of a confession. Because I don't remember much about the actual . . . well . . . acts. Beadie does them, and I kind of . . . I don't know . . . go unconscious. Get amnesia. Some damn thing.'

Oh, you liar. You remember everything. It's in your eyes, it's even in the way your mouth turns down at the corners.

'And now . . . everything's in Darcellen's hands.' He raised one of her hands to his lips and kissed the back of it, as if to emphasize this point. 'You know that old punchline, the one that goes, "I could tell you, but then I'd have to kill you"? That doesn't apply here. I could never kill you. Everything I do, everything I've built . . . modest as it would look to some people, I guess . . . I've done and built for you. For the kids too, of course, but mostly for you. You walked into my life, and do you know what happened?'

'You stopped,' she said.

He broke into a radiant grin. 'For over twenty years!'

Sixteen, she thought but didn't say.

'For most of those years, when we were raising the kids and struggling to get the coin business off the ground – although that was mostly you – I was racing around New England doing taxes and setting up foundations—'

'You were the one who made it work,' she said, and was a little shocked by what she heard in her voice: calmness and warmth. 'You were the one with the expertise.'

He looked almost touched enough to start crying again, and when he spoke his voice was husky. 'Thank you, hon. It means the world to hear you say that. You saved me, you know. In more ways than one.'

He cleared his throat.

'For a dozen years, BD never made a peep. I thought he was gone. I honestly did. But then he came back. Like a ghost.' He seemed to consider this, then nodded his head very slowly. 'That's what he is. A ghost, a bad one. He started pointing out women when I was traveling. "Look at that one, she wants to make sure you see her nipples, but if you touched them she'd call the police and then laugh with her friends when they took you away. Look at that one, licking her lips with her tongue, she knows you'd like her to put it in your mouth and she knows you know she never will. Look at that one, showing off her panties when she gets out of her car, and if you think that's an accident, you're an idiot. She's just one more snoot who thinks she'll never get what she deserves."'

He stopped, his eyes once more dark and downcast. In them was the Bobby who had successfully evaded her for twenty-seven years. The one he was trying to pass off as a ghost.

'When I started to have those urges, I fought them. There are magazines . . . certain magazines . . . I bought them before we got married, and I thought if I did that again . . . or certain sites on the Internet . . . I thought I could . . . I don't know . . . substitute fantasy for reality, I guess you'd say . . . but once you've tried the real thing, fantasy isn't worth a damn.'

He was talking, Darcy thought, like a man who had fallen in love with some expensive delicacy. Caviar. Truffles. Belgian chocolates.

'But the point is, I stopped. For all those years, I *stopped*. And I could stop again, Darcy. This time for good. If there's a chance for us. If you could forgive me and just turn the page.' He looked at her, earnest and wet-eyed. 'Is it possible you could do that?'

She thought of a woman buried in a snowdrift, her naked legs exposed by the careless swipe of a passing plow – some mother's daughter, once the apple of some father's eye as she danced clumsily across a grammar-school stage in a pink tutu. She thought of a mother and son discovered in a freezing creek, their hair rippling in the black, ice-edged water. She thought of the woman with her head in the corn.

'I'd have to think about it,' she said, very carefully.

He grasped her by the upper arms and leaned toward her. She had to force herself not to flinch, and to meet his eyes. They were his eyes . . . and they weren't. *Maybe there's something to that ghost business after all*, she thought.

'This isn't one of those movies where the psycho husband chases his screaming wife all around the house. If you decide to go to the police and turn me in, I won't lift a finger to stop you. But I know you've thought about what it would do to the kids. You wouldn't be the woman I married if you hadn't thought about that. What you might not have thought about is what it would do to you. Nobody would believe that you were married to me all these years and never knew . . . or at least suspected. You'd have to move away and live on what savings there are, because I've always been the breadwinner, and a man can't win bread when he's in jail. You might not even be able to get at what there is, because of the civil suits. And of course the kids—'

'Stop it, don't talk about them when you talk about this, don't you *ever*.'

He nodded humbly, still holding lightly to her forearms. 'I beat BD once – I beat him for twenty years—'

Sixteen, she thought again. *Sixteen, and you know it.*

'—and I can beat him again. With your help, Darce. With your help I can do anything. Even if he were to come back in another twenty years, so what? Big deal! I'd be seventy-three. Hard to go snoot-hunting when you're shuffling around in a walker!' He laughed cheerily at this absurd image, then sobered again. 'But – now listen to me carefully – if I were ever to backslide, even one single time, I'd kill myself. The kids would never know, they'd never have to be touched by that . . . that, you know, *stigma* . . . because I'd make it look like an accident . . . but *you'd* know. And you'd know why. So what do you say? Can we put this behind us?'

She appeared to consider. She *was* considering, in fact, although such thought processes as she could muster were probably not trending in a direction he would be likely to understand.

What she thought was: *It's what drug addicts say. 'I'll never take any of that stuff again. I've quit before and this time I'll quit for good. I mean it.' But they don't mean it, even when they think they do they don't, and neither does he.*

What she thought was: *What am I going to do? I can't fool him, we've been married too long.*

A cold voice replied to that, one she had never suspected of being inside her, one perhaps related to the BD-voice that whispered to Bob about the snoots it observed in restaurants, laughing on street corners, riding in expensive sports cars with the top down, whispering and smiling to each other on apartment-building balconies.

Or perhaps it was the voice of the Darker Girl.

Why can't you? it asked. *After all . . .* he *fooled* you.

And then what? She didn't know. She only knew that now was now, and now had to be dealt with.

'You'd have to promise to stop,' she said, speaking very slowly and reluctantly. 'Your most solemn, never-go-back promise.'

His face filled with a relief so total – so somehow boyish – that she was touched. He so seldom looked like the boy he had been. Of course that was also the boy who had once planned to go to school with guns. 'I would, Darcy. I do. I *do* promise. I already told you.'

'And we could never talk about this again.'

'I get that.'

'You're not to send the Duvall woman's ID to the police, either.'

She saw the disappointment (also weirdly boyish) that came over his face when she said that, but she meant to stick to it. He had to feel punished, if only a little. That way he'd believe he had convinced her.

Hasn't he? Oh, Darcellen, hasn't he?

'I need more than promises, Bobby. Actions speak louder than words. Dig a hole in the woods and bury that woman's ID cards in it.'

'Once I do that, are we—'

She reached out and put her hand to his mouth. She strove to make herself sound stern. 'Hush. No more.'

'Okay. Thank you, Darcy. So much.'

'I don't know what you're thanking me for.' And then, although the thought of him lying next to her filled her with revulsion and dismay, she forced herself to say the rest.

'Now get undressed and come to bed. We both need to get some sleep.'

10

He was under almost as soon as his head hit the pillow, but long after he'd commenced his small, polite snores, Darcy lay awake, thinking that if she allowed herself to drift off, she would awake with his hands around her throat. She was in bed with a madman, after all. If he added her, his score would be an even dozen.

But he meant it, she thought. This was right around the time that the sky began to lighten in the east. *He said he loves me, and he meant it. And when I said I'd keep his secret — because that's what it comes down to, keeping his secret — he believed me. Why wouldn't he? I almost convinced myself.*

Wasn't it possible he could carry through on his promise? Not all drug addicts failed at getting clean, after all. And while she could never keep his secret for herself, wasn't it possible she could for the kids?

I can't. I won't. But what choice?

What goddam choice?

It was while pondering this question that her tired, confused mind finally gave up and slipped away.

She dreamed of going into the dining room and finding a woman bound with chains to the long Ethan Allen table there. The woman was naked except for a black leather hood that covered the top half of her face. *I don't know that woman, that woman is a stranger to me*, she thought in her dream, and then from beneath the hood Petra said: 'Mama, is that you?'

Darcy tried to scream, but sometimes in nightmares, you can't.

11

When she finally struggled awake — headachey, miserable, feeling hungover — the other half of the bed was empty. Bob had turned his clock back around, and she saw it was quarter past ten. It was the latest she'd slept in years, but of course she hadn't dropped off until first light, and such sleep as she'd gotten was populated with horrors.

She used the toilet, dragged her housecoat off the hook on the back of the bathroom door, then brushed her teeth — her mouth tasted foul. *Like the bottom of a birdcage*, Bob would say on the rare mornings after he'd taken an extra glass of wine with dinner or a second bottle of beer during a baseball game. She spat, began to put her brush back in the toothglass, then paused, looking at her reflection. This morning she saw a woman who looked old instead of middle-aged: pale skin, deep lines bracketing the mouth, purple bruises under the eyes, the crazed bed-head you only got from tossing and turning. But all this was only of passing interest to her; how she looked was the last thing on her mind. She peered over her reflection's shoulder and through the open bathroom door into their bedroom. Except it wasn't theirs; it was the Darker Bedroom. She could see his slippers, only they weren't his. They were obviously too big to be Bob's, almost a giant's slippers. They belonged to the Darker Husband. And the double bed with the wrinkled sheets and unanchored blankets? That was the Darker Bed. She shifted her gaze back to the wild-haired woman with the bloodshot, frightened eyes: the Darker Wife, in all her raddled glory. Her first name was Darcy, but her last name wasn't Anderson. The Darker Wife was Mrs Brian Delahanty.

Darcy leaned forward until her nose was touching the glass. She held her breath and cupped her hands to the sides of her face just as she had when she was a girl dressed in grass-stained shorts and falling-down white socks. She looked until she couldn't hold her breath any longer, then exhaled in a huff that fogged the mirror. She wiped it clean with a towel, and then went downstairs to face her first day as the monster's wife.

He had left a note for her under the sugarbowl.

Darce —
 I will take care of those documents, as you asked.
 I love you, honey.
 Bob

He had drawn a little Valentine heart around his name, a thing he hadn't done in years. She felt a wave of love for him, as thick and cloying as the scent of dying flowers. She wanted to wail like some woman in an Old Testament story, and stifled the sound with a napkin. The refrigerator kicked on and began its heartless whir. Water dripped in the sink, plinking away the seconds on the porcelain. Her tongue was a sour sponge crammed into her mouth. She felt time — all the time to come, as his wife in this house — close around her like a straitjacket. Or a coffin. This was the world she had believed in as a child. It had been here all the time. Waiting for her.

The refrigerator whirred, the water dripped in the sink, and the raw seconds passed. This was the Darker Life, where every truth was written backward.

12

Her husband had coached Little League (also with Vinnie Eschler, that master of Polish jokes and big enveloping manhugs) during the years when Donnie had played shortstop for the Cavendish Hardware team, and Darcy still remembered what Bob said to the boys – many of them weeping – after they'd lost the final game of the District 19 tourney. Back in 1997 that would have been, probably only a month or so before Bob had murdered Stacey Moore and stuffed her into her cornbin. The talk he'd given to that bunch of drooping, sniffling boys had been short, wise, and (she'd thought so then and still did thirteen years later) incredibly kind.

I know how bad you boys feel, but the sun will still come up tomorrow. And when it does, you'll feel better. When the sun comes up the day after tomorrow, a little better still. This is just a part of your life, and it's over. It would have been better to win, but either way, it's over. Life will go on.

As hers did, following her ill-starred trip out to the garage for batteries. When Bob came home from work after her first long day at home (she couldn't bear the thought of going out herself, afraid her knowledge must be written on her face in capital letters), he said: 'Honey, about last night—'

'Nothing happened last night. You came home early, that's all.'

He ducked his head in that boyish way he had, and when he raised it again, his face was lit with a large and grateful smile. 'That's fine, then,' he said. 'Case closed?'

'Closed book.'

He opened his arms. 'Give us a kiss, beautiful.'

She did, wondering if he had kissed *them*.

Do a good job, really use that educated tongue of yours, and I won't cut you, she could imagine him saying. *Put your snooty little heart into it.*

He held her away from him, his hands on her shoulders. 'Still friends?'

'Still friends.'

'Sure?'

'*Yes.* I didn't cook anything, and I don't want to go out. Why don't you change into some grubbies and go grab us a pizza.'

'All right.'

'And don't forget to take your Prilosec.'

He beamed at her. 'You bet.'

She watched him go bounding up the stairs, thought of saying *Don't do that, Bobby, don't test your heart like that.*

But no.

No.

Let him test it all he wanted.

13

The sun came up the next day. And the next. A week went by, then two, then a month. They resumed their old ways, the small habits of a long marriage. She brushed her teeth while he was in the shower (usually singing some hit from the eighties in a voice that was on-key but not particularly melodious), although she no longer did it naked, meaning to step into the shower as soon as he'd vacated it; now she showered after he'd left for B, B & A. If he noticed this little change in her modus operandi, he didn't mention it. She resumed her book club, telling the other ladies and the two retired gentlemen who took part that she had been feeling under the weather and didn't want to pass on a virus along with her opinion of the new Barbara Kingsolver, and everyone chuckled politely. A week after that, she resumed the knitting circle, Knuts for Knitting. Sometimes she caught herself singing along with the radio when she came back from the post office or the grocery store. She and Bob watched TV at night — always comedies, never the forensic crime shows. He came home early now; there had been no more road trips since the one to Montpelier. He got something called Skype for his computer, saying he could look at coin collections just as easily that way and save on gas. He didn't say it would also save on temptation, but he didn't have to. She watched the papers to see if Marjorie Duvall's ID showed up, knowing if he had lied about that, he would lie about everything. But it didn't. Once a week they went out to dinner at one of Yarmouth's two inexpensive restaurants. He ordered steak and she ordered fish. He drank iced tea and she had a Cranberry Breeze. Old habits died hard. Often, she thought, they don't die until we do.

In the daytime, while he was gone, she now rarely turned on the television. It was easier to listen to the refrigerator with it off, and to the small creaks and groans of their nice Yarmouth house as it settled toward another Maine winter. It was easier to think. Easier to face the truth: he would do it again. He would hold off as long as he could, she would gladly give him that much, but sooner or later Beadie would gain the upper hand. He wouldn't send the next woman's ID to the police, thinking that might be enough to fool her, but probably not caring if she saw through the change in MO. *Because*, he would reason, *she's a part of it now. She'd have to admit she knew. The cops would get it out of her even if she tried to hide that part.*

Donnie called from Ohio. The business was going

great guns; they had landed an office products account that might go national. Darcy said hooray (and so did Bob, cheerily admitting he'd been wrong about Donnie's chances of making it so young). Petra called to say they had tentatively decided on blue dresses for the bridesmaids, A-line, kneehigh, matching chiffon scarves, and did Darcy think that was all right, or would outfits like that look a bit childish? Darcy said she thought they would look sweet, and the two of them went on to a discussion of shoes – blue pumps with three-quarter heels, to be exact. Darcy's mother got sick down in Boca Grande, and it looked like she might have to go into the hospital, but then they started her on some new medication and she got well. The sun came up and the sun went down. The paper jack-o'-lanterns in the store windows went down and paper turkeys went up. Then the Christmas decorations went up. The first snow flurries appeared, right on schedule.

In her house, after her husband had taken his briefcase and gone to work, Darcy moved through the rooms, pausing to look into the various mirrors. Often for a long time. Asking the woman inside that other world what she should do.

Increasingly the answer seemed to be that she would do nothing.

14

On an unseasonably warm day two weeks before Christmas, Bob came home in the middle of the afternoon, shouting her name. Darcy was upstairs, reading a book. She tossed it on the night table (beside the hand mirror that had now taken up permanent residence there) and flew down the hall to the landing. Her first thought (horror mixed with relief) was that it was finally over. He had been found out. The police would soon be here. They would take him away, then come back to ask her the two age-old questions: what did she know, and when did she know it? News vans would park on the street. Young men and women with good hair would do stand-ups in front of their house.

Except that wasn't fear in his voice; she knew it for what it was even before he reached the foot of the stairs and turned his face up to her. It was excitement. Perhaps even jubilation.

'Bob? What—'

'You'll never believe it!' His topcoat hung open, his face was flushed all the way to the forehead, and such hair as he still had was blown every which way. It was as if he had driven home with all his car windows open. Given the springlike quality of the air, Darcy supposed he might've.

She came down cautiously and stood on the first riser, which put them eye-to-eye. 'Tell me.'

'The most amazing luck! Really! If I ever needed a sign that I'm on the right track again – that *we* are – boy, this is it!' He held out his hands. They were closed into fists with the knuckles up. His eyes were sparkling. Almost dancing. 'Which hand? Pick.'

'Bob, I don't want to play g—'

'Pick!'

She pointed to his right hand, just to get it over with. He laughed. 'You read my mind . . . but you always could, couldn't you?'

He turned his fist over and opened it. On his palm lay a single coin, tails-side up, so she could see it was a wheat penny. Not uncirculated by any means, but still in great shape. Assuming there were no scratches on the Lincoln side, she thought it was either F or VF. She reached for it, then paused. He nodded for her to go ahead. She turned it over, quite sure of what she would see. Nothing else could adequately explain his excitement. It was what she expected: a 1955 double-date. A double-*die*, in numismatic terms.

'Holy God, Bobby! Where . . . ? Did you buy it?' An uncirculated '55 double-die had recently sold at an auction in Miami for over eight thousand dollars, setting a new record. This one wasn't in that kind of shape, but no coin dealer with half a brain would have let it go for under four.

'God no! Some of the other fellows invited me to lunch at that Thai place, Eastern Promises, and I almost went, but I was working the goddarn Vision Associates account – you know, the private bank I told you about? – and so I gave Monica ten bucks and told her to get me a sandwich and a Fruitopia at Subway. She brought it back with the change in the bag. I shook it out . . . and there it was!' He plucked the penny from her hand and held it over his head, laughing up at it.

She laughed with him, then thought (as these days she often did): *HE DID NOT 'SUFFER!'*

'Isn't it great, honey?'

'Yes,' she said. 'I'm happy for you.' And, odd or not (*perverse* or not), she really was. He had brokered sales of several over the years and could have bought one for himself any old time, but that wasn't the same as just coming across one. He had even forbidden her to give him one for Christmas or his birthday. The great accidental find was a collector's most joyous moment, he had said so during their first real conversation, and now he had what he had been checking handfuls of change for all his life. His heart's desire had come spilling out of a white sandwich-shop paper bag along with a turkey-bacon wrap.

He enveloped her in a hug. She hugged him back,

then pushed him gently away. 'What are you going to do with it, Bobby? Put it in a Lucite cube?'

This was a tease, and he knew it. He cocked a finger-gun and shot her in the head. Which was all right, because when you were shot with a finger-gun, you did not 'suffer.'

She continued to smile at him, but now saw him again (after that brief, loving lapse) for what he was: the Darker Husband. Gollum, with his precious.

'You know better. I'm going to photo it, hang the photo on the wall, then tuck the penny away in our safe deposit box. What would you say it is, F or VF?'

She examined it again, then looked at him with a rueful smile. 'I'd love to say VF, but—'

'Yeah, I know, I know – and I shouldn't care. You're not supposed to count the teeth when someone gives you a horse, but it's hard to resist. Better than VG, though, right? Honest opinion, Darce.'

My honest opinion is that you'll do it again.

'Better than VG, definitely.'

His smile faded. For a moment she was sure he had guessed what she was thinking, but she should have known better; on this side of the mirror, she could keep secrets, too.

'It's not about the quality, anyway. It's about the finding. Not getting it from a dealer or picking it out of a catalogue, but actually finding one when you least expect it.'

'I know.' She smiled. 'If my dad was here right now, he'd be cracking a bottle of champagne.'

'I'll take care of that little detail at dinner tonight,' he said. 'Not in Yarmouth, either. We're going to Portland. Pearl of the Shore. What do you say?'

'Oh, honey, I don't know—'

He took her lightly by the shoulders as he always did when he wanted her to understand that he was really serious about a thing. 'Come on – it's going to be mild enough tonight for your prettiest summer dress. I heard it on the weather when I was driving back. And I'll buy you all the champagne you can drink. How can you say no to a deal like that?'

'Well . . .' She considered. Then smiled. 'I guess I can't.'

15

They had not just one bottle of very pricey Moët et Chandon but two, and Bob drank most of it. Consequently it was Darcy who drove home in his quietly humming little Prius while Bob sat in the passenger seat, singing 'Pennies from Heaven' in his on-key but not particularly melodious voice. He was drunk, she realized. Not just high, but actually drunk. It was the first time she had seen him that way in ten years. Ordinarily he watched his booze intake like a hawk, and sometimes, when someone at a party asked him why he wasn't drinking, he'd quote a line from *True Grit*: 'I would not put a thief in my mouth to steal my mind.' Tonight, high on his discovery of the double-date, he had allowed his mind to be stolen, and she knew what she intended to do as soon as he ordered that second bottle of bubbly. In the restaurant, she wasn't sure she could carry it through, but listening to him sing on the way home, she knew. Of course she could do it. She was the Darker Wife now, and the Darker Wife knew that what he thought of as his good luck had really been her own.

16

Inside the house he whirled his sport coat onto the tree by the door and pulled her into his arms for a long kiss. She could taste champagne and sweet crème brûlée on his breath. It was not a bad combination, although she knew if things happened as they might, she would never want either again. His hand went to her breast. She let it linger there, feeling him against her, and then pushed him away. He looked disappointed, but brightened when she smiled.

'I'm going upstairs and getting out of this dress,' she said. 'There's Perrier in the refrigerator. If you bring me a glass – with a wedge of lime – you might get lucky, mister.'

He broke into a grin at that – his old, well-loved grin. Because there was one long-established habit of marriage they had not resumed since the night he had smelled her discovery (yes, smelled it, just as a wise old wolf may smell a poisoned bait) and come rushing home from Montpelier. Day by day they had walled up what he was – yes, as surely as Montresor had walled up his old pal Fortunato – and sex in the connubial bed would be the last brick.

He clicked his heels and threw her a British-style salute, fingers to forehead, palm out. 'Yes, ma'am.'

'Don't be long,' she said pleasantly. 'Mama wants what Mama wants.'

Going up the stairs, she thought: *This will never work. The only thing you'll succeed in doing is getting yourself killed. He may not think he's capable of it, but I think he is.*

Maybe that would be all right, though. Assuming he didn't hurt her first, as he'd hurt those women. Maybe any sort of resolution would be all right. She couldn't spend the rest of her life looking in mirrors. She wasn't a kid anymore, and couldn't get away with a kid's craziness.

She went into the bedroom, but only long enough to toss her purse onto the table beside the hand mirror. Then she went out again and called, 'Are you coming, Bobby? I could really use those bubbles!'

'On my way, ma'am, just pouring it over ice!'

And here he came out of the living room and into the hall, holding one of their good crystal glasses up before him at eye level like a comic-opera waiter, weaving slightly as he crossed to the foot of the stairs. He continued to hold the glass up as he mounted them, the wedge of lime bobbing around on top. His free hand trailed lightly along the banister; his face shone with happiness and good cheer. For a moment she almost weakened, and then the image of Helen and Robert Shaverstone filled her mind, hellishly clear: the son and his molested, mutilated mother floating together in a Massachusetts creek that had begun to grow lacings of ice at its sides.

'One glass of Perrier for the lady, coming right uh—'

She saw the knowledge leap into his eyes at the very last second, something old and yellow and ancient. It was more than surprise; it was shocked fury. In that moment her understanding of him was complete. He loved nothing, least of all her. Every kindness, caress, boyish grin, and thoughtful gesture – all were nothing but camouflage. He was a shell. There was nothing inside but howling emptiness.

She pushed him.

It was a hard push and he made a three-quarters somersault above the stairs before coming down on them, first on his knees, then on his arm, then full on his face. She heard his arm break. The heavy Waterford glass shattered on one of the uncarpeted risers. He rolled over again and she heard something else inside him snap. He screamed in pain and somersaulted one final time before landing on the hardwood hall floor in a heap, the broken arm (not broken in just one place but in several) cocked back over his head at an angle nature had never intended. His head was twisted, one cheek on the floor.

Darcy hurried down the stairs. At one point she stepped on an ice cube, slipped, and had to grab the banister to save herself. At the bottom she saw a huge knob now poking out the skin on the nape of his neck, turning it white, and said: 'Don't move, Bob, I think your neck is broken.'

His eye rolled up to look at her. Blood was trickling from his nose — that looked broken, too — and a lot more was coming out of his mouth. Almost gushing out. 'You pushed me,' he said. 'Oh, Darcy, why did you push me?'

'I don't know,' she said, thinking, *We both know*. She began to cry. Crying came naturally; he was her husband, and he was badly hurt. 'Oh God, I don't know. Something came over me. I'm sorry. Don't move, I'll call 911 and tell them to send an ambulance.'

His foot scraped across the floor. 'I'm not paralyzed,' he said. 'Thank God for that. But it *hurts*.'

'I know, honey.'

'Call the ambulance! Hurry!'

She went into the kitchen, spared a brief glance for the phone in its charger-cradle, then opened the cabinet under the sink. 'Hello? Hello? Is this 911?' She took out the box of plastic GLAD bags, the storage-size ones she used for the leftovers when they had chicken or roast beef, and pulled one from the box. 'This is Darcellen Anderson, I'm calling from 24 Sugar Mill Lane, in Yarmouth! Have you got that?'

From another drawer, she took a dishwiper from the top of the pile. She was still crying. *Nose like a firehose*, they'd said when they were kids. Crying was good. She needed to cry, and not just because it would look better for her later on. He was her husband, he was hurt, she needed to cry. She remembered when he still had a full head of hair. She remembered his flashy breakaway move when they danced to 'Footloose.' He brought her roses every year on her birthday. He never forgot. They had gone to Bermuda, where they rode bikes in the morning and made love in the afternoon. They had built a life together and now that life was over and she needed to cry. She wrapped the dishwiper around her hand and then stuffed her hand into the plastic bag.

'I need an ambulance, my husband fell down the stairs. I think his neck might be broken. Yes! Yes! Right away!'

She walked back into the hall with her right hand behind her back. She saw he had pulled himself away from the foot of the stairs a little, and it looked like he'd tried to turn over on his back, but at that he hadn't been successful. She knelt down beside him.

'I didn't fall,' he said. 'You pushed me. Why did you push me?'

'I guess for the Shaverstone boy,' she said, and brought her hand out from behind her back. She was crying harder than ever. He saw the plastic bag. He saw the hand inside clutching the wad of toweling. He understood what she meant to do. Perhaps he had done something like it himself. Probably he had.

He began screaming . . . only the screams weren't really screams at all. His mouth was filled with blood, something had broken inside of his throat, and the sounds he produced were more guttural growls than screams. She jammed the plastic bag between his lips and deep inside his mouth. He had broken a number of teeth in the fall, and she could feel the jagged stumps. If they tore into her skin, she might have some serious explaining to do.

She yanked her hand free before he could bite, leaving the plastic bag and the dishwiper behind. She grabbed his jaw and chin. The other hand she put on top of his balding head. The flesh there was very warm. She could feel it throbbing with blood. She jammed his mouth shut on the wad of plastic and cloth. He tried to beat her off, but he only had one arm free, and that was the one that had

been broken in the fall. The other was twisted beneath
him. His feet paddled jerkily back and forth on the hardwood floor. One of his shoes came off. He was gurgling.
She yanked her dress up to her waist, freeing her legs,
then lunged forward, trying to straddle him. If she could
do that, maybe she could pinch his nostrils shut.

But before she could try, his chest began to heave
beneath her, and the gurgles became a deep grunting in
his throat. It reminded her of how, when she was learning
to drive, she would sometimes grind the transmission
trying to find second gear, which was elusive on her
father's old Chevrolet standard. Bob jerked, the one eye
she could see bulging and cowlike in its socket. His face,
which had been a bright crimson, now began to turn
purple. He settled back onto the floor. She waited, gasping
for breath, her face lathered with snot and tears. The eye
was no longer rolling, and no longer bright with panic.
She thought he was d—

Bob gave one final, titanic jerk and flung her off.
He sat up, and she saw his top half no longer exactly
matched his bottom half; he had broken his back as well
as his neck, it seemed. His plastic-lined mouth yawned.
His eyes met hers in a stare she knew she would never
forget . . . but one she could live with, should she get
through this.

'Dar! Arrrrrr!'

He fell backward. His head made an egglike cracking
sound on the floor. Darcy crawled closer to him, but not
close enough to be in the mess. She had his blood on
her, of course, and that was all right – she had tried to
help him, it was only natural – but that didn't mean she
wanted to bathe in it. She sat up, propped on one hand,
and watched him while she waited for her breath to come
back. She watched to see if he would move. He didn't.
When five minutes had gone by according to the little

jeweled Michele on her wrist – the one she always wore
when they went out – she reached a hand to the side of
his neck and felt for a pulse there. She kept her fingers
against his skin until she had counted all the way to thirty,
and there was nothing. She lowered her ear to his chest,
knowing this was the moment where he would come
back to life and grab her. He didn't come back to life
because there was no life left in him: no beating heart,
no breathing lungs. It was over. She felt no satisfaction
(let alone triumph) but only a focused determination to
finish this and do it right. Partly for herself, but mostly
for Donnie and Pets.

She went into the kitchen, moving fast. They had to
know she'd called as soon as she could; if they could tell
there had been a delay (if his blood had a chance to
coagulate too much, for instance), there might be awkward
questions. *I'll tell them I fainted, if I have to*, she thought.
They'll believe that, and even if they don't, they can't disprove
it. At least, I don't think they can.

She got the flashlight from the pantry, just as she
had on the night when she had literally stumbled over
his secret. She went back to where Bob lay, staring up
at the ceiling with his glazed eyes. She pulled the plastic
bag out of his mouth and examined it anxiously. If it
was torn, there could be problems . . . and it was, in two
places. She shone the flashlight into his mouth and
spotted one tiny scrap of GLAD bag on his tongue. She
picked it out with the tips of her fingers and put it in
the bag.

Enough, that's enough, Darcellen.

But it wasn't. She pushed his cheeks back with her
fingers, first the right, then the left. And on the left side
she found another tiny scrap of plastic, stuck to his gum.
She picked that out and put it in the bag with the other
one. Were there more pieces? Had he swallowed them? If

so, they were beyond her reach and all she could do was pray they wouldn't be discovered if someone – she didn't know who – had enough questions to order an autopsy.

Meanwhile, time was passing.

She hurried through the breezeway and into the garage, not quite running. She crawled under the worktable, opened his special hiding place, and stowed away the blood-streaked plastic bag with the dishwiper inside. She closed the hidey-hole, put the carton of old catalogues in front of it, then went back into the house. She put the flashlight where it belonged. She picked up the phone, realized she had stopped crying, and put it back into its cradle. She went through the living room and looked at him. She thought about the roses, but that didn't work. *It's roses, not patriotism, that are the last resort of a scoundrel*, she thought, and was shocked to hear herself laugh. Then she thought of Donnie and Petra, who had both idolized their father, and that did the trick. Weeping, she went back to the kitchen phone and punched in 911. 'Hello, my name is Darcellen Anderson, and I need an ambulance at—'

'Slow down a little, ma'am,' the dispatcher said. 'I'm having trouble understanding you.'

Good, Darcy thought.

She cleared her throat. 'Is this better? Can you understand me?'

'Yes, ma'am, I can now. Just take it easy. You said you needed an ambulance?'

'Yes, at 24 Sugar Mill Lane.'

'Are you hurt, Mrs Anderson?'

'Not me, my husband. He fell down the stairs. He might only be unconscious, but I think he's dead.'

The dispatcher said she would send an ambulance immediately. Darcy surmised she'd also send a Yarmouth police car. A state police car as well, if one were currently in the area. She hoped there wasn't. She went back into the front hall and sat on the bench there, but not for long. It was his eyes, looking at her. Accusing her.

She took his sport coat, wrapped it around herself, and went out on the front walk to wait for the ambulance.

17

The policeman who took her statement was Harold Shrewsbury, a local. Darcy didn't know him, but did know his wife, as it happened; Arlene Shrewsbury was a Knitting Knut. He talked to her in the kitchen while the EMTs first examined Bob's body and then took it away, not knowing there was another corpse inside him. A fellow who had been much more dangerous than Robert Anderson, CPA.

'Would you like coffee, Officer Shrewsbury? It's no trouble.'

He looked at her trembling hands and said he would be very happy to make it for both of them. 'I'm very handy in the kitchen.'

'Arlene has never mentioned that,' she said as he got up. He left his notebook open on the kitchen table. So far he had written nothing in it but her name, Bob's name, their address, and their telephone number. She took that as a good sign.

'No, she likes to hide my light under a bushel,' he said. 'Mrs Anderson – Darcy – I'm very sorry for your loss, and I'm sure Arlene would say the same.'

Darcy began to cry again. Officer Shrewsbury tore a handful of paper towels off the roll and gave them to her. 'Sturdier than Kleenex.'

'You have experience with this,' she said.

He checked the Bunn, saw it was loaded, and flipped it on. 'More than I'd like.' He came back and sat down. 'Can you tell me what happened? Do you feel up to that?'

She told him about Bob finding the double-date penny in his change from Subway, and how excited he'd been. About their celebratory dinner at Pearl of the Shore, and how he'd drunk too much. How he'd been clowning around (she mentioned the comic British salute he'd given when she asked for a glass of Perrier and lime). How he'd come up the stairs holding the glass high, like a waiter. How he was almost to the landing when he slipped. She even told about how she'd almost slipped herself, on one of the spilled ice cubes, while rushing down to him.

Officer Shrewsbury jotted something in his notebook, snapped it closed, then looked at her levelly. 'Okay. I want you to come with me. Get your coat.'

'What? Where?'

To jail, of course. Do not pass Go, do not collect two hundred dollars, go directly to jail. Bob had gotten away with almost a dozen murders, and she hadn't even been able to get away with one (of course he had planned his, and with an accountant's attention to detail). She didn't know where she'd slipped up, but it would undoubtedly turn out to be something obvious. Officer Shrewsbury would tell her on the way to the police station. It would be like the last chapter of an Elizabeth George.

'My house,' he said. 'You're staying with me and Arlene tonight.'

She gaped at him. 'I don't . . . I can't . . .'

'You can,' he said, in a voice that brooked no argument. 'She'd kill me if I left you here by yourself. Do you want to be responsible for my murder?'

She wiped tears from her face and smiled wanly. 'No, I guess not. But . . . Officer Shrewsbury . . .'

'Harry.'

'I have to make phone calls. My children . . . they don't know yet.' The thought of this brought on fresh tears, and she put the last of the paper towels to work on them.

Who knew a person could have so many tears inside them? She hadn't touched her coffee and now drank half of it in three long swallows, although it was still hot.

'I think we can stand the expense of a few long-distance calls,' Harry Shrewsbury said. 'And listen. Do you have something you can take? Anything of a, you know, calming nature?'

'Nothing like that,' she whispered. 'Only Ambien.'

'Then Arlene will loan you one of her Valiums,' he said. 'You should take one at least half an hour before you start making any stressful calls. Meantime, I'll just let her know we're coming.'

'You're very kind.'

He opened first one of her kitchen drawers, then another, then a third. Darcy felt her heart slip into her throat as he opened the fourth. He took a dishwiper from it and handed it to her. 'Sturdier than paper towels.'

'Thank you,' she said. 'So much.'

'How long were you married, Mrs Anderson?'

'Twenty-seven years,' she said.

'Twenty-seven,' he marveled. 'God. I am so sorry.'

'So am I,' she said, and lowered her face into the dishtowel.

18

Robert Emory Anderson was laid to rest in Yarmouth's Peace Cemetery two days later. Donnie and Petra flanked their mother as the minister talked about how a man's life was but a season. The weather had turned cold and overcast; a chilly wind rattled the leafless branches. B, B & A had closed for the day, and everyone had turned out. The accountants in their black overcoats clustered together like crows. There were no women among them. Darcy had never noticed this before.

Her eyes brimmed and she wiped at them periodically with the handkerchief she held in one black-gloved hand; Petra cried steadily and without let-up; Donnie was red-eyed and grim. He was a good-looking young man, but his hair was already thinning, as his father's had at his age. *As long as he doesn't put on weight like Bob did*, she thought. *And doesn't kill women, of course*. But surely that kind of thing wasn't hereditary. Was it?

Soon this would be over. Donnie would stay only a couple of days — it was all the time he could afford to take away from the business at this point, he said. He hoped she could understand that and she said of course she did. Petra would be with her for a week, and said she could stay longer if Darcy needed her. Darcy told her how kind that was, privately hoping it would be no more than five days. She needed to be alone. She needed . . . not to think, exactly, but to find herself again. To re-establish herself on the right side of the mirror.

Not that anything had gone wrong; far from it. She didn't think things could have gone better if she had planned her husband's murder for months. If she had done that, she probably would have screwed it up by complicating things too much. Unlike for Bob, planning was not her forte.

There had been no hard questions. Her story was simple, believable, and almost true. The most important part was the solid bedrock beneath it: they had a good marriage stretching back almost three decades, and there had been no recent arguments to mar it. Really, what was there to question?

The minister invited the family to step forward. They did so.

'Rest in peace, Pop,' Donnie said, and tossed a clod of earth into the grave. It landed on the shiny surface of the coffin. Darcy thought it looked like a dog turd.

'Daddy, I miss you so much,' Petra said, and threw her own handful of earth.

Darcy came last. She bent, took up a loose handful in her black glove, and let it fall. She said nothing.

The minister invoked a moment of silent prayer. The mourners bowed their heads. The wind rattled the branches. Not too far distant, traffic rushed by on I-295. Darcy thought: *God, if You're there, let this be the end.*

19

It wasn't.

Seven weeks or so after the funeral – it was the new year now, the weather blue and hard and cold – the doorbell of the house on Sugar Mill Lane rang. When Darcy opened it, she saw an elderly gentleman wearing a black topcoat and red muffler. Held before him in his gloved hands was an old-school Homburg hat. His face was deeply lined (with pain as well as age, Darcy thought) and what remained of his gray hair was buzzed to a fuzz.

'Yes?' she said.

He fumbled in his pocket and dropped his hat. Darcy bent and picked it up. When she straightened, she saw that the elderly gentleman was holding out a leather-cased identification folder. In it was a gold badge and a picture of her caller (looking quite a bit younger) on a plastic card.

'Holt Ramsey,' he said, sounding apologetic about it. 'State Attorney General's Office. I'm sorry as hell to disturb you, Mrs Anderson. May I come in? You'll freeze standing out here in that dress.'

'Please,' she said, and stood aside.

She observed his hitching walk and the way his right hand went unconsciously to his right hip – as if to hold it together – and a clear memory rose in her mind: Bob sitting beside her on the bed, her cold fingers held prisoner by his warm ones. Bob talking. Gloating, actually. *I want them to think Beadie's dumb, and they do. Because they're dumb. I've only been questioned a single time, and that was as a witness, about two weeks after BD killed the Moore woman. An old guy with a limp, semi-retired.* And here that old guy was, standing not half a dozen steps from where Bob had died. From where she had killed him. Holt Ramsey looked both sick and in pain, but his eyes were sharp. They moved quickly to the left and right, taking in everything before returning to her face.

Be careful, she told herself. *Be oh so careful of this one, Darcellen.*

'How can I help you, Mr Ramsey?'

'Well, one thing – if it's not too much to ask – I could sure use a cup of coffee. I'm awfully cold. I've got a State car, and the heater doesn't work worth a darn. Of course if it's an imposition . . .'

'Not at all. But I wonder . . . could I see your identification again?'

He handed the folder over to her equably enough, and hung his hat on the coat tree while she studied it.

'This RET stamped below the seal . . . does that mean you're retired?'

'Yes and no.' His lips parted in a smile that revealed teeth too perfect to be anything but dentures. 'Had to go, at least officially, when I turned sixty-eight, but I've spent my whole life either in the State Police or working at SAG – State Attorney General's Office, you know – and now I'm like an old firehorse with an honorary place in the barn. Kind of a mascot, you know.'

I think you're a lot more than that.

'Let me take your coat.'

'No, nope, I think I'll wear it. Won't be staying that long. I'd hang it up if it was snowing outside – so I wouldn't drip on your floor – but it's not. It's just boogery cold, you know. Too cold to snow, my father would have said, and at my age I feel the cold a lot more than I did fifty years ago. Or even twenty-five.'

Leading him into the kitchen, walking slowly so Ramsey could keep up, she asked him how old he was.

'Seventy-eight in May.' He spoke with evident pride. 'If I make it. I always add that for good luck. It's worked so far. What a nice kitchen you have, Mrs Anderson – a place for everything and everything in its place. My wife would have approved. She died four years ago. It was a heart attack, very sudden. How I miss her. The way you must miss your husband, I imagine.'

His twinkling eyes – young and alert in creased, pain-haunted sockets – searched her face.

He knows. I don't know how, but he does.

She checked the Bunn's basket and turned it on. As she got cups from the cabinet, she asked, 'How may I help you today, Mr Ramsey? Or is it Detective Ramsey?'

He laughed, and the laugh turned into a cough. 'Oh, it's been donkey's years since anyone called me Detective. Never mind Ramsey, either, if you go straight to Holt, that'll work for me. And it was really your husband I wanted to talk to, you know, but of course he's passed on – again, my condolences – and so that's out of the question. Yep, entirely out of the question.' He shook his head and settled himself on one of the stools that stood around the butcher-block table. His topcoat rustled. Somewhere inside his scant body, a bone creaked. 'But I tell you what: an old man who lives in a rented room – which I do, although it's a nice one – sometimes gets bored with just the TV for company, and so I thought, what the hell, I'll drive on down to Yarmouth and ask my few little questions just the same. She won't be able to answer many of them, I said to myself, maybe not *any* of them, but why not go anyway?

You need to get out before you get potbound, I said to myself.'

'On a day when the high is supposed to go all the way up to ten degrees,' she said. 'In a State car with a bad heater.'

'Ayuh, but I have my thermals on,' he said modestly.

'Don't you have your own car, Mr Ramsey?'

'I do, I do,' he said, as if this had never occurred to him until now. 'Come sit down, Mrs Anderson. No need to lurk in the corner. I'm too old to bite.'

'No, the coffee will be ready in a minute,' she said. She was afraid of this old man. Bob should have been afraid of him, too, but of course Bob was now beyond fear. 'In the meantime, perhaps you can tell me what you wanted to talk about with my husband.'

'Well, you won't believe this, Mrs Anderson—'

'Call me Darcy, why don't you?'

'Darcy!' He looked delighted. 'Isn't that the nicest, old-fashioned name!'

'Thank you. Do you take cream?'

'Black as my hat, that's how I take it. Only I like to think of myself as one of the white-hats, actually. Well, I would, wouldn't I? Chasing down criminals and such. That's how I got this bad leg, you know. High-speed car chase, way back in '89. Fellow killed his wife and both of his children. Now a crime like that is usually an act of passion, committed by a man who's either drunk or drugged or not quite right in the head.' Ramsey tapped his fuzz with a finger arthritis had twisted out of true. 'Not this guy. This guy did it for the insurance. Tried to make it look like a whatchacallit, home invasion. I won't go into all the details, but I sniffed around and sniffed around. For three years I sniffed around. And finally I felt I had enough to arrest him. Probably not enough to convict him, but there was no need to tell *him* that, was there?'

'I suppose not,' Darcy said. The coffee was hot, and she poured. She decided to take hers black, too. And to drink it as fast as possible. That way the caffeine would hit her all at once and turn on her lights.

'Thanks,' he said when she brought it to the table. 'Thanks very much. You're kindness itself. Hot coffee on a cold day – what could be better? Mulled cider, maybe; I can't think of anything else. Anyway, where was I? Oh, I know. Dwight Cheminoux. Way up in The County, this was. Just south of the Hainesville Woods.'

Darcy worked on her coffee. She looked at Ramsey over the rim of her cup and suddenly it was like being married again – a long marriage, in many ways a good marriage (but not in all ways), the kind that was like a joke: she knew that he knew, and he knew that she knew that he knew. That kind of relationship was like looking into a mirror and seeing another mirror, a hall of them going down into infinity. The only real question here was what he was going to do about what he knew. What he *could* do.

'Well,' Ramsey said, setting down his coffee cup and unconsciously beginning to rub his sore leg, 'the simple fact is I was hoping to provoke that fella. I mean, he had the blood of a woman and two kiddies on his hands, so I felt justified in playing a little dirty. And it worked. He ran, and I chased him right into the Hainesville Woods, where the song says there's a tombstone every mile. And there we both crashed on Wickett's Curve – him into a tree and me into him. Which is where I got this leg, not to mention the steel rod in my neck.'

'I'm sorry. And the fellow you were chasing? What did he get?'

Ramsey's mouth curved upward at the corners in a dry-lipped smile of singular coldness. His young eyes sparkled. 'He got death, Darcy. Saved the state forty or fifty years of room and board in Shawshank.'

'You're quite the hound of heaven, aren't you, Mr Ramsey?'

Instead of looking puzzled, he placed his misshapen hands beside his face, palms out, and recited in a singsong schoolboy's voice: '"I fled Him down the nights and down the days, I fled Him down the arches of the years, I fled Him down the labyrinthine ways . . ." And so on.'

'You learned that in school?'

'No, ma'am, in Methodist Youth Fellowship. Lo these many years ago. Won a Bible, which I lost at summer camp a year later. Only I didn't lose it; it was stolen. Can you imagine someone low enough to steal a Bible?'

'Yes,' Darcy said.

He laughed. 'Darcy, you go on and call me Holt. Please. All my friends do.'

Are you my friend? Are you?

She didn't know, but of one thing she was sure: he wouldn't have been Bob's friend.

'Is that the only poem you have by heart? Holt?'

'Well, I used to know "The Death of the Hired Man,"' he said, 'but now I only remember the part about how home is the place that, when you go there, they have to take you in. It's a true thing, wouldn't you say?'

'Absolutely.'

His eyes – they were a light hazel – searched hers. The intimacy of that gaze was indecent, as if he were looking at her with her clothes off. And pleasant, for perhaps the same reason.

'What did you want to ask my husband, Holt?'

'Well, I already talked to him once, you know, although I'm not sure he'd remember if he was still alive. A long time ago, that was. We were both a lot younger, and you must've been just a child yourself, given how young and pretty you are now.'

She gave him a chilly spare-me smile, then got up

to pour herself a fresh cup of coffee. The first one was already gone.

'You probably know about the Beadie murders,' he said.

'The man who kills women and then sends their ID to the police?' She came back to the table, her coffee cup perfectly steady in her hand. 'The newspapers dine out on that one.'

He pointed at her – Bob's finger-gun gesture – and tipped her a wink. 'Got that right. Yessir. "If it bleeds, it leads," that's their motto. I happened to work the case a little. I wasn't retired then, but getting on to it. I had kind of a reputation as a fellow who could sometimes get results by sniffing around . . . following my whatdoyoucallums . . .'

'Instincts?'

Once more with the finger-gun. Once more with the wink. As if there were a secret, and they were both in on it. 'Anyway, they send me out to work on my own, you know – old limping Holt shows his pictures around, asks his questions, and kind've . . . you know . . . just *sniffs*. Because I've always had a nose for this kind of work, Darcy, and never really lost it. This was in the fall of 1997, not too long after a woman named Stacey Moore was killed. Name ring a bell?'

'I don't think so,' Darcy said.

'You'd remember if you'd seen the crime scene photos. Terrible murder – how that woman must have suffered. But of course, this fellow who calls himself Beadie had stopped for a long time, over fifteen years, and he must have had a lot of steam built up in his boiler, just waiting to blow. And it was her that got scalded.

'Anyway, the fella who was SAG back then put me on it. "Let old Holt take a shot," he says, "he's not doing anything else, and it'll keep him out from underfoot."

Even then old Holt was what they called me. Because of the limp, I should imagine. I talked to her friends, her relatives, her neighbors out there on Route 106, and the people she worked with in Waterville. Oh, I talked to them plenty. She was a waitress at a place called the Sunnyside Restaurant there in town. Lots of transients stop in, because the turnpike's just down the road, but I was more interested in her regular customers. Her regular *male* customers.'

'Of course you would be,' she murmured.

'One of them turned out to be a presentable, well-turned-out fella in his mid or early forties. Came in every three or four weeks, always took one of Stacey's booths. Now, probably I shouldn't say this, since the fella turned out to be your late husband — speaking ill of the dead, but since they're *both* dead, I kind've figure that cancels itself out, if you see what I mean . . .' Ramsey ceased, looking confused.

'You're getting all tangled up,' Darcy said, amused in spite of herself. Maybe he *wanted* her to be amused. She couldn't tell. 'Do yourself a favor and just say it, I'm a big girl. She flirted with him? Is that what it comes down to? She wouldn't be the first waitress to flirt with a man on the road, even if the man had a wedding ring on his finger.'

'No, that wasn't quite it. According to what the other waitstaff told me — and of course you have to take it with a grain of salt, because they all liked her — it was *him* that flirted with *her*. And according to them, she didn't like it much. She said the guy gave her the creeps.'

'That doesn't sound like my husband.' Or what Bob had told her, for that matter.

'No, but it probably was. Your husband, I mean. And a wife doesn't always know what a hubby does on the road, although she may think she does. Anyway, one of the

waitresses told me this fella drove a Toyota 4Runner. She
knew because she had one just like it. And do you know
what? A number of the Moore woman's neighbors had
seen a 4Runner like that out and about in the area of the
family farmstand just days before the woman was murdered.
Once only a day before the killing took place.'

'But not on *the* day.'

'No, but of course a fella as careful as this Beadie
would look out for a thing like that. Wouldn't he?'

'I suppose.'

'Well, I had a description and I canvassed the area
around the restaurant. I had nothing better to do. For a
week all I got was blisters and a few cups of mercy-coffee
– none as good as yours, though! – and I was about to
give up. Then I happened to stop at a place downtown.
Mickleson's Coins. Does *that* name ring a bell?'

'Of course. My husband was a numismatist and
Mickleson's was one of the three or four best buy-and-sell
shops in the state. It's gone now. Old Mr Mickleson died
and his son closed the business.'

'Yep. Well, you know what the song says, time takes
it all in the end – your eyes, the spring in your step, even
your friggin jump shot, pardon my French. But George
Mickleson was alive then—'

'Upright and sniffin the air,' Darcy murmured.

Holt Ramsey smiled. 'Just as you say. Anyway, he
recognized the description. "Why, that sounds like Bob
Anderson," he says. And guess what? He drove a Toyota
4Runner.'

'Oh, but he traded that in a long time ago,' Darcy
said. 'For a—'

'Chevrolet Suburban, wasn't it?' Ramsey pronounced
the company name *Shivvalay*.

'Yes.' Darcy folded her hands and looked at Ramsey
calmly. They were almost down to it. The only question

was which partner in the now-dissolved Anderson marriage this sharp-eyed old man was more interested in.

'Don't suppose you still have that Suburban, do you?'

'No. I sold it about a month after my husband died. I put an ad in *Uncle Henry's* swap guide, and someone snapped it right up. I thought I'd have problems, with the high mileage and gas being so expensive, but I didn't. Of course I didn't get much.'

And two days before the man who'd bought it came to pick it up, she had searched it carefully, from stem to stern, not neglecting to pull out the carpet in the cargo compartment. She found nothing, but still paid fifty dollars to have it washed on the outside (which she didn't care about) and steam-cleaned on the inside (which she did).

'Ah. Good old *Uncle Henry's*. I sold my late wife's Ford the same way.'

'Mr Ramsey—'

'Holt.'

'Holt, were you able to positively identify my husband as the man who used to flirt with Stacey Moore?'

'Well, when I talked to Mr Anderson, he admitted he'd been in the Sunnyside from time to time – admitted it freely – but he claimed he never noticed any of the waitresses in particular. Claimed he usually had his head buried in paperwork. But of course I showed his picture – from his driver's license, you understand – and the staff allowed as how it was him.'

'Did my husband know you had a . . . a particular interest in him?'

'No. Far as he was concerned, I was just old Limpin' Lennie looking for witnesses who might have seen something. No one fears an old duck like me, you know.'

I fear you plenty.

'It's not much of a case,' she said. 'Assuming you were trying to make one.'

'No case at all!' He laughed cheerily, but his hazel eyes were cold. 'If I could have made a case, me and Mr Anderson wouldn't have had our little conversation in his office, Darcy. We would have had it in *my* office. Where you don't get to leave until I say you can. Or until a lawyer springs you, of course.'

'Maybe it's time you stopped dancing, Holt.'

'All right,' he agreed, 'why not? Because even a box-step hurts me like hell these days. Damn that old Dwight Cheminoux, anyway! And I don't want to take your whole morning, so let's speed this up. I was able to confirm a Toyota 4Runner at or near the scene of two of the earlier murders – what we call Beadie's first cycle. Not the same one; a different color. But I was also able to confirm that your husband owned another 4Runner in the seventies.'

'That's right. He liked it, so he traded for the same kind.'

'Yep, men will do that. And the 4Runner's a popular vehicle in places where it snows half the damn year. But after the Moore murder – and after I talked to him – he traded for a Suburban.'

'Not immediately,' Darcy said with a smile. 'He had that 4Runner of his well after the turn of the century.'

'I know. He traded in 2004, not long before Andrea Honeycutt was murdered down Nashua way. Blue and gray Suburban; year of manufacture 2002. A Suburban of that approximate year and those *exact* colors was seen quite often in Mrs Honeycutt's neighborhood during the month or so before she was murdered. But here's the funny thing.' He leaned forward. 'I found one witness who said that Suburban had a Vermont plate, and another – a little old lady of the type who sits in her living room window and watches all the neighborhood doins from first light to last, on account of having nothing better to do – said the one *she* saw had a New York plate.'

'Bob's had Maine plates,' Darcy said. 'As you very well know.'

'Acourse, acourse, but plates can be stolen, you know.'

'What about the Shaverstone murders, Holt? Was a blue and gray Suburban seen in Helen Shaverstone's neighborhood?'

'I see you've been following the Beadie case a little more closely than most people. A little more closely than you first let on, too.'

'Was it?'

'No,' Ramsey said. 'As a matter of fact, no. But a gray-over-blue Suburban *was* seen near the creek in Amesbury where the bodies were dumped.' He smiled again while his cold eyes studied her. 'Dumped like garbage.'

She sighed. 'I know.'

'No one could tell me about the license plate of the Suburban seen in Amesbury, but if they had, I imagine it would have been Massachusetts. Or Pennsylvania. Or anything but Maine.'

He leaned forward.

'This Beadie sent us notes with his victims' identification. Taunting us, you know – daring us to catch him. P'raps part of him even *wanted* to be caught.'

'Perhaps so,' Darcy said, although she doubted it.

'The notes were printed in block letters. Now people who do that think such printing can't be identified, but most times it can. The similarities show up. I don't suppose you have any of your husband's files, do you?'

'The ones that haven't gone back to his firm have been destroyed. But I imagine they'd have plenty of samples. Accountants never throw out anything.'

He sighed. 'Yuh, but a firm like that, it'd take a court order to get anything loose, and to get one I'd have to show probable cause. Which I just don't have. I've got a number of coincidences — although they're not coincidences in my mind. And I've got a number of . . . well . . . *propinquities*, I guess you might call them, but nowhere near enough of them to qualify as circumstantial evidence. So I came to you, Darcy. I thought I'd probably be out on my ear by now, but you've been very kind.'

She said nothing.

He leaned forward even further, almost hunching over the table now. Like a bird of prey. But hiding not quite out of sight behind the coldness in his eyes was something else. She thought it might be kindness. She prayed it was.

'Darcy, was your husband Beadie?'

She was aware that he might be recording this conversation; it was certainly not outside the realm of possibility. Instead of speaking, she raised one hand from the table, showing him her pink palm.

'For a long time you never knew, did you?'

She said nothing. Only looked at him. Looked *into* him, the way you looked into people you knew well. Only you had to be careful when you did that, because you weren't always seeing what you thought you were seeing. She knew that now.

'And then you did? One day you did?'

'Would you like another cup of coffee, Holt?'

'Half a cup,' he said. He sat back up and folded his arms over his thin chest. 'More'd give me acid indigestion, and I forgot to take my Zantac pill this morning.'

'I think there's some Prilosec in the upstairs medicine cabinet,' she said. 'It was Bob's. Would you like me to get it?'

'I wouldn't take anything of his even if I was burning up inside.'

'All right,' she said mildly, and poured him a little more coffee.

'Sorry,' he said. 'Sometimes my emotions get the better

of me. Those women . . . all those women . . . and the boy, with his whole life ahead of him. That's worst of all.'

'Yes,' she said, passing him the cup. She noticed how his hand trembled, and thought this was probably his last rodeo, no matter how smart he was . . . and he was fearsomely smart.

'A woman who found out what her husband was very late in the game would be in a hard place,' Ramsey said.

'Yes, I imagine she would be,' Darcy said.

'Who'd believe she could live with a man all those years and never know what he was? Why, she'd be like a whatdoyoucallit, the bird that lives in a crocodile's mouth.'

'According to the story,' Darcy said, 'the crocodile lets that bird live there because it keeps the crocodile's teeth clean. Eats the grain right out from between them.' She made pecking motions with the fingers of her right hand. 'It's probably not true . . . but it *is* true that I used to drive Bobby to the dentist. Left to himself, he'd accidentally-on-purpose forget his appointments. He was such a baby about pain.' Her eyes filled unexpectedly with tears. She wiped them away with the heels of her hands, cursing them. This man would not respect tears shed on Robert Anderson's account.

Or maybe she was wrong about that. He was smiling and nodding his head. 'And your kids. They'd be run over once when the world found out their father was a serial killer and torturer of women. Then run over again when the world decided their mother had been covering up for him. Maybe even helping him, like Myra Hindley helped Ian Brady. Do you know who they were?'

'No.'

'Never mind, then. But ask yourself this: what would a woman in a difficult position like that do?'

'What would *you* do, Holt?'

'I don't know. My situation's a little different. I may be just an old nag – the oldest horse in the firebarn – but I have a responsibility to the families of those murdered women. They deserve closure.'

'They deserve it, no question . . . but do they *need* it?'

'Robert Shaverstone's penis was bitten off, did you know that?'

She hadn't. Of course she hadn't. She closed her eyes and felt the warm tears trickling through the lashes. *Did not 'suffer' my ass*, she thought, and if Bob had appeared before her, hands out and begging for mercy, she would have killed him again.

'His father knows,' Ramsey said. Speaking softly. 'And he has to live with that knowledge about the child he loved every day.'

'I'm sorry,' she whispered. 'I am so, so sorry.'

She felt him take her hand across the table. 'Didn't mean to upset you.'

She flung it off. 'Of course you did! But do you think I haven't been? Do you think I *haven't* been, you . . . you nosy old man?'

He chuckled, revealing those sparkling dentures. 'No. I don't think that at all. Saw it as soon as you opened the door.' He paused, then said deliberately: 'I saw everything.'

'And what do you see now?'

He got up, staggered a little, then found his balance. 'I see a courageous woman who should be left alone to get after her housework. Not to mention the rest of her life.'

She also got up. 'And the families of the victims? The ones who deserve closure?' She paused, not wanting to say the rest. But she had to. This man had fought considerable pain – maybe even excruciating pain – to come here, and now he was giving her a pass. At least, she thought he was. 'Robert Shaverstone's father?'

'The Shaverstone boy is dead, and his father's as good as.' Ramsey spoke in a calm, assessing tone Darcy recognized. It was a tone Bob used when he knew a client of the firm was about to be hauled before the IRS, and the meeting would go badly. 'Never takes his mouth off the whiskey bottle from morning til night. Would knowing that his son's killer — his son's *mutilator* — was dead change that? I don't think so. Would it bring any of the victims back? Nawp. Is the killer burning in the fires of hell for his crimes right now, suffering his own mutilations that will bleed for all of eternity? The Bible says he is. The Old Testament part of it, anyway, and since that's where our laws come from, it's good enough for me. Thanks for the coffee. I'll have to stop at every rest area between here and Augusta going back, but it was worth it. You make a good cup.'

Walking him to the door, Darcy realized she felt on the right side of the mirror for the first time since she had stumbled over that carton in the garage. It was good to know he had been close to being caught. That he hadn't been as smart as he'd assumed he was.

'Thank you for coming to visit,' she said as he set his hat squarely on his head. She opened the door, letting in a breeze of cold air. She didn't mind. It felt good on her skin. 'Will I see you again?'

'Nawp. I'm done as of next week. Full retirement. Going to Florida. I won't be there long, according to my doctor.'

'I'm sorry to hear th—'

He abruptly pulled her into his arms. They were thin, but sinewy and surprisingly strong. Darcy was startled but not frightened. The brim of his Homburg bumped her temple as he whispered in her ear. 'You did the right thing.'

And kissed her cheek.

20

He went slowly and carefully down the path, minding the ice. An old man's walk. *He should really have a cane,* Darcy thought. He was going around the front of his car, still looking down for ice patches, when she called his name. He turned back, bushy eyebrows raised.

'When my husband was a boy, he had a friend who was killed in an accident.'

'Is that so?' The words came out in a puff of winter white.

'Yes,' Darcy said. 'You could look up what happened. It was very tragic, even though he wasn't a very nice boy, according to my husband.'

'No?'

'No. He was the sort of boy who harbors dangerous fantasies. His name was Brian Delahanty, but when they were kids, Bob called him BD.'

Ramsey stood by his car for several seconds, working it through. Then he nodded his head. 'That's very interesting. I might have a look at the stories about it on my computer. Or maybe not; it was all a long time ago. Thank you for the coffee.'

'Thank you for the conversation.'

She watched him drive down the street (he drove with the confidence of a much younger man, she noticed – probably because his eyes were still so sharp) and then went inside. She felt younger, lighter. She went to the mirror in the hall. In it she saw nothing but her own reflection, and that was good.

AFTERWORD

The stories in this book are harsh. You may have found them hard to read in places. If so, be assured that I found them equally hard to write in places. When people ask me about my work, I have developed a habit of skirting the subject with jokes and humorous personal anecdotes (which you can't quite trust; never trust anything a fiction writer says about himself). It's a form of deflection, and a little more diplomatic than the way my Yankee forebears might have answered such questions: *It's none of your business, chummy*. But beneath the jokes, I take what I do very seriously, and have since I wrote my first novel, *The Long Walk*, at the age of eighteen.

I have little patience with writers who *don't* take the job seriously, and none at all with those who see the art of story-fiction as essentially worn out. It's not worn out, and it's not a literary game. It's one of the vital ways in which we try to make sense of our lives, and the often terrible world we see around us. It's the way we answer the question, *How can such things be?* Stories suggest that sometimes – not always, but sometimes – there's a *reason*.

From the start – even before a young man I can now hardly comprehend started writing *The Long Walk* in his college dormitory room – I felt that the best fiction was both propulsive and assaultive. It gets in your face. Sometimes it shouts in your face. I have no quarrel with literary fiction, which usually concerns itself with extraordinary people in ordinary situations, but as both a reader and a writer, I'm much more interested by ordinary people in extraordinary situations. I want to provoke an emotional, even visceral, reaction in my readers. Making them think *as they read* is not my deal. I put that in italics, because if the tale is good enough and the characters vivid enough, thinking will supplant emotion when the tale has been told and the book set aside (sometimes with relief). I can remember reading George Orwell's *1984* at the age of thirteen or so with growing dismay, anger, and outrage, charging through the pages and gobbling up the story as fast as I could, and what's wrong with that? Especially since I continue to think about it to this day when some politician (I'm thinking of Sarah Palin and her scurrilous 'death-panel' remarks) has some success in convincing the public that white is really black, or vice-versa.

Here's something else I believe: if you're going into a very dark place – like Wilf James's Nebraska farmhouse in '1922' – then you should take a bright light, and shine it on everything. If you don't want to see, why in God's name would you dare the dark at all? The great naturalist writer Frank Norris has always been one of my literary idols, and I've kept what he said on this subject in mind for over forty years: 'I never truckled; I never took off my hat to Fashion and held it out for pennies. By God, I told them the truth.'

But Steve, you say, you've made a great many pennies during your career, and as for truth . . . that's variable, isn't it? Yes, I've made a good amount of money writing my stories, but the money was a side effect, never the goal. Writing fiction for money is a mug's game. And sure, truth is in the eye of the beholder. But when it comes to fiction, the writer's only responsibility is to look for the truth inside his own heart. It won't always be the reader's truth, or the critic's truth, but as long as it's the *writer's* truth – as long as he or she doesn't truckle, or hold out his or her hat to Fashion – all is well. For writers who knowingly lie, for those who substitute unbelievable human behavior for the way people really act, I have nothing but contempt. Bad writing is more than a matter of shit syntax and faulty observation; bad writing usually arises from a stubborn refusal to tell stories about what people actually do — to face the fact, let us say, that murderers sometimes help old ladies cross the street.

I have tried my best in *Full Dark, No Stars* to record what people might do, and how they might behave, under certain dire circumstances. The people in these stories are not without hope, but they acknowledge that even our fondest hopes (and our fondest wishes for our fellowmen and the society in which we live) may sometimes be vain. Often, even. But I think they also say that nobility most fully resides not in success but in trying to do the right thing . . . and that when we fail to do that, or willfully turn away from the challenge, hell follows.

'1922' was inspired by a nonfiction book called *Wisconsin Death Trip* (1973), written by Michael Lesy and featuring photographs taken in the small city of Black River Falls, Wisconsin. I was impressed by the rural isolation of these photographs, and the harshness and deprivation in the faces of many of the subjects. I wanted to get that feeling in my story.

In 2007, while traveling on Interstate 84 to an auto-graphing in western Massachusetts, I stopped at a rest area for a typical Steve King Health Meal: a soda and a candybar. When I came out of the refreshment shack, I saw a woman with a flat tire talking earnestly to a long-haul trucker parked in the next slot. He smiled at her and got out of his rig.

'Need any help?' I asked.

'No, no, I got this,' the trucker said.

The lady got her tire changed, I'm sure. I got a Three

Musketeers and the story idea that eventually became 'Big Driver.'

In Bangor, where I live, a thoroughfare called the Hammond Street Extension skirts the airport. I walk three or four miles a day, and if I'm in town, I often go out that way. There's a gravel patch beside the airport fence about halfway along the Extension, and there any number of roadside vendors have set up shop over the years. My favorite is known locally as Golf Ball Guy, and he always appears in the spring. Golf Ball Guy goes up to the Bangor Municipal Golf Course when the weather turns warm, and scavenges up hundreds of used golf balls that have been abandoned under the snow. He throws away the really bad ones and sells the rest at the little spot out on the Extension (the windshield of his car is lined with golf balls – a nice touch). One day when I spied him, the idea for 'Fair Extension' came into my mind. Of course I set it in Derry, home of the late and unlamented clown Pennywise, because Derry is just Bangor masquerading under a different name.

The last story in this book came to my mind after reading an article about Dennis Rader, the infamous BTK (bind, torture, and kill) murderer who took the lives of ten people – mostly women, but two of his victims were children – over a period of roughly sixteen years. In many cases, he mailed pieces of his victims' identification to the police. Paula Rader was married to this monster for thirty-four years, and many in the Wichita area, where Rader claimed his victims, refuse to believe that she could live with him and not know what he was doing. I did believe – I *do* believe – and I wrote this story to explore what might happen in such a case if the wife suddenly found out about her husband's awful hobby. I also wrote it to explore the idea that it's impossible to fully know anyone, even those we love the most.

All right, I think we've been down here in the dark long enough. There's a whole other world upstairs. Take my hand, Constant Reader, and I'll be happy to lead you back into the sunshine. I'm happy to go there, because I believe most people are essentially good. I know that I am.

It's *you* I'm not entirely sure of.

Bangor, Maine
December 23, 2009

HODDER
PRESENTS

UNDER THE WEATHER

A NEW STORY FROM
STEPHEN KING ...

'Under the Weather' copyright © 2011
by Stephen King.

Published by arrangement with the Author.
All rights reserved.

I've been having this bad dream for a week now, but it must be one of the lucid ones, because I'm always able to back out before it turns into a nightmare. Only this time it seems to have followed me, because Ellen and I aren't alone. There's something under the bed. I can hear it chewing.

You know how it is when you're really scared, right? Your heart seems to stop, your tongue sticks to the roof of your mouth, your skin goes cold and goose bumps rise up all over your body. Instead of meshing, the cogs in your head just spin and the whole engine heats up. I almost scream, I really do. I think, *It's the thing I don't want to look at. It's the thing in the window seat.*

Then I see the fan overhead, the blades turning at their slowest speed. I see a crack of early morning light running down the middle of the pulled drapes. I see the graying milkweed fluff of Ellen's hair on the other side of the bed. I'm here on the Upper East Side, fifth floor, and everything's okay. The dream was just a dream. As for what's under the bed—

I toss back the covers and slide out onto my knees, like a man who means to pray. But instead of that, I lift the flounce and peer under the bed. I only see a dark shape at first. Then the shape's head turns and two eyes gleam at me. It's Lady. She's not supposed to be under there, and I guess she knows it (hard to tell what a dog knows and what it doesn't), but I must have left the door open when I came to bed. Or maybe it didn't quite latch and she pushed it open with her snout. She must have brought one of her toys with her from the basket in the hall. At least it wasn't the blue bone or the red rat. Those have squeakers in them, and would have wakened Ellen for sure. And Ellen needs her rest. She's been under the weather.

'Lady,' I whisper. 'Lady, come out of there.'

She only looks at me. She's getting on in years and not so steady on her pins as she used to be, but – as the saying goes – she ain't stupid. She's under Ellen's side, where I can't reach her. If I raise my voice she'll have to come, but she knows (I'm pretty sure she knows) that I won't do that, because if I raise my voice, that will wake Ellen for sure.

As if to prove this, Lady turns away from me and the chewing recommences.

Well, I can handle that. I've been living with Lady for eleven years, nearly half my married life. There are three things that get her on her feet. One is the rattle of her leash and a call of 'Elevator!' One is the thump of her food dish on the floor. The third—

I get up and walk down the short hall to the kitchen. From the cupboard I take the bag of Snackin' Slices, making sure to rattle it. I don't have to wait long for the muted clitter of cocker-claws. Five seconds and she's right there. She doesn't even bother to bring her toy.

I show her one of the little carrot shapes, then toss it into the living room. A little mean, maybe, and I know she didn't mean to scare the life out of me, but she did. Besides, the fat old thing can use the exercise. She chases her treat. I linger long enough to start the coffee-maker, then go back into the bedroom. I'm careful to pull the door all the way shut.

Ellen's still sleeping, and getting up early has one benefit: no need for the alarm. I turn it off. Let her sleep a little later. It's a bronchial infection. I was scared for a while there, but now she's on the mend.

I go into the bathroom and officially christen the

day by brushing my teeth (I've read that in the morning a person's mouth is as germicidally dead as it ever gets, but the habits we learn as children are hard to break). I turn on the shower, get it good and hot, and step in.

The shower's where I do my best thinking, and this morning I think about the dream. Five nights in a row I've had it. (But who's counting.) Nothing really awful happens, but in a way that's the worst part. Because in the dream I know – absolutely *know* – that something awful *will* happen. If I let it.

I'm in an airplane, in business class. I'm in an aisle seat, which is where I prefer to be, so I don't have to squeeze past anybody if I have to go to the toilet. My tray table is down. On it is a bag of peanuts and an orange drink that looks like a vodka sunrise, a drink I've never ordered in real life. The ride is smooth. If there are clouds, we're above them. The cabin is filled with sunlight. Someone is sitting in the window seat, and I know if I look at him (or her, or possibly *it*), I'll see something that will turn my bad dream into a nightmare. If I look into the face of my seatmate, I may lose my mind. It could crack open like an egg and all the darkness there is might pour out.

I give my soapy hair a quick rinse, step out, dry off. My clothes are folded on a chair in the bedroom. I take them and my shoes into the kitchen, which is now filling with the smell of coffee. Nice. Lady's curled up by the stove, looking at me reproachfully.

'Don't go giving me the stinkeye,' I tell her, and nod toward the closed bedroom door. 'You know the rules.'

She puts her snout down on the floor between her paws.

I choose cranberry juice while I wait for the coffee. There's OJ, which is my usual morning drink, but I don't want it. Too much like the drink in the dream, I suppose. I have my coffee in the living room with CNN on mute, just reading the crawl at the bottom, which is all a person really needs. Then I turn it off and have a bowl of All-Bran. Quarter to eight. I decide that if the weather's nice when I walk Lady, I'll skip the cab and walk to work.

The weather's nice all right, spring edging into summer and a shine on everything. Carlo, the doorman, is under the awning, talking on his cell phone. 'Yuh,' he says. 'Yuh, I finally got hold of her. She says go ahead, no problem as long as I'm there. She don't trust nobody, and I don't blame her. She got a lot of nice things up there. You come when? Three? You can't make it earlier?' He tips me a wave with one white-gloved hand as I walk Lady down to the corner.

We've got this down to a science, Lady and I. She does it at pretty much the same place every day, and I'm fast with the poop bag. When I come back, Carlo stoops to give her a pat. Lady waves her tail back and forth most fetchingly, but no treat is forthcoming from Carlo. He knows she's on a diet. Or supposed to be.

'I finally got hold of Mrs Warshawski,' Carlo tells me. Mrs Warshawski is in 5-C, but only technically. She's been gone for a couple of months now. 'She was in Vienna.'

'Vienna, is that so,' I say.

'She told me to go ahead with the exterminators. She was horrified when I told her. You're the only one on four, five, or six who hasn't complained. The rest of them . . .' He shakes his head and makes a *whoo* sound.

'I grew up in a Connecticut mill town. It pretty well wrecked my sinuses. I can smell coffee, and Ellie's perfume if she puts it on thick, but that's about all.'

'In this case, that's probably a blessing. How *is* Mrs Nathan? Still under the weather?'

'It'll be a few more days before she's ready to go

back to work, but she's a hell of a lot better. She gave me a scare for a while.'

'Me, too. She was going out one day – in the rain, naturally—'

'That's El,' I say. 'Nothing stops her. If she feels like she has to go somewhere, she goes.'

'—and I thought to myself, "That's a real graveyard cough."' He raises one of his gloved hands in a *stop* gesture. 'Not that I really thought—'

'It was on the way to being a hospital cough, anyway. But I finally got her to see the doctor, and now . . . road to recovery.'

'Good. Good.' Then, returning to what's really on his mind: 'Mrs Warshawski was pretty grossed out when I told her. I said we'd probably just find some spoiled food in the fridge, but I know it's worse than that. So does anybody else on those floors with an intact smeller.' He gives a grim little nod. 'They're going to find a dead rat in there, you mark my words. Food stinks, but not like that. Only dead things stink like that. It's a rat, all right, maybe a couple of them. She probably put down poison and doesn't want to admit it.' He bends down to give Lady another pat. '*You* smell it, don't you, girl? You bet you do.'

There's a litter of purple notes around the coffeemaker. I take the purple pad they came from to the kitchen table and write another.

Ellen: Lady all walked. Coffee ready. If you feel well enough to go out to the park, go! Just not too far. Don't want you to overdo now that you're finally on the mend. Carlo told me again that he 'smells a rat.' I guess so does everyone else in the neighborhood of 5-C. Lucky for us that you're plugged up and I'm 'olfac'rarlly challenged.' Haha! If you hear people in Mrs. W's. it's the exterminators. Carlo will be with them, so don't worry. I'm going to walk to work. Need to think summore about the latest male wonder drug. Wish they'd consulted us before they hung that name on it. Remember, DON'T OVERDO. Love you — love you.

I jot half a dozen X's just to underline the point, and sign it with a *B* in a heart. Then I add it to the other notes around the coffeemaker. I refill Lady's water dish before I leave.

It's twenty blocks or so, and I don't think about the latest male wonder drug. I think about the exterminators, who will be coming at three. Earlier, if they can make it.

The walk might have been a mistake. The dreams have interrupted my sleep cycle, I guess, and I almost fall asleep during the morning meeting in the conference room. But I come around in a hurry when Pete Wendell shows a mock-up poster for the new Petrov Vodka campaign. I've seen it already, on his office computer while he was fooling with it last week, and looking at it again I know where at least one element of my dream came from.

'Petrov Vodka,' Aura McLean says. Her admirable breasts rise and fall in a theatrical sigh. 'If that's an example of the new Russian capitalism, it's dead on arrival.' The heartiest laughter at this comes from the younger men, who'd like to see Aura's long blond hair spread on a pillow next to them. 'No offense to you intended, Pete, it's a great leader.'

'None taken,' Pete says with a game smile. 'We do what we can.'

The poster shows a couple toasting each other on a balcony while the sun sinks over a harbor filled with expensive pleasure boats. The cutline beneath reads SUNSET. THE PERFECT TIME FOR A VODKA SUNRISE.

There's some discussion about the placement of the Petrov bottle — right? left? center? below? — and Frank

Bernstein suggests that actually adding the recipe might prolong the page view, especially in mags like *Playboy* and *Esquire*. I tune out, thinking about the drink sitting on the tray in my airplane dream, until I realize George Slattery is calling on me. I'm able to replay the question, and that's a good thing. You don't ask George to chew his cabbage twice.

'I'm actually in the same boat as Pete,' I say. 'The client picked the name, I'm just doing what I can.'

There's some good-natured laughter. There have been many jokes about Vonnell Pharmaceutical's newest drug product.

'I may have something to show you by Monday,' I tell them. I'm not looking at George, but he knows where I'm aiming. 'By the middle of next week for sure. I want to give Billy a chance to see what he can do.' Billy Ederle is our newest hire, and doing his break-in time as my assistant. He doesn't get an invite to the morning meetings yet, but I like him. Everybody at Andrews-Slattery likes him. He's bright, he's eager, and I bet he'll start shaving in a year or two.

George considers this. 'I was really hoping to see a treatment today. Even rough copy.'

Silence. People study their nails. It's as close to a public rebuke as George gets, and maybe I deserve it. This hasn't been my best week, and laying it off on the kid doesn't look so good. It doesn't feel so good, either.

'Okay,' George says at last, and you can feel the relief in the room. It's like a light cool breath of breeze, there and then gone. No one wants to witness a conference room caning on a sunny Friday morning, and I sure don't want to get one. Not with all the other stuff on my mind.

George smells a rat, I think.

'How's Ellen doing?' he asks.

'Better,' I tell him. 'Thanks for asking.'

There are a few more presentations. Then it's over. Thank God.

I'm almost dozing when Billy Ederle comes into my office twenty minutes later. Check that: I *am* dozing. I sit up fast, hoping the kid just thinks he caught me deep in thought. He's probably too excited to have noticed either way. In one hand he's holding a piece of poster board. I think he'd look right at home in Podunk High School, putting up a big notice about the Friday night dance.

'How was the meeting?' he asks.

'It was okay.'

'Did they bring us up?'

'You know they did. What have you got for me, Billy?'

He takes a deep breath and turns his poster board around so I can see it. On the left is a prescription bottle of Viagra, either actual size or close enough not to matter. On the right – the power side of the ad, as anyone in advertising will tell you – is a prescription bottle of our stuff, but much bigger. Beneath is the cutline: PO-10s, TEN TIMES MORE EFFECTIVE THAN VIAGRA!

As Billy looks at me looking at it, his hopeful smile starts to fade. 'You don't like it.'

'It's not a question of like or don't like. In this business it never is. It's a question of what works and what doesn't. This doesn't.'

Now he's looking sulky. If George Slattery saw that look, he'd take the kid to the woodshed. I won't, although it might feel that way to him because it's my job to teach him. In spite of everything else on my mind, I'll try to do that. Because I love this business. It gets very little respect, but I love it anyway. Also, I can hear Ellen say, you don't let go. Once you get your teeth in something, they stay there. Determination like that can be a little scary.

'Sit down, Billy.'

He sits.

'And wipe that pout off your puss, okay? You look like a kid who just dropped his binky in the toilet.'

He does his best. Which I like about him. Kid's a tryer, and if he's going to work in the Andrews-Slattery shop, he'd better be.

'Good news is I'm not taking it away from you, mostly because it's not your fault Vonnell Pharmaceutical saddled us with a name that sounds like a multivitamin. But we're going to make a silk purse out of this sow's ear. In advertising, that's the main job seven times out of every ten. Maybe eight. So pay attention.'

He gets a little grin. 'Should I take notes?'

'Don't be a smartass. First, when you're shouting a drug, you *never* show a prescription bottle. The logo, sure. The pill itself, sometimes. It depends. You know why Pfizer shows the Viagra pill? Because it's blue. Consumers like blue. The shape helps, too. Consumers have a very positive response to the shape of the Viagra tab. But people *never like to see the prescription bottle their stuff comes in*. Prescription bottles make them think of sickness. Got that?'

'So maybe a little Viagra pill and a big Po-10s pill? Instead of the bottles?' He raises his hands, framing an invisible cutline. '"Po-10s, ten times bigger, ten times better." Get it?'

'Yes, Billy, I get it. The FDA will get it, too, and they won't like it. In fact, they could make us take ads with a cutline like that out of circulation, which would cost a bundle. Not to mention a very good client.'

'*Why?*' It's almost a bleat.

'Because it *isn't* ten times bigger, and it isn't ten times better. Viagra, Cialis, Levitra, Po-10s, they all have about the same penis-elevation formula. Do your research, kiddo. And a little refresher course in advertising law wouldn't hurt. Want to say Blowhard's Bran Muffins are ten times tastier than Bigmouth's Bran Muffins? Have at it, taste is a subjective judgment. What gets your prick hard, though, and for how long . . .'

'Okay,' he says in a small voice.

'Here's the other half. "Ten times more" anything is – speaking in erectile dysfunction terms – pretty limp. It went out of vogue around the same time as Two Cs in a K.'

He looks blank.

'Two cunts in a kitchen. It's how advertising guys used to refer to their TV ads on the soaps back in the fifties.'

'You're joking!'

'Afraid not. Now here's something I've been playing with.' I jot on a pad, and for a moment I think of all those notes scattered around the coffeemaker back in good old 5-B – why are they still there?

'Can't you just tell me?' the kid asks from a thousand miles away.

'No, because advertising isn't an oral medium,' I say. 'Never trust an ad that's spoken out loud. Write it down and show it to someone. Show it to your best friend. Or your . . . you know, your wife.'

'Are you okay, Brad?'

'Fine. Why?'

'I don't know, you just looked funny for a minute.'

'Just as long as I don't look funny when I present on Monday. Now – what does this say to you?' I turn the pad around and show him what I've printed there: po-10s . . . FOR MEN WHO WANT TO DO IT THE HARD WAY.

'It's like a dirty joke!' he objects.

'You've got a point, but I've printed it in block caps.

Imagine it in a soft italic type, almost a girly type. Maybe even in parentheses.' I add them, although they don't work with the caps. But they will. It's a thing I just know, because I can see it. 'Now, playing off that, think of a photo showing a big, burly guy. In low-slung jeans that show the top of his underwear. And a sweatshirt with the sleeves cut off, let's say. See him with some grease and dirt on his guns.'

'Guns?'

'Biceps. And he's standing beside a muscle car with the hood up. Now, is it still a dirty joke?'

'I . . . I don't know.'

'Neither do I, not for sure, but my gut tells me it'll pull the plow. But not quite as is. The cutline still doesn't work, you're right about that, and it's got to, because it'll be the basis of the TV and 'Net ads. So play with it. Make it work. Just remember the key word . . .'

Suddenly, just like that, I know where the rest of that damn dream came from.

'Brad?'

'The key word is *hard*,' I say. 'Because a man . . . when something's not working – his prick, his plan, his *life* – he *takes* it hard. He doesn't want to give up. He remembers how it was, and he wants it that way again.'

Yes, I think. Yes he does.

Billy smirks. 'I wouldn't know.'

I manage a smile. It feels god-awful heavy, as if there are weights hanging from the corners of my mouth. All at once it's like being in the bad dream again. Because there's something close to me I don't want to look at. Only this isn't a lucid dream I can back out of. This is lucid reality.

After Billy leaves, I go down to the can. It's ten o'clock, and most of the guys in the shop have off-loaded their morning coffee and are taking on more in our little caf, so I have it to myself. I drop my pants so if someone wanders in and happens to look under the door he won't think I'm weird, but the only business I've come in here to do is thinking. Or remembering.

Four years after coming on board at Andrews-Slattery, the Fasprin Pain Reliever account landed on my desk. I've had some special ones over the years, some breakouts, and that was the first. It happened fast. I opened the sample box, took out the bottle, and the basis of the campaign – what admen sometimes call the heartwood – came to me in an instant. I ditzed around a little, of course – you don't want to make it look *too* easy – then did some comps. Ellen helped. This was just after we found out she couldn't conceive. It was something to do with a drug she'd been given when she had rheumatic fever as a kid. She was pretty depressed. Helping with the Fasprin comps took her mind off it, and she really threw herself into the thing.

Al Andrews was still running things back then, and he was the one I took the comps to. I remember sitting in front of his desk in the sweat-seat with my heart in my mouth as he shuffled slowly through the comps we'd worked up. When he finally put them down and raised his shaggy old head to look at me, the pause seemed to go on for at least an hour. Then he said, 'These are good, Bradley. More than good, terrific. We'll meet with the client tomorrow afternoon. You do the prez.'

I did the prez, and when the Dugan Drug VP saw the picture of the young working woman with the bottle of Fasprin poking out of her rolled-up sleeve, he flipped for it. The campaign brought Fasprin right up there with the big boys – Bayer, Anacin, Bufferin – and by the end of the year we were handling the whole Dugan account. Billing? Seven figures. Not a low seven, either.

I used the bonus to take Ellen to Nassau for ten days. We left from Kennedy, on a morning that was pelting down rain, and I still remember how she laughed and said, 'Kiss me, beautiful,' when the plane broke through the clouds and the cabin filled with sunlight. I did kiss her, and the couple on the other side of the aisle – we were flying in business class – applauded.

That was the best. The worst came half an hour later, when I turned to her and for a moment thought she was dead. It was the way she was sleeping, with her head cocked over on her shoulder and her mouth open and her hair kind of sticking to the window. She was young, we both were, but the idea of sudden death had a hideous possibility in Ellen's case.

'They used to call your condition "barren," Mrs Franklin,' the doctor said when he gave us the bad news, 'but in your case, the condition could more accurately be called a blessing. Pregnancy puts a strain on the heart, and thanks to a disease that was badly treated when you were a child, yours isn't strong. If you did happen to conceive, you'd be in bed for the last four months of the pregnancy, and even then the outcome would be dicey.'

She wasn't pregnant when we left on that trip, but she'd been excited about it for two weeks before. The climb up to cruising altitude had been plenty rough . . . and she didn't look like she was breathing.

Then she opened her eyes. I settled back into my aisle seat, letting out a long and shaky breath.

She looked at me, puzzled. 'What's wrong?'

'Nothing. The way you were sleeping, that's all.'

She wiped at her chin. 'Oh God, did I drool?'

'No.' I laughed. 'But for a minute there you looked . . . well, dead.'

She laughed, too. 'And if I was, you'd ship the body

back to New York, I suppose, and take up with some Bahama mama.'

'No,' I said. 'I'd take you, anyway.'

'What?'

'Because I wouldn't accept it. No way would I.'

'You'd have to after a few days. I'd get all smelly.'

She was smiling. She thought it was still a game, because she hadn't really understood what the doctor was telling her that day. She hadn't – as the saying goes – taken it to heart. And she didn't know how she'd looked, with the sun shining on her winter-pale cheeks and smudged eyelids and slack mouth. But I'd seen, and I'd taken it to heart. She *was* my heart, and I guard what's in my heart. Nobody takes it away from me.

'You wouldn't,' I said. 'I'd keep you alive.'

'Really? How? Necromancy?'

'By refusing to give up. And by using an adman's most valuable asset.'

'Which is what, Mr Fasprin?'

'Imagination. Now can we talk about something more pleasant?'

The call I've been expecting comes around three-thirty. It's not Carlo. It's Berk Ostrow, the building super. He wants to know what time I'm going to be home, because the rat everybody's been smelling isn't in 5-C, it's in our place next door. Ostrow says the exterminators have to leave by four to get to another job, but that isn't the important thing. What's important is what's wrong in there, and by the way, Carlo says no one's seen your wife in over a week. Just you and the dog.

I explain about my deficient sense of smell, and Ellen's bronchitis. In her current condition, I say, she wouldn't know the drapes were on fire until the smoke detector went off. I'm sure Lady smells it, I tell him, but to a dog, the stench of a decaying rat probably smells like Chanel No. 5.

'I get all that, Mr. Franklin, but I still need to get in there to see what's what. And the exterminators will have to be called back. I think you're probably going to be on the hook for their bill, which is apt to be quite high. I could let myself in with the passkey, but I'd really be more comfortable if you were—'

'Yes, I'd be more comfortable, too. Not to mention my wife.'

'I tried calling her, but she didn't answer the phone.' I can hear the suspicion creeping back into his voice. I've explained everything, advertising men are good at that, but the convincing effect only lasts for sixty seconds or so.

'She's probably got it on mute. Plus, the medication the doctor gave her makes her sleep quite heavily.'

'What time will you be home, Mr Franklin? I can stay until seven; after that there's only Alfredo.' The disparaging note in his voice suggests I'd be better off dealing with a no-English wetback.

Never, I think. I'll never be home. In fact, I was never there in the first place. Ellen and I enjoyed the Bahamas so much we moved to Cable Beach, and I took a job with a little firm in Nassau. I shout Cruise Ship Specials, Stereo Blowout Sales, and supermarket openings. All this New York stuff has just been a lucid dream, one I can back out of at any time.

'Mr Franklin? Are you there?'

'Sure. Just thinking.' What I'm thinking is that if I leave right now, and take a taxi, I can be there in twenty minutes. 'I've got one meeting I absolutely can't miss, but why don't you meet me in the apartment around six?'

'How about in the lobby, Mr Franklin? We can go up together.'

I think of asking him how he believes I'd get rid of my murdered wife's body at rush hour – because that *is* what he's thinking. Maybe it's not at the very front of his mind, but it's not all the way in back, either. Does he think I'd use the service elevator? Or maybe dump her down the incinerator chute?

'The lobby is absolutely okey-fine,' I say. 'Six. Quarter of, if I can possibly make it.'

I hang up and head for the elevators. I have to pass the caf to get there. Billy Ederle's leaning in the doorway, drinking a Nozzy. It's a remarkably lousy soda, but it's all we vend. The company's a client.

'Where are you off to?'

'Home. Ellen called. She's not feeling well.'

'Don't you want your briefcase?'

'No.' I don't expect to be needing my briefcase for a while. In fact, I may never need it again.

'I'm working on the new Po-10s direction. I think it's going to be a winner.'

'I'm sure,' I say, and I am. Billy Ederle will soon be movin' on up, and good for him. 'I've got to get a wiggle on.'

'Sure, I understand.' He's twenty-four and understands nothing. 'Give her my best.'

We take on half a dozen interns a year at Andrews-Slattery; it's how Billy Ederle got started. Most are terrific, and at first Fred Willits seemed terrific, too. I took him under my wing, and so it became my responsibility to fire him – I guess you'd say that, although interns are never actually 'hired' in the first place – when it turned out he was a klepto who had decided our supply room was his private game preserve. God knows how much stuff he lifted before Maria Ellington caught him loading reams of paper into his suitcase-sized brief one afternoon. Turned out he was a bit of a psycho, too. He went nuclear when I told him he was through. Pete Wendell called security while the kid was yelling at me in the lobby and had him removed forcibly.

Apparently old Freddy had a lot more to say, because he started hanging around my building and haranguing me when I came home. He kept his distance, though, and the cops claimed he was just exercising his right to free speech. But it wasn't his mouth I was afraid of. I kept thinking he might have lifted a box cutter or an X-ACTO knife as well as printer carridges and about fifty reams of copier paper. That was when I got Alfredo to give me a key to the service entrance, and I started going in that way. All that was in the fall of the year, September or October. Young Mr Willets gave up and took his issues elsewhere when the weather turned cold, but Alfredo never asked for the return of the key, and I never gave it back. I guess we both forgot.

That's why, instead of giving the taxi driver my address, I get him to let me out on the next block. I pay him, adding a generous tip – hey, it's only money – and then walk down the service alley. I have a bad moment when the key doesn't work, but when I jigger it a little, it turns. The service elevator has brown quilted movers' pads hanging from the walls. Previews of the padded cell they'll put me in, I think, but of course that's just melo-drama. I'll probably have to take a leave of absence from the shop, and what I've done is a lease breaker for sure, but—

What *have* I done, exactly?

For that matter, what have I been doing for the last week?

'Keeping her alive,' I say as the elevator stops at the fifth floor. 'Because I couldn't bear for her to be dead.'

She *isn't* dead, I tell myself, just under the weather.

It sucks as a cutline, but for the last week it has served me very well, and in the adverising biz the short term is what counts.

I let myself in. The air is still and warm, but I don't smell anything. So I tell myself, and in the advertising biz imagination is *also* what counts.

'Honey, I'm home,' I call. 'Are you awake? Feeling any better?'

I guess I forgot to close the bedroom door before I left this morning, because Lady slinks out. She's licking her chops. She gives me a guilty glance, then waddles into the living room with her tail tucked way down low. She doesn't look back.

'Honey? El?'

I go into the bedroom. There's still nothing to be seen of her but the milkweed fluff of her hair and the shape of her body under the quilt. The quilt is slightly rumpled, so I know she's been up – if only to have some coffee – and then gone back to bed again. It was last Friday when I came home and she wasn't breathing and since then she's been sleeping a lot.

I go around to her side and see her hand hanging down. There's not much left of it but bones and hanging strips of flesh. I gaze at this and think there's two ways of seeing it. Look at it one way, and I'll probably have to have my dog – Ellen's dog, really, Lady always loved Ellen best – euthanized. Look at it another and you could say Lady got worried and was trying to wake her up. Come on, Ellie, I want to go to the park. Come on, Ellie, let's play with my toys.

I tuck the reduced hand under the sheets. That way it won't get cold. Then I wave away some flies. I can't remember ever seeing flies in our apartment before. They probably smelled that dead rat Carlo was talking about.

'You know Billy Ederle?' I say. 'I gave him a slant

on that damn Po-10s account, and I think he's going to run with it.'

Nothing from Ellen.

'You can't be dead,' I say. 'That's unacceptable.'

Nothing from Ellen.

'Do you want coffee?' I glance at my watch. 'Something to eat? We've got chicken soup. Just the kind that comes in the pouches, but it's not bad when it's hot. What do you say, El?'

She says nothing.

'All right,' I say. 'That's all right. Remember when we went to the Bahamas, hon? When we went snorkeling and you had to quit because you were crying? And when I asked why, you said "Because it's all so beautiful."'

Now *I'm* the one who's crying.

'Are you sure you don't want to get up and walk around a little? I'll open the windows and let in some fresh air.'

Nothing from Ellen.

I sigh. I stroke that fluff of hair. 'All right,' I say, 'why don't you just sleep for a little while longer? I'll sit here beside you.'

COMING IN AUTUMN 2011 – STEPHEN KING'S BRAND NEW NOVEL

What if you could go back in time and change the course of history?

What if the watershed moment you could change was the Kennedy assassination?

What happens when a young teacher from Lisbon Falls, Maine, 2011 gets the chance to stop Lee Harvey Oswald from shooting JFK?

Read Stephen King's brilliant new novel:

11/22/63

The date that Kennedy was shot – unless . . .

In his incredibly ambitious, heartstoppingly dramatic time travel novel, King takes his readers on a fascinating journey back to the late fifties and early sixties – from a world with mobile phones and iPods, to a world of Elvis, James Dean, Plymouth Furies, signs reading WINSTON TASTES GOOD, LIKE A CIGARETTE SHOULD, of root beer and Lindy Hopping.

With extraordinary imaginative power, King weaves the social, political and popular culture of his baby-boom American generation into an unputdownable, unforgettable book.

Visit www.hodder.co.uk for more information

CAN'T WAIT FOR THE NEW BOOK?

Then why not try one of Stephen King's previous bestsellers?

If you like suspense try the following:

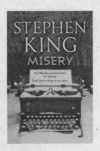

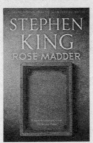

HODDER

STEPHEN KING

DOLORES CLAIBORNE

'Only a novelist of the very first rank could combine comedy and tragedy so judiciously' – *Sunday Telegraph*

Dolores Claiborne has a story to tell.
But not quite what the police had expected.
Dolores Claiborne has a confession to make . . .

She will take her time. Won't be hurried. Will do it her way, sparing neither details nor feelings. Hers or anyone else's.

This is the truth, the whole truth and nothing but the truth. Truth that takes you to the edge of darkness.

Dolores Claiborne has a story to tell and you'd better pay attention – or else.

'The tension is unrelenting and the narrator/heroine with her vivid colloquialisms and her sharp, homespun wit, is a *tour de force* . . . This is a work not just of imagination but genuine pathos' – *Daily Telegraph*

HODDER

STEPHEN
KING

GERALD'S GAME

You can't help admiring King's narrative skills and his versatility as a storyteller' – *Sunday Telegraph*

A game. A husband–and–wife game. Gerald's Game.

But this time Jessie doesn't want to play. Lying there, spreadeagled and handcuffed to the bedstead while he looms and drools over her, she feels angry and humiliated.

So she kicks out hard. Aims to hit him where it hurts.

He isn't meant to die, leaving Jessie alone and helpless in a lakeside holiday cabin. Miles from anywhere. No-one to hear her screams.

Alone. Except for the voices in her head that begin to chatter and argue and sneer . . .

'An incredibly gifted writer' – *Guardian*

HODDER

STEPHEN
KING
MISERY

Paul Sheldon used to write for a living. Now he's writing to stay alive.

Misery Chastain is dead. Paul Sheldon has just killed her – with relief, with joy. Misery made him rich; she was the heroine of a string of bestsellers. And now he wants to get on to some *real* writing.

That's when the car accident happens, and he wakes up in pain in a strange bed. But it isn't hospital. Annie Wilkes has pulled him from the wreck, brought him to her remote mountain home, splinted and set his mangled legs.

The good news is that Annie was a nurse and has pain-killing drugs. The bad news is that she has long been Paul's Number One Fan. And when she finds out what Paul has done to Misery, she doesn't like it. She doesn't like it at all . . .

'Not since Dickens has a writer had so many readers by the throat' – *Guardian*

HODDER

STEPHEN KING

ROSE MADDER

'A superb suspense novel' – *The Sunday Times*

Roused by a single drop of blood, Rosie Daniels wakes up to the chilling realisation that her husband Norman is going to kill her. And she takes flight – with his credit card.

Alone in a strange city, Rosie begins to build a new life: she meets Bill Steiner and she finds an odd junk shop painting, 'Rose Madder', which strangely seems to want her as much as she wants it.

But it's hard for Rosie not to keep looking over her shoulder. Rose-maddened and on the rampage, Norman is a corrupt cop with a dog's instinct for tracking people. And he's getting close. Rosie can feel just how close he is getting . . .

'Relentlessly paced and brilliantly orchestrated . . . one of King's most engrossing and topical' – *Publishers Weekly*

HODDER

STEPHEN KING

THE GIRL WHO LOVED TOM GORDON

'A compelling battle for survival that you dare not put down' – *Daily Mail*

'The world had teeth and it could bite you with them anytime it wanted. Trisha McFarland discovered this when she was nine years old. Lost in the woods.' In her panic to get back to her family, she takes a turning that leads deeper into the tangled undergrowth.

At first it's just the bugs, midges and mosquitoes. Then comes the hunger. For comfort she tunes her Walkman into broadcasts of the Red Sox baseball games and the performances of her hero Tom Gordon.

As darkness begins to fall, Trisha realises that she is not alone. There's something else in the woods – watching. Waiting . . .

'Moving, gripping. One of his best . . . A literary home run' – *Mirror*

HODDER

And if you want an epic thriller try:

**Visit Hodder website for details
of all Stephen King's books
www.hodder.co.uk**

We hope you enjoyed *Full Dark, No Stars*. If you'd like to see the video trailers which were made by Hodder in conjunction with Future Shorts of *1922*, *Big Driver*, *Fair Extension* and *A Good Marriage* you can scan this code with your smart phone or go straight to our site www.stephenking.co.uk